Praise for *Henry and Clara*

"A pitch-perfect rendering . . . Mesmerizing and assiduously researched."
—*The Philadelphia Inquirer*

"A powerful reconstruction of actual events."
—*New Orleans Times-Picayune*

"From the footnotes of American history, Mallon has pulled authentic figures and embroidered a compelling novel."
—*Booklist*

". . . a masterly blend of fact and fiction."
—*Albany Times Union*

"Mallon . . . outdoes himself in this re-creation."
—*Publishers Weekly*

"All written history is a work of the imagination, but seldom is it rendered as skillfully as in *Henry and Clara*."
—*Raleigh News and Observer*

"Beautifully written, *Henry and Clara* is marked by tender passion, and its characters are, for all their faults, endearing."
—*National Review*

"A stately and elegant historical novel of classic proportions."
—*Los Angeles Times*

D0057720

Henry
Clara
and

Henry and Clara

THOMAS MALLON

Picador USA
NEW YORK

HENRY AND CLARA. Copyright © 1994 by Thomas Mallon. All rights
reserved. Printed in the United States of America. No part of this book
may be used or reproduced in any manner whatsoever without written
permission except in the case of brief quotations embodied in critical
articles or reviews. For information, address Picador USA,
175 Fifth Avenue, New York, NY 10010.

Picador® is a U.S. registered trademark and is used by St. Martin's Press
under license from Pan Books Limited.

Cover design by Henry Sene Yee

Clara Harris's letter on pages 201–202 is quoted
courtesy of the New-York Historical Society. Extracts from the
correspondence of Ira Harris and William Hamilton Harris are
quoted courtesy of Rare Books and Manuscripts Division, The New
York Public Library, Astor, Lenox, and Tilden Foundations.

Library of Congress Cataloging-in-Publication Data

Mallon, Thomas
Henry and Clara / Thomas Mallon.
p.   cm.
ISBN 0-312-13508-4 (trade paperback)
1. Lincoln, Abraham, 1809–1865—Assassination—Fiction.
2. Presidents—United States—Assassination—Fiction.   3. Rathbone,
Henry Reed, 1837–1911—Fiction.   4. Married people—United
States—Fiction.   5. Rathbone, Clara—Fiction.   I. Title.
PS3563.A43157H46   1995b
813'.54—dc20   95-23938   CIP

First published in the United States by Ticknor & Fields

First Picador USA Edition: September 1995
10 9 8 7 6 5 4 3 2 1

To my sister

CONTENTS

Prologue
APRIL 14, 1865
10:17 P.M.

"'AND FALL upon the ground,'" he pants, spurring the horse with his good leg. "'Taking the measure of an unmade grave.'" He tries to remember the lines as tears of pain and self-pity and sheer excitement stream down his face. The horse races into Judiciary Square.

At the beginning of his flight, two minutes ago, he had been calm, even precise, noting each turn — from the Public Alley into F Street, through the gate he'd arranged to be open, then across Ninth, past the Patent Building — amazed that he'd not been pursued or shot in the back. The noise of the theatre was far behind him. But as soon as he thought that no one would catch him, it seemed too good to be true, and the tears came, along with this wave of fear. The moon and the gas lamps are too bright; the city, a week after Appomattox, too nervous. Someone is bound to wonder why, at this hour, this horse is galloping through Washington. Someone is bound to thwart his path.

He'd felt no pain until a moment ago, but he knew he'd shattered the leg as soon as he hit the stage. The exact same spot on the boards! Just where he'd nicked himself with his dagger a year and a half ago, throwing himself down with too much feeling in Friar Laurence's cell. When he'd leapt from the box — three minutes ago? had he covered a mile yet? one of the three between Ford's and the Navy Yard Bridge? — he'd forgotten the slope of the stage. If he'd remembered, he could have landed clean, he was sure, even after the flag caught his spur. But no one will ever forget *him*. Tomorrow morning he will be the most famous man in America.

He spurs the horse again, cursing the animal, though it isn't her fault. She's racing down Fourth to Indiana as fast as she can go. She is as scared as he, baffled about being spurred with one boot, frightened by the smell of blood that clings to her rider. It isn't the Ape's blood, of course. The one little ball from the derringer went too perfectly into his head to make a mess. The blood belongs to the other fellow, the one who should have been Grant. He hadn't known until ten minutes ago, when Johnny Buckingham, reading the *Star* in the ticket booth, let him in as the third act was on. "Is the general with him?" he'd asked. "Naw," said Johnny, "the paper says he was supposed to be, but it's just some major and his girl."

It was the only thing amiss, if you didn't count forgetting about the stage. He'd made his way down the dress circle and caught a distant glimpse of Lincoln, leaning forward and grinning his ape's grin over the line Harry Hawk was hamming for dear life. The sight so sickened him, made him so wild with purpose, he'd only wished he could shoot him full in the face instead of from behind.

But how everything else cooperated! He reached the passageway to the box, and his luck astonished him: the white chair, empty. The fat patrolman who should have been in it had gone off to watch the play or get a drink at Taltavul's. So he slipped in and jammed the door with the pine board he'd planted there in the afternoon. From that moment on — still less than five minutes ago — absolutely nothing could have stopped him. Could anyone deny that fate had wanted him to do it? Let the preachers spend tomorrow writing their Easter sermons and looking for another explanation.

"Freedom." That's what he thinks he said to the major when he thrust the knife into him. What brought the word to mind, he doesn't know. A thought of this mute statue — for that's what they call it — catching the moonlight atop the Capitol? As the horse races over the south grounds, he gives the dome a backward glance. Its marble looks like the bone of a giant skull. The Ape, whose own skull now is surely shattered, had moved heaven and earth to get it finished in spite of the war. Well, now they can lay his body out beneath it, and all the ladies, even the secesh ones who love a good cry, can pass by, snuffling into their silk handkerchiefs. His own girls, Ella and Lucy, would love it, poor things, but they'll be too afraid to show their faces after the newspapers reach the breakfast tables.

{4}

A mile and a half to go. Will he have to kill the sentry at the bridge? He guesses that he won't. Lincoln himself has abetted his escape — lifting the ban on travel between Washington and the Confederacy. One week after Lee had given up! Did the Ape think everyone would forget and forgive so soon? Virginia was still full of men whose blood boiled in their breasts, and they would welcome John Wilkes Booth as a hero, once he reached them and safety.

He might not have to kill the sentry, but had he killed the major? His blood, which the horse can smell, had sprung forth like a fountain. Had he bled to death by now? If there was a doctor in the house, was he still trying to dislodge the pine board to get through the door to the box? No matter. The Metropolitan Police's night scrivener could draw up two murder indictments instead of one. What difference did it make after a half million dead on both sides? Let the major's girl mourn for him.

She wasn't a girl, actually. He'd gotten a good look at her through the peephole, and even in the box's shadowy light he could tell she was thirty. Had she been waiting for the major through four years of war? Had he at last come home to her, only to die amidst the cushioned sofas and flowered wallpaper of box number 8? She'd seemed bored with the play, wasn't even looking at the stage, was looking across the way instead, at the empty box on the other side of the theatre, as if she were disappointed no one was in it to watch her and the major lap up the limelight with the Ape and his consort.

He, too, had wanted the other balcony occupied: he would have liked an audience. By now everyone knew who'd done it, but they hadn't *seen* him do it. He wishes someone had been watching as he went through the last door, a moment too soon, and stood there, looking at the back of the Ape's hairy skull, waiting a last ten seconds for the cue he'd picked for himself, the line that would leave just Hawk onstage and fill the house with laughter, enough to muffle the pistol's crack and give him a precious, confused instant more to make it over the railing and onto the stage.

Pennsylvania Avenue, at last. Straight on from here to Eleventh Street and the bridge. His leg is aflame, and he wants to cry out into the night at the injustice of it all. He curses his fall, and wishes he could somehow have been hoisted into the flies, set free from the theatre like an angel, and spared this pain that is cutting him in two.

Until his foot hit the stage, it had gone so perfectly. He'd heard the line, *Don't know the manners of good society, eh? Well, I guess I know enough to turn you inside out, old gal — you sockdologizing old man-trap,* and with it the Ape laughed his last. The ball went into his brain. He dropped the pistol as if it were no more than some spent taper he'd used to light a fireplace. But then the major was on him. The fellow had been so inert, he was surprised to see him come to life at all. But he'd been ready for this halfhearted attempt at stopping him, and he plunged the knife into him, the knife he'd been ready to use on the policeman, and which he'll use on the sentry a minute from now if he has to. The blood came so fast, a shower of it every-where. Even now he's not sure where the dagger entered. He could hear the moaning as he made his leap and rushed toward the wings, staggering past the callboy and Miss Keene, made up like an ancient procuress, twenty years too old for what she was playing. He'd wanted to douse the gaslights but couldn't find the wheel, and there was no time to search for it. The major was shouting *Stop that man!* and the audience beginning to pick up his cry. He made it to the alley with no time to spare, kicking the nigger who held his horse and racing it away down Baptist Alley.

Eleventh Street. Through the navy yard's stretches of timber, all the hulls and masts being hewn for engagements that now won't be fought. Finally he sees the bridge. Giddy with pain, he's whistling "When Johnny Comes Marching Home Again." There it is, the river he will cross. He sees its water catch the moon-light, and remembers the last word he heard as he ran out the stage door and into the alley. *Water!* someone had screamed in a high voice, a voice he knows must be beautiful when it isn't stretched by panic. *Water!* It was the major's girl, he realized. Who was she? As he looks for the sentry box, he wonders: Would her major recover, or had he died in her arms? Had John Wilkes Booth destroyed her evening or her life?

Part One
1845–1861

→ 1 ←

"AND TOMORROW I shall be forty-three years old," whispered Ira Harris while writing down the date, May 30, 1845. As he sat alone at his desk, it was not the rapid advance of years that prompted his disbelief; it was rather his youthfulness, his being too young to be a widower left with four motherless children, as he had been for the past two weeks.

The Irish mouse of a parlor maid had kept the Argand lamps so funereally low these last twelve days that it was doubly hard for him to perform the task for which he'd set aside this night: answering the notes of condolence that started coming the morning after Louisa passed away. There, on her last year's birthday present to him, the tin tray with its painted picture of Cortland apples growing in their orchard outside, lay all the sympathetic communications he must attend to. He rose to turn up the flame in the bronze sconces over the mantel. He'd finally bought them last Christmas to replace the pewter ones about which his wife would always jokingly complain. So many letters; a tribute to Louisa's sweet nature, to be sure, but also to his own increasing prominence. Amidst all those from neighbors and friends were short, solemn expressions from his new colleagues in the state assembly, and one from the governor himself. But none had surprised him more than the letter from Pauline Rathbone, widow of the just-deceased Albany mayor. Though Mr. Rathbone had left office four years ago, the stationery still bore the mayor's seal.

May 23, 1845

My dear Mr. Harris,
    My shock at the death of Louisa is exceeded only by my sorrow at the news. To have lost my own dear husband ten

days ago, never knowing that your wife was lying ill with the same dreadful pleurisy. My grief kept me from being with you at Pearl Street for her service, which truly shames me, as I recall your appearance at the rites for Mr. Rathbone — accompanied by your darling daughter! — a mere four days before. I know that your generous nature, so widely and justly known, will forgive me.

May God grant peace to Jared and to Louisa — and may he save and comfort our dear children!

Mrs. Jared Rathbone

Beneath the signature there was a tiny, parenthetical "Pauline" — perhaps in apology for the pompous mayoral paper, or in bafflement at her own new widowhood. Harris could recall the tears in her eyes as she stood below the steps outside the church two weeks ago, her hands on the shoulders of her seven-year-old son, Henry. He'd gone past them, holding his daughter Clara's hand and never imagining, sick though she was, that his own dear wife would be in a coffin just days later. Mrs. Rathbone's expression had touched his heart, and he could remember nodding to her. But what stayed with him more vividly was having to tug at young Clara, who could not stop staring at the stiff, noble face of Mrs. Rathbone's young son as he watched his father's coffin being hoisted onto the funeral wagon.

Among his four children, ten-year-old Clara was Ira Harris's darling, and on July 22, while sitting on a hard bench in Schenectady's Reformed Dutch Church and listening to the venerable Reverend Sweetman, he diverted himself with the thought of how yesterday afternoon she had informed her younger brother that "Father is going to school tomorrow."

What she meant, of course, was that as a loyal member of the class of 1824, Ira Harris would be going from Albany to Schenectady to attend the semicentennial celebrations for Union College. It would be the biggest gathering the city had ever seen, and up until the time Louisa became ill, he had been in the thick of the planning for it. How odd that at this moment he should be sitting not by her but by Pauline Rathbone, a woman whose husband he had never really gotten to know, not even when they'd served together on the church's board of trustees. After their simultaneous losses and her initial letter of condolence, Mrs. Rathbone had continued responding to his notes of thanks, drawing him into a long volley of reciprocated courtesies. Jared Rathbone had not been a Union man, but last week it struck Ira Harris as being seemly to invite the Albany mayor's widow to the college's festivities, since he would be without his own Louisa and since most of the celebrations would be open to the ladies. (This had been decided after great debate within the semicentennial committees, and with the reluctant progressivism that was becoming his political hallmark, Ira Harris had voted to invite the fair sex.)

Though it was unclear whether Reverend Sweetman, class of 1797, had actually finished speaking, he was now being led away from the pulpit, never losing the seraphic smile that had illuminated his old, unperspiring face throughout his long oration, during which the assembled men of Union sweated through their collars and tried to catch any breeze made by the ladies' fans. The congregants could only hope that Alonzo Potter, '18, the just-named bishop of Pennsylvania now coming to the lectern, a man whose expression bespoke more ambition than beatitude, would be quicker about the business of collegial gratitude.

"That no college," said Dr. Potter, "can claim credit for all the merit of its children is certain; but the concurrent judgment of mankind must be greatly at fault if such seminaries do not exert immense and almost unequaled influence on the foundation of character." Ira Harris, whom Union College had certainly helped make into a good man, listened attentively straight through to the bishop's benediction, and then gave Pauline Rathbone his right arm. They rose from the bench and made their way out of the church, on whose steps, in the hot sunlight, stoically indifferent to the coats and dresses sweeping past him, waited young Henry Reed Rathbone, the eldest of Pauline's two surviving sons.

"Well, Henry," said Ira Harris, "in nine years' time, if your mother is so inclined, you can be a Union man yourself. If I calculate correctly, Dr. Nott will be presiding over his fiftieth commencement just as you're entering the gates. A great summer that will be." Harris tapped Henry's shoulder and attempted to read the boy's expression. The child was looking up at his mother, as if trying to see whether she regarded Mr. Harris's suggestion as complimentary or presumptuous.

Pauline Rathbone's face evinced nothing but delight. "That would be splendid," she said, looking first at Harris and then at Henry. "Dr. Nott is one of our greatest educators," she informed her son. "What a wonderful thing it would be for you to learn from him. Just look, Henry, right over there. That's Dr. Nott himself, isn't it, Mr. Harris?"

"Indeed it is, Mrs. Rathbone," said her escort. The little president, whose white hairs stuck out from under his high hat, was trying to break through a circle of handshaking well-wishers and begin the short walk that the emerging throng would now make to the college grounds. "I've always been happy to be led by Dr. Nott," said Ira Harris. "Shall we follow his lead now?" Pauline Rathbone flung back her head in determined appreciation of her companion's wit, and nudged her son forward with her free hand.

Harris was surprised by Mrs. Rathbone's energy, the spirit she seemed able to summon so soon after her loss. It put her in high contrast to her silent son. The two of them walked on different sides of Harris's tall, manly figure, near the front of the chattering procession making its way to Union's main gates. Keeping a protective eye on Dr. Nott's bobbing hat, Ira Harris recalled the most powerful speech he'd ever heard him give, the Phi Beta Kappa address twenty-one years before, when Harris, ranking first in his class, had sat at the head of the table of initiates. What an extraordinary talk it had been, with Dr. Nott speculating on the very "inhabitability of the planets." The young men had sat open-mouthed as that endlessly inquisitive man, who even then had the ancient aspect of a wizard, declared that "discovery will go on until the worlds are put in communication, and mutual signalings are made from every part of God's kingdom." Twenty years later, as word of Morse's telegraph spread, Harris had shivered with the memory of Dr. Nott's suggestive prophecies. No, he had never heard a speech to equal it, not in twenty years of law school lectures and bar association meetings and legislative debates.

Nor would he this afternoon, as the roster of speakers went on and on under the hot sun. Governor Wright threatened to be interminable, and now, after dinner under the great broiling canopy, as the supper dishes were cleared, Mr. Spencer of Albany, head of the festivities, repeated motifs from the day's long rhetorical music: "The subjects of study have been so selected as to prepare men, not for the cloister, not for the retired literary life, but for the world — a world of wonderful activity and enterprise, where passion and interest stimulate to the utmost tension of energy."

Actually, thought Ira Harris, looking around the table at his contemporaries, the world was now a much less rough-and-tumble place than what they had left dear Union to enter twenty years ago. On the whole, this new world was to his liking. Gone were the foolishly tight red and blue jackets they'd sported as young fellows; everyone in this accomplished throng now wore a dignified black coat. And one would be hard put to find any of them eating with their knives, as they would have back in the twenties. No, the fork's civilizing triumph was complete, just as the nation pushed toward a second ocean and telegraphy promised eventual communication with those other men on other planets.

Pauline Rathbone's thoughts, taking place behind the vivacious, attentive gaze she granted every speaker, were at this hour strictly microcosmic, centered upon the nearby city of Albany and the scenes she had so recently played on its social stages. Being surrounded today by all this male accomplishment made her miss Mr. Rathbone's political dinners at the Eagle Tavern; the balls at Stanwix Hall; the four o'clock dinners in the house of every great merchant in the city; even prize day at the Albany Academy, when she, the mayor's wife, would bestow the penmanship award. Mr. Rathbone's vitality and ambition had been marvelous to her: nearly fifty-five at his sudden death, he always gave the impression of a man ten years younger, whereas Mr. Harris, who at forty-three (she had inquired) *was* ten years younger than Mr. Rathbone, looked, for all his fine frame and full crop of hair, rather older than her husband had done. But he was still a rising man — new to the state assembly, and thought a likely prospect for the upper chamber or a judgeship or even something beyond that. This was the essential thing to ponder, and as Dr. Nott began his climactic remarks, Pauline swelled with excitement over the achievements of men in the civic arena.

In a voice amazingly strong for his years, the president hit his oratorical stride: "Preceding generations bequeathed to us a noble inheritance — and shall we not add something to that inheritance, ere it be left to those who shall come after us?" The assembled graduates leaned toward him with renewed attention.

"Yes, Henry," whispered Pauline to her young son, who throughout the day's long proceedings had sat nearly wordless between her and Mr. Harris. "You *shall* be a Union man." The boy just nodded as he stared straight ahead, letting his mother know this was nothing he looked forward to. But his impassivity could not quench the high spirits of Pauline Rathbone, who a second before squeezing her son's hand had decided that she would marry Ira Harris.

→ 2 ←

LOUISE AND AMANDA HARRIS were scarcely heard as they shrieked, at the top of their little girls' lungs, over the sight they could see from the dining room window of the Delavan hotel. Jared Rathbone, four years old, was outside chasing a frightened pig, one of the roaming thousands that kept down the garbage on Albany's streets. He nearly had it by the tail, and the closer he got, the louder Louise and Amanda cried with disgust and delight.

The army of wedding-breakfast guests were making too much social din to notice. Judge Harris, on the other side of the huge room, was having trouble finding his new wife, who had organized this party on a scale that astonished him. Pauline had been a widow for more than three years, so there was no reason she couldn't arrange for festivities that were actually festive, but this was beyond any of Harris's expectations. Instead of having something at home on Eagle Street, or in the more modest Albion Hotel, she'd chosen this great place on Broadway, which seemed hardly large enough for all the people with whom she'd filled it. On Harris's right, a large lady in a green silk dress was speaking loudly to a gentleman squeezed up against her other side, talking about the latest boy the papers were reporting killed by Niagara Falls. She was practically shouting the details — the naked body, the crushed forehead. The gentleman she had cornered nodded and smiled, appealing for rescue from Ira Harris, who knew neither of the parties in this conversation but assumed them to be some of the dozens of Rathbones. Harris was too busy looking for Pauline to help the man.

There she was, chatting with Erastus Corning and Reverend

Welch, who an hour ago had performed the marriage at the Pearl Street Baptist Church. She was still in her bonnet and clutching her violets, pretty as a picture in her powder-blue dress, unwilling to don the old maroon mourning they used to stuff widows into. He needed her now, for something important. If he could only catch her eye.

During the past three years, Pauline Rathbone had rarely let herself lose sight of Ira Harris. The rising man she spotted at the time of their mutual bereavement had quickly passed from the assembly to the state senate and onto the supreme court of New York; for one thrilling month not long ago, it had even appeared as if he might be nominated for governor. But the judge had been slower about matters of the heart. Season after season he had gone on raising his four children by himself, aided only by a housekeeper. He continued to escort Pauline Rathbone to one social function after another, but the question of an alliance never quite arose. Did he imagine the acquisition of her own sons would push his household toward levels of noise and bustle for which even the addition of a mother would not compensate? Certainly the financial considerations weighed favorably with him — or did they? Did the prospect of marrying into the piles of Rathbone money Pauline had inherited embarrass his sense of manhood?

It had taken Mr. Fillmore — thank goodness for his arrival on the scene! — to move matters forward. Late this spring, before General Taylor selected him to run for Vice President, the former congressman had been with the judge at a Whig dinner in Albany. When he heard that Ira Harris was slowly courting Pauline Pinney, one of the Pinneys from his home city of Buffalo, the happily married Fillmore boisterously asked the cautious widower what he was waiting for. And so: the morning after he'd been clapped on the back at the Eagle Tavern, Ira Harris walked around to Pauline Pinney Rathbone's door and asked for her hand in marriage.

In the weeks since, things had moved with a swiftness matching Niagara Falls'. This morning she had been given away by her former brother-in-law, Joel Rathbone, so rich from manufacturing stoves that he had retired from business seven years ago at the age of thirty-five. He was the greatest man here, she believed, even if one put Mr. Corning, Dr. Nott, and Thurlow Weed into the reckoning.

Mr. Weed, the editor of the *Albany Evening Journal,* was only one of the political men she had made sure was here this morning. All of her late husband's colleagues from the city government were present, too, along with the friends he'd acquired long before, while making his fortune as a wholesale grocer. Add to all these the swarms of Rathbones, and the Harris clan. Ira's young son, Will, so prematurely judicious, so unnaturally obedient, seemed to her particularly lacking in spirit. There he was, just ten years old, listening dutifully to his uncle Hamilton, another lawyer, as the rest of the room shook with singing and laughter and the feet of children running between tables laden with food. The Rathbone boys provided a contrast that she was proud to note. Little Jared had run off on his own, while Henry and his cousin Howard, thirteen-year-old son of the masterly Joel, were swallowing pastries, balancing crockery, and teasing girls who'd come up on steamboats from as far downriver as Poughkeepsie.

Ira had been doing his best to introduce everyone to everyone else, a process complicated by his own formality and the fact that so many of those he was presenting to others were unknown to himself. Right now — she'd just seen him waving to her — he seemed to have something important on his mind. He had his hands on the shoulders of his daughter Clara — what was she, thirteen? — and he was making a gesture to indicate that Pauline should come toward them and bring Henry with her. While collecting her son from a table piled high with pudding, she thought about how during the last three years she had taken care to keep her boys in the background; they had yet to meet their new stepfather's own children.

"Henry," said Ira Harris when the boy came face to face with his daughter, "this is Clara."

With the polish that so pleased his mother, Henry smiled and extended his hand to the girl, at which point Pauline noticed that her eleven-year-old son's thumb was wearing the wedding ring Mr. Rathbone had presented to her years before, and which at home this morning, keeping with custom, she had removed. Uncertain of what to do with it, she had, during the carriage ride to the church, presented it to Henry as a memento of his father.

Clara, who took the boy's hand without removing her gaze from his eyes, seemed confused enough even without seeing the ring.

"Are you my brother?" she asked.

Ira Harris, who was seeing some carefully delivered paternal explanation come apart, looked flustered. Pauline smiled and patted Clara's curls. "Think of Henry as your cousin, darling." She looked at her new husband and flashed the sort of smile she knew would please him. "Let's defeat complexity with inaccuracy," she said.

THE UNITED Harrises and Rathbones had trouble fitting under one roof. Jared Rathbone's old house at the corner of Eagle and State streets, into which the judge moved his family after marrying Pauline, was a large affair, but it teemed like a beehive on nights when all the boys and girls doubled up in its small bedrooms. Even the judge's farmhouse in Loudonville was barely big enough to hold all the children.

On the last Friday evening of October 1851, the city house was empty. Pauline had taken Amanda Harris and Lina, the baby girl she and the judge had unexpectedly produced together, down to Kenwood, Joel Rathbone's great estate south of the city. They would spend the weekend there, while out in Loudonville Judge Harris presided over his other daughters, his son Will, and the Rathbone boys. At twilight he and Will made the short journey over the plank road out of Albany, and upon arriving, Will ran into the house full of excitement. "Father has a letter from Mr. Fillmore," he said to Clara, pompously setting the White House stationery on a table near Pauline's sewing basket, which Clara and Louise had been organizing. Louise seemed uncertain who Millard Fillmore actually was and what he had to do with Papa. Clara, now seventeen, knew exactly how he'd become President when General Taylor died two summers ago, and she reminded her younger sister that they'd met the handsome, white-haired President at Papa's wedding.

But Papa himself was all that mattered to Clara right now, and she rushed out to his carriage to greet him. "My darling," he said, dropping a satchel of legal papers to embrace his favorite daughter. They walked back to the house and into the parlor, where Will was again poring over Mr. Fillmore's letter. Clara hoped it contained good news, since lately she had noticed that whenever talk in the house turned to politics or Mr. Weed or the state of the country, her papa seemed troubled and her stepmother impatient.

In truth, Mr. Fillmore's letter contained little more than the courteous greetings of a genial man, one who remained friendly toward his old friend Ira Harris despite all provocations from "the Dictator" — Fillmore's former patron and Harris's present one, Thurlow Weed. The falling-out of Weed and Fillmore had begun as soon as the latter became Vice President — a position he owed, everyone felt, to Mr. Weed, who soon took offense at Fillmore's assertiveness over the spoils of office. When President Taylor died — after drinking too much iced milk on a hot Fourth of July — the quarrel over patronage evolved into a war of principle. Thurlow Weed adopted the antislavery views of his most promising protégé, Senator Seward, the man he now hoped to make President, causing a rift with those Whigs who backed Fillmore's efforts to enforce last year's great Compromise, which might ensure the survival of slavery but would at least preserve the Union.

Judge Harris had been triply distressed by these developments. Temperamentally, he was with Mr. Fillmore, a man more interested in respect than power; morally, he was with Mr. Seward, whose boldness in citing God's "higher law" against slavery was something Harris himself could never have managed; and politically, he seemed to be nowhere at all. Mr. Weed, who had been so attracted by the abilities he displayed in the legislature, had cooled toward him: the more brilliant Seward now claimed the Dictator's attentions, while Harris, taken care of with a seat on the court, was more or less forgotten, except on those occasions when the editor of the *Evening Journal* needed a special favor, and Harris, rather to his shame, was willing to provide it.

Clara could sense that Pauline Harris's frustrations were even greater than her husband's. Not long ago she had heard her stepmother remark to one of her Rathbone in-laws, who was standing right beside Ira Harris, "Alas, there isn't much supremacy to the supreme court."

Now Ira Harris asked Clara, "Have you and Louise had your supper?"

"Yes, Papa. We ate with the boys."

"Where are they now?" asked the judge.

"Out near the orchard, playing ball."

"Well, my lady," said Ira Harris, relaxing a bit now that everyone was accounted for, "as soon as I get cook to feed me and Will, perhaps you and I can read a little of Mr. Irving together. Would that suit you?"

"Yes," said Clara, smiling up at Ira Harris's graying head.

"Good. I'll find you upstairs."

Clara was willing to agree that Washington Irving was the greatest man the Hudson Valley had produced, because her papa said so, and she always looked forward to the tales that Ira Harris read in a fine baritone. Her own adolescence was being lived between boys who might themselves be the magnetic poles of a fairy tale. The studious, flaxen-haired Will Harris had had little to do with the dark, choleric Henry since he came into their house three years ago. Right now, in the last available daylight, Henry was out in the orchard with his cousin Howard, batting fallen apples. From her bedroom window Clara watched and listened without making a sound, smoothing the silk cover of a diary that Howard had brought her back from Germany last year, when all the Joel Rathbone family made a six-month tour of the Continent.

Howard pitched from a supply of apples continually replenished by Henry's little brother, Jared, who would scamper to the edges of the orchard for armfuls of fruit to lay at his cousin's feet. Howard would throw the apples toward Henry, who swung a broom handle into them, sending the hard ones sailing high and away, and pulverizing the ones that had gone soft, exploding them into jets of pulp and water. His fourteen-year-old frame was already as strong as a man's, and whenever he missed a swing, Clara heard the sound of the air being sliced, like the stroke of a handsaw through a block of wood.

From the moment she saw him six years ago, on the church steps after his father's funeral, she had wanted him to notice her; during the three years of their parents' courtship, when the children were never introduced to one another, she had remembered his face, his expression, and had always asked her papa, whenever he came home from Mrs. Rathbone's, what her eldest son had said or done. After the wedding and the decision to move the Harrises into the Rathbone house on Eagle Street, she knew that Henry looked upon their coming as an invasion. She could see him, still disapproving, when Ira Harris crossed the threshold into Mayor Rathbone's old bedroom, or picked up a carving knife with the Rathbone monogram, or just took down one of the books in the mayor's library. Henry had taken the arrival of Clara's younger sisters as an irritant, a feminine smothering. Within the family this reaction was regarded as comic, just a case of a boy being a boy. But in observing Henry's discomfort, Clara had taken pains to differentiate herself from the rest of the girls, using the chief advantage she had, her age, to treat him in a way that Louise and Amanda couldn't. She would mother him a little, straighten his tie, smooth his cowlick, brush a speck of lint from his pretty face, ask him if he remembered to pack his paper and nibs when he went out the door to school in the morning.

Gradually, he came to depend on her as someone who seemed to understand him, though to her he was like a magic-lantern slide she could never keep in focus very long. In the evenings, they were often wordless company to each other, sitting on opposite sides of the dining room table, she with a book and he with the string and sticks and knife he needed to make a model ship. Now that she was seventeen, the rest of the family had begun to make gentle jokes about possible suitors, which she disliked, but which Henry made thrilling one night by declaring, "Anyone who comes calling on Clara will have to have my approval." The remark was considered funny by Will and Amanda — this boy of fourteen laying down the law — but Clara realized it was true: she wouldn't want any beaux without his approval.

She was thinking of all these things as she watched the ball game below her window, losing interest in it when Henry wasn't swinging the stick. At the moment Howard was out of apples.

He reached down, found none, and looked around for his young cousin, whose attention had been captured by a squirrel that couldn't decide whether to head into the orchard or back to the cherry trees along the driveway. Howard smiled, but Henry was annoyed by the boy's dereliction, and before Jared knew it, the backs of his legs were smarting from a blow delivered by his older brother. He erupted in wails, squatting down and grasping his bare calves, feeling the apple grease left by Henry's stick. Howard shook his head, and up at her second-story window Clara clasped her book more tightly. "Game's over," pronounced Henry, abandoning the stick with a debonair toss. "And it's Jared's fault. Now stop whining. You'll know to pay attention next time."

"Come on, Jared," said Howard. "I'll help you carve your pumpkin." Halloween was just a few nights away.

Henry, left alone, began throwing apples. Gracefully twisting his torso, he sent them into high, lonely arcs over the treetops before they plunged into the darkness of the orchard. Clara watched as they flew, and once, as Henry turned around to take another apple from the ground, he caught sight of her up at the window. He smiled and made a low, beseeching bow, sure the eager reader above him knew the balcony scene in *Romeo and Juliet,* which he and his classmates had studied at the Albany Academy. To tease her further, he fell to one knee and mimed the offering of a bouquet.

Suddenly, for the first time tonight, Henry saw Ira Harris, who had stepped out onto the back porch of the house. He was giving his stepson a puzzled, discomfited look, but after turning to look up at the window, he chose to say only, "I'll be up in a moment, Clara." Henry nodded to him before disappearing into the orchard.

Ira Harris went as promised to his daughter's room and together they read some pages of the *Sketch Book.* More than an hour passed before he kissed her good night and went back down to his study to answer Mr. Fillmore's letter. Throughout the storytelling, Clara had stolen glances out the window, looking for a sign of Henry. Now, after getting into her nightgown, she propped herself up on the windowsill and leaned out into the darkness. But still, the only face she saw was the fiery, cackling one of the jack-o'-lantern Howard had carved for Jared. She watched it flicker until she grew sleepy, and lowered her head to her folded arms on the ledge. She didn't know how long she had dozed before she heard a low whistling sound, and awoke with a start. The flaming pumpkin had begun to move, was dancing on the night air.

"I'm the Headless Horseman," she heard a voice say — a boy's imitation of an old man.

She laughed. "Henry, you're a fool." He had his jacket pulled up over his head and the jack-o'-lantern riding above it, like a substitute skull.

"Was that tonight's tale from Mr. Irving?"

"No," she hissed, still laughing. "The Spectre Bridegroom."

"He's dull, dull, *dull!*" he shouted.

"Henry, you'll wake the girls."

"Probably wake Will, too. I'm sure he's already asleep."

"If you want to talk, come up here." She shut the window and smiled, hoping he'd take her invitation. A moment later she heard him on the stairs, knew he had already gone past Papa's study and was on his way to her.

He flung open the door and stood there, his jacket once more pulled above his head, the candle he held lighting nothing but the empty space above.

"Will you *stop?*" She laughed, taking the candle and pulling down his coat. "There's no predicting you whenever your mother's gone away."

"Well, you can't be my mother, too," he said, flopping down on the bed but keeping his boots off the counterpane. "You're already my sister, and everyone calls you my cousin."

"I'll be your teacher," she said. "I think you're in the mood to be read to. I think you're envious of me and Papa and Mr. Irving."

He pulled the pillow over his head and groaned.

She laughed again. "All right, no Mr. Irving. The truth is, even Papa wasn't much in the mood for him tonight. He could hardly stop talking about Mr. Fillmore."

"Politicians," he said with exaggerated disgust.

"How can you say that?" she scolded. "Your father was a politician of a kind."

"Only for a while. He was a merchant, even when he was mayor. He helped put the food on your table."

"And we cooked it in a stove made by your uncle. That's what you're going to tell me next."

"That's right," said Henry, brightening. "We Rathbones make things."

Clara smiled at the manful little "we," but she could see how serious he was.

"Politicians don't make anything," he said.

"You're wrong," she replied. "They make history."

He rolled his eyes over the riddle she'd made of his words, and retaliated with a ball of yarn thrown in her direction. "Good catch!" he cried.

"*Shh*," she whispered. "You'll wake the dead."

"You mean Will."

"Henry, *stop*." To change the subject, she asked, "Did your father ever read to you?"

"No. I read to him."

"You couldn't have," she said. "You were only seven when he passed away."

"But I did. While he was sick in bed. I read him the marine lists and the weather tables out of the *Evening Journal*."

Clara could see him concentrating on this memory. She wanted to reach over from her chair and pat him, but then she remembered he was a boy, and only fourteen. He wouldn't want her to.

Suddenly he brightened up. "I made some mistakes, but I stumbled through them."

She wanted him to talk more, about his father and the hurt he must have felt when still so small, the same hurt she had felt when her mother died. She wanted them to exchange these two stories, which they had never really done since he'd come into the house three years ago, so full of reserve and resentment, so full, she was sure, of a deeper pain, still more fresh and raw than her own.

"Let's go out, Clara!" he exclaimed, bringing himself upright on the bed.

"Where? It's long since dark."

"Come on," he said, tossing her her shawl and taking her hand. "We'll go for a walk in the woods. The leaves are already thick on the ground. Like a carpet."

"But everyone's —"

He pulled on her arm and dragged her after him, through the door and down the stairs, both of them stifling giggles as they passed Judge Harris's study and noticed candlelight through a crack in the door. "He's writing old Fillmore, I'll bet," whispered Henry. The two of them crossed the threshold out of the house and began to run, past the jack-o'-lantern Henry had set down on the porch, out onto the grass, past the cherry trees along the driveway, and finally into the orchard, where each of them took a great gulp of the mulchy air. In the dark, Henry took her hand. She looked at her stepbrother's silhouette and wondered if he was feeling happy now, even smiling. He was taller than she, and with the moonlight blocked by the treetops it was easy to think he was older, too, a real young man. The rustle of leaves beneath their feet made her want to keep running, so she squeezed his fingers and the two of them laughed and began to race, hand in hand, away from her father's house and deeper into the woods.

→ 4 ←

IN THE YEARS before the Civil War, Clara Harris became well acquainted with Southern girls and boys without ever traveling below New York City. It was in Newport — in those days summer home to more Southern planters than Northern millionaires — that she got to know girls like Sybil Bashford, from Camden, South Carolina, with whom she was now, late in August 1854, finishing an unpleasant walk along Bailey's Beach. Sybil had just turned eighteen, and was not about to let anyone forget that last summer she had been left here by her mama to spend the whole year at the Newport Academy. Even at nineteen, Clara simply could not compete with history like this, and she was relieved when the two of them came back in sight of the Ocean House Hotel, where Pauline Harris, looking up from her newspaper, waved them toward the veranda. Sybil immediately abandoned Clara for the company of a young man in a sailor's cap, leaving her to settle into a wicker chair beside her stepmother. Pauline passed her a sketchpad and pencil and went on reading her paper.

Most of the other adults on the hotel porch favored *Town Topics* and the Newport *Mercury,* even if these publications were written mostly for year-round residents who professed alarm (and kept quiet about their financial satisfaction) over the growing number of summer cottagers and hotel guests. More than sixty houses had been built this past winter alone, one of them by Sybil Bashford's father. Pauline Harris — who owned no home in Newport, but each year took one or two of the Harris girls with her to the Ocean House — preferred reading the *Providence Journal.* She wished to know what was happening on the contested landscapes of Kansas and the Crimea, not just the lawns of Bellevue Avenue. The newly founded Republican Party was a matter of special interest to her — and one she wished her husband would regard more carefully. Ira Harris was, to Pauline's way of thinking, far too complacent about the imminent demise of the Whigs. If he didn't take care, he would find himself without a party and a future. He might take Pauline's advice about keeping his relations with Thurlow Weed in good repair, but to the broader movements of this turbulent decade he seemed resigned, as if large matters of destiny were impervious to manipulation by individuals. In contrast, Pauline was sure that, however wild a ride it might take him on, history offered a man its reins, to pull or slacken while he set the course. She could see her husband's measure of vanity, and was glad he possessed it; she only wished it would overwhelm his dignity, which made him sit and wait for the advancement he was ashamed to pursue.

Ambitious for him and her two sons, and pleased by the little girl she and Ira had created themselves, Pauline found herself uninspired by the band of stepchildren she had acquired with her second marriage. Her relations with Will were cordial but more or less irrelevant, and with the Harris girls she had settled into a sort of chaperonage. Her presence was friendly, authoritative, and rarely emotional. In the six years she had been Clara's stepmother, scarcely a scene or secret had arisen between them. Her own sons spoke to her in a way outsiders found curiously intimate, but she remained a sort of endlessly visiting aunt to the three Harris girls, whose memories of their real mother had begun to fade.

At this moment there was nothing Clara could say about her walk with Sybil Bashford that might compete for interest with the front-page columns of the *Providence Journal,* and Pauline was untouched by guilt. "There's a letter from Henry you might want to read," she said, pointing to a little stack of envelopes on the wicker table between their chairs, glad there was something besides the sketchpad to keep her stepdaughter occupied now that her friend had run off.

Clara reached toward the pile out of reflex obedience and a measure of real excitement. Each letter had an Albany postmark — daily communications from her kind and dutiful papa — except for a single Schenectady one, the first letter she'd seen from Henry since his departure for Union College a month before. The words in bold black ink were addressed to Pauline, and reading them gave Clara a thrill of intrusion:

Dear Mother,

I have found some pretty good fellows, Hastings and Van Voast, with whom I wrestle and ride. Even amidst the sea breezes of Newport you probably realize that it is too hot to be doing any of this, but these activities seem far more sensible than what we spend the rest of our summer hours doing — reading Tacitus and working Geometry and saying prayers in that stifling chapel. (The Little Wizened One leads us in them like a happy wind-up cricket.) Perhaps I will bear all this more cheerfully in the fall term. Nonetheless, I remain quite unsure that I should be here at all. Ah, the things I do to please my mama.

When you get back to Albany, you may embrace the Rathbones and give mere regards to the Harrises. While in Newport you may kiss lovely Clara for me.

Your loving son,
Henry

Clara was so agitated by this letter that she couldn't remember the name of the girl now shyly asking if she minded her taking the chair beside her. No, said Clara, adjusting her own so that she might face Mary Hall — that was it — the daughter of an Episcopal priest in New York City.

"It's from my brother," said Clara, noticing Mary's interest in the letter she held. "He's away at college."

"Oh, that sounds so exciting," said Mary. "I think even Sybil Bashford might envy having a learned brother." The two of them shared a laugh against the belle at the other end of the porch. "Could I hear some of it?" asked Mary.

Clara read her the first paragraph, and was again disturbed by the conspiratorial tone between Henry and his mother. The expressions of frustration with studying in the summertime were understandable, she supposed, but calling Dr. Nott the Little Wizened One, and comparing him to a toy cricket! That would crush Ira Harris. And yet the epithet was used as if Pauline already knew it, perhaps even used it herself, with Henry. At the least, Henry seemed to know that she could be counted on to laugh at this most revered of all the Harris household's gods. Looking over toward her stepmother, Clara decided she must have been too occupied by events in the newspaper to remember the letter's containing this terrible reference to Eliphalet Nott.

At home she often heard Pauline and Henry talking behind a closed door. Clara would stand in the hall, fussing with herself at the mirror, pushing up her brown hair to give herself a higher forehead, admiring the fullness of her breasts and wishing the family lived in a warmer climate, where she might have more occasions to dress them to advantage. But before she could ever hear anything Pauline and Henry were saying, she would grow bored with her attempts at allure, and come away from the mirror, doubly frustrated.

This letter was such a fraud upon poor Papa. But Clara was conscious of having just perpetrated her own fraud, upon shy Mary Hall. She knew why she hadn't read the letter's salutation, and why she'd stopped before the short paragraph containing Henry's wishes — including the astonishing one that she be kissed. It was that she wanted Mary to think Henry had written this letter not to his mother, who remained too deep in the *Providence Journal* to hear any of its recitation, but to herself. She wanted to impress Mary and regain confidence after the walk with Sybil, but it was not just a matter of enhancing her status. If Mary Hall and Sybil Bashford had been nowhere around on this summer afternoon, she would still be wishing that Henry had written this sarcastic, flirtatious, and seditious letter just to her and her alone.

→ 5 ←

"AND THIRTEEN CENTS for the broken glass."

"But it's yet to be repaired!" said Henry.

"It will be, Rathbone, before the summer's out. The carpenters have quite a bit else to do the day before commencement," said Professor Pearson, not looking up from his desk in the treasurer's office, just writing silently, forcing the young man to listen to the hammers and saws out on the lawn on this warm midsummer day in 1856. The young hothead said nothing, just stood there in front of him, seething. "I hope you don't think I'm unaware of how the window broke, either," said Pearson, proud of how little escaped him, pleased with how much he could get a junior proctor to divulge. "I'll just add it to the fines for missed prayers and recitations. So," he said, subtracting the $24 paid in May, at the beginning of term, "that makes one dollar and forty-four cents to be carried forward." The precision, the paltriness; the boy would soon burst his collar, thought Pearson, if he had to listen to much more of this. But that's what Pearson would make him do, just a little more. This boy could use a bit of toning down. There was too much blood in him for his own good.

"And shall I send the bill to Judge Harris?" he asked.

The judge's ward, listed as such in large black letters of Pearson's handwriting on the piece of paper directly between them, nodded with as angry a look as he dared.

"He's quite a man, your stepfather." Professor Pearson put his pen back in the holder and looked up at the young man, as if to say, You don't agree?

"Yes," said Henry.

Pearson kept going. "Yes, Rathbone, the judge was graduated first in his class, as you no doubt know." He pasted a copy of the term's charges into the college bill book.

"Is that all, sir?"

"He was a legend," said Pearson. "Nothing less, even in his own college days. Not long ago President Nott remarked to me, 'Pearson, I don't know which runs higher in Ira Harris, probity or perspicacity. It's a splendidly close race between the two.' A marvelous compliment, don't you think? His service to the college has been exemplary, of course, but we all look forward to the time when he might be persuaded to do even more. Though goodness knows," said Pearson, sighing so ostentatiously that he nearly laughed at his own sadistic success, "a man with his talents and sense of duty is bound to be spread pretty thin." He just couldn't prolong it anymore; it was indecently delicious. The boy's little red whiskers looked as if they were about to pop, like a porcupine's quills. "Very well, Rathbone. Have a pleasant summer, but do make some preparation for the fall. Moral Philosophy, Optics, and Electricity will make for no small set of burdens. They wouldn't for even a gifted scholar."

The boy began to withdraw.

"Our best to the judge, of course."

Out in the sunlight, returning to North College, Henry broke into a run, just for the pleasure of feeling his feet hit the ground as hard as he could make them. He imagined smashing his shoes, again and again, into Pearson's soft, womanish face. Mounting the steps to North College, he struck blows against the handrail with his fist.

Back in his third-floor room, he had a few minutes to sit on his packed trunk and wait for the carriage. The driver was hired to take him to the Schenectady train depot, from which he would travel home to Albany and Eagle Street. But could he really stand that? Going back there straightaway and handing his marks to the judge, who would be terribly understanding and fatherly about them? Could he bear to sit at the dinner table tonight, the disreputable center of attention, with no breeze to stir the hot air emanating from the noble milksop Will, who would be back from his second year at the University of Rochester, carrying marks as high as his father's, full of Greek and Cicero and goodness to pour over them all? And all of them would drink it up — except for Will's stepmother, Henry's own mother, still less a Harris than a Rathbone, less proud to be part of a family that dealt in civic virtue and learning than the family she first married into, one that spun gold from iron and groceries. He could hear Will going on and on in his reedy preacher's voice, sounding like one of his letters home. Actually, there was someone on the Harris side who wouldn't be taken in. That was Clara, he thought, picturing the way she'd catch his glance at some point in the piety, and slyly roll her eyes, hiding behind the glass she sipped.

She was so different from Louise and Amanda and Will. Once in a while he imagined that she was his real sister and had somehow managed to keep the gaiety that had gone out of life and left him so unhappy when his father died. He thought back to his earliest memories, stories his mother had later filled in, of how, no more than three or four years old, he'd gone with his parents to Stanwix Hall and the Albany Burgesses ball, and the St. Patrick's dinner at the Eagle, and clapped with delight at the sight of his dancing parents, who at some point in their whirlings would pick him up and dance him between them. Everyone loved the sight of the mercantile mayor, who'd stayed a bachelor past forty, doting on his child and being dazzled by his wife. All the young matrons who for years had plied him with invitations before settling for someone duller couldn't help joining in the applause and enjoyment.

When a few years later the city's politicans tired of him, he accepted his time's being up, laughing as he walked away from office, looking as happy as when he'd entered. Which is how he continued to look, brave and gay, all through his painful, ugly sickness, as Henry sat by his bed and read him the newspaper.

In the three years after he died, Henry thought that, like his younger brother, he was getting over it — growing up and "becoming a little man," as his mother liked to put it. And so he had been, until she married the judge, who moved his family into the Rathbone house and himself into Jared Rathbone's room and bed. Instead of feeling as if he had a father once more,

Henry felt orphaned, as if now his mother had been taken from him, too. When the Harris regime of cold-water baths, morning prayers, and egg whites was fully imposed, she seemed to realize her mistake. But she could not admit it, and he remained lonely, with only Clara's protective attention for solace.

The gap between them had grown ever smaller — she was now twenty-one and he nineteen — but would her loving company, her mischief, be enough to get him through tonight?

Once back in Albany, why not make for Elk Street instead of Eagle? Aunt Emeline would be glad to give him a bed at her house, where he could have a night of honest Rathbone noise instead of Harris hush. If cousin Howard was home, they could go see what was on at the Levantine, maybe afterward go flirt with the girls under the gas lamps on Maiden Lane.

Where was the blasted driver? Henry got off the trunk and lay down on the stripped bed, taking care not to hurt the crease in his pants. His fastidious dress and toilet were a joke in his small circle of friends; even now, alone in the room, he positioned himself like a ramrod. He looked out the broken window at the tops of the trees ringing the empty circle where the huge Central Building, the domed centerpiece of the architect's grand plan for this pretentious seat of learning, was supposed to have gone. Even Eliphalet Nott, in his fifty-two years here, despite all the help of civic-minded disciples like Ira Harris, had yet to find the money to get it built. How many times Henry had had to hear about this folly, during wistful sermons in the chapel and forward-looking utterances at the Harris dining room table. He looked at the trees circling nothing but grass, before he closed his eyes and wondered just what he would tell the judge about his latest collection of bad marks and petty fines.

"Rathbone!"

He started. It wasn't the driver who'd arrived, but his classmate Leander Reynolds.

"Now, old boy, how can you lie there with your eyes closed and miss the splendid clarity of this view? Why, there's not so much as a piece of glass to dull it." Imitating an unctuous shopkeeper, he traced the outlines of the missing pane.

Henry lay back and closed his eyes. "Reynolds, go away."

"Go? Without the chance to reminisce about that grand recent occasion leading to the *ventilation* of this prospect of Nott's arbored nothingness? Go? With no opportunity to be nostalgic for the celebration, three weeks ago, in this room, of the nineteenth birthday of Henry Reed Rathbone, at which festivity Messrs. Leander Reynolds, Bowen Moon, Gerrit Van Voast, Peter Wyckoff, and James B. Beveridge did toast the guest of honor six, or eight, or was it twelve times? However many, with great gusto, until the honoree terminated the proceedings by hurling a tumbler — with the whiskey still in it, more's the pity — straight through the glass and out onto the college lawn. By the way, Rathbone, how much did old poncy Pearson dun you for the window?"

"Thirteen cents, Reynolds," said Henry without opening his eyes. "Are you through?"

"Not just yet," he said, serious now, sitting down at the foot of the bed. "Not until you tell me just what made you so mad at Van Voast. You damn near broke his head along with the window when you threw that glass. We tried all the next day to figure out what set you off, and we quite honestly couldn't."

"It was something about his face," Henry said softly. "I decided I didn't like the look on it."

Reynolds laughed and got up from the bed. "All right, Rathbone. I see I won't be getting anything out of you. We'll just hope your twentieth is more peacefully festive. See you in the fall, old man." He waved goodbye and, spotting the coachman in the corridor, directed him into the room.

Henry said nothing, just pointed to the trunk, which the driver and his boy assistant hoisted between them. He followed them out of North College.

"To the train, sir?"

"Yes," said Henry, sighing.

The coach set off, beginning a circle toward the main gates, passing the treasurer's office, where Jonathan Pearson looked up and smiled.

From inside the carriage, Henry pondered the circle of trees ringing the bare patch of ground where the unbuilt rotunda should have been. Without it Union College looked curiously empty, its two main buildings, North and South colleges, facing each other in distant, nearsighted bafflement over the large expanse of intervening landscape. The sight of the treetops made Henry recall the perspective from which he'd regarded them minutes ago, up in the third-floor rooms, when Reynolds had asked why he threw the glass. The strange thing, he now realized, is that when he told him it had only to do with the look on Gerrit Van Voast's face — and the inexplicable impulse of a single instant — he had been telling the truth.

Henry returned to Eagle Street after all, having decided it was better to get his homecoming over with. As the parlor maid took his coat, Pauline came out from the dining room to kiss him. "Only one more year of it," she said soothingly. "The heat is terrible, isn't it? Jared and the girls, all of them but Clara, are in the country. Everyone else is at the table."

Henry shook hands with Ira Harris and Will. His cousin Howard, who'd come over to give him a surprise welcome home, got a hearty clap on the back. "What have I been missing here?" whispered Henry.

"Clara is wondering who will act as Mr. Buchanan's First Lady if he's elected."

"Perhaps he won't have anyone at all," she said of the Democrats' bachelor candidate. "If England could have a Virgin Queen, why can't we have a Virgin President?"

"Clara, really," said Pauline. Henry and Howard laughed loudly, while Will looked scandalized. Judge Harris, at the head of the table, said nothing, but was amused at Clara's remark. During the last year she'd found her tongue. She read every newspaper that came into the house and tore through all manner of novels and poems, sometimes making fun of his fondness for native bards like Whittier over Englishmen like Tennyson. She would be twenty-two this year, and he was proud of all the learning she'd accumulated on her own — though he drew the line at Lord Byron, and had asked her to return *Don Juan* to the bookshop as soon as he'd seen her with it.

"So politics is the evening's topic?" asked Henry.

Ira Harris glanced down at his soup, leaving Pauline to respond, "Can there be any other?" This summer, after John Brown's party had massacred the Kansas slavers at Pottawatomie, and Mr. Sumner had been thrashed within an inch of his life on the Senate floor, it would be hard to challenge her point.

"There's a torchlight rally for Fillmore tonight. Care to go?" Howard asked Henry.

"No, Howard," said Pauline, giving him a hard look. "No."

"Not even to rally for an old friend?" asked Henry, toying with her, knowing how frustrated she was by all the events painting her second husband into an irrelevant corner.

Judge Harris continued to eat in silence. Millard Fillmore, after four years' absence, was trying to return to the White House at the head of the American Party ticket. The judge would have liked to be able to vote for him, but there were too many reasons he couldn't. The Nativists and Know-Nothings were using Fillmore, and Harris had little resentment in his own heart against the immigrants and Catholics who so frightened the followers of this new third party. For God's sake, it was an Irish girl, a cheerful little thing named Matilda, who was setting a plate of fish in front of him this very minute. There were always a couple of them in the house, singing away as they worked. In any event, Mr. Weed had virtually ordered the Whigs into the Republican Party, through which he might one day succeed in making Senator Seward President of the United States. Harris had been on the bench for ten years now, and would probably die on it. If not for Pauline, he might be content to watch the whole political parade go past, but she insisted that he keep on marching behind Mr. Weed, along with all the others still dependent on the Dictator's favor. So he would vote for Frémont and prepare to spend what remained of his career with the infant Republican Party, while Pauline kept hoping, with less and less reason, that the forces pulling on the poor Union might somehow toss her husband up to new heights, like a morsel of bread from a loaf being ripped in two.

"I'll be happy to go and hurrah for Mr. Fillmore," said Henry, provoking an appalled look from Will, who remained in all things his father's loyal son.

"I know why Henry is for Mr. Fillmore," said Clara.

"Oh, you do?" asked Howard, smiling.

"Yes, it's because he . . . knows . . . nothing."

Henry joined his cousin in laughter. "No," he said. "It's because I'm sentimental about old things that are coming apart, like Mr. Fillmore and the United States of America."

"Henry," said Ira Harris sternly, "you go too far."

Will declared, "Henry fancies he can take his lack of principle to such lengths that it becomes a principle in itself."

"Very good, Will," said Henry. "I've heard reports of the high marks you were getting in Moral Philosophy out there at Rochester. You can't expect me to keep up. I'm just a poor Know-Nott."

Clara was the only one at the table to recognize the pun, and she broke into a peal of laughter, which she quickly stifled for her poor papa's sake. Will looked quizzically at Henry, who turned his eyes away, too bored by his stepbrother to give him the fight he wanted. "Clara, will you come along with Howard and me? Another torch for old Mr. Fillmore?"

Before Clara could answer, Pauline stood up and threw her napkin onto her plate. "Good night." She waved off her husband, too bent on getting away from the table to wait for any gallantry with the back of her chair. The whole situation left her furious: having to play the prudent partner of her futureless husband and his spotless son. With the exception of Henry, she was tired of all these children, tired of Albany itself, and wishing right now that she'd spent at least another week in Newport.

Everyone was silent as she exited the room. When she'd crossed the threshold of the parlor, she turned around and said, "Clara, you are to stay inside tonight."

Clara appealed to Ira Harris with a look, but before his wife was out of earshot he said, "You must do what your mother says."

Henry got up and gestured for Howard to come with him. "I suppose we should apologize. Then we can head out."

The three Harrises finished eating. "I'm sorry, Papa," said Clara at last. "I do love you." She walked around to the head of the table and gave him a kiss before going upstairs to the room she usually shared with Louise. She was sulky about the lonely evening she had to look forward to, while Henry and Howard got to carry torches through the streets of Albany. From her reading, Clara was aware of melancholy's pleasures, so she took down Tennyson's *Poems, Chiefly Lyrical* from its place on the shelf beside bundles of Henry's and Will's letters. She opened to "Mariana" and tried to puff up her own plight into something worthy of verse six:

> *All day within the dreamy house,*
>   *The doors upon their hinges creaked;*
> *The blue fly sung in the pane; the mouse*
>   *Behind the mouldering wainscot shrieked,*
> *Or from the crevice peered about.*
>   *Old faces glimmered through the doors,*
>   *Old footsteps trod the upper floors,*
> *Old voices called her from without.*
>   *She only said, 'My life is dreary,*
>   *He cometh not,' she said;*
>   *She said, 'I am aweary, aweary,*
>   *I would that I were dead!'*

Too cranky to achieve the grander depths of despair, Clara put the book aside and spent the next two hours fidgeting and sewing and sketching, until she went to sleep from sheer boredom, without getting up from the window seat. Except for the kitchen maid tidying up downstairs, the house was soundless.

Then, around ten o'clock, with her sleeping face still turned toward the window, Clara began to hear a distant roar of voices, just loud enough to make her open her eyes and see a hundred orange tufts of flame, like a sea of marigolds, a half block away. The torchlight parade for Mr. Fillmore was coming up Eagle Street. Its sight and sound were suddenly as desirable as the lover Mariana sighed for. Swinging her legs down from the window seat, she put on her shoes, did up her laces, and tiptoed to the door. Satisfied that her stepmother and father were asleep, and that Will was in his room, absorbed by a book, she hurried down the stairs and out of the house. She ran up the street, smiling, as the torchlights brightened and the voices swelled. Reaching the crowd, she squeezed through row after row of it, excusing herself as politely as she could, until she had a clear view of the man standing atop the ship's crate and holding forth for Mr. Fillmore in Mr. Fillmore's own words: " 'If there be those either North or South who desire an administration for the North as against the South, or for the South as against the North, they are not the men who should give their suffrages to me. For my own part, I know only my country, my whole country, and nothing but my country!' "

There wasn't anything in this speech to give a fright to the Harrises' Irish maids, and as the crowd realized it wouldn't be thrown the red meat of nativism, its members quieted down. But since the speaker was warning them against national breakup — something far more perilous than the peculiar habits of new arrivals to the American shore — they remained attentive, and Clara took advantage of everyone's fixed position to make an orderly scan for Henry and Howard. She spotted the latter with his arm around a pretty girl and Henry on the other side of him. After pushing toward them, she tapped Henry on the shoulder from behind and said, "I see who gets Howard's support."

Henry turned around, delighted. "What a surprise, Cous'! Have you run away from the familial tomb, or have you converted Judge Harris to the hopeless cause of the Know-Nothings? I must say you were well spoken at the table tonight." He took hold of her arm and gracefully parted the crowd around them, two by two, until he had steered her back to its edges.

Clara could remember only a handful of occasions in the last eight years when she'd been truly alone with Henry, and though she was hardly alone with him now, the lack of Harrises and Rathbones in the immediate vicinity gave this moment, lit by torches and the moon, such a complete feeling of privacy that she had trouble speaking.

"Must you provoke Papa so?" she finally asked. "You know that he was much more upset than your mother, don't you?"

"Of course I do, Cous'." He raised her chin with his hand so her gaze met his. "I also know that he's *your* papa. And as for *my* mama, she can take care of herself." Seeing he had not yet made her smile, he argued: "Haven't I pleased him? Spending two years at bloody Union?" A cheer rose behind him as one speaker finished and another took his place. Henry glanced over his shoulder and then, with a smile, back at Clara. "It will soon enough be the only Union left."

"You don't really believe that," she said.

"Oh, yes. It will all go up in flames." He took his torch and held it under his chin and made a scary face, all bared teeth and flaring eyes. Clara remembered the night with the jack-o'-lantern, years before, and she laughed.

"But what will happen to us?"

"I don't know," he said. "But more than silly dining room arguments and silly elections like this one. The terrible time of our lives." His face took on a certain sadness. But he immediately cleared it, like a slate being wiped with a sponge, and put on a joking expression. He stripped off his Fillmore rosette and offered it to Clara like a bouquet.

⇸ 6 ⇷

A YEAR LATER, on the hot morning of July 22, 1857, Clara watched as Henry was graduated from Union College. She sat between Pauline and Will in the front row of spectators, a position accorded them not because of any distinction Henry had achieved during his three years in Schenectady, but as befitting the family of Judge Ira Harris, distinguished member of the class of 1824, who was on the dais and soon to make remarks.

As Pauline looked at the sea of black-robed graduates, she was aware of being on almost the exact spot where twelve years before she had set her widow's cap for Ira Harris. Their amalgamated sets of children, who took up nearly this entire row, had since grown into adolescence and beyond, and their own Lina was now seven. But how little everything else had changed! Dr. Nott, who had just finished speaking on the wonders of the transatlantic cable, looked just as he had in 1845, neither more nor less ancient. Ira himself was heavier, his hair now completely silver, but he was otherwise much less transformed than she would have imagined a dozen years ago: he was soon scheduled to serve a brief term on the court of appeals — a step above the state supreme court, though it sounded a step below — before resuming his usual seat and the settlement of such dull disputes as managed to get started in Albany County.

Pauline had put on some matronly weight herself, and the heat made her more uncomfortable than it used to. Fanning herself with the program, which promised a long series of student orations on everything from "Modern Chivalry" to "Civil Engineering as a Science and an Art," she wondered how she would stand it all; Henry's short speech would not come until almost the end of the long afternoon. She knew, though, that it would be more inspired than the one she was now hearing, her husband's. Really just a series of quotations from the *New York Times*'s July 4 editorial — which clung to the idea of "a glowing American nationality" and disbelieved that Northerners and Southerners really hated one another — Judge Harris's remarks provoked somnolent nods of approval from the crowd. The only man who could possibly object was the Dictator, who would not be pleased to have one of his men retailing from the *Times* sentiments he might as easily have found in the *Albany Evening Journal*. Pauline twisted this way and that to see if she could find anyone likely to report back to Mr. Weed on the judge's performance, though at this point she had to wonder why she even bothered.

Will Harris, on the other side of Clara, nodded vigorously over each paragraph of his father's rehashings, as if that might inspire the judge to work on his political fortunes the kind of transformation that Will had, over the past year, worked in himself: he had inflated his physique with dumbbells and pulleys, forsaken Greek and the University of Rochester, and prevailed upon the judge to prevail upon the Dictator to prevail upon a pliant congressman to get him admitted to West Point. He had been there for a month, full of new zeal and ambition that, were he Pauline's son, might have excited her support. As it was, she rather agreed with Henry on the subject of his stepbrother's metamorphosis: "He's made his body as hard as his head."

Clara knew that her papa hadn't done very well with the crowd, but she put it down to their impatience for what was to follow, the brief appearances of their own sons and brothers. She herself was looking forward to Henry's performance too much to think about her poor father now. If only there weren't so many others to sit through first! As the boys went about their stiff oratorical business under the hot sun, they presented a comical aspect to Clara. They might have been a small regiment, all in black uniforms, first one and then another standing up and sitting down, like musketeers daring to fire over the top of a trench and then be shot. The embarrassment of so many of them as they stood on gangly limbs in oversized robes, their manful attempts at whiskers hiding, or not hiding, boyish complexions, endeared them to her. But the dreariness of what they spoke made her glad of her own haphazard education, gained on the window seat in her bedroom with books carried up from her father's library. Surely she had found more beauty and truth in that manner than these poor boys had found in three years of compulsory lectures.

At last, after a dozen more speeches and two musical interludes, it was time for Henry, who crossed the platform with the casual gait of a beau approaching a dance partner. Without breaking stride, he shook hands with Ira Harris, a gesture that touched Clara and made her wonder if Henry might somehow be ready to put away the animosities he had carried with him into the family ten years ago. He took the podium with a confident smile, and Clara noticed the sun glint off his whiskers and crown, from which his hairline had begun a slight, manly recession.

"The American Idol" was his subject, and it seemed that the object of national veneration he had in mind was, thankfully, good character. He began by quoting Mr. Emerson, surely something that would please Ira Harris and Eliphalet Nott: "We think our civilization near its meridian, but we are yet only at the cock-crowing and the morning star. In our barbarous society the influence of character is in its infancy." By speaking sentiments such as these, Henry was performing much like those who spoke before him, though Clara took proud note of the way his clear, piercing tenor stirred the air as his predecessors hadn't managed to.

But within a minute she realized that Henry's speech was something altogether different; he was bringing up Mr. Emerson not as visionary but as false prophet. By Henry's reckoning, it was neither dawn nor noon but rather a few minutes before midnight. No recitation of American promise and plenty was forthcoming. Instead, the audience, increasingly amazed, heard the young man speak of police riots in New York City, polygamy in the Utah Territory, and William Walker's self-coronation in the jungles of Nicaragua. "We pretend that history is a snake charmer, a piper who will uncoil men's individual mysteries and set them marching in a straight line toward sunlight and progress. But only at our peril do we think of ourselves as domestic creatures. When we honestly reckon the intractable stirrings within men, we will speak more humbly about the future of Man. We claim the ability to undo history's repetitions, to turn history into civics, but if we are truthful and if we are strong, we will admit that history's whirlwinds are not ours to tame. The American Idol is civility, and that idol is shaking in the winds that now besiege the national temple. I look out upon these rows of friends and urge them to pay less heed to the slack tongues of reason and more attention to the gusts gathering behind them: 'Not in the air shall these my words disperse, / Though I be ashes; a far hour shall wreak / The deep prophetic fullness of this verse, / And pile on human heads the mountain of my curse!'"

It was Lord Byron himself, Clara realized, as Henry took his seat to stunned silence, angry faces, and concerted cheering from a few pockets of the graduating seniors. A quotation from the libertine bard of *Childe Harold* seemed even more brazen than Henry's own words, which had left the gray heads on the platform looking like a Roman senate forced to witness a stabbing in the chamber. Clara strained to read the expression on her father's face, but the distress it must be exhibiting was hidden by the young form of Mr. Abner P. Brush, who had just gotten up to follow Henry's jeremiad with some brief remarks on "The Scholar, his Trials and Triumphs."

A susurrus traveled from the gowned graduates to the spectators behind them. It was clear that the boys, who within minutes would cast their votes for the two best speakers, were already fighting among themselves. Small groups swept away by Henry's icon-smashing were determined, in a carnival spirit, to make a little revolution and bestow one of the Blatchford Medals on him. Clara could feel this happening, just as beside her she could feel Will twitching to put out the anarchic fire Henry had lit. Pauline strained to see the blank ballots being passed into the rows of graduates before poor Mr. Brush had even finished his oration.

The counting was accomplished as degrees were conferred. First prize went to Mr. Daniel W. Richardson of Middleton, Massachusetts, for his remarks on "Freedom of Thoughts," and second prize to Henry Rathbone, the orator who had unexpectedly carried Mr. Richardson's bland prescription into distant territory. Though the conventional students got to see their man take top prize, the real victory belonged to Henry's impulsive party, who had succeeded in conferring one of the college's honors on a highly unsuitable candidate. Their hurrahing had yet to cease when Dr. Nott began his benediction, sending these newest sons of Union "into the light, to serve their land and Lord."

With that, the band struck up the alma mater. The black pool of graduates dissolved into the parti-colored one of friends and family. Henry Rathbone, never the most popular man in his class, now received the backslappings of his new claque, who were ready to revel in the way he had turned Schenectady, for one afternoon, into the Land of Cockaigne. Will went off in search of his father, and Clara made her way toward Henry.

"You were wonderful," she said.

"It was nothing," said Henry, blowing his mother a kiss and promenading Clara away from his troops. "As it is, passion came in second to prudence." But his expression belied his words, and he took Clara in his arms and made her dance with him to the recessional airs the band was piping. "It was a silly speech," he said.

"But you meant it," she argued.

He did not slow their dance, but his expression became more serious. "I meant all my fears of the war. And what it will do to every man in this class if these politicians bring it upon us. I can think of nothing else."

"You won't go to it," said Clara, unsure if she meant this as a question or just her own pointless wish.

"Oh, I'll go to it," said Henry. "With relish. From the same part of me that relished being up here today."

"The best part."

"The impulsive part. The part that can't help itself."

They laughed together at this last elaboration.

"The best part of me is the one you bring out," he declared.

She lowered her eyes, unsure of what to say.

"Have they sent you to attend me as a nurse?" he asked, whirling her across a patch of the lawn. "Are they afraid my departure from the arms of Union will mean the end of all restraints on my behavior? Are you to be your brother's keeper?"

Clara only laughed, silently thanking God that Henry Rathbone was not her brother, since he was, she now realized, looking into his eyes, the man with whom she had fallen in love.

→ 7 ←

IRA HARRIS'S younger brother, Hamilton, had a thriving law practice in the Exchange Building. His clientele was a mixture of commercial men and criminal defendants, the latter made up partly of people he had prosecuted during his three-year term as Albany County's district attorney. That had ended in 1856 and now, two years later, he kept himself and a small team of copyists busy with a steady flow of deeds, affidavits, and motions for dismissal. He had also taken on a law student, his nephew Henry Reed Rathbone. This was done at the request of Ira Harris, who had suggested his stepson give the law a try while waiting for his true vocational desire to make itself known. Henry, who had shown scant anxiety about this delayed revelation, agreed to the arrangement, much to the judge's surprise and Pauline's satisfaction. The political ambitions of her brother-in-law Hamilton were, in contrast to her husband's, still waxing, and should Henry decide that he himself had aspirations in that realm (something Pauline hoped for), she knew he would learn more of what he needed to know by toiling in Hamilton's busy law offices than idling in Ira's august chambers.

In fact, on this July afternoon a year after his graduation, Henry was not working terribly hard. He and one of the scriveners were engaged in a contest to see who could more accurately pitch balls of paper into the unlit Rathbone stove standing in the corner. (John Finley Rathbone, who had been started in business by Howard's father, Joel, was now making thousands of them each year in a foundry on North Ferry Street.) Every few minutes, after a particularly good or bad shot, the two young men would shout loud enough to make Hamilton Harris scowl at his desk behind the screen, where he was deposing a client. He wished Henry would take things a bit more seriously, but he didn't count on it. He'd seen the boy grow up in his brother's house and knew that he was more than a little mercurial. Still, Hamilton Harris didn't mind having him around; he had brains and a certain rhetorical flair, which Hamilton might one day usefully deploy, if he could get the young man to learn the basics of the law. So far Henry's progress had been sporadic; he seemed no more inclined to stick with a book during the day than he was to stay in one place at night. Hamilton never knew when, or from where, his nephew would roll in each morning: Loudonville, Eagle Street, his Aunt Emeline's house on Elk, they were all possibilities, along with, Hamilton feared, rooms where Henry spent the night with girls who sold themselves along Quay Street. He was scattering his wild oats in a gloomy, peevish way that alarmed Ira and even Pauline. But given a choice, Hamilton would take Henry over his "solid" stepbrother, Will, who might have wound up in this office if he hadn't gone off to the Point.

A few minutes before five o'clock the doorbells jingled, and in came Pauline and Clara. They'd been out shopping all afternoon, and Clara was in a rush to tell Henry what they'd just heard: "Mrs. Hartung has been captured!"

"You don't say," replied Henry, taking Clara's bonnet from her and setting it on his pigeonholed desk. "Have you got all the details?"

"Just a few," said Clara, still breathless, as Pauline took a chair near the scrivener who'd been playing ball with Henry. "They found her in New Jersey, in a town called Guttenberg, like the Bible, and they're bringing her back."

"Was her 'paramour' with her?" asked Henry, playing with the word Mr. Weed's *Evening Journal* liked to use for William Reimann, who was widely thought to have helped Mary Hartung poison her husband before the two of them fled Albany several weeks ago.

"I think so," said Clara. "Do you think they'll put them on trial together?"

Henry laughed. "Appeals to your sense of romance, doesn't it?"

"Oh, it's a wonderfully romantic story, all right. Especially the part about how the coroner found enough arsenic in Mr. Hartung to do away with a whole family." Clara leaned over, laughing, and Henry gave a playful swat to the hair piled atop her head.

The bells on the door jingled once again. "So what are you two delighting in?" Howard Rathbone asked as he entered the office. "Oh, I'm sorry, Aunt Pauline. I didn't see you. I should have said three."

"Except that she's not delighting, are you, Mother?" Henry said.

"No, dear. I've got to think about *feeding* my husband to-night, not poisoning him. That's why we're here, in fact. I want to know if I can count on you for dinner. Mr. Morgan is coming."

Henry made a face. Edwin D. Morgan, the Republican candidate for governor, Mr. Weed's man this year, was not much of an enticement. "Will the Dictator be around?"

"No," said Pauline, "I'm afraid not."

"Probably over in Auburn having dinner with the Sewards," said Henry. This succeeded in exasperating his mother, which Henry thought was good for her: once she gave up the last of her ambitions for the judge, she would be more content.

"Howard, how about yourself?"

"I'm afraid I can't, Aunt Pauline."

"Howard has his own constituents to court, Mother." Clara smiled at her blade of a stepcousin. "Who is it tonight? Not the widow Hartung, I hope. She's spoken for. But did you know she'll soon be back in town?"

"So I just heard, up the street."

"I'd love to get a glimpse of her," said Clara.

"You'll probably get the chance for a good deal more than that," said Hamilton Harris, emerging from behind the screen to get a statute book that lay near the stove. "I suspect this one will be tried before your father, when he's come back down from the court of appeals."

"Really?" said Clara, her eyes brightening. "How do you know?"

"From a little discussion I heard last night at the sheriff's office. I do maintain a few connections among the constabulary," said the ex–district attorney, smiling at his niece before returning to his client.

Pauline was clearly not enamored of the prospect of Ira Harris refereeing the combatants in this sordid spectacle, which had already engrossed Albany for months. "Clara," she said, "we're off."

When they had gone, Howard sat down on Henry's desk and said, "That girl is in love with you. You know that, don't you?"

"I'm aware of it," said Henry, balling up another paper and preparing to resume his game of skill with the Rathbone stove.

"So is my mother aware of it," said Howard. "And so is yours."

"And so is Will," said Henry calmly. "And so are Amanda and Louise and Jared. Probably even little Lina. Though I'm not quite sure it's sunk below the silver dome of the paterfamilias."

"In one family discussion down at Kenwood this was elevated to the level of a 'problem.'"

"So?" asked Henry.

"I should think you'd be interested to know that that's how it's discussed."

"Howard, this afternoon I have *no* problems, none at all, and to demonstrate my freedom from all care I'm going to take you to dinner." From the pocket of his waistcoat Henry pulled a silver money clip that held a thick clutch of bills.

Howard laughed with recognition. "Your inheritance," he said.

"The first installment of it. Having turned twenty-one more than two weeks ago, I decided to visit the State Bank of Albany this morning. It's rather an interesting feeling," said Henry, tapping the pocket into which he'd reinserted the cash.

"Well, Cousin," said Howard, "I've *always* been rich, so I can't appreciate the novelty. But if it adds to your enjoyment, you can buy us two plates of oysters at the Delavan."

Within an hour Henry had done just that, and when the

dishes were set on the table, he took his fork and pointed first to the pewter plate and then to one of the oysters. "Emblems of our fortunes, Howard. Mr. Joel Rathbone, metal goods; Mr. Jared Rathbone, wholesale comestibles."

"Speaking of metal goods, have you thought about going to work for Cousin John? If you like all this money you've come into, you'll find there's plenty more to be made with him. Making stoves might be more of a challenge than pitching legal papers into them."

"So you've noticed I seem less than excited at my Uncle Hamilton's. Well, for the moment it's all right. I can wait."

"Ah, yes," said Howard. "You and your approaching apocalypse. Or what is it Mr. Seward calls it now?"

"'Irrepressible conflict,'" Henry replied. "Coming ever closer."

"Which is why I hope to be far away from it," said Howard, swallowing another oyster. "I just hope my enlistment in the Marines — when I get around to it — lasts long enough to keep me on the high seas and in friendly ports while everybody back here knocks each other's brains out. I was built for love, Cousin, not contention. Now buy us another bottle with your new wealth and tell me what's going on at home — though I hear you're never around long enough for the word to mean much."

"Alas," said Henry, "the flames of the Harris hearth reach out and singe me no matter how far I roam. So I can give you the news. The judge will be over at Union next week, laying a cornerstone and speechifying with Dr. Nott, who's finally going to see his big Graduates Hall built. Will sends the family his every-other-day letter from the Point, all about bayoneting sacks of straw and refighting Napoleon's battles on blackboards. He ends these heroic missives with pleas to Clara and Louise to send him fresh collars and the latest piece of sheet music."

"Yes," said Howard, "back to Clara."

"Thank God she's still different from the rest of them. Streaked with some mischief. Not weighed down by all that dutifulness, all that need to be 'well thought of' that crushes the life out of her father."

"Henry," said Howard, pushing his plate to one side, "someday you're going to tell me just why you've never let yourself feel the slightest affection for this man who's clothed and schooled and sheltered you from the time you were eleven."

"You're wrong about that, Howard." Henry paused to fill his glass, noting his cousin's expectant expression. "I'll *never* tell you why I don't feel the slightest affection for this man who's clothed and schooled and sheltered me from the time I was eleven."

Howard shook his head and smiled. "You make Clara sound rather like yourself. Do you think she *makes* herself different from the rest of them?"

"You mean, to please me?"

"Yes. And you still haven't told me what you think of the problem."

"I don't think it *is* a problem. I think it's a pleasure."

"Maybe that's what it was for her once. She had a face to picture and moon over when she read all those poems to herself. But she's getting ready to turn twenty-four. If her feelings for you persist, how much of a pleasure will they be for her? When —"

"For *me*, Howard. I think it's a pleasure for me."

"Basking in her hopeless love? A cruel sort of entertainment, if you ask me."

"I didn't ask you. But since you keep on asking me, I'll tell you that the pleasure it gives me is not a matter of 'entertainment.' It's a matter of serious satisfaction."

"You can't persist in this, Cousin. The two of you were raised as brother and sister from the time she was thirteen."

"And now, as you say, she's nearly twenty-four." Henry looked at Howard, his gaze still level.

Howard was embarrassed. "I can't see any good coming from it," he said, lifting his wine glass to signal the waiter. "Maybe we ought to talk about something else."

Which is what they did for another hour or two, over another couple of bottles, before walking out into the summer night, a warm one that made the two young men seek whatever breeze would be coming off the Hudson. As they strolled eastward, the gaslights, which had replaced the old whale-oil ones the year

Henry's father died, began to come on. Henry pointed to one that had just flared into life at the end of the lamplighter's pole. "I know a street where some of these lights have a pleasant reddish hue. Care to venture there with me? I've got lots of money left to spend."

"Another time," said Howard. He was eager to go to the girl he'd been steadily courting the past few weeks. "I'll leave the night to you."

Henry clapped him on the back and said he didn't know what he was missing. They parted with a handshake and went in opposite directions, but before they were separated by twenty paces, Howard Rathbone, still disturbed by their conversation at the Delavan, and hoping to sound more generous than he had, called out, "Henry?"

His cousin turned around.

"Wouldn't it be better to spend the rest of the evening with Clara?"

Henry just waved before continuing off into the night. It *would* be better to spend the evening with Clara, his true home, in whose presence he could be his truest self. But tonight, as on half the nights of his life, it seemed, he wanted to lose that self, to take it off with his clothes, and think no more of it 'til morning.

→ 8 ←

EACH NEW YEAR'S DAY at their home on Elk Street, Mr. and Mrs. Joel Rathbone received the cards of over a hundred callers, Albany revelers who would drop by after visiting the Eagle Street residence of Judge and Mrs. Ira Harris. In 1859, the New Year's rounds left many of the Rathbones and Harrises so sated with sociability that it was February 10 before the families once again commingled. The occasion was an evening sermon in Tweddle Hall by the Reverend Henry Ward Beecher of Brooklyn's Plymouth Church. The house was packed, abuzz with anticipation, when Howard Rathbone noticed his cousin Henry far down the aisle, which set the Rathbone party, just come from dinner at the Albion, waving to the Harris one. Clara raised her arm in response, though she was busy renewing an old acquaintance: Mary Hall, whom she'd not seen since two summers ago at Newport, had just spotted her and come running up from the back of the auditorium. It seemed that Mary's father, the Reverend William T. Hall, had come from Manhattan to join abolitionist forces with Reverend Beecher at a string of upstate rallies. As the audience awaited a thrilling oratorical display, Clara and Mary clasped each other's hands like pairs of reins and hurried through a conversation that dealt in large part with news of the impossible Sybil Bashford of South Carolina.

The young women were only a little more agitated than the rest of the audience. Rumors were everywhere that John Brown, who had come back east to raise money from the radical abolitionists, was planning to finance a slave rebellion. These days Pauline Harris was so swept up by national events that she neglected to test each one's relevance to the political career of her husband. Reverend Beecher was, of course, Horace Greeley's chosen preacher, not something to please Mr. Weed, but lately the Dictator himself seemed a small thing, just one more perplexed politician trying to ride the tide of news. Pauline was determined to hear Beecher no matter whose protégé he was.

The crowd settled itself while an usher filled the water glass at the platform. Howard Rathbone, who had gone down to his cousin Henry's aisle seat, thought he'd better now double back to his own. He took just enough time to say, "Perhaps you *are* a great prognosticator, Cousin. The crowd seems worked up for Armageddon."

When Henry Ward Beecher at last took the stage, he struck Clara as a compressed version of her handsome father. Though quite a bit younger, and wearing long hair that had not gone so gray, the minister had a broad face and chest that might have belonged to a shorter Ira Harris. There was power in Beecher's form, the suggestion of great energy too long pent up and needing loud, immediate release. He flung his first words at the audience like a lightning bolt, punctuating them with a stomped foot: "Did I, when I became a minister, cease to be a man or a citizen? No! A thousand times no! Have I not as much interest in our government as though I were a lawyer, a ditch digger, or a wood sawyer?" He was soon pounding his fists and throwing back his hair, and when he came to utter the name of John Brown, it was with a force that shook even the Rathbones at the back of the hall: "I may disapprove of his bloody forays and of those feeble schemes we hear rumored, and I may shrink likewise from the judicial bloodshed that doubtless would follow them." He paused and stood stock still. Not a cough interrupted the silence. *"But if such schemes unfold, let no man pray that Brown be spared!"* Raising his clenched fists heavenward, Beecher cried, "Let the South make him a martyr! His work will have been miserable. But a cord and a gibbet will redeem all that and round up his failure with heroic success!"

The crowd was too stunned even to applaud.

When it came to Brown's feeble schemes and bloody forays, Henry Rathbone realized he felt no disapproval at all. Neither, he knew, did Beecher. Passion was passion, and Beecher had it, a lust for drama and catastrophe and redemption that he might have satisfied equally as a stage tragedian. So long as the action was spectacular, its moral end was beside the point. John Brown, Henry felt sure, was the same: after fomenting an insurrection, he would be the perfect man to lead the avenging mob against himself. They were, Henry thought unhappily, three of a kind, himself and Brown and Beecher.

Beecher dropped his voice to a hush. "If an enslaved man, acting from the yearnings of his own heart, desires to run away, who shall forbid him? I stand on the outside of this great cordon of darkness, and every man that escapes from it, running for his life, shall have some help from me." He trailed off into complete silence, which was soon broken by clapping at the back of the auditorium, a smattering that gathered noise and gusto as it rolled forward toward the stage. Listening to its full thunder, Beecher cast his eyes modestly downward.

No hands contributed more fervently to the ovation than the small gloved ones belonging to Mary Hall, who was imagining how eagerly she would help any slave found tapping at her family's door on a cold night like this. She had already had her gentle heart impassioned by the novel Beecher's sister had written, and only wished there were some way to stop the sufferings of gentle souls like Topsy. The thought of one of them showing up to seek her aid, right on Beekman Place, was almost unbearably affecting.

Clara certainly had no sympathy for any institution that permitted the likes of Sybil Bashford to own other human beings, but she could not help seeing the comic side of Reverend Beecher's exertions. The man's vanity coated every syllable he coddled from his throat, and all the foot-stomping and arm-flailing reminded her of some Indian dance in one of Mr. Cooper's novels. She leaned forward and looked leftward, and when she succeeded in catching Henry's eye, she did a quick imitation of the preacher, rolling her eyes and clenching her fists. Henry laughed hard enough to make Ira Harris cast a perplexed glance toward each of them.

Tonight Clara's poor papa was too preoccupied by other things to keep his mind on the lecture, let alone the mischief of his daughter and stepson. Right now even the Fugitive Slave Act troubled him less than the fate of Mrs. Mary Hartung, over whose trial he had begun presiding ten days ago. It was a dreadful business, and for the life of him he couldn't tell who had driven whom, the wife or the paramour, to kill the wretched husband. The normal disappointments between man and wife were a sad part of our earthly existence, to be borne with charity and understanding (he was well aware of the extent to which he had disappointed Pauline these past eleven years); but violent betrayal of the sort that had sundered Mr. and Mrs. Hartung was past reckoning. What if the woman had been the one to make the plan and serve the poison? Would she not then deserve to hang, just as the man, were he the chief evildoer, surely would? Farther down the valley, his friend Matthew Vassar, the brewer, was planning to build a college for women, one that would educate them as fully as Union College educated men. Well, if men and women were to have equality in all things, should not hanging be one of them?

Onstage Reverend Beecher was talking of an equality so broad it spanned all the races and peoples of the globe: "The glory of intelligence, refinement, genius, has nothing to do with men's rights. The rice slave, the Hottentot, are as much God's children as Humboldt or Chalmers."

How blessed he was, able to utter these sentiments with such confidence! The judge could appreciate their nobility, but right now their forceful expression would be beyond the capacities of his own depressed soul. Last week Will's letter from West Point contained a story that troubled Ira Harris greatly: a cadet named Randol from down at Newburgh had a father, once a happy and prosperous man, who'd just killed himself in a fit of delirium. The elder Randol, according to Will, "was very much excited about spiritualism, or something of the sort." One more poor, forked creature, the judge now reflected, just trying to find some wings to take him over the walls of this vale of tears. And look at the result.

There were terrible times approaching, Henry was right about that. The judge himself would be too far past his prime to play any part in the coming cataclysm, and his only impulse was to shield those he loved from it, to gather them inside the house, like the apples in his orchard, against the advance of a frost.

Reverend Beecher was gone from the stage, and the whole of Tweddle Hall was shaking with applause, before the judge even noticed that the lecture was over. As people put on their coats, chattering and arguing about what the minister had said, Harris could barely find the energy to rise from his seat. He was still in it when Clara, who already had her bonnet tied, put a loving hand on his shoulder and said, "Come, Papa. Henry's Aunt Emeline has asked all of us back for some hot cider. It will drive out the hot air we've absorbed."

Clara's sarcasm always charmed the judge, even though he knew it was born as much from a desire to please Henry as from her own nature. The intimacy between the two young people had grown up with him barely noticing it, and was growing still stronger, though he hoped Henry's appetite for female conquest, and Clara's desirability to other beaux, would eventually lead them away from each other. For the moment, however, Ira Harris welcomed his daughter's sharp remarks as a sort of smelling salt. She took his arm as they left the hall, but it was really his beleaguered spirit that was leaning on her vitality. Pauline had taken the free arm of the masterly Joel Rathbone, who had his wife Emeline on the other. All the young people and their friends formed a gay convoy around the parents — even shy Mary Hall had been swept into it — and after a fast walk through the chilly February air, the whole party, more than a dozen strong, arrived at 3 Elk Street.

Though less grand in size and decoration than Kenwood, the Rathbones' mansion south of the city, this townhouse had a sumptuousness that made Mary Hall's modest jaw drop. She had never seen its equal in New York City, and as her eyes raced from Venetian bottles to Swiss clocks to German crystal, she supposed there wasn't its like in any one country of Europe — so many different countries had been necessary to furnish it!

The increasing frequency of the Rathbones' grand tours was a sore point with Pauline Harris, and it pained the judge that his wife now had to listen with polite impatience as Emeline Rathbone regaled her with tales of recent destinations and acquisitions. No, Pauline hadn't seen those Meissen jars before tonight, and yes, it was fascinating to think that they'd been in a shipping crate somewhere on the ocean between Hamburg and New York when everyone was sipping coffee here on New Year's morning. Ira Harris winced anew at the thought of how his wife's ambitions, social and material, were rubbing themselves raw in the rut she walked between Albany and Loudonville, with only rare escapes to Newport and New York.

Frustrated by watching Emeline propel Pauline from painting to bibelot to drapery, he shifted his eyes to their usual source of comfort and pride: the face of his Clara. But it was only a profile he was seeing now, the left side of a face whose attention was in the full possession of Henry Rathbone, as the two of them delighted in each other's skill at teasing Mary Hall. Behind him and to the right, the judge could hear Howard Rathbone talking to his latest sweetheart in a low voice about the Hartung trial, speculating upon what had been in the murderous lovers' minds, and what now went on in the jurors'. Were Howard to ask what lay inside the magistrate's, Ira Harris could tell him about a tumult of uncertainty. He had always been a "cold water" man, in politics and by his pledge to the Pearl Street Baptist Church, but he had just taken a second cup of hard cider to fortify his mood against the melancholy that was sapping it. He loved his city, loved his work and wife and family, but how he longed to lay down the burden of daily judiciousness, to escape the disappointed expressions that Pauline wore, and to remove his daughter from the gaze of his stepson.

It was a collection of small events — the taking of a third cup of cider; the sight of Pauline as Emeline Rathbone held some Limoges porcelain a few inches from her face; and the sound of one of Henry Rathbone's whisperings to his daughter, detected during a momentary drop in the noise filling the room — that made Ira Harris, before he fully knew what he was doing, tap the side of his cup with a spoon and declare, with a gaiety more nervous than real, that he had an announcement to make. "As we stand amidst all these treasures of the Old World, I realize that the time has come for the Harrises to walk in the footsteps of the Rathbones who have preceded them — or, more literally, to follow in their wake. I hope that these two tribes can gather again a few months from now, sometime in the early summer, so that one of them may bid a temporary goodbye to the other." Pauline gave him a perplexed expression. He met her look with a smile, and declared, "Come July, the Harrises will be setting sail for Europe."

A happy gasp emanated from the judge's wife; the normally timid Louise swung round to hug her sisters Clara and Amanda; and Henry's younger brother, Jared, who would surely be amongst the party, clapped his head in such delight that Pauline laughed with a heartiness she rarely displayed these days. But it was Clara's expression that most pleased the judge. His daughter was looking at him with a wide, calm smile, as if to say, Why, you dear old Papa, how did you succeed in keeping this a secret? Of course, there had been no secret to keep, no plan at all, but having said what he just had, the judge was smiling in self-congratulation, even if the cider deserved some credit for his action. He was enough emboldened to risk turning toward his stepson.

Henry had his glass in the air and was about to make a toast. "To the expedition!" he cried, to the two families' applause.

Howard called out across the room, "And as it proceeds, what shall you be doing with two empty houses, Cousin?" Everyone laughed.

"I shall be nowhere near them," Henry replied to more laughter, though of a somewhat nervous kind, since his nocturnal ramblings were more and more remarked upon.

"For I shall be," he continued, "on the rue de Rivoli and the Ponte Vecchio, clearing a path for my sisters, who will need a chaperone to make a safe way for them through the Old World." The laughter grew relaxed once more, as heads turned toward one another, nodding with the realization that the judge must have told Henry about these plans some time ago, along with his intention to include him. "I think," said Henry, recommandeering everyone's attention, "that Clara will be in the greatest danger from cynical Old World charms. So, along with my protection, the price of her passage will be my next birthday present to her. After all, her father will have quite enough to look after and pay for." He began a comic inventory of all the other Harris girls, pointing a finger toward each of them and pretending to lose count. Real laughter mixed with a politer kind from those used to discussing "the problem" posed by the so-called cousins' mutual attentiveness.

"You must write to me from every city, Clara!" exclaimed Mary Hall.

Clara, thrilled by the promise of Henry's presence on the unexpected journey, gave her a tight hug. Henry, raising his glass once more, looked at the judge. Ira Harris managed to nod in response, even though his moment of inspiration had recoiled upon him like a gunstock.

→ 9 ←

TEN WEEKS LATER, on the afternoon of April 22, the Rathbones' house on Elk Street stood drenched in rain and bereft of
gaiety. Even before Reverend Beecher's lecture there had been
much sickness in the city, more than usual for winter, and many
of the season's balls and parties were never held. By April every
family seemed to have someone ill, and the Joel Rathbones were
no exception.

It was Howard, who for all his good looks and cheer had
never had a robust constitution. Dr. Cox had long suspected the
young man's stomach and lungs were weak, and a desire to force
some sea air into himself was one of the things behind Howard's
oft-expressed wish to sign up with the United States Marines.
When, late in February, he came down with the same cold plagu-
ing half the city, he refused to give in to it, traveling instead to
Brooklyn, where he made his enlistment and received a fast
week's training. He'd gotten his orders just the other day and
was due to ship out a week from tomorrow. He had returned to
Albany to pack his trunk and make his goodbyes, but as soon
as he arrived he came down with a chest cold. Hot brandy and
sweat walks had done no good, and this morning he'd had to
stay in bed. Emeline had come up to read her son the paper, and
her daughter Sarah played his favorite songs on the parlor piano, hitting the pedal hard enough for the music to drift upstairs
through his open bedroom door. No one could imagine how he
would put to sea in only eight days.

Even if he succeeded, his cousin Henry and the whole Harris
family would be on the ocean well before he. Their departure
for Europe had been pushed up from the summer to tomorrow

afternoon, the change in plans coming not from uncontainable enthusiasm but rather a condition that Ira Harris had never before experienced in his public life: unpopularity. The jurors in his courtroom had found Mrs. Hartung guilty of her husband's murder, and after a good deal of agonizing, the judge had stunned the citizens of Albany County by sentencing her to hang on April 27. As soon as he pronounced her fate, a great outcry arose at the prospect of a woman swinging from the scaffold. The same people who had reveled in details of Mary Hartung's adultery became eager to demonstrate their fine sensibilities by signing petitions against the judicial outrage soon to be perpetrated in their names.

They met with quick success: Mrs. Hartung was granted another trial while the state assembly fashioned a new capital punishment law with a loophole that made it unlikely she would ever be executed. Her supporters congratulated themselves on their mercifulness, as the judge withered under a storm of criticism over his supposed haste and hardness. When his brother Hamilton agreed to defend the paramour, Reimann, Ira Harris decided to inquire about the next sailing date of the *Vanderbilt*.

"Howard!" cried the familiar voice charging upstairs. "Back on your feet! Do you expect the government of the United States to soothe you with sisterly song when your stomach does a flip some night on the bounding main?" Howard smiled at his cousin's roar, and motioned for Henry to take the chair at the foot of his sickbed. Downstairs, Sarah's piano fell silent. Clara followed Henry into the bedroom and handed Howard a wrapped tin of candy.

"I should be giving one of these to you," said Howard. "I intended to get you a *bon voyage* present before this business came to visit." He tapped his congested chest.

"We wouldn't have a cubic inch of room for it," Clara replied, patting his hand and urging him to untie the ribbon. "Besides, you'll need to bring more of your own treats than we will. I understand President Buchanan's ships are not so luxuriously stocked as Commodore Vanderbilt's liner."

Howard was twisting the wrapper off a peppermint when

Sarah came up with a tea tray. She wanted to get another look at her cousin Henry, who always scared her a little, in a thrilling way. "Goodness," she said, setting the tray down before hurrying back out, "everyone here will soon be out on the ocean."

"So what is the plan?" asked Howard.

"To the station," said Henry, "about an hour from now behind a great hill of trunks. Since Manhattan can't come to the mountain, the mountain will come to Manhattan."

Clara groaned and gave him a gentle elbow in the ribs.

"The judge," said Henry, "has been amazingly vociferous — for the judge, at least — on the subject of excess baggage. Amanda and Louise are afraid to pack another handkerchief."

"We'll be at the Gramercy House before dark," said Clara, "and after dinner at Delmonico's everyone will get to bed — *early.*" She looked at Henry with mock fierceness.

"I hear," said Howard, "that Senator Seward will be following in the Harris wake."

"For the first and no doubt last time," said Henry.

"Don't be horrible, Henry," said Clara. "But it's true about Mr. Seward, Howard. He's leaving for England next month on the *Ariel.* A mere paddle wheeler, as my stepmother likes to point out."

"Nothing less than the commodore's steam for aristocrats like us," said Henry. "But the purpose of both journeys is the same: a last look at the Old World before the New one calls us home to participate in its destruction."

"If there ever is a war," said Clara, "Henry should raise a regiment of cavalry. He'll already have had so much experience riding with the Four Horsemen of the Apocalypse."

Howard laughed, and coughed.

"There will be enough civil strife right aboard ship, I'm sure," said Henry.

"What do you mean?" asked Howard.

"Oh, it's awful," said Clara, commencing a rapid explanation of the Harris family's woes. "Papa can't be cheered up about the trial. It's a terrible way to end his term on the court. Twelve years and then this. He really can't bear not being loved by everyone. When we return, he'll be only a professor at the Albany Law School, and —"

"My mama," cried Henry, "a mere don's wife! The insupportability of it!"

"If we're talking about an absence of support," said Clara, "we ought to talk about Uncle Hamilton."

"It's true, then?" asked Howard.

"Yes," said Clara.

"Well, a case is a case," said Howard, without much conviction. "Everyone is entitled to representation. Even Reimann."

"Still," said Clara, "it will just keep people thinking of Papa in connection with this terrible business."

"Oh, so now it's a terrible business," said Henry, laughing. "Last year it was the most colorful topic of your conversation." He pulled the ribbon behind Clara's neck. "There's nothing wrong with your father passing into local legend, even if it's on the coattails of spouse murder. The point is that he'll be remembered for *something*. I tell you, Clara, if I hadn't made a solemn commitment to guarding the virtue of you and your sisters on European soil, I'd be helping out your Uncle Hamilton with more relish than I've brought to any other business in that office."

"There's no use arguing with him," said Clara, smiling down at Howard. "You can only hope he'll change the subject."

"All right, Howard," said Henry, "I will change the subject, at least slightly. The word is that *you'll* never get the chance to commit uxoricide — at least not against Annie Martin."

"Oh, Henry," said Clara. "For heaven's sake!"

"I'm afraid that rumor is also true," said Howard, who couldn't help laughing. "I've decided Miss Martin is a better ballroom dancer than a marriage prospect. There's just not much passion there." Sighing over his renewed fecklessness in matters romantic, he went on, "It's no great disappointment to her either, I think."

"Well, it should be," said Clara. "And it should be only a relief to you. You deserve a lot more vitality than Miss Annie Martin can provide." She made a face.

"Thank you, dear Clara," said Howard. "I just wish Dr. Cox could provide *me* with a little vitality. If I only had the strength to get out of this bed and stay on my feet. All I wanted to do in coming back here was bid a fond farewell to Kenwood and my women here." He nodded toward his mother and sister, who were coming through the door. "Now I'm not sure this whole enlistment was a good idea."

"Nonsense," said Clara. "You'll be as good as new before you embark, and even better once you're out upon the water. I can't *wait* to be past the seventieth meridian."

Henry and Howard laughed at her newly acquired geography, but she meant what she said. Clara had never in her life looked forward to anything so much as the coming journey, and not because of all the books she'd read and all the ocean voyages she'd heard about from the traveling Rathbones. She felt that once she and Henry were transplanted to a new land, even in the midst of the family, all would change. In the ancient precincts of Europe, life's arrangements and rules would be redrawn, making everything possible between the two of them. "In fact," she burst out, "I should like to go and never come back!"

"Well," said Henry, rising to his feet and putting his arm over her shoulders, "in that case we had better get moving. We can't have you missing your dreams because you've missed the train."

"Do come back," said Howard to Clara as she kissed him goodbye. "I couldn't stand it if you didn't."

Through the bedroom window Sarah and her mother watched Henry and Clara disappear down Elk Street. "Clara told me they're going to Tivoli, Mother. Do you remember how lovely it was?"

"Yes," said Emeline. "Lovely." She peered unsmilingly at the receding figures in the street.

From his pillow Howard could not see Henry and Clara, only the backs of his mother and Sarah, and the sparkling raindrops on the window. He too remembered the lights of Tivoli, from whatever Rathbone family tour he'd seen them on. Right now he tried to picture how Clara would look, some night several weeks from now, in those faraway gardens and under those lights. He was also, he realized, trying to imagine himself next to her. But Henry refused to leave the picture.

The Vanderbilt Line
April 26, 1859

My dear Will,

We are three days out of New York — so distantly east that I imagine the sunset we had hours ago is reaching the bluffs of West Point only now.

I'm thinking back to my visits there, because the stateroom I write from is very much a female version of your old plebe barracks. Lina, Louise, Amanda, and I are all in one large room, a small ruffled regiment, though one entirely without discipline. We live in a constant uproar of chatter, combing, and lacing. Our things are strewn everywhere, and we are so completely pampered that we never think of picking up a single scrap ourselves. Commodore Vanderbilt's notions of decorating have their odd aspects — one of our walls has a print of his Staten Island manse and the other a very grave engraving of Mr. Henry Clay! But the premises are so comfortable that for hours on end we are unconscious of being on the "high seas" at all; the vessel is so huge — 355 feet from stem to stern! — that one experiences it more as a great island than a simple ship. I'm sure Versailles will seem paltry after the expanses of rosewood and mirror we sit amidst each evening in the grand saloon. (The jaw of Mr. Joel Rathbone himself would drop upon seeing it.)

Poor Papa nearly made us late for the embarkation. Right at dockside he insisted on stopping at the Equitable Life offices to take out insurance policies on all of us. Mother declared this to be unnecessary in our age of safety, but he patiently went on filling out form after form. I suppose it made him feel better. Alas, nothing else seems to. He hasn't spoken of the trial, but I know it is still on his mind; I can tell by the way he jumps whenever the ship's boilers shift and groan. (These mechanical monsters leave me completely indifferent; they irritate our stepmother; they terrify Louise.)

The crew are quite refined, as if they'd come straight off the Commodore's own yacht, but life for the stokers and those in steerage is, I suppose, less genteel than what we experience on the higher promenades. Of all us Harrises, only Father and Louise have ventured down to see them — joining the lower orders for evening prayers, and earning a stern rebuke from Pauline. ("Do you want to pick up something that will get us quarantined?")

I myself can't imagine getting sick in these circumstances — the air has given me the lungs and appetite of an alpinist! We've all just had the most enormous dinner, and as soon as I seal this I'm going to join Amanda for a post-prandial promenade. We all wish you were here, but I know how much you prefer parading in ranks with a rifle to dancing on polished sandalwood with a different girl each night!

Your loving sister,
Clara

She put the letter into its envelope, quickly, before she could think about the two little lies in its last paragraph. Not everyone was missing Will (Henry couldn't have borne his presence), and it was of course Henry, not Amanda, with whom she was going to stroll.

"I'll be back," she said to her sisters, who looked up from their novels and knitting and curling papers to nod at Clara and, after she'd closed the cabin door, one another.

She knew just where he'd be, and in the dark she walked with careful speed along the damp wooden deck, trying not to slide toward rail or rigging. She felt the vibrations of the boilers beneath her feet as she looked for the air funnel behind which

Henry had stood waiting for her each of the past two nights. She thought she had the right funnel in view, but there were so many of them; perhaps she was wrong. Or maybe she was early. Or perhaps he'd decided not to come. She pulled her shawl tighter and hoped no one would see her and wonder what she was doing by herself.

It was so dark that when the voice came she nearly screamed.

"You're not below, praying with your papa?"

"No!" she shouted, before realizing who it was. Then relief made her angry. "I nearly jumped out of my skin! And don't scoff at Papa!"

"I'm not scoffing at your papa," the voice said, laughing. "I'm too occupied with his daughter."

Her fear gave way to a different sort of excitement, though another, delicious sort of fear was mixed into it. She tried to calm herself, to keep him from thinking she was scared of the dark. "Do you think," she asked, in too much of a rush to sound as casual as she wished, "that our Italian trip will be spoiled? It's a shame the Piedmont may be torn up by war just because the French and Austrian emperors can't get along."

He laughed. "Have you been writing to Will? On affairs of state?"

She tried to laugh with him, but was still worried that anyone who saw them, tucked into this dark alcove, might start some talk. "There's a woman over there," she said, pointing toward the railing.

"Do you think she's going to jump?" he asked. "A jilted maiden who purchased a ticket to come out upon the ocean and do away with herself? They say it happens, you know, even on the commodore's ships."

"I think she's a happily married mother," said Clara, not pleased at the way he was spooking her tonight. She wanted to get out of this small space, to see his face. "I think," she added, trying to push him away from her, back into some moonlight, "I think she's probably trying to get away from a roomful of beautiful, noisy children who haven't given her a moment's peace all day."

He laughed at her hypothesis and at her pushing, and he took her wrist and pushed back, gently at first and then harder, until she whispered "Henry!" loud enough, she hoped, to make him stop what he was doing, but not so loud the woman at the railing would be alarmed. But now the woman was out of her view, erased by the black silhouette of Henry's head, which was moving closer, blocking everything else from sight, until his face reached her own and he pressed his lips against hers. He took hold of her with both arms and squeezed her, so hard he forced the breath out of her mouth and into his. He removed his lips and brought them to her neck, and when she realized her mouth was free, and open, she expected to hear herself crying out, to the woman at the railing, for help. But the sound she heard coming from herself was a soft moan, a series of murmurs keeping time with the strokes of Henry's hands upon her breasts. Her thoughts went back again to the woman, who now seemed only an annoyance, a hindrance to this moment her own body wanted to continue, this moment that her hands, pulling on Henry's shoulders — and her face, biting at his whiskers — were trying to prolong.

And just when she thought her pounding heart might burst, the moment was stopped by the sound of footsteps. Two evening strollers were approaching, and as she closed her eyes, breathing with fear, several seconds passed before she realized that Henry had slipped away into the dark. She was alone.

→ 11 ←

ON THE LAST Friday morning in May, Pauline Harris sat on a bench in the Tuileries, reading the copy of the London *Times* she had purchased at Galignani's. Henry and three of his sisters were taking a turn about the statuary, still near enough for Pauline to hear their feet scrunching the gravel paths that ran beside the orange trees and lilacs. Judge Harris, complaining of indigestion (the result of having had too late a supper after last night's opera), was back at the hotel, being cared for by Amanda.

A brief look around convinced Pauline that it was unusual for a woman to sit here by herself reading the newspaper, but none of the strolling dandies and mothers with children seemed to be paying her much mind. More likely these days to crave solitude than attention, she took a long, slow breath and appreciated the momentary absence of the chattering girls, and of her husband, too, who remained almost as fretful and self-pitying as he'd been the day of Mary Hartung's conviction. It had never been like him to find fault with trifles, but so far his progress through Europe had been a parade of small, nervous complaints about everything from how the breakfast eggs had gone off to the way the fabulous sets at the Opéra only distracted one from the music. Over the years, he had learned to watch *her* for signs of irritation, but these past several weeks their parts had been reversed, and she was grateful for the escape his indigestion was affording her this morning.

Alas, there was no escaping Mr. Seward. Along with news of the fighting in Italy, the London paper was full of his English trip: the way the *Ariel*'s band had piped him aboard with "Hail to the Chief," how he'd been presented at court and entertained at Lord Palmerston's home in Piccadilly. It was as if the Harris party had been in London just to sweep an anonymous path before him: Mr. Seward's French plans included a visit to Napoleon's tomb, which Henry had insisted on their seeing just the other afternoon. At least they would be gone from Paris by the time Mr. Weed's favorite caught up with them. After that, their paths would diverge, Mr. Seward going off to see the pope in Rome and the Harrises proceeding east into Germany.

A few dozen yards away from Pauline, Clara's gaze paid less attention to the sculptures and flowering trees than to the gravel at her feet. She and her sisters followed Henry as he recited from Baedeker's and delivered an ironic commentary on the guidebook's account of the treasures they were passing. Even solemn Louise giggled at his cleverness, but Clara walked in silence, confused and humiliated: the girls might as well be pigeons trotting behind a priest, as he strolled through the matutinal passages of his breviary.

Had she dreamed those nighttime walks on the deck of the *Vanderbilt?* From the moment they docked at Southampton, Henry had made not the slightest allusion, by word or glance, to them — not even to counsel secrecy. Her instincts and shame kept her from making any reference herself. Would this whole grand tour have to be a mere interval, until they were embarked for home and she and Henry could once more safely meet amidst the shipboard shadows?

Since their arrival in England, every day had been smothered in a jabbering fuss about carriages, trunks, itineraries, and meals, all of it made worse by Papa's sulkiness. The exasperation she felt with him and with all the touristic nonsense should have drawn Henry closer to her, made him realize she could finally appreciate the way he'd endured the whole past noisy decade of doubled family life. But all the bother of travel seemed to trouble him not at all. In fact, Amanda had taken to teasing him about his cheerful new disposition.

An hour later, among the tangled vines and leering funerary monuments of Père Lachaise, Clara continued to worry. Pauline had gone back to the hotel with Louise to check on Papa, leaving her and nine-year-old Lina to stumble with Henry over the illustrious corpses. The Gothic gloom didn't fret Lina; she went gamboling among the sarcophagi, popping up here and there in imitation of a gargoyle's eyes and open mouth, while Henry looked up from his guidebook just long enough to laugh.

Clara felt sick with frustration, wondering why, even in this threatening place, Henry seemed unable to resurrect his doom-saying self. "Give me that voice again, my Porphyro," she wanted to cry out. "Those looks immortal, those complainings dear!" But he remained horribly merry and fraternal. Only Howard, who Clara hoped was out of his sickbed and on the high seas, could have been gladdened by this new incarnation. The afternoon wore on, and during a long walk through Les Halles, the noise and smells and butcher's blood succeeded only in further animating Henry and Lina. After they had all, at Henry's ciceronian insistence, crossed the Pont Neuf and walked clear through Montparnasse, Clara was still unable to find her nerve and demand an explanation of his good spirits.

Now the three of them were prowling the dark aisles of Saint Sulpice. Each ecclesiastical pillar rested on a huge block of streaked marble resembling the great slabs of fatty beef they'd seen at the market, and as she passed them Clara thought she would be sick. She hurried ahead, keeping her eyes on the plain straw chairs, as if this bland visual food might settle her stomach. In the first row, just before the altar, she sat down. Papa would never forgive her if she knelt in this popish place, but she wished she could pray to the sculpture before her: the Virgin Mary, standing upon a stone globe over some stone clouds, her Infant in her arms. Clara longed to ask for an end to the confusion she was feeling, but no matter how sweet the carved face, her Baptist soul would not permit her to petition this graven surrogate.

What she truly needed was the light of day, an escape from history and the dead and all this obligatory looking at them. She rose from her seat, intent on fleeing, and reached the nave after skirting the complexities of the floor by the altar, a series of wooden trap doors and hinges leading farther into the violent past. As her heels clicked across the marble toward the sunlight, she closed her eyes and imagined her father's apple trees in Loudonville — a sight Parisians ought to be crossing the ocean to see.

Outside in the square she sat on a ledge of the fountain, wondering if Henry and Lina had taken notice of her absence and if she might be able to find her way back to the hotel, halfway across the city, without them.

"*Eh bien. La poupée.*"

A loud American accent coming from the church steps made her look up. It was Henry, waving off Lina, giving her permission to visit the dollmaker's shop they'd passed on their way to the church, the one whose front window was filled by the figure of Marie Antoinette wearing a bell-shaped gown the dollmaker had fashioned entirely from starched doilies. As Lina ran off, Henry strode toward the fountain. The last thing Clara now wanted was what she'd wished for all morning, to be alone with him. Even so, she could feel the frustration drain from her all at once, as if her body were a lock on the Erie Canal; what rushed in to refill it was the excitement she remembered from the ship.

Suddenly she had the courage to stand up and fling questions at him: "Why are you treating me this way? Why are you being so horrible to me, after . . ." She couldn't finish.

"After what?" asked Henry, smiling at her.

"After all that's happened," she answered.

"All that's happened?"

"On the ship!" she cried.

"Nothing's happened," said Henry, as if trying to soothe some childish misapprehension.

"Nothing!" shouted Clara.

"Nothing yet," said Henry.

She fell quiet, until his laughter brought her back to angry life. "*Yet?* Does that mean something is supposed to *follow* all this indifference? Why are you testing me! And what are you testing? My strength? My discretion?"

"*Our* strength," he whispered, creating new hope in her tired face. "*Our* discretion."

Sensing she might let herself collapse in a tearful heap on the fountain's ledge, Henry swept his arm around her waist and projected her into the square. "Come," he said, getting her feet to scamper across the cobblestones. "Let's go buy Lina the decapitated queen."

"IT'S JUST LIKE the Pitti Palace," said Mrs. Alexander Stafford, pointing to the Königsbau. "You'll realize that as soon as you get down to Florence. Mark my words."

"I'm sure," said Pauline. The Staffords and their two plain daughters had run into the Harrises an hour ago at the cathedral and agreed to join forces in exploring the old city of Munich. The Königsbau having been dismissed as a replica, the combined group went on to the small theatre nearby, where the Staffords' hotelkeeper had assured them small parties of tourists were, during the noon hour, welcome to stand at the back and glimpse the players in rehearsal.

"The costliness of that victory at Solferino was nothing short of astonishing," declaimed Mr. Stafford, clapping Judge Harris's back as they mounted the steps together.

"From what I read," replied the judge, "even beyond what he paid at Magenta." The appearance of Mr. Stafford, a bluff Alabama planter, had contributed to a rise in the judge's spirits that had been perceptible since crossing the Rhine. The Hartung fiasco had at last begun to fade, and he was finally taking an interest in their sightseeing and the news of the day, which this month consisted chiefly of Napoleon III's victories over the Austrians down in Italy.

"Wait until the political conversation turns to matters domestic," Henry said to Clara as the two of them followed behind. "You can wager the bonhomie won't last when yo' pa heahs about Massa Stafford's chained-up Negroes — of whom I suspect there are plenty." Pauline, walking arm in arm with Mrs. Stafford, looked over her shoulder to give Henry a cautioning glance. She wanted nothing to confound the morning's pleasant turn of events. Whatever the reason Mr. Stafford acted as a tonic to the judge's spirits — perhaps the amiable Southerner buoyed his belief in the chances of preserving the Union — Pauline wanted nothing to dilute its effect; she only wished there were enough of it left over to dose Clara, who during the past few weeks of travel had been terribly glum.

Laertes was making his first-act goodbyes to Ophelia — in German — when the Harrises and Staffords were startled by some incomprehensible barking from a man standing near them at the back of the auditorium. He was apparently the director and, as nearly as one of the Stafford girls could figure out from her pre-travel language lessons, he was trying to indicate that this whole exercise in Bavarian bardolatry would collapse if Laertes couldn't manage to talk to Ophelia like a brother instead of a householder scolding a servant. *Dummkopf!* The object, he assured the actor, was to get her to stay away from Hamlet, not to dust more assiduously.

"This is our cue," whispered Henry to Clara, easing her through a red velvet curtain, back into the lobby and out to the street, where he showed the driver of an empty diligence a city map with an X penciled on the outskirts. The driver nodded and helped the two Americans to their seats before clattering off with them in the direction of the Isar River.

"All right, Henry," said Clara, determined to be calm, even hopeful. "Tell me where we'll be while Papa spends the rest of the afternoon worrying himself sick."

"X marks the spot. A little studio inhabited by my old Union friend Leander Reynolds. The great artist of my set in North College. He came here a year ago, determined to become the new Kaulbach by taking advantage of the scenery and the prices. I think he's probably spent more time drinking beer in the Bock-keller than he has painting, but we'll probably find one or two canvases propped up in his lair."

"Is he expecting us?"

"I hope not, since he's in Paris at the moment. But when I wrote to tell him I'd be over, he said I should feel free to have a look around whether he was there or not. The door is never bolted."

Clara remained silent, and Henry took her hand. As they drove through the old city, she told herself that she was on her way to her heart's desire, that she could not wait another day for it, that she and Henry would now bring themselves together forever in the way they were meant to be. Their union as man and woman would now be accomplished, and be so evident to others that no one would any longer be able to look at them as brother and sister. And yet, in the back of her mind, as they drove on, she wondered if this submission were wise, and if perhaps there really wasn't some good reason they remain apart. Yes, she would have her Lord Byron, but might people now look at Henry as they had looked at the poet, whispering about what he'd done to his sister? No, she decided, closing her eyes decisively. She and Henry were not brother and sister, and never had been. There was no blood between them, and nothing to stop them from loving each other.

Leander Reynolds's studio was really a little cottage in sight of the river, surrounded by a fence and flowers. Henry paid the driver and helped Clara down. He waved to the *hausfrau* in the next yard, pushing open the cottage door as if he were returning home for the thousandth time.

Determined to look brave — unsure whether she was alarmed or relieved at what might finally be about to happen — Clara took off her bonnet and began exploring the little studio, which was, in fact, full of spun-sugar landscapes, so many that it seemed like one more museum on the Harris family itinerary.

"Awful, aren't they?" asked Henry, picking up a pastel-colored oil of the Aukirche's tower.

"Terrible," Clara agreed, wondering what her father would be thinking when the Harrises and Staffords explored that very church this afternoon. Poor Papa. Just when he was regaining his old self, she joins with Henry in betraying him. But would they really be betraying him by doing what they might soon be . . . doing where? She looked into the cottage's only other room and spotted Mr. Reynolds's unmade bed.

"Why do you hate Papa so?" she asked, surprised at the question, at the ease with which it had escaped her lips. She was right now so anxious that Henry's unconquerable dislike of his stepfather seemed almost a conversational matter, like Leander Reynolds's pictures, just a way to pass the time until the moment arrived and they went into the other room.

"All right, I will tell *you*," said Henry, recalling the day he'd come into his inheritance and told Howard over oysters at the Delavan that he would never explain his feelings for Ira Harris.

"You remember your real mother," he began, as Clara tried keeping her eyes on one of the paintings. "And I remember mine. The way she was before my father died. She had a beauty and a brazen confidence beyond anything you can imagine. My father was mad for her, and dared anybody else not to be. He'd march all of us into the Eagle Tavern with him on Friday nights and hold court. He'd put Jared and me on his backers' laps and sit my mother right beside him, without her hat, her curls glinting under the whale-oil lamps. She was like some cask of booty he'd flung open to make them gape. He knew they didn't want her there, but he knew they couldn't stop looking at her either, couldn't stop being envious, because this was the woman who'd made him more than a grocer looking for votes, made him into something they could never be. She turned the two of them into a thing the others had to watch. And then he died."

Henry had sat down on the edge of a paint-splattered table. Afraid he might not finish the story, Clara pulled over the stool by one of the easels and sat in front of him. She took his hand in hers.

"You never truly met her, Clara. She was transformed, shrunken, immediately after he died. I remember that summer when she took me off to Schenectady so she could be with your father at the Union commencement. I was eight years old and I watched her coquette with him. What I was most aware of was her fear. She needed him because she was afraid of being alone with only the money my father had left her. She was afraid of never again being an important man's wife, afraid of no longer being allowed to sit and shine in the lamplight at the tavern. My father had left her an appetite, but the men at the Eagle had no more need of her. Without someone like your father, she wouldn't have anybody looking at her the way those men had looked at her on Friday nights."

"Are you saying my father let her down? By not rising as high as she expected him to?" Clara kept her voice neutral, inquiring. She was trying to be Henry's ally, not his opponent, on this unexpected journey into the past.

"No," said Henry softly. "I don't blame him for that." Clara squeezed his hand encouragingly. "I blame him for being so little from the start." She drew away as if he'd clawed her. "My mother was something magnificent, almost wild. Then fear made her small. She was afraid to look back and to remember what she was, who *he* was — my father — and what they'd been together. It would be easier if your father had been some terrible usurper. But he's not Claudius. He's just Polonius, asked to play Claudius's part." He paused to look into her astonished eyes.

"You are disgusting!" she said, pushing the stool out from under herself and slapping his face. "You ungrateful, horrible . . ." But she couldn't get the words out; he'd spun her around and squeezed her waist so hard she could barely breathe. He was carrying her into the next room and onto Leander Reynolds's bed. She was screaming now, struggling to get off the dingy linen.

"I hate you!" she cried.

"No, you don't. You love me, and I love you, and have for years and years, watching you read in your window seat, looking at you across the dinner table as you struggled not to say all the clever things in your head because your manners told you to let your father and your brother have the floor."

He began to unlace her dress. Her hand rose, and he thought she was about to fight him again, but before he counterattacked, he saw that she had lifted her hand only to undo the dress herself. "I'm not Ophelia," she whispered, through tears. "And you're not Hamlet. We're not any of those people."

He said nothing as he rose to remove his coat and shirt. When he got back to the bed, she had unpinned her long dark hair and was reaching up for him, recalling summer nights in Loudonville when there would be a storm, and she would put her arms out the window and try to coax the lightning down. As he pressed upon her, she struggled for one last moment, until he whispered that it was too late for that. And then he entered her, like a knife, and she screamed until the pain was gone, replaced with a joy and fierceness that, as they moved together, each seemed to borrow from the other. When it was over, they smoothed each other's hair. He saw her look down at the bedclothes and once more take fright, but then he soothed her, saying softly that the blood was nothing to worry about.

→ 13 ←

"A WASTE of gunpowder, if you ask me." Thus the masterful Joel Rathbone on the evening of December 3, 1859, sitting with friends and kinsmen in the main drawing room of Kenwood, grand site of his premature retirement just south of Albany, where yesterday morning, at the hour of his hanging, a one-hundred-gun salute had been fired in tribute to John Brown. The *Albany Evening Journal* was full of the details: the brave and dignified appearance Brown made while climbing to the scaffold; Colonel J. T. L. Preston's declaration, "So perish all such enemies of Virginia"; the thirty-seven minutes that the body was left to hang. Most prominently featured was Brown's written prophecy, handed to a bystander as the prisoner left his cell: "I, John Brown, am now quite certain that the crimes of this guilty land will never be purged away but with Blood. I had, as I now think, vainly flattered myself that without very much bloodshed it might be done."

"The body's to be buried in North Elba," said Joel's cousin John Finley Rathbone, repeating what everyone already knew, "and to come through Troy on its way. Giving the abolitionists righteous fits at every stop." He could not say that a civil war's lucrative effect on his foundry hadn't crossed his mind, but outwardly this richest of the Rathbones continued to support President Buchanan and the commercial creed that peace was always the best prescription for prosperity.

"Lucky for Seward to be abroad until the New Year," said Hamilton Harris, alluding to the absence of any comment from the senator in Mr. Weed's paper. "Waiting to see what the Dictator wants him to say, I suppose." Judge Harris's younger brother took loyal pains to disparage the Albany boss's favorite whenever Ira was around, particularly since the latter had had to return from Europe and find that Hamilton had succeeded in winning an acquittal for Reimann, paramour of the still-imprisoned Mary Hartung.

"Seward's waiting," said John Finley Rathbone, "to see which comment can provoke maximum inflammation from Boston to Birmingham. A year from now he'll have the presidency and we'll all have his war."

"A shame mankind can't put all its energies into things like this Suez Canal," said Ira Harris with a nobility no one could dispute.

"Seward's proposing a canal?" squawked Mr. Osborne, an ancient friend of Joel Rathbone's father. "*Suez*," corrected several voices at once, reassuring the old man that this was something being undertaken very far away and not the sort of internal improvement Andy Jackson, rest his soul, had spent his years in Washington fighting.

"Henry?" asked Ira Harris, puffing on his pipe, content enough to risk drawing his stepson into the conversation. "You've been rather mum this evening."

"Oh, I'm in firm agreement with Uncle Joel. They wasted the gunpowder. Consider the need they'll have for it soon." Given the discussion's overall inclination toward the dire, Henry seemed less of a doomsayer than usual. But he kept the full measure of his feelings hidden. There was a part of himself, a part he feared, that would have been perfectly willing to drop the trap door beneath John Brown's feet yesterday morning; and as Brown swung in the breeze, he'd have been happy to shake his hand, the one that had lit the fuse now lying in a straight line across a very dry field. As he had told Clara, the moving spark was visible just over the horizon. No one could deny that it was getting brighter, and closer, and heading toward them.

Attracted by the sound of her son's voice, her old political instincts telling her what the men were discussing, Pauline Harris ventured in from the parlor and put her hands on Henry's shoulders. "No, don't get up," she told the men, deciding after a brief look at them against entering this conversation. Like her husband, she had lost her touch for it. "Mr. Harris," she said to Ira, "what was the name of the silversmith who sold you this beautiful pin for me? The man whose little shop was near Santa Felicita?" She had been engaged with Emeline Rathbone in some traveler's one-upmanship, a game she could finally play since their return in October; she'd be better off going back to that than trying to heat up any tepid remarks Ira might make about the political situation.

"Papi, my dear. Mr. Giuseppe Papi."

"Thank you," said Pauline, brushing her son's cheek. "Although I expect he calls himself *Signor* Papi." She exited to polite male chuckles.

"John Brown, of course," reported Pauline when she retook her seat in the parlor between Emeline and Clara. Emeline twisted her mouth in displeasure, as if the boring nature of such a topic were self-evident, and Clara wondered what pitch of agitation her next letter from Mary Hall would reach. In the forty-five days since Brown's capture at Harper's Ferry, Mary had sent her one distressed missive after another, two of them tear-stained, so goodness knew what yesterday's martyrdom might provoke. Clara had responded with appropriate expressions of concern, but except for its effect on Henry, the John Brown affair hardly engaged her. She wished that she could shift the subject of her correspondence with Mary to what she herself had been going through in the eight weeks since they'd arrived home. She was without anyone to confide in. Pauline was out of the question, and her sisters were too immature to be considered. Alas, sweet-natured Mary seemed to have no room inside her brain for anything but the bad case of abolitionist fever she'd caught during her father's winter tour with Beecher.

If it were otherwise, Clara would tell her about that afternoon in Munich, and its single repetition in London just before sailing home; of her father's hoping-against-hope silences when they returned with excuses Henry put little effort into fabricating; of Pauline's stern glances and Clara's fear that she had guessed or, even worse, been told by Henry. Worst of all was Henry's inscrutability, his disinclination to speak of what had happened between them, or to discuss the future of it.

It was the only future she wished to contemplate, though she knew it was an impossible one for her father and Pauline, and even for Henry himself, to accept right now. Social awkwardness would be the chief item on the bill of particulars drawn up against the idea of their becoming man and wife. But each passing month, she felt, could be made to work to her advantage: she was willing to keep a distance from him, to minimize their joint appearance at family occasions such as this, until everyone eventually got it into their heads that Clara Harris and Henry Rathbone shared less blood than the second cousins whose weddings they were forever attending up and down the Hudson Valley. She would keep to herself, to Wordsworth and the window seat, as Henry, on his way to seeing the logic of his ardor, put in his lazy hours in Uncle Hamilton's office and spent his inheritance too freely. Even if he spent it on the girls of Quay Street, she would be patient. He would see his war — she'd become certain of that today — but she would have him, before he and Will went off to fight it.

Pauline and Emeline were disputing the merits of Florentine coffee when Howard Rathbone abandoned the drawing room for the parlor. He took a seat beside Clara, who hoped his arrival might save her from this new twist of the continental competition between her stepmother and Henry's aunt. How sadly pale he looked! Months on the ocean had left him no more hardy than he'd been that day in April when they'd all said goodbye; she wondered if there was more than holiday generosity to the shore leave he'd been granted.

"You're quiet tonight," said Howard, inching his chair closer to hers. He had actually enjoyed her silences at dinner, preferred them to the sarcastic chatter he remembered from the months before she went abroad, all that mimicry of Henry which continued in her letters, as she attempted to keep up with him and appear more formidable to Pauline.

"I've already bored half of Albany with my 'European impressions,'" she responded. "Besides, what can compete with John Brown?"

"Real life?" sighed Howard, who had none of the family taste for politics. "The things right in front of us?"

"You need to find yourself a new girl, Howard." Clara smiled at him and patted his knee.

He realized he was a little in love with her, knew she was the real reason he could never stick with any girl for long. "What's wrong with an *old* girl?" he asked, taking her hand and squeezing it, but not daring to lose his smile and show this was more than a jape. "What's wrong with a girl you've known practically forever?"

"Why, Howard Rathbone," she replied, keeping up the illusion of playfulness, swatting his hand once she'd withdrawn her own. "You and I are cousins by marriage. Don't you think that's dangerously close for a man to be to a girl he wants to court?"

She regretted the joke as soon as she made it. She had no desire to hurt dear Howard, whose cheeks had just gone as red as his hair. She didn't particularly resent his opposition to the idea of Henry and herself getting together. Howard's objections were sweetly intentioned, and they would be the least of the obstacles she and Henry would have to overcome. She knew perfectly well that Howard was in love with her, but she was sure he would get over it. When he did, he might even be persuaded to help them with the rest of the family. And now she'd gone and embarrassed him by making a joke — in Henry's exact style, too — about his well-meant alarm.

"I'm just a silly tease, Howard." She gave his thin rib cage a good-natured poke. "Let's go into the other room. Mother, Aunt Emeline: I've asked Howard to see if his presence will be enough to secure me admission to the drawing room." Emeline gladly waved her away and Pauline smiled, a bit nostalgically. Taking Howard's arm, Clara crossed the threshold over which the sliding doors ran, and the gentlemen stood up through a cloud of their pipe smoke to greet her. Howard relinquished her to Henry, who made a place for her beside himself on the sofa. "Proceed, Uncle," he said to Hamilton Harris.

"Not much more to say," said the crisp attorney. "The invitation was issued weeks ago, and he'll be talking in Brooklyn on the twenty-seventh of February. If you're interested in seeing somebody other than Mr. Seward move into the White House a year from now, you might think about going down to hear him."

"Whom are they talking about?" Clara whispered to Henry.

"Abraham Lincoln," he replied.

"U GH — U GH — U GH," chanted Sybil Bashford on the porch of Ocean House in Newport. She scratched her stomach, too, in ape-like imitation of the Republican candidate for President — all to infuriate poor Mary Hall.

"Stop it, Sybil," she cried. "That's awful!"

Clara Harris just laughed.

"He's not at *all* like that," Mary said. "My father took me to see him at the Cooper Institute in February, after they'd moved the meeting from Reverend Beecher's church. The crowd was *enormous,* and he couldn't have been more eloquent. 'Let us have faith that right makes might, and in that faith, let us —' "

"Oh, Lord, she's committed it to memory! Someone make her stop!" shrieked Sybil. "If that abolitionist wins, he's liable to spoil my whole wedding next May." She pouted, and returned her gaze to the illustrations of bridal accessories she'd been perusing on this hot summer day.

"He's not an abolitionist," Clara offered as correction to Miss Bashford, a graduate of the Newport Academy whose interest in national affairs knew many bounds.

"If only he were," cried Mary. "But he's still the least equivocal of any of the candidates about slavery — it's *wrong,* Sybil — and he'll keep it from entering any more territories, that's certain."

"Oh, pooh," said Sybil. "There's nothing wrong with slaves. They're the reason even this town got built. The triangular trade. We learned about it in the academy."

"Why, Sybil," purred Clara, stirring the ice in a pitcher of lemonade. "I'm surprised by your scholarship."

"A lot of lovely slaves are even part of my dowry," Sybil continued.

"I shall scream!" cried Mary.

"It would do you good," said Sybil, flipping over the sketch of a lace train and asking Clara to pour her another glass of lemonade.

"Stop it, both of you," said Clara, quite calmly. The slavery question did not agitate her as it did Mary, who she had decided was a better person than she. But the ascendancy of Mr. Lincoln interested her deeply. She had discussed it over and over with Henry and Papa in the six months since Uncle Hamilton came back all excited from the Cooper Institute speech. It had happened so fast. After Harper's Ferry, Mr. Seward, at the Dictator's insistence, had tried to mollify the Southerners, convince them he wasn't as extreme as they feared. It didn't work, and the Republicans decided at their Chicago convention that only Lincoln stood a real chance of carrying what was being called the "lower North," and thereby the presidency. Ira Harris had sent Seward his fulsome condolences, while Mr. Weed, shocked by defeat, journeyed to Springfield, his big black hat in hand, to call on the plain man who'd vanquished the brilliant creature he'd been grooming for the last dozen years.

"Sybil, think of it this way. It could be much worse. You could be faced with Mr. Seward instead."

"Oh, him," said Sybil, disgusted. "The 'irresistible contest.'"

"'Irrepressible conflict,'" corrected Mary, as if Sybil had misquoted a psalm.

"They're the same thing," Sybil said, putting her glass of lemonade down rather hard. "Oh, I *hate* August. No one even sends us letters now. They're tired of writing the same thing they've written since the beginning of the summer, and they're too hot to move in any case."

"Have you had anything from Will?" asked Mary, who thought Clara's brother a figure of wonderful rectitude.

"Nothing since he got back to Loudonville last month."

"Then read us one of the letters he sent from West Point, back in June."

Clara rummaged among the envelopes in her sewing basket as Sybil made a face. "Here's the one about the dining hall," said Clara. "How about that?"

"Oh, yes, read it," said Mary.

"'As an instance of the fare at our mess, the other day a cadet who sits opposite me tied a shoestring to a piece of crust, saying, "Let's see if that comes in our pudding tomorrow." Sure enough, the next day a lieutenant found it in his pudding, fished it out, and carried it on the point of his sword about the hall. Pudding is suspicious to me, and I quit eating it before I had been here three months.'"

Mary beamed over this display of healthy spirit. "Is he really the highest officer in his class?" she asked.

"Yes," said Clara. "The sergeant major of the corps."

Sybil moaned. "I shall spit if we have to sit here forever."

"Let's go up to Boston," suggested Mary.

"It's too hot," said Clara.

"No, Mary's right. Let's go," said Sybil. "My mama can get the carriage to take us to Providence, and we can take the train from there. It will be fun. We can look at bridal gloves."

"And hear Mr. Seward," said Mary.

"What?" cried Sybil.

"He's speaking in Boston this evening," Mary said.

Clara looked amused. "I'm beginning to think this is a good idea after all."

"Absolutely not!" cried Sybil.

"Then neither of us will go with you. Isn't that right, Clara?"

"I'm afraid Mary's correct, Sybil. If she's going to be dragged through the shops with you, there's got to be something in it for her, too."

Sybil growled, in a torment of indecision. "You are a *sneak*, Mary Hall. That abolitionist is the only reason you suggested Boston." Losing ground, she raised conditions: "You can't tell my mama we're going to do anything but look at the gloves."

Mary and Clara nodded.

"And I'm allowed to stuff my ears when he speaks."

"Perhaps you should bring your salts," said Clara.

It was a hot day, and even in this ocean-drenched little state, nothing could keep down the dust on the roads. By the time the young women reached Providence, Sybil was so parched and cranky that Mary and Clara could get her onto the train only by buying her two different-flavored ices from the Italian man on the platform. The trip to Boston took nearly two hours, but the rush of air through the open windows refreshed the girls before they arrived. Once in the city, they had time for Sybil to visit just three shops in Newbury Street, none of them adequate to her demands. The young ladies were soon swept into the throngs moving toward Revere House, on whose steps Mr. Seward would deliver his remarks. It was a dreadful experience for Sybil, who hated being jostled. Her tortures were increased by Clara's pointing to a Republican women's banner — WE LINK ON TO LINCOLN, AS OUR MOTHERS DID TO CLAY — and by Mary's knowing the words to every campaign ditty being sung. The wait for Mr. Seward seemed endless, but finally Governor Banks led him to the lectern, where he acknowledged the crowd's cheers, none of them more lusty than those shouted by pale little Mary Hall. Clara divided her attention among Sybil's theatrical agonies, Mary's ecstatic partisanship, and the eagle-like face of Mr. Seward, whose thick planes of sharply cut hair hung immobile in the breezeless evening.

"It behooves you, solid men of Boston, if such are here" — great cheers — "and if the solid men are not here, then the lighter men of Massachusetts" — great laughter followed by an even greater cheer — "to bear onward, and forward, first in the ranks, the flag of freedom." It was a performance Clara's father never could have given; it had a gaiety Papa would never allow to scamper out from under the heavy folds of his rhetoric. Late this spring the gossip in Uncle Hamilton's law office was that Mr. Seward had taken his defeat hard, been too distressed to stir from Auburn; but to Clara's eyes, and judging from his schedule of campaign speeches, his recovery was admirably complete. Should Mr. Lincoln win, the new President would have a formidable ally in the Senate. If only her papa had had such resiliency after the case of Mrs. Hartung — a far smaller thing to endure than the loss of the White House.

"Come," said Clara, catching Sybil and Mary at the elbows

as soon as Mr. Seward showed signs of finishing. "Let's make our escape. The other speakers will go on all night." Mary looked wistfully back at the Revere House steps, but deferred to Clara's authority. The clamor of the rally and the rare victory of her own will over Sybil Bashford's had left her tired.

They stayed overnight at a small hotel on Beacon Hill, and the following day, in a mood to make things up to Sybil, Mary and Clara gave over the whole morning and most of the afternoon to bridal shopping. By the time they finished the train ride back to Providence and a steamship run down to Newport, during which Clara knitted and Sybil snored, it was nearly midnight. As the boat docked, Mary realized that the day's excitement wasn't over. Marching toward them along the shore were crooked lines of young men in capes and shiny hats, carrying torches in a loud procession. "Clara, look! Some Wide-Awakes!" A lusty party of Lincoln cadres, the sort now found on the streets of Albany and other Northern cities almost every night, were marching to one of their songs, whose lyrics Mary joined in singing:

> This is no time in idle dreams
>   A glorious rest to take;
> What man that loves the right and true
>   He must be Wide-Awake!

"Sybil," called Clara, poking her in the ribs. "Wake up."

"*Mmnnh,*" said Sybil, ostentatiously rubbing her eyes. "What is it?"

"Men," said Clara. "Yankee men, but young and good looking nonetheless."

This intelligence roused Sybil to life. She sat up in her deck chair and squinted. "Where are we?" she asked.

"Home," said Clara.

"Speak for yourself," she replied. "And will *you*," she added, turning toward Mary and pinching her on the arm, "stop that caterwauling?"

Back at Ocean House the women were surprised to find Pauline

Harris still up, sitting on the porch and staring out toward the sea. She greeted them wearily: "Did you have a good time?"

"Yes," said Clara. "Sybil saw some lovely wedding things." She knew better than to talk of Mr. Seward.

"There's a letter for you from Henry," said Pauline, pointing to it on a nearby table.

Sybil, who had been thoroughly revived by a long look at the broad shoulders of the Wide-Awakes, said, "Clara, you need a beau. The only letters you get are from brothers."

"I *have* a beau," said Clara.

Mary's eyes widened, and Pauline picked this moment to raise her ample form from the wicker chair and announce her retirement for the night.

"Who?" insisted Sybil as soon as Mrs. Harris had gone in.

Clara said nothing, just lightly ran her fingers over Henry's letter and tenderly grazed it against her cheek. Before Mary could drop her jaw and Sybil begin an interrogation, Clara left the porch to go inside and up to the second floor. She found Pauline in the front room of the suite the two of them were sharing with Louise.

"Your sister is asleep," whispered Pauline, indicating the door of the girls' room as she unpinned her hair.

"I saw the look on your face," said Clara. "But you should know that I'm going to marry Henry."

"No," said Pauline. "You are not. Your father will never permit it."

"What can he object to? There's no blood between us."

"It isn't right," said Pauline, brushing out her hair and pretending casually to consider her looks in the vanity's mirror. "You have been brought up too closely for too long. A marriage like this would not bring you happiness."

"Why are you now so interested in me?" asked Clara, trying to equal her in nonchalance as she removed a tortoise-shell comb from her own hair.

"I've always been interested in you," said Pauline.

"That's not true!" said Clara, unable to control herself. "Isn't your real thought that I'm not worthy of Henry? That he'd be another Rathbone wasted on another Harris?"

"You're being ridiculous," said Pauline, whose composure did not desert her as she swept her hairpins into a china dish. "You must wait for someone else."

"I'm nearly twenty-six. I've done my waiting — for Henry!"

"Calm down, you're going to wake Louise. This discussion is concluded. You are not right for Henry, and that is all there is to it."

Clara's whisper was a hiss. "Who *would* be right for Henry? Someone more like his mother?"

Pauline ignored whatever suggestion hung in the room. She merely repeated her main point. "You've been joined as brother and sister for a dozen years."

"We've been joined more closely than that for some time. Since an afternoon in Munich last summer."

Clara saw Pauline's silhouette stiffen in the mirror. She ran back downstairs, not because any display of wrath was likely to emanate from her stepmother, but because she feared the secret, the thing itself, that she had let loose, like an animal, into the dark. There was just a single candle burning in the hotel parlor, enough to let her find her way out to the porch.

Mary Hall pretended to be asleep in one of the wicker chairs. From the chaise longue Sybil Bashford reached up and grabbed Clara's gingham sleeve. "Tell us *everything*," she demanded.

✦ 15 ✦

THE POLLS CLOSED AT 4:47 P.M., sunset, on November 6, but the sun had been so little in evidence all day that its departure was hardly noticed. Rain had fallen steadily on the crowds lining up to vote throughout the city, from Franklin Street in the First Ward to Elm and Swan in the Tenth. Mr. Weed's paper exhorted the citizenry to BEWARE OF SPLIT TICKETS, WATCH FOR FRAUDULENT VOTERS, and do all they could to secure A GLORIOUS VICTORY for the Republican Party in the county, state, and nation. In a further effort to whip up fervor, the City News column reported an assault on a Wide-Awake that had taken place during the previous night's procession down Pearl Street.

After an early dinner at his brother's home, Hamilton Harris enlisted Ira, Henry, old Mr. Osborne, and John Finley Rathbone to accompany him to the Central Club, at 356 Broadway, where the returns would come in by messenger and telegraph. Clara insisted on coming as well, which led to little Lina's insistence, too — at which point Hamilton Harris said all right, but that's it, hoping the bustle of the evening would keep anyone down at the Central Club from objecting to the girls' presence.

As soon as they had secured their seats and cups of cider, Ira Harris withdrew from his pocket a letter that Will had written from West Point just two days ago. The soothing baritone in which he shared it could not conceal the doubtfulness it prompted in him: "'I suppose you are looking forward to the results of next Tuesday's election as already settled in favor of Lincoln. It seems to be conceded by all parties, as near as I can judge, that his election is certain, and of course you must be glad of it.'"

"Well, let's hope it's certain," said Hamilton Harris, looking at the scanty totals on the chalkboards. "Be damned glad if it *is* certain," he added, making an apologetic nod for his language toward the girls.

Judge Harris continued reciting: "'But I think it would pain you, as it has me, to witness the effect which this struggle has produced in the army and especially in the corps of cadets. Some of my own class who are appointed from South Carolina have received positive orders from home to come there immediately in the case of Lincoln's being elected. I am glad for you that the Republican Party is coming to power, but I sincerely trust that it will not allow those incessant slavery agitators to be their representatives and spokesmen. Slavery may be a curse but I cannot help thinking that anti-slavery is a greater one.'"

What would Mary Hall think of this? wondered Clara, intrigued by the way Will's unionist sentiments had defeated his abolitionist ones.

"He's right about the anti-slavers," said John Finley Rathbone between puffs of his pipe. "That's why I went for Douglas."

Hamilton Harris laughed. "You're riding the wave of the past, Jack. Now, Henry, if you don't mind my asking, how did you vote?"

"For Mr. Bell."

"In four years Henry's gone from being a Know-Nothing to a do-nothing," explained Clara to the laughter of the men. John Bell, the fourth-party candidate, had campaigned by saying nothing whatsoever about slavery.

"You girls know better than your brother, eh?" asked Hamilton. "Two lasses for Lincoln, isn't that so, Lina?"

Ten-year-old Lina just blushed. Except for the Wide-Awake parades that passed under her window some nights, the election was a dull thing. She didn't know how they could talk about it night after night in the dining room on Eagle Street, and down at Kenwood, and out in Loudonville, but they did, even though it only made her papa look left out and unhappy.

For something to do, Clara took her little sister's hair and began braiding it, a sight that always enchanted Henry.

"Yes," Clara said, "I'm still for Lincoln, Uncle Hamilton."

"That's my girl."

"Good for you, dear," said Ira Harris, without much conviction.

"What else does Will say, Papa? Aside from politics."

"Well," said Ira Harris, "there's a bit about Howard: 'The last time I saw Miss Carroll, she told me she was introduced to Lieutenant Rathbone of the U.S. Marines at Lady Napier's ball and danced with him.'" Everyone laughed at news of the family blade, while Clara, joining the strands of her sister's brown hair, thought about the letter she had had from Howard last month, one that could only be called a love letter, vaguely warning her against Henry. She had spoken of it to no one — not even Mary Hall, who, the day after her argument with Pauline, had at last become Clara's confidante. (She had told Sybil Bashford absolutely nothing, despite being beseeched through half the night on the porch at Ocean House.)

"Well," said Hamilton Harris, teasing his niece, "you won't have to put up with all this politics for too much longer. Did you see Mr. Weed's pledge in the *Evening Journal?*" He reached for the newspaper and put on his spectacles. "'We are sure our lady readers are weary of the mass of political matters with which our columns have teemed for months past. But they are no more weary of them than we ourselves —'"

"As if Thurlow Weed ever tired of politics!" said John Finley Rathbone.

"'— so it is our ambition to make the *Journal* more a family than a political newspaper, and we hope to hereafter be able to fully gratify this ambition. We have schemes of improvement in embryo which, when developed, will render the *Journal* more welcome than ever to the family circle.'"

Henry burst out laughing. "Oh, I'm sure there will be no political news at all for the next four years. Can't imagine anything that will be worth noticing!" He took the paper from his uncle. "Let's have a look at some of the welcome tidings Mr. Weed has managed to bring to the 'family circle' even now. Oh, here's matter fit for home and hearth: 'About eleven o'clock last night Patrolman Manning, while going his rounds, discovered smoke issuing from the premises of One Twenty-three Broad Street, occupied by Peter Mullen and his family. He immediately rushed into the house and, upon entering the room, he beheld a horrid spectacle. He found a straw bed on fire and upon it laid a female wholly unconscious of what was going on. With a few pails of water and some assistance, he quenched the flames when he ascertained that the female upon the bed was Mrs. Mullen. She was in a beastly state of intoxication —'"

"Enough, Henry," said Ira Harris, taking the paper from his stepson and nodding in the direction of Lina. Still, Henry had succeeded in making the others laugh. They were growing silly with waiting, and when old Mr. Osborne, who'd been deaf to every word of everyone's recitation, just smiled over their laughter and said, "Good cider, isn't it?" there were contagious guffaws.

Ira Harris, as if calling the proceedings to order, drew attention to one last item in Mr. Weed's paper, a report out of Portsmouth, Virginia: "'The greatest crowd that was ever witnessed in this city, gathered together on Saturday to listen to Honorable Henry A. Wise.'" The man who had hanged John Brown eleven months ago "'DECLARED BEFORE GOD THAT HE WOULD NEVER SUBMIT TO THE ELECTION OF ABRAHAM LINCOLN.'" Mr. Weed's writer went on to explain, in the *Journal*'s impartial way: "'This was telegraphed all over the Union yesterday, in hopes that Wise's crazy ravings would scare some timid voter.'"

"Some more cider for you," said Clara to Mr. Osborne, patting his knee and getting up to fetch him another cup. On her way to the punch bowl she was nearly knocked over by three boys racing in with tallies. The returns were at last flooding in, and soon the telegraphs were clattering without letup, the operators pressing headsets to their ears in order to hear over the noise of the clubroom, which was now packed tight with men arriving by the dozen, shaking the rain from their hats and stroking their whiskers as they watched the numbers fill the boxes on the blackboard.

Ira Harris kept his seat beside his brother while the messengers posted totals from Beaver Street in the Fourth Ward and Orange in the Eighth, as the operators of the "divine signaler" prophesied by Dr. Nott so many years ago heard the word from up and down and across the state, from Brooklyn to Allegheny to Erie, and then, as the evening drew on, from Boston to Pittsburgh to Cleveland. There was no single moment of mathematical certainty; it was only the growing confidence of the alcoholic roar which eventually made apparent the truth of all the digits, dots and dashes: Abraham Lincoln was to be the sixteenth President of the United States. At one A.M. Hamilton Harris, a careful man, finally allowed himself to rise with an exultant expression. Once on his feet, he seemed at a loss for something to do. He settled for quietly patting the judge's shoulder. "Well, brother, Mr. Seward will have to endure the Senate; the Executive Mansion will never be his." This was cold comfort to Ira Harris, who had left the bench months ago and supposed he would teach at the Albany Law School for a few more years before retiring out to Loudonville.

"Come on, Ira. Let's you and Jack and I go upstairs for a brandy."

The three gentlemen left for a more private room. Mr. Osborne and Lina had already been brought home, leaving Henry to walk Clara back to Eagle Street. He held the umbrella over her with his left hand, tilting it in from the street, so that his right was free to grasp her waist. She could smell the whiskey he had drunk all night instead of cider. It had left him drowsy — peaceful, she thought.

Arriving at number 28, where Pauline and Jared and the girls had gone to bed, Henry spread the *Evening Journal* on the steps for Clara to sit upon. The rain was slackening, and he closed the umbrella. He sat down beside her and unpinned her hair. She shut her eyes and let her head fall back as he separated her long damp tresses, the way she had Lina's. He didn't know how to make braids, but he stroked the different strands, folding and unfolding them, one over another, in a way that made his breath fall faster on the back of her neck. And then he gently let go, letting her hair fall to its full length, down to the wet pages of the newspaper.

She was thrilled by this tenderness; she'd never had it before.

"So," she said, "has our hour come round with Mr. Lincoln's?"

She saw him smile before he nestled his head, childishly, into her bosom.

"Soon," he said. After another moment he brought his lips to her ear and whispered, "Yes."

"Yes?"

"Yes," he said. "I do love you, Clara." And then he replaced his head upon her breast. As she looked down Eagle Street — determined that she would manage her father, and that he would manage Pauline — Henry fell asleep in her arms.

⇥ 16 ⇤

SHORTLY AFTER TEN P.M. on February 2, 1861, Hamilton
Harris and John Finley Rathbone were finishing supper at the
Delavan.

"Do you think he really wants it?" Rathbone asked.

Hamilton Harris laughed. "Don't let the Olympian demeanor
fool you. He wants it as heaven 'wanted one immortal song.'"
Then Hamilton's face turned grave, and he looked around the
dining room for a clock. "I just hope he doesn't come up dry. A
month ago he wouldn't dream of the possibility. But for the past
three weeks he's thought of nothing else. I can't stand the idea
of his hopes being crushed."

"Not to mention Pauline's."

"Damn it all," said Hamilton, bringing his hand down hard
enough to rattle the silverware. "He deserves it after all these
years in the wilderness."

What Ira Harris deserved, according to his younger brother,
and what he just might get tonight, was the Senate seat occupied
for the last twelve years by William Henry Seward. To the surprise of nearly everyone, Mr. Lincoln had asked the eagle-nosed
wizard of Auburn to serve as secretary of state in the unity
Cabinet he was trying to assemble, leaving New York's legislators with the task of sending someone to the U.S. Senate in
Seward's place. Thurlow Weed was determined it wouldn't be
his enemy Horace Greeley, the *New York Tribune*'s editor, about
whom the Dictator grumbled, "The man never met a reform he
couldn't chant for." A few weeks ago he'd given the machine's
blessing to William M. Evarts, a New York lawyer.

But the Greeley forces, scenting blood from the wounds Weed

suffered last May in Chicago, had proved formidable through-out a bruising series of ballots, the eighth of which had given 47 to Greeley, 39 to Evarts — and 19 to Ira Harris, the sentimental favorite of a third faction that saw the chance to keep both Greeley and Weed from having their ways. But earlier tonight the Dictator, fearing Greeley was about to go over the top, put out the word that his Evarts men were to shift to Harris — anything to keep his rival editor from getting the seat he'd plumped Seward onto a dozen years ago.

"Do you think he'll be able to swing enough of them over?" asked John Finley Rathbone for the third time tonight.

"It will be close," replied Hamilton Harris, as he had twice before. What he would not tell him was that even before Evarts ran into trouble, the Dictator had privately asked Ira to serve as backup man. There was life yet in the wily old boss, and the original Harris backers would be surprised to know they hadn't been as independent a faction as they'd believed. Hamilton felt there was something unseemly to the alacrity with which Ira, after being passed over and ignored for a dozen years, had agreed to cooperate with his tormentor, but whatever shame was in the bargain would make victory only a little less sweet: the Dictator would still be humbled by the loss of Evarts, and Ira would see his youthful promise blaze up after such a long time sputtering. If, that is, the Greeley forces didn't yet carry the day. The wait was maddening. Hamilton Harris refilled his pipe and tried to change the subject.

"Have you seen any more of the letters Will's been sending from West Point?" he asked. "Enough to break one's heart. Clara showed me one she'd got right after New Year's. Tells how one of his best friends in the class, boy from Alabama, was summoned home after three and a half years at the academy. A wonderful fellow apparently, wanted to be a cavalry officer, no sort of secessionist at all. Will says he and his mates treated this boy and another one from the South to a bottle of wine before carrying them to the dock on their shoulders. They're all keeping up their spirits, he says, but it's a terrible thing. Best young men in the world being sundered from one another."

"Likely to be killing one another soon," said John Finley Rathbone. "Boys slaughtering boys."

"Speaking of boys and slaughter," said Hamilton Harris. "I'm going to slaughter this damned office boy of mine. Where is he? I told him to be over at the State House, and he swore he'd race over here as soon as there was any news."

"He's probably been enticed into a card game by Henry," grunted John Finley Rathbone. "I don't know how you keep him on."

"Oh," said Hamilton Harris, "Henry just needs a good challenge. When one comes along, he'll come into his own. Damn it, let's go over there ourselves. I can't stand this waiting any longer."

A brisk walk took the two men to the State House and up the stairs leading to the Governor's Room, where they knew Thurlow Weed was keeping his command. As they reached the top of the flight, they saw a small clamor of activity. Weed had just emerged into the corridor. His cigar twitching in his mouth, his black hat clamped over his wild white hair, the old man had one arm around a young assemblyman and the other around a reporter from the Albany *Argus,* who was putting a question to him so timidly that Hamilton Harris and John Finley Rathbone couldn't overhear it. Weed's reply, however, boomed out loud and clear: "Do I *know* Judge Harris *personally?*" He roared with laughter. "I should rather think I do. I invented him!"

Ira Harris had defeated Horace Greeley by eleven votes, and Mr. Weed was, if all these gentlemen would kindly let him through, on his way over to 28 Eagle Street to congratulate the new junior senator from the state of New York, "and his wife, Pauline, a lovely woman, used to be married to Mayor Rathbone back in the forties. Fine woman, fine woman."

Hamilton Harris looked at the lined face of Thurlow Weed and, despite all the Dictator had inflicted upon his brother, could feel only admiration for the vitality that had kept the man charging through life ever since his days as a drummer boy in the War of 1812. He'd just suffered a defeat, whether the boy from the *Argus* understood that or not, and he'd never again be as powerful as he'd been before the advent of the Rail Splitter, but his head was high and his step still quick, so quick that Hamilton had to nudge John Finley Rathbone, telling him to hurry down the stairs if they were going to make it over to Ira's house before Weed got there.

Upon entering his brother's parlor, Hamilton Harris saw Pauline, *in excelsis,* wearing a great purple garlanded dress, a pearl bracelet, and feathers in her hair. By now she was quite stout, tending toward Queen Victoria, but still beautiful — and newly radiant. She must have started dressing hours ago. Bless her — the chance she'd taken of having her heart broken! They had only gotten the word a moment or two ago: Jared had been up at the capitol with instructions from his mother to fly down the hill like Mercury as soon as there was news, and the young man had done just that. (How Hamilton would box his office boy's ears when he saw him!)

He kissed Pauline's hand and shook Ira's. "Brother, the people of this great state could be no better served in this time of trial. Their tribunes have chosen well."

"Because they didn't choose the *Tribune,*" cried Clara, who breezed in from the hallway to greet her Uncle Hamilton and John Finley Rathbone. She straightened the antimacassar behind her father's head, and he reached up to squeeze her hand. She was happy, but also, Hamilton Harris thought, agitated with something besides pure pleasure in her father's elevation. In contrast to her regal stepmother, she couldn't keep still.

For the past three months she had been forced to wait upon events. After Will's time home for Christmas, his leavetaking for the Point had been dreadful; her father had looked at his son as if he might never see him again, and Henry told her this was no time to ask her papa to give up his favorite daughter — "certainly not to the likes of me." She had argued with him and let the weeks pass, and then the Senate rumors suddenly began. She'd given them no credit until last week, and now here she was, standing behind her father — who had been resurrected, she feared, as something more formidable than the man she'd counted on dealing with.

"Was Henry at the capitol?" she asked Uncle Hamilton.

"No, he wasn't, and when I get my hands on young Georgie Ensor . . ."

Before he could finish, Clara bustled back toward the dining room.

"Thank you for your confidence, Ham," said Ira Harris. "I'm truly grateful, as well as quite unworthy."

"Nonsense," said John Finley Rathbone.

"Must look alive now," said Hamilton Harris. "Mr. Weed is on his way over."

"Is he?" asked the senator-elect, genuinely surprised. By reflex he began to rise, until Pauline reached over and pulled his elbow back to the armrest.

The door knocker sounded, and Clara rushed past the parlor maid. Pauline and Ira Harris straightened up in their chairs, and the whole house fell silent in anticipation of the Dictator's entrance. But it was only Henry, with Georgie Ensor, who, as John Finley Rathbone suspected, had never made it from Hamilton Harris's law office to the capitol. Spotting his boss's glare, the boy ventured into the parlor to take his punishment. Clara pushed Henry back out onto the front steps.

His grudging congratulation of her papa could wait. She needed to speak to him this instant, because she knew he would be the only one to grasp the real implications of what was happening.

"You know?" she asked.

"Yes," he said. "State Street's buzzing with it."

"The two of them don't understand it at all," she said in a rush. "Perhaps it's still too much of a shock, but all they can think of is Mr. Weed and all the little humiliations of the past. Your mother is acting as if she's back at the Eagle Tavern with your father. She thinks she's been given a second chance, allowed to go back."

"And so she has," said Henry.

"No," said Clara. "They're not thinking of what lies ahead. Their lives, all our lives, have just been turned upside down. We're about to go off to a city they're not even sure the new President will reach alive. We're being thrown into this cauldron, and all they can attend to are feathers and bracelets and restored pride."

"Let me go in. I must see her."

"Henry, surely *you* understand what it means."

"Yes, I do."

"Then marry me. *Now.* Before we're all stirred into the catastrophe."

He took her in his arms and kissed her, and when she opened her eyes she could see, over his shoulder, the fast-approaching figure of the Dictator.

"I must get in there," said Henry.

He opened the door and stepped into the house, leaving her on the steps to greet Mr. Weed, who threw his dead cigar into the shrubbery as he came bustling up. "Clara Harris," he called. "Dear child."

Within half an hour the house was full. Lina, Amanda, and Louise rushed about with trays, making sure Emeline had her second glass of sherry; that the telegraph boy bearing Mr. Seward's congratulations received his dime; that Will's friends had their sandwiches. Judge Harris kept his seat throughout, as did Pauline, flanked on her right side by Henry, who sat on an ottoman and scarcely took his eyes off her.

"Father," whispered Clara when she could wait no longer, "may I see you alone for a moment? Upstairs?"

"Of course, my darling."

They went to the window seat in her bedroom. She took both his hands in hers and looked into his eyes. "Papa, I want to marry Henry. Before we go off to Washington."

He turned his head away, but she gently pulled on his arms, demanding he look her once more in the eye.

"No, Clara."

"Papa, this is going to happen! You can deny it to yourself as long as you like, but it's going to happen."

"I fear so, my dear, though I cannot say it will ever have my blessing."

She had not expected this resignation, and now that she heard it, she wanted to protect him from the hurt he must be feeling.

She started to say something when he interrupted: "Not now, Clara. Not now."

"But none of us knows what lies ahead. There may be a war, and —"

"That only makes it worse," he said. "I want to shield you from as many unpleasant eventualities as I can."

"Let my marriage shield me from them."

"It won't shield you from widowhood," he said.

She looked away from him, through the glass and into the street.

"Clara." He sighed. "My darling. Let us wait until we know some more. There is still a chance this whole crisis will pass, and if it does, I'll think anew. But I wish you would find another man, the right man. If you did, I'd march you down the aisle of the Pearl Street Baptist Church, as proud as any man in Albany, and happier than all the city's brokenhearted bachelors."

"Oh, Papa," she said, turning back toward him. The din of the impromptu party was still coming up the stairs. She thought of all the young men she knew, most of whom were in the house. She doubted she'd ever leave them brokenhearted, but she wondered which among them might soon be dead.

→ 17 ←

WHEN, on the morning of March 4, 1861, Ira Harris finished taking his oath of office, he looked up from the floor of the Senate to make two dignified nods, the first to his wife and the second to Abraham Lincoln, who sat in the gallery's center beside Mr. Buchanan. For another half hour or so Lincoln would be no more than a former congressman: his own swearing-in would come only when that for the new senators and Vice President Hannibal Hamlin was complete. But to the crowd filling the gallery, Lincoln had already taken on strangeness. Impending history had not draped him in a mantle; it had stripped him bare. His presence spoke more of vulnerability than power. That he had made it unharmed to this place and hour was thought remarkable, and the riflemen perched at the windows of the Capitol only served to remind the new President's observers of the constant dangers to his person. The incompleteness of the Capitol dome made the building feel like a crater, as if it were inviting the heavens to fling a lightning bolt at this rustic titan who dared to say he would hold together a continent so manifestly wanting to split apart.

As Mr. Hamlin went on, and on, with his own inaugural speech, Clara, sitting at the end of the row of Harris women, watched Mr. Lincoln and recalled her first sight of him exactly two weeks ago today. He had arrived in Albany on the afternoon of February 18, the windows of his railway car hung with blue silk and embroidered stars, to be met by loud, shoving crowds and chaos before his parade up State Street to Public Square. Because of his new position, her papa had been picked to head the city's reception committee, an honor that so dazzled him and Pauline that even now the two of them couldn't admit what was evident to everyone else: the day had been a fiasco.

The friendly noise of the parade had soon given way to a terrible stiffness inside the legislative chamber, where the bitter feelings of the Senate contest still persisted. That night, at the Delavan, chaos resumed. The separate ladies' reception planned for the following morning had to be canceled due to the press of Mr. Lincoln's schedule, so the fair sex was left to fight its way through the hotel's Broadway entrance, along with everyone else, on Monday night. Pauline lost a pearl button while pushing through a crowd of inebriates, and the resulting imperfection preoccupied her as she stood on the receiving line. Mr. Lincoln showed a kindly patience, Clara thought, when she herself was presented to him as Ira Harris's daughter.

"So it's your father who is responsible for this day," he'd said.

"Yes," she replied. "And I hope you won't hold it against him, sir."

Pauline later told her that this response had been unbecoming, even if it had made the President-elect smile, and produced an enchanted titter from his spouse. Back home in the parlor of 28 Eagle Street, Mrs. Harris had pronounced Mr. Lincoln "somewhat common" and the wife "unexpectedly stout." Clara bit her tongue, except to remind the pot that the kettle in question was known to share her antipathy for Mr. Seward.

Henry and Will had not been at the reception, nor were they here now, as Mr. Hamlin finally prepared to perorate. Will could hardly secure leave from the Point at a time like this, and Henry had elected to stay in Albany. His slender excuses for not sharing his stepfather's hour of triumph were accepted as a gesture of generosity: Ira Harris would have no coolness or sarcasm to fear, and every detail of Pauline's social renaissance would be left fresh for her to tell her son; she would be the protagonist of each tale, something that would please both her and Henry.

The applause for Mr. Hamlin died quickly into an awed silence. Mr. Lincoln rose to his full height and helped Mr. Buchanan up to his much lesser one, so that the proceedings could move to the Capitol steps. There would be a place on the platform only for Senator Harris, so Pauline hustled Clara and her sisters out of the Senate chamber and down into the East Plaza. As fast as they went, they were not fast enough. The crowd, much of it rougher than what had been outside the Delavan in February, was packing the area so tight that Pauline and her stepdaughters could barely make out whether up on the platform that was really Senator Douglas holding Mr. Lincoln's stovepipe hat. The President's voice — disappointingly high, thought Clara — managed to travel eastward on the air with enough strength for the Harris women to hear the address that preceded the oathtaking. The treetops in the park were full of young men, Clara noticed, the boy-filled branches looking as frail as a field of puffballs waiting for the mower.

It was peace that Mr. Lincoln wanted. To keep it, he was even willing to enforce the Fugitive Slave Law. It was "the declared purpose of the Union that it *will* constitutionally defend and maintain itself," but some of what the new President was saying sounded so mild ("The mails, unless repelled, will continue to be furnished in all parts of the Union") that she could imagine Henry's unspoken surprise as he pored over the *Evening Journal* in Uncle Hamilton's law office. As Clara strained to listen, she realized that all the parallel sentences and rhetorical questions had great beauty, like the balance of a sculpture. Reason *was* sweet, and perhaps this huge gaunt man could hold the Union together by its exercise. In the last few weeks her papa and Uncle Hamilton had muttered much about how it would really be Mr. Seward running the country, from the State Department, but from the sound of this speech she wasn't so sure.

Still, Mr. Lincoln had seemed so friendless during the procession this morning. Since the Harrises had taken their house at Fifteenth and H streets (just behind Lafayette Square, little more than a stone's throw from the White House), the city had filled up with visitors — the rich ones trenchering at Willard's, the poor ones washing in the fountains. But these gawkers would go home soon, and the city's regular residents, judging from this morning's parade, seemed anything but well disposed toward the new chief magistrate. So many of them wouldn't even open their shutters to see him pass!

The city's uncertainty matched her own. Rumor was the daily

fare, a gruel that left one famished and nervous and asking for more. From the second-floor study where she had begun writing letters to Henry and Mary Hall and Howard, she heard the footsteps and voices of each pair of passersby. Their words came bouncing up from the cobblestones, like sparks. For all the anxiety she could detect in their conversations, she imagined them going home to domestic comforts and certainty. In her own room in this new house there was nothing but the struggle to wait. It was only in her confidential letters to Mary, and in the cautioning ones she received from Howard, that she felt allowed to live her real life, to ponder and acknowledge her heart's desire. Henry had come to regard Mr. Lincoln's approaching inaugural as almost a new Law of Motion: until it took effect the world's whole direction was unforeseeable. In such a period of uncertainty, he could not be expected to discuss the question of marriage. The need to defer to political developments was perhaps the sole point upon which he agreed with her father, and Pauline had never raised the issue since Newport.

If Mr. Lincoln was the god of the new world in which all their lives would proceed, he seemed reluctant to let his creation begin spinning. "I am loth to close," Clara could hear him saying. "We are not enemies, but friends. We must not be enemies. Though passion may have strained . . ." She was distracted from the President's main clause when Pauline tapped her on the arm, directing her attention to the sight of an old man on the edge of the crowd, walking north with a depressed sort of step, away from the Capitol. It seemed odd that anyone, friend or foe, could be indifferent to anything Mr. Lincoln had to say this morning. It was not the man's hat or white hair or cigar that finally allowed Clara to identify him; it was the quiet smile on Pauline Harris's face that made her stepdaughter realize the old man was Thurlow Weed.

→ 18 ←

15th & H Sts.
Washington, D.C.
April 25, 1861

Dear Mary,

Since Virginia announced its secession from the Union last week, we have lived in fear of imminent siege. The city is so aware of its defenselessness that the last inches of everyone's nerves are beginning to shred. Even Papa — a United States Senator, you may recall — came home from the Riggs National Bank yesterday afternoon having withdrawn a large sum of money — for what purpose I am not certain, since most of the shops in the city have closed. Mother has sent my sisters back to Albany and has tried to send me home, too, though I have so far successfully resisted.

She is quite calm herself, determined that a mere civil war will not disturb the six years she intends to spend as the wife of Senator Ira Harris. She thanks you, I've forgotten to mention, for the New York newspaper clippings about the inaugural. I am afraid, however, that no item can compete with the one from the *Albany Evening Journal* that made mention of her presence at the Union Ball. The combination of being noticed by Mr. Weed's paper and having the clip sent to her by Emeline has assured its perpetual residence under the glass top of her dressing table. In my stepmother's boudoir it will forever be late evening, March 4, 1861.

Most of what these dispatches say is true — Mrs. Lincoln did dance a quadrille with Senator Douglas (just as I danced one with Senator Harris), and Mr. Seward did arrive with his daughter-in-law. And the flags and shields made a handsome sight. But I can assure you that *I* did *not* wear a hoop skirt and have no intention of wearing one — ever. I refuse to live as the clapper inside a great swinging bell. These dancing, perambulating monstrosities were the most humorous sight we've seen in the two months we have been here.

Mother's pleasure in her new role is undiminished by the fact that we are relatively friendless. The Southern ladies who dominate society here have no desire for our company — nor for Mrs. Lincoln's either, though she is close to being one of them herself. We have been to one of her levees, and she did, to my astonishment, remember me from the Delavan in Feb. I like her, though few others seem to. She is terribly nervous — says whatever flies into her head ("The Chief Usher will scold me for telling you this, but Mr. Lincoln found such a big creepy crawly thing in his shaving basin that he mistook it for his comb"), but she is smart for all that, and truly anxious for her husband. Papa now concedes that Mr. Lincoln is running his own administration.

He (Papa) was growing in happiness and confidence even through Fort Sumter, but since then two events have made him frail and gloomy. One is Virginia's secession, and the other is the arrival of Henry.

He got here on the 15th, the day Mr. Lincoln called for 75,000 troops, and of course he showed up at the door with a mock salute (and more clippings for Mother). "At the service of the Republic," he announced, coming into the parlor. I fear he will be in the army very soon, but he tells me little, and I think his exact plans are uncertain. He reached Washington just in time, since right now nothing is getting in or out. We are "protected" by the District Militia — who are no smart set of Zouaves, I assure you — and we await *relief*, the word on every set of lips in every conversation.

I await my own relief, of course, but bringing up the question of marriage right now would be an enterprise whose hopelessness bordered on teaching Sybil Bashford manners. (At least these national troubles have unburdened us of any obligation to witness her exchanging rings and slaves with her beau ideal next month. The last I heard

Clara never finished this letter. It was rendered obsolete by the event she heard being shouted in the street below. "They've come!" cried two girls to three others, who took up the cry until there was a great rush of women and men and small children and dogs, all of them heading to the depot, where, if the rumor was true, the Sixth Massachusetts Regiment was now arriving.

By the next morning, relief of the city was well under way, principally through the appearance of the Seventh New York, a bewildered few of whom still reverently carried the sandwiches that Delmonico's had provided at their departure. Their encampment ended up being the Capitol building itself, inside the House chambers and galleries. The Eighth Massachusetts moved into the Rotunda, the Sixth having taken over the furnace room. During the next week the city's population cheered all of them on their daily parades up and down Pennsylvania Avenue. Inside their legislative premises, the city's saviors put their feet up on the desks, played the banjo, and pretended to bellow speeches on the issue that had brought them here in the first place. The guard around the Capitol was no more disciplined than the rest of the carnival going on inside, and on most mornings any citizen who appeared vaguely familiar or just respectable was permitted to wander in. Ladies took food baskets, and boys brought their wooden swords to be signed and admired.

Curiosity led Henry and Clara up the Hill on the morning of May 3. Miss Harris's recognition by a doorkeeper, who remembered flirting with her on the morning of the inaugural, gained the couple access to the House gallery. Henry spotted an acquaintance from the Seventh and waved down to him. "Hurrah for Old Abe!" shouted the young man in greeting. Some of his companions made it into a chant, as if the President who had summoned them here had occupied the house at the other end of the avenue for eight years instead of eight weeks.

"Join us!" they shouted with hands cupped to the sides of their mouths.

Henry shook his head no, but cried down "Soon!" before flashing first ten fingers and then another two.

"The Twelfth," he said to Clara.

"Do you mean the twelfth of May?" she asked with alarm.

"It's not a date," he explained. "It's a regiment. Or it will be. Tomorrow Old Abe is going to direct that it be organized at Fort Hamilton, up in New York harbor."

"How do you know this?"

"Have you forgotten, Cous', that we now have family connections to the great powers?"

"Papa told you?"

"Last night. It appears I could go in as a captain, which I'm not likely to do anywhere else."

Clara said nothing. Henry's entry into the army had been inevitable since April 15. She was determined not to erupt in a flood of silly tears, which she felt no impulse toward in any case. She was simply overwhelmed with weariness at her design's defeat. Looking down on the hundreds of boys below, some of Albany's bachelors among them, she thought that she would probably never marry anyone, let alone Henry.

"Where is your regiment likely to go?"

"Nowhere for ages. Once it's raised, it's got to be trained. You can bet, however, that when it's ready we'll be sent to only the most hazardous places — that is, if your father has any influence with General Scott and Old Abe."

"Don't make jokes like that. How can you even imagine such horrors about Papa?"

The two of them were swept aside by a twenty-year-old private in pursuit of an eight-year-old boy, who'd succeeded in beaning him with an orange. Henry brought Clara over to the balcony's railing.

"Why do you look so glum?" he asked her.

"Oh, Henry," she said wanly.

"*Oh, Henry,*" he mimicked. "Cheer up, my darling. It will be a short war. Your father — the senator — says he's sure of it. It will probably be finished before the Twelfth ever leaves Fort Hamilton." He raised her chin with his fingers. "And I'll never make jokes about Senator Ira Harris again. He may not be my father, but he's agreed to be my father-in-law, once the war is over, so I'll desist."

"What?" Her expression changed completely.

"Yes. It was all approved by him and the mater during last night's regimental discussion, conducted after you'd gone to bed. I'm rather surprised you were able to sleep through it."

"How did you convince them?"

"I told them that if they refused, I would invest my money in the South and sit out the war in England and write inconvenient letters to the Albany and Washington press."

She laughed. "Did they think you were serious?"

"How do you know I wasn't?"

In fact, she didn't. "I'm so happy!" she cried. "Maybe this war *is* a blessing — God forgive me for saying it — but if it's what brought them around . . ." She could never have foreseen that in February, but she should have. Mr. Lincoln's world *was* a new one; all the old laws were repealed.

"That and one more thing brought them around," he said.

"What was that?"

"I told them I would start pursuing Louise if they refused me you."

He covered her open mouth with his hand. "That *was* a jest, Clara. J-e-s-t."

She bit down on his finger, and when he didn't withdraw it she closed her eyes and began caressing it with her lips. Giddy and thrilled and fearful, she had only one question: "When do you go?"

"Tomorrow morning, now that the rail line to Annapolis is open again."

She pressed her face against his chest.

"Courage, Clara. Remember, your sagacious papa says it will be over in a trice. And while you're living here," he said, turning her head so she could see over the balcony to the noisy spectacle below, "think of what a play you'll get to watch."

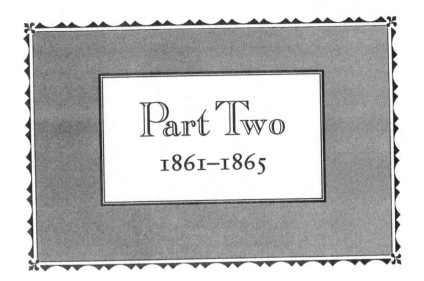

Part Two
1861–1865

"No," said Pauline, sternly, to eleven-year-old Lina Harris. She likewise forbade Clara and Louise to open the letter that had come an hour ago and lay in the front parlor, ticking with the unknown, on a marble tabletop beside a vase of hollyhocks. The arrival of the letter, whose envelope showed it was from Colonel William Harris of the Fourth U.S. Artillery, had occasioned peals of joy from the Harris girls, and even a silent thanks from the author's stepmother. But Pauline insisted that the letter, which proved Will's survival in Sunday's battle at Manassas Junction, remain sealed until Ira Harris arrived home from the Senate, which was meeting in special session all through this hot July. "Not another word," she said, telling the girls to busy themselves however they could. The letter continued to lie near the open window, through which a smell of the capital's sewage came to mingle with the scent of the hollyhocks.

Clara went up to her room, feeling that the war, which these past three months had been firmly declared but otherwise unreal, was at last upon them. It had entered their house, like a sniper's bullet, with this letter. Will was alive, but in what condition? At this moment, she could hear the sound of soldiers marching on a nearby street. Since April, parades and reviews had been a daily occurrence, part of a pageant, not a war. Thaddeus Lowe's observation balloons flew gaily above the city, the delight of all who saw them; the balloons' actual purpose — to spy on the movement of Confederate soldiers whose guns would be murdering the boys of the Union — was all but disregarded.

Her own days had been quiet, sewing havelocks with her sisters for the Christian Commission down H Street; supervising

Lina's reading; and endlessly writing letters, batting them back and forth like shuttlecocks, to her Albany cousins, Mary Hall in New York, Will with the Fourth, and Henry, training at Fort Hamilton. Her nights were quiet except for Fridays, when she would walk across Lafayette Square with Papa and Pauline to the Lincolns' evening receptions. She would stay straight through, from "Hail to the Chief" to "Yankee Doodle," the usual recessional, and return home feeling so lively that her sisters joked about her becoming a rival to Kate Chase, the socially ambitious daughter of the secretary of the treasury.

Mrs. Lincoln had taken a liking to her, and three times had had her to the Red Room for one of her "afternoons," when between more formal courtesies the First Lady would seize her arm and wail confidentially about her ague, or her husband's burdens, or the cost of entertaining, until the fretful monologue was interrupted by an appearance of the elfin, peculiar Tad, who had learned to greet her as "Mith Cwawa."

Before this week, it was in the East Room of the Mansion that Clara had felt the closest approach of the war. Late in May the beautiful body of Colonel Ellsworth had lain there; he'd been killed when his Zouaves marched across the Long Bridge and retook Alexandria for the Union. The feat had given the capital's morale a great lift, a euphoria tempered only by the slaying of Ellsworth himself. Mrs. Lincoln set a wax laurel wreath on his casket and gushed tears, which was not surprising, though the visible distress of the President himself shocked Clara and everyone else present. The colonel's corpse was marched up Pennsylvania Avenue to the music of a new march by Sousa and then sent home to New York — preceded by an especially florid letter that Clara wrote for the pleasure of Mary Hall.

But even this episode, with the colonel lying demonstrably dead before their eyes, had not seemed real. The romantic effect had lingered all the way through this Sunday morning, when the sound of cannon told the city that rebel forces were being engaged at Bull Run. Half the ladies in Lafayette Square had jumped into their carriages, some of them with picnic hampers, to be spectators at the instant victory they expected. Lina had begged to join the rush, and Louise and Amanda — just as bored as Clara with the months of sewing and bandage rolling — were about to say yes when Senator Harris, vibrating with a wholly new paternal severity, informed his daughters that their brother Will was probably manning one of the guns they could hear booming across the river. From that moment the day froze into a vigil, a long and eventually frightened one: word came late in the afternoon that the Federals were racing back toward the city in panicked disarray.

In the four days since, the Harris family had waited for news of Will, whose exact fate was at last revealed after six P.M., when Clara saw her father, returning from a caucus of Republicans on the Judiciary Committee, cross Fifteenth Street with his long stride. Pauline presented him the envelope, and he gathered his women into the front parlor, where he read the letter in its entirety, his voice as steady as if he were once more routinely charging a jury, his feelings betrayed only by the slight shaking of the thin brown paper.

> Fort Albany, Monday evening
> July 22, 1861
> 5:30 P.M.

Dear Father

I am well & have lost no blood. Our army, or rather that part of it commanded by McDowell is disorganized, routed & demoralized. I was in the saddle all night & then most of the past 48 hours. I fired two of our guns for several hours yesterday. We need reinforcements in the shape of *reliable* infantry & some cavalry & somewhat expect an attack at this point within twenty-four hours. Cushing is supporting a regiment of skirmishers with his 2 guns & as Green is not at all well, I have much to do yet this evening. If I can I will come and see you to-morrow morning. If I do not, I expect to stay here until our men & horses can receive some provisions & forage & our guns, ammunition.

I have worked hard, but suffered nothing but regret &

disappointment that my first battle should have terminated in a retreat — a *rout*.

Believe me faithfully
Your aff. son
Wm. H. Harris

Senator Harris allowed himself a sigh as he put the letter back in its envelope. Little Lina sobbed with relief as Amanda and Louise went into the kitchen, sniffing quietly into the fancy handkerchiefs they had sewn during breaks from havelocks and mufflers. Their father paced the parlor in a mixture of pride and frustration, while Pauline rubbed her hand across his broad back with a trace of the new wifely tenderness Clara had seen her display since her husband's sudden political ascent. But by tomorrow at breakfast, Clara knew, her stepmother's mood would have shifted like a powerful loom. Pauline would be in full-throttled argument about military appropriations and strategy, pressing her mild Whiggish husband with all the radical force of Senators Sumner and Stevens, insisting on a fuller, bloodier, faster prosecution of the war — whatever it took to get it over before Henry left his training for a battlefield like the one Will had just escaped. Pauline intended to have her son safe, the country reunited, and her husband part of a truly national Senate instead of a rump parliament. She wanted the atmosphere of constant emergency replaced by one permitting her more ceremony and notice. In this, thought Clara, she was not unlike the Southern ladies who still ran the serious social business of the town, and would settle for normality if they couldn't have a Confederate victory.

All Clara wanted was her wedding.

She crossed the room to kiss her papa and lead him into the dining room for supper. When the meal was over, the evening's letter writing would begin, with Papa conveying Will's story to Uncle Hamilton; her stepmother sending it to Aunt Emeline and Joel; and her sisters passing it on to young Jared, who was still in Albany and hoping to be admitted to West Point, if his stepfather's new adroitness at securing favors could get him the appointment. Clara herself would recount it to Henry, hoping that he would find some sympathy for Will's ordeal. As she ate her mutton soup, she concentrated on the letter she would write first, to Mary Hall. She might be forbidden to share the secret of her engagement, but she could at least describe the dress she planned to wear, nine nights hence, at the Lincolns' dinner for Prince Napoleon.

⇥ 20 ↤

"THE GIRL IN THE OPERA was just like Clara, wasn't she, Mother?" Sarah Rathbone's question to Emeline was irritating, and Clara was glad when the ever-solicitous Mary Hall clarified matters: "Oh, I don't think so, Sarah. Clara reads all sorts of serious things. Norina only read silly novels."

Actually, Clara had not entirely escaped identifying with the heroine of *Don Pasquale*; she only wished there were a Dr. Malatesta in her own life, some well-intentioned schemer with the power to remove what stood between herself and her marriage. Putting an end to the civil war was a tall order, but to anyone who could manage it (even General Beauregard, she secretly thought), she would be forever grateful.

"I didn't mean anything nasty," Sarah insisted.

"No quarreling now," said her mother. "The night is far too lovely for that." It was fine October weather, dry and cool with a hint of smokiness on the Hudson Valley air. Clara breathed in deeply, remembering the awful Washington summer she'd lived through. It was good to be home in Albany for a week. She and Pauline had stopped in New York, collecting Mary Hall as they continued north. Tonight the party of Harrises and Rathbones — Uncle Hamilton, Emeline, Joel, and Sarah — was smaller than it would have been a year ago, but as it proceeded from Tweddle Hall to Elk Street, passing en route a barracks and a new hospital, its members tried to act as if these were old, normal times.

Waiting in the Rathbones' dining room was a table piled with cake and Roman punch. Mary Hall, who cherished any new story about the leader of the Union, was eager to know if this was the sort of party fare Mrs. Lincoln served at the White House. The cake, said Pauline, speaking before her stepdaughter could, *was* similar to what Prince Napoleon had been given in August. That this knowledge was less than firsthand, that it had been communicated to her by Clara, the only member of the Harris family invited to the state dinner, was left unsaid. Clara herself went on to describe the affair, choosing details Mary would enjoy (the prince's crimson sash, Mrs. Lincoln's entry on his arm) and avoiding her own essential memory, which was that she hadn't enjoyed the evening at all. Much of the conversation had been in French, a point of pride with Mrs. Lincoln, and beyond what Clara had taught herself on the window seat in her father's house. And while the prince may have reviewed the Union army and inspected some camps, many of the legislators at the party had grumbled that he was here merely for the sport of seeing the New World's rustics knock one another's brains out. Looking past the back lawn of the White House at the unfinished Washington Monument (as hopeless a sight as the unfinished dome over the Capitol), Clara had felt futile and incomplete. She danced with some frail young men who had yet to join the army, but after hearing some matchmaking chatter from the old ladies, she decided to sit the next ones out, which succeeded only in angering her toward those who assumed she was already a spinster. All this endured to protect a secret she wanted to shout from the bandstand!

By the morning after the visit, the administration's critics were already complaining about its cost — the injustice of which criticism Clara would hear about from Mrs. Lincoln for weeks, during afternoons in the Red Room.

"It was terribly hot that night," added Pauline, safely enough, to Clara's narrative.

"Why don't you spend more time up here?" asked Emeline.

"Yes, we miss you and the girls," said Uncle Hamilton.

"Oh, there's far too much we'd miss," Pauline insisted.

"Mother is right," said Clara. "Just the other week we got to see beautiful Mrs. Greenhow dragged off to the Capitol Hill prison as a Confederate spy."

"What news is there of Henry?" asked Joel.

Before Pauline could preempt this subject, too, Clara's hand dove into her purse for a letter. "Still at the fort," she said, rushing to extract the paper from its envelope. "Would you like to hear what he has to say?"

"Of course," said Uncle Hamilton. "Give us a recitation, my dear."

In comic imitation of Henry's sarcastic baritone, Clara read out the following: "'I'll be a captain before Christmas, I'm assured, and that should keep me the kind of clubable man General Franklin always said he wanted for this regiment. He's been heard to quote Caesar, about how fops make the best soldiers, something your textbook-trained brother wouldn't want to hear.'" The family smiled nervously, and Mary Hall looked at the carpet, even though she had resigned herself to losing the noble Will, ever since he'd begun talking, in his own letters, of a girl named Emma Witt.

"'As it is,'" Clara continued, "'here inside the not terribly defensible walls of Fort Hamilton (our guns couldn't repel an assault by Lina and her schoolmates), we listen to more dull instruction that I ever heard at Union. The rest is drilling and what Major Clitz still likes to call recruiting. He ought to call it kidnapping. I've already snatched willing fourteen-year-olds off the thoroughfares of Manhattan island, but as most of them have at one time or another already resided in government facilities — those of the police — the change in life is less abrupt than it might be. "The highest bounties will be paid, and good quarters, rations and uniforms furnished": this is what we promise, in handbills and in speech, over the shouts of hecklers. But the first batches of uniforms sent by the Brooks Brothers were in truth somewhat less than durable. The pockets could be so easily ripped from the rest of the cloth that it was all the easier for the recruits to rob one another. It is a strange life here, for certain. Old Colonel Martin Burke, who entered the army forty years ago, parades around in dressing gown and slippers, chatting up all the dissenters who've been imprisoned within our walls (with no heed paid, by the way, to their real degree of dangerousness, not to mention their constitutional rights).'"

Clara looked up when she realized how quiet everyone was. Mary was kneading her handkerchief, Emeline fussing with some crumbs on her silk sleeve. Joel Rathbone looked scandalized, and young Sarah was on her way upstairs. Clara turned to Uncle Hamilton. "Go on, dear," he said. "Henry's unorthodox point of view is good for us all, I'm sure."

"Senator Harris depends on it," Pauline said. "As you can imagine, we're surrounded by flatterers in Washington."

"Of course," sighed Emeline.

"Henry is always good for a dose of reality," said Hamilton Harris.

"At least his own sort of reality," said Joel.

"I'll read just a bit more," said Clara. "'I've still no idea when we'll be permitted to travel south and join the Army of the Potomac. At the present rate of things, I fear it won't be until the war is over. There are all sorts of ways to define readiness, and I am ready in all the important ones.'"

"Hear, hear," said Hamilton Harris.

Clara decided to stop there. As it was, she had never intended to read them the letter's last page, though she could have done so from memory: "You remember the crannies of the *Vanderbilt*, don't you, darling? Well, on one recent voyage its non-paying carriage consisted of the boys of Billy Wilson's Sixth Regiment, on their way down toward the war, throughout which they will have to suspend their dog fights and rat-baiting. If you knew what a filthy business all this really is — even hundreds of miles from the lines! Your innocent friend Mary should see what we send to fight for precious freedom. A recent night spent camped at the Palace Garden on Sixth Avenue, after a day of dragooning Paddies into the Rail Splitter's service, left me yearning for the rough linen inside the walls of Fort Hamilton — let alone the ironed masterpieces brought up every third morning by our maid on Eagle Street. I long for their smell, and yours — the clean secret message of your unperfumed skin as I used to pass it in the hall, after breakfast, as we observed the enforced decorum of our familial mornings. I also long for killing, with an ardor that frightens me. But that is what we were assembled to do. Perhaps I'll have the chance to do it soon, and exhaust the worst that's in me on what others call the national purpose. But my real goal, darling, is to come home to you."

After silently playing Henry's latest Byronic song, Clara became alert to the room's still uncomfortable feeling and declared, "Perhaps I should find Sarah." Emeline quickly said, "No, Clara, that's not necessary." But Clara, rising from her chair, insisted: "No, I ought to. I should have remembered that the sound of Henry always scares her." To more awkward laughter in the room, she went up the stairs, and became aware of Sarah's soft voice, talking, Clara imagined, to one of her white cats.

"Sarah?" she called, moving down the hall to Howard's room, where the cat was probably playing inside one of his old valises. But there was no cat in the room, only Sarah and Howard himself, whose presence so startled Clara that the younger girl quickly exited into the hall, as if she had spilled a secret.

"Yes, it's only me," said Howard jauntily, patting the bedclothes and urging Clara to take the spot Sarah had occupied. "Another bout of lungs and stomach, I'm afraid. So I'm home once more. I seem to have a pattern. I alternate four months on the high seas with two atop soaked sheets. I've just about sweated this one out, I think."

"Howard, don't joke," said Clara, touching his thin face, which remained handsome and merry at all its sharp angles. "Why didn't your parents tell us you were up here?"

"They would rather keep these recurrences quiet. As would I. If they continue, I shall be one of the few men forced to exercise family influence to stay *in* the service."

Clara shook her head, angry at Emeline and furious at the thought Pauline may have known about this.

"Now, Clara," said Howard, reaching for her hand, "you're not to worry. I shall soon be good as new, and permanently this time. By Christmas I'll be blasting through the Confederacy's coastline, just you wait and see. So let's change the subject. Sarah tells me you've been downstairs spreading sedition."

She laughed. "Not sedition, just Henry."

"Yes," said Howard. "Henry." They were silent for a moment. Clara rose to straighten the bottles of powder and ointment on Howard's dresser. "Tell me something," she heard him say from behind. "What exactly is it?"

"It?"

"What is it that still attracts you to him?"

"Howard," she said flatly.

"No, I must know. I've thought and thought, but I only come up with explanations for the long ago. There you were, a girl of thirteen in a house full of other little girls and one overly responsible brother. In blew this dark strong boy with his temper and tongue. How could your little girl's eyes not have widened?"

"Howard, stop. Right now. Please."

"But that was thirteen years ago. How has it lasted? You're no longer a girl, and the novelty is long since gone."

"I love Henry," she said, turning around. "I can't say why."

"Can't or won't?" he asked.

"Won't. Can't. I don't know. How does one explain love? How do you explain what you felt for Annie Martin and all the rest of them?"

"That wasn't love."

"Well, this is, and I can't say any more about it. Why must you be so wary of Henry? He's your cousin and your friend. Life isn't finished with him, Howard," she said, sitting down on the bed once more, as if prepared to point out some delightful fact he'd overlooked. "The war will change him, I know it. He hints at that himself in his letters. It will purge him of all that aggression he has inside."

"Then he'll be the first man war ever changed for the better." Howard took her hand. "As for me, I am as I am. Why not love me instead?"

She looked in his eyes and knew he meant it. "Howard."

"I am healthy, Clara," he said, sitting up straighter against the headboard. "In all the ways that count. And I soon shall be in all the others, too. We can be rich and idle and happy once this war is over. We'll raise a beautiful tribe of children down at Kenwood. I'll buy you every book ever printed. I'll buy you Tennyson himself. I'll pay him to recite his poems every night at the dinner table."

"It's a lovely vision, Howard, for some other girl. But I'm going to marry Henry when the war is over. You're the only one I've told, but it's going to happen. Papa and my stepmother have agreed."

"Reluctantly, no doubt."

"That's being generous," she admitted.

"All right," said Howard, suddenly approximating his old gaiety. "We'll never speak of this again. Tell me about the opera instead. I should have gone. I would probably have gotten more sleep there than I did here."

Clara laughed, but she longed to get away. "I can hear them downstairs, Howard. They're getting ready to go."

"Yes, you'd better return to them. As it is, they'll be annoyed that you've discovered the invalid in the attic."

She kissed him and started for the door.

"Clara," she heard him call. She turned around and saw that his smile was gone.

"I love you," he said.

She went quickly down the stairs, trying to think of anything but these words and why they couldn't move her. Was there something wrong with her heart? Did she even *want* the war to change Henry? Didn't she really just want the war to make him miss her?

The Rathbones' butler helped her with her coat as Emeline tried to think of an explanation to offer about Howard. "We thought it best . . ." she murmured.

"It's all right," said Clara, whose distress was taken by everyone as a sign of worry about the young man upstairs.

"Give our love to the judge," said Emeline, kissing Clara and speaking loudly enough for Pauline to hear her and understand that Albany remained the real world, and that its titles mattered more than such remote and temporary ones as Senator.

→ 21 ←

15th and H Sts.
Washington
February 24, 1862

My dearest Henry,

They buried Willie Lincoln today, amidst howling winds and rain. He had been sick with the bilious fever for days, and I spent the greater part of them with his mother, who from the beginning of his ordeal seemed more abstracted from reality than he. He was such a brave boy, religious and poetic (do you remember? he wrote a lovely verse when Colonel Baker was killed), and yet for all that a *boy*, still just eleven years old, romping with his younger brother up and down the stairs all this winter. I cannot imagine Mrs. L's recovering: she is *mad* with grief, transformed utterly from the woman Mrs. Keckley and I wrapped in white satin three weeks ago and sent down to her 800 guests, guests who shouted their admiration (and whispered their contempt). It was the Lincolns' first ball in the Mansion, and I should not be surprised, even if the war ended tomorrow, if it were their last.

As the weekend began, I gave up my attempts at consolation, let her push me away, and turned my attentions to soothing the distress of little Bud Taft, Willie's favorite playmate. He has put his head upon my bosom and cried his eyes out. During the vigil, when it appeared Willie might survive, I promised Bud that I would take him to see the illuminations; all the public buildings had been ordered lit to celebrate the capture of Fort Henry. Then, on Thursday, Willie was gone, and the lights were cancelled.

All has been darkness since. This afternoon, at 2:00, I ran back across Lafayette Square, through thunder and lightning, to fetch Papa and your mother to the East Room, to join the mourners. Among them one could find much of the Congress, along with McClellan, Bob Lincoln and the President. He was so tired from watching at the bedside; his lined face looks scarcely like the one that smiled at us in Albany a year ago. He took my hand for a moment, and managed a weak smile, addressing me as "Aunt Clara," which Willie had called me once or twice. "You must soon have some children of your own," Mr. Lincoln said. Then they began the procession to Oak Hill. Willie will be in a mausoleum there until the day comes when the whole family return to Illinois, carrying his tiny body with them.

What will become of young Tad, with a mother laid waste by her feelings, and a father whose every hour is consumed with the prosecution of this war? Robert will have to be as much father as brother to him; and yet Robert must soon go back at Harvard. Somehow the President manages to find moments for the child — such a strange one — who clings to him like a small, fretful animal, completely without the dignified little-manly comportment of Willie. What a contrast they made: another fairy-tale pair like you and Will, one dark and one light — and now one gone!

Oh, Henry, I miss you so tonight. Not a candle burns in any window of the Mansion, and the rain brought by the storm has puddled into ice all over Lafayette Park. Andy Jackson stands frozen — a statue of a statue — and suddenly no one dares hope for the victory needed to end everybody's woe. We hear rumors that at last — but too soon! — the Twelfth will be moving to Virginia. That your being nearer to me depends upon the commencement of your danger is just one more cruel method this war has devised for breaking hearts.

Take my love and let it keep you safe. And tell us where you are —

Your loving bride
(for that I shall finally be),
Clara

Fort Monroe
Virginia
March 29, 1862

Darling Clara,

We arrived yesterday at Fort Monroe and are now in camp at Hampton. Our march down from New York ended in a few small skirmishes with the rebels. I am unscathed, but three or four others were hit.

Being fired upon was the most extraordinary experience — *personally* thrilling. Each bullet, it seemed, was intended just for me. In fact, I was probably no more visible to whichever soldier was firing from behind the trees than he was to me. But, whoever he was, I wanted to dash into the brush after him, to find him and slash his throat with the blade of my bayonet. I would have done so entirely without malice, with only a strong desire to know just who he was, to gaze upon his face, as if it were another side of my own.

This is no sort of letter to write to one's love — and that you are, my darling Clara. But if this frightens you, I know you will indulge it, for we have never spoken to each other only as lovers; I can share with you my secrets and fears, as if we really *were* the sister and brother most of the family still take us for.

My fears are not really *for* myself. They are *of* myself. I wonder what this war will unleash inside me, what it will do to my will and spirit. If my heart beats faster at a mere sprinkling of gunfire, what will it do when hurling itself at Jackson's whole army? I am sitting on an old dry chestnut-tree log as I write this; for how many years it's been sleeping in the sun, I don't know. For all its apparent lifelessness, I know that, cracked open with an axe, it would release all manner of crawling insects upon its little patch of the world. This is what I fear the war may do to many of us fighting it.

Your letter, more than a month old, the one about the Lincolns' son, was waiting for me when we arrived at Monroe. It had ricocheted down from Fort Hamilton ahead of our slowly marching feet. It is only the first one atop a small stack from you, but I want to answer each one by itself — to do otherwise would be like giving you back a single kiss for a dozen you've showered on me. After five weeks, the letter's perfume is still fresh, and I have again taken it out in the morning brightness, to smell the paper and imagine you in my arms.

I am sorry for your distress, but I must tell you, darling, how paltry a thing Willie Lincoln's death looks from here. I do not underestimate the Pres.'s woe, but the national fuss: is it seemly? It is as if a dauphin had died. Mother sends me a cutting from the *Star:* Lying in state in the Green Room? Before a funeral in the East one? Children die each day in the normal order of things: think of the ones my mother lost, Charles and Anna, infants, more than twenty years ago. The President's grief for his son is ill-proportioned to the merely abstract sorrow he can feel at reports of grown men dying in quantity, just across the river from Washington. Madame President should come downstairs and get out to the hospitals, so that she can see all the boys, older than her Willie, but still boys for all that, dying far from their own mothers' comforting arms.

I sit only yards from one of the fellows hit by a rebel bullet the day before yesterday. He moans persistently, and every once in a while gives out with a sharp cry. Last night I saw the doctor change his dressing. I looked into the wound itself, a deep depression in the muscle of the boy's right chest. Red blood bubbled to life amidst the discoloration, like a strange flower from a latitude we have never seen. I was repelled — but conscious, too, of my fascination. I longed to see deeper inside the boy, to glimpse whatever secret lay inside his being, the way I wish I could open myself up for a look inside. The boy's blood, pulsing almost imperceptibly to the beating of his heart, was wonderful to see, until one remembered that it was shedding itself for nothing. The passions of the individual are a glorious mystery, before which we should tremble with respect; to see them squandered, spilt, for the dry creeds of the old men who insist upon this war, far away from where it is actually fought, is to feel one's spirit crushed.

But mine will soon revive and soar, so don't you worry. Once we march into battle, I shall be bellowing with delight, out for blood and greedy for glory.

You are love of the deepest kind; our connection is absolute, full, unbreakable. We could not be closer if we *did* share the same blood. As it is, we *shall* share each other's blood, in the beautiful children we create together. I shall give you boys of your own, Clara, great strong boys who will grow healthy into manhood and not be wasted on war such as this.

> Your own,
> Henry

He put the brown paper into its rough envelope and sealed it up, wondering if he should have been quite so firm on the subject of the Lincoln boy. Yes, he decided, Clara needed to read what he had written. In her own letter she didn't sound herself. She was morbidly sentimental, filled with the sighs and tears of a maiden aunt. ("Aunt Clara" indeed!) Her own deepest feelings were being pressed into service by the Abraham Lincolns, distracted toward an object unnatural to them. *Everyone's* nature was being snatched from itself, displaced, by the man directing this war.

Clara's grief, thought Henry, however false its object, was at least better than the crocodile tears of the men who'd gone to the East Room to make a proper display of lamentation before the boss. And as for Madame! He had no doubt she would be back in her white dress within weeks, just as Miss Donnelly's poem, clipped from the newspaper and tucked into Pauline's letter, made so bitterly clear:

> *What matter that I, poor private,*
> *Lie here on my narrow bed,*
> *With the fever gripping my vitals,*
> *And dazing my hapless head!*

What matter that nurses are callous,
  And rations meagre and small,
So long as the beau monde *revel*
  At the Lady-President's Ball!

He read the verse again before inclining his ear to the hospital
tent.

→ 22 ←

> Our loss was 1 killed and 3 wounded . . . The follow-
> ing officers were present guarding the bridge, and after-
> ward on skirmish duty or supporting Tidball's battery:
> Capt. M. M. Blunt, commanding battalion; Capt.
> H. R. Rathbone, acting field officer, commanding
> Company C . . .

A COPY OF Captain Matthew Blunt's report on the Twelfth
Infantry's performance at Antietam Creek had lain on Clara
Harris's night table for three days, just one less than the original
had been in Secretary Stanton's office. In the week after September 17, 1862 — a day on which the Northern and Southern
armies inconclusively killed 5,000 of one another's men — the
hunger for news was like a great, persistent moan in Lafayette
Square. Every house with a soldier in the battle contributed to
it. Knowing that Henry had been fighting in those bleeding
Maryland cornfields, Clara urged her father, each morning, to
see if a report from the Twelfth had arrived at the War Department. Senator Harris disliked Mr. Stanton's perfumed whiskers
as much as the secretary disliked Harris's frequent favor-seeking,
but every morning the senator had gone around to check. When
he at last secured Captain Blunt's report — technical, confusing,
but absolutely affirming Henry's safety — Clara wept with joy.
Neither General Lee nor General McClellan had gotten what he
wanted from the apocalypse, but she had, and she kept the
paper on her table so that she might prove the fact, over and
over, to her own satisfaction.

Since the Twelfth had joined the Army of the Potomac in

May, it had seen some fighting at Mechanicsville and Bull Run, but Henry's letters had been more about building corduroy roads than battling Stonewall Jackson, and throughout the heat of this second summer in Washington — or at least those weeks of it she hadn't escaped with Pauline and her sisters to Newport — Clara found it hard to believe that Henry was any more likely to die of the malaria he mentioned than she was to perish from the germs and stink suffocating the capital. But when news of the battle near Sharpsburg started coming, there was a terrible change in her feelings. What took place was on a scale so titanic that it seemed impossible for anyone near it to have survived. Imagine, said her father, someone obliterating the whole center of Albany with wagon loads of gunpowder: *that* might give you 5,000 killed and 20,000 wounded. Surely, Clara thought, the word "Antietam" would replace some older one in the language — Leviathan, perhaps — becoming forevermore the synonym for pitiless devouring. She so wanted to shut her eyes and ears to the thought of it, and to all the excited, horrified chatter that filled the square and the Executive Mansion, that she had actually been averse to opening what at last arrived today, Tuesday the thirtieth, a letter from Henry himself:

Near Sharpsburg
Sept. 18

Darling Clara,
    Am completely safe.
    We spent 19 hours guarding one of the two small bridges. We were well to the rear of everything, with McClellan further back still, using his field glasses to watch us watch. In the distance was the slaughter in the cornfield, men hacking at each other, and at stalks as tall as themselves, until they couldn't tell the difference. A New York fellow told me today it was like swinging a hammer in a forest of mirrors. The firing was so constant that the brief moments of quiet rang in our ears like explosions. The world had gone mad: thousands upon thousands killing themselves for a small white church and a

tiny patch of land. We were not at all eager to get into it, but then at noon came the order to cross the bridge. The cavalry and guns galloped into heavy fire, but our skirmishers drove back what was opposing us. Our losses were small, our part in the whole thing minuscule. Still, everything changed for me, completely, at that moment, as if I had come up through water and taken in a great gulp of air. It was over quickly, but not before I'd seen a fat boy from Newburgh, in the middle distance, exploding like a flour sack.

I shot a man of theirs I was close enough to see, in the arm, and I heard him scream, more in annoyance, I thought, than pain.

Today we worked, shirtless, picking up bodies, some of them with their mouths still open from when they tried to catch last night's rain. What they are calling Bloody Lane was once a sunken path, worn from being trod; but this morning the corpses were thick enough to make it level, like a ditch that had been filled with human water. Everywhere the green leaves are so dappled with blood that I imagine myself walking past a long Christmas table covered with holly.

Now, when all is bloated bodies, tallies, and terrible pictures, I should feel foolish at the smallness of our part — the bridge we set such store by crossed a creek no one had bothered to try fording; had they troubled themselves, they would have discovered that every man could have waded across it without wetting his belt. But I do not feel foolish. I remember myself instead at the moment we crossed — screaming, alive, *complete* — which is how I remained until we pulled back east.

We are safely camped and you are not to worry.

These days Pauline received her own letters from Henry and no longer asked for Clara's, and the other girls in the house knew that no amount of wheedling could induce their sister to show them any more of Henry's correspondence than she wished. If her father had not just asked her to bring this letter to him in his study, Clara would have kept it from him as well. It was not any intimacy in it that made her shy of sharing the letter; it was the lack of intimacy, except perhaps that between Henry and himself, a thing that would distress Senator Harris, whose hair, after a year and a half of war, was going from gray to white, and whose impatience with General McClellan now exceeded President Lincoln's. The senator knew every opportunity had been squandered, and that the slaughter at Antietam was nobody's triumph. But he had marveled these past few nights at supper over the way the President was bent on treating it as one. "Stalemate surpasses defeat," Mr. Lincoln had told him, "and since losing is what we're used to, I see no reason not to call this victory." So that's just what the President had been doing, to the extent of proclaiming the emancipation of the slaves the other morning at a Cabinet meeting.

"Sit down, my darling," the senator said to Clara, "and tell me what Henry has to say." She handed him the letter and took up the *Evening Star*, avoiding his expression as he read.

"It is good that he is well" was all he said when finished. "Now I have something to share with you," he added, smiling for the first time. "A letter from your friend Mary."

"A letter from Mary Hall to you?"

"Read it," he said, and as soon as she began, she laughed. "Of course. The proclamation." The long letter, which Clara skimmed, was a fountain of joy and gratitude. "'To think,'" Clara quoted, "'that only twenty-five miles from Harper's Ferry lay the spot where the slaves would see their freedom won! What a day the first day of 1863 will be!'"

"You see?" said Ira Harris. "This is just what the President wanted. He's got everyone from Horace Greeley to your friend Mary thinking we've won a splendid victory. She now puts me in her personal pantheon, along with Sumner and Beecher and the rest of them."

Clara laughed. "Poor Papa. Everyone's a radical now."

"That's the trouble," the senator replied. "This is beyond what was intended. Officers are already grumbling that they didn't go to this war to 'free the niggers,' certainly not before they'd subdued the South. You may even be hearing such sentiments from Henry, if he can come down from whatever private exaltation he's feeling."

"Papa," said Clara, "Henry is doing only what Mr. Lincoln is. He's trying to turn a calamity into a victory, just a small personal one in his case. Would you rather, at the moment of truth, that he'd found himself cowardly?"

"Well, it's a strange sort of alchemy, if you ask me. By him *and* the President."

Clara did not want to argue. The truth was, she thought Mr. Lincoln wholly different from any of them. There he was, calmly unshackling slaves in the South and suspending habeas corpus in the North — feeling transcendent if not serene. He was remade, never again to be the man he had been eighteen months ago. It was the rest of them who were somehow unchanged, incapable of being anything but what they were. Mrs. Lincoln might be mad with grief over Willie, dead for seven months now, but not so distracted that she couldn't each day find new slights to rail at. The war's enormities weighed Papa down with sorrow, but his vision could not encompass any meaning it might finally hold. In the Senate his greatest energy and clarity came when arguing small matters of right and wrong, whether Mr. Stark had the credentials to be seated or Senator Bright the guilt requiring expulsion.

Now he broke the silence. "I'm afraid I have one piece of bad news, my darling, and I must tell it to you, since it isn't likely to come by any other means. It concerns another of your old friends, Miss Bashford. Her husband, a lieutenant, died at Sharpsburg last week. Mr. Stanton manages to get some of the rebel newspapers, and while I waited in his office trying to get word of the Twelfth, I scanned one from Charleston. Quite by chance I noticed the name Edmund Lodge Baxter on their casualty list. I'm sure it is he. I haven't known whether to tell you."

"It's good that you did, Papa." Clara tucked Mary Hall's letter into its envelope. "Poor Sybil," she said, shaking her head. "Losing her husband and her slaves, all in the same week." The joke was more in Henry's line than her father's, but from behind his desk Ira Harris managed a smile.

She leaned over to kiss him good night, and as she went upstairs to bed she realized that she, too, a year and a half into the war, was still what she was. Her mind was not on Sybil, or the soon to be liberated slaves, or the thousands of men whose blood soaked the Maryland soil. She was thinking only of Henry, of his bare chest and arms beneath the hot sun, walking amongst the dead, himself still alive, glistening, the blood still inside him, pumping.

⇀ 23 ↽

THROUGHOUT 1863, Clara and her father became occasional members of Mrs. Lincoln's Blue Room salon, evening gatherings of what the First Lady liked to call the *beau monde,* a shifting company of writers, politicians, and adventurers who came to talk about literature and stayed to gossip about everyone but themselves. Pauline Harris's exclusion was unremarkable: few wives were ever in evidence. Clara realized that she herself was allowed to accompany her father because she was young enough not to be regarded by Mrs. Lincoln as feminine competition. If anything, the First Lady thought of her as a social protégée, someone perhaps witty and comely enough to deploy as a rival to Secretary Chase's daughter, if the war ever ended and a full social life bloomed in the capital. As for Papa, he had a soothing effect on Mrs. Lincoln, and since the real point of these gatherings was to distract her from endless grief over Willie, that was reason enough for him to be here.

Her moods kept the congregants on edge, but her peculiar charm kept them coming back, or at least added to the pleasure of being near the most powerful President in the Republic's history. Senator Sumner, an even more unlikely guest than Ira Harris, was always glad to further the radical cause by his presence in the Mansion, but in the Blue Room he seemed to forget his political self and take the evenings' nervous froth as a tonic. Uncomfortable as they might be with each other in the Senate chamber, he and Ira Harris got on well here, united by a certain disdain for the less serious men who occupied a large number of the chairs. Nathaniel Willis, editor of a ladies' magazine, was a fussy little mince, and Henry Wikoff, when he wasn't spying for the English, was hardly more than a gigolo.

Tonight, three weeks before Christmas, Clara took a seat on the left of Emilie Helm, Mrs. Lincoln's "Little Sister," as she was always addressed. Mrs. Helm was much younger than the First Lady, and the solace she had been receiving, during an extended visit to the Mansion, was more motherly than anything else: her husband, a Confederate officer, had been killed at Chattanooga, leaving her with three children and a terrible burden of grief that Mary Todd Lincoln was eager to meld with her own. Mrs. Helm's visit had raised eyebrows among the radicals, but Clara thought all the more of the President for clutching this pretty young woman to the family bosom. As it was, since her arrival she'd given more comfort than she'd received, steering the First Lady away from her spiritualist, as well as taking her mind off Tad's recent illness and the President's mild case of smallpox, which Mrs. Lincoln said would not permit him to come down and say hello this evening.

Clara was amused to see crazy Dan Sickles take the chair on Mrs. Helm's right. Flushed with drink and not quite used to the wooden leg he'd acquired at Gettysburg, he ignored the particulars of Mrs. Lincoln's introduction of her sister, but he didn't let the young widow's black dress keep him from making an appreciative survey of her form. Before he'd commanded Third Corps at Gettysburg (with such zest he nearly got all his men slaughtered), he had been famous as the congressman who murdered his wife's lover — the major episode in a career whose eccentricities once included advocating New York City's secession from the Union. He was, everyone agreed, an impossible man, and just as impossible to dislike: his loud arrival, as he thumped his way across the Blue Room's thin carpet, had brightened up Senators Harris and Sumner.

Clara was amused by his inventory of Little Sister's charms. Perverse as she knew it to be, she herself couldn't look at the widow's black dress without a certain envy, almost as much as she'd felt three Saturdays ago at the sight of Sarah Rathbone's white satin dress when it came down the aisle of the Second Presbyterian Church in Albany. Sarah's wedding to Frederick Townsend had taken place the same afternoon as Mr. Lincoln's oratorical success at Gettysburg, and upon Clara's return to

Washington, Mrs. Lincoln, who had been present at neither occasion (and had made sure she was absent from Kate Chase's wedding on the twelfth), was eager for details of the dress. But Clara found it so hard to talk about someone else's public badge of love that her description was less ample than it might have been.

Conversation, a word Mrs. Lincoln liked to give its French pronunciation, was tonight, as always, about everything but the war. An exception was sometimes made to discuss the incompetence of particular generals, but this evening the talk seemed to be staying on the degree to which Mr. and Mrs. Tom Thumb and the Prince and Princess of Wales, both couples newly married, might be enjoying happiness. If peace ever came, Mr. Willis wondered, might Mrs. Lincoln invite the Prince and Princess to the White House? It was a fawning inquiry, a chance for "Madame" to speak from the lofty heights she occupied, but she never got a chance to answer, because General Sickles interrupted. "Not likely, I should think. I can't imagine them wanting to pass through the Celtic mobs of New York City after disembarking." The summer's draft riot, which had left good Republican families like Mary Hall's shaking inside their houses, had been forgotten by no one here, including Ira Harris. "Imagine the reward presented to some soldiers who'd just survived Gettysburg," Sickles continued, deliberately shifting his wooden leg. "'Now that you've beaten back the rebels, please nip over to New York and put down the Irish in Gramercy Park!'" He was fairly roaring.

"A battalion of Henry's regiment was there," said Clara. "He wrote me about it."

"And where is Henry now?" asked Mrs. Lincoln, hoping this new line of inquiry might keep Dan Sickles under control.

"In the winter camp at Rappahannock," Clara replied.

"After a very, very long year," said her father, shaking his head and murmuring the names of battles like an old priest telling beads: "Fredericksburg, Chancellorsville . . ." The worst fighting was yet to come, and Ira Harris wondered how long his own family would continue to be spared. As if the ordinary familial afflictions, the kind that came without war, weren't enough for human creatures to bear. Since Joel Rathbone's sudden death in Paris in September, just two months before Sarah's wedding, he'd had to offer Emeline all kinds of personal and practical comfort, from being with her to meet the body when it came off the ship to straightening out the enormous estate. He was as careworn as he ever hoped to be, and just an hour ago, while fixing his cravat, he'd told Pauline he prayed this would be the last Christmas of the war.

"And where did you say you came from, little lady?" shouted General Sickles, unsubdued, to Mrs. Helm.

"I didn't say," she replied, recoiling slightly from his breath. "But my sister, Mrs. Lincoln, may have explained to you the circumstances of my visit. Since my husband's death, I have been trying to get to my mother in Lexington, Kentucky, but the war has prevented that. My daughter and I reached Fort Monroe but were prevented from going on from there. At that point Mr. Lincoln was kind enough to ask us here."

A light went on inside General Sickles. This was the Little Sister whose presence in the Mansion he'd been hearing about. His admiring gaze narrowed into something else. "You were prevented from leaving Fort Monroe, I take it, because you wouldn't swear an oath of allegiance to the United States?"

"My son Will spent some time at Fort Monroe," said Ira Harris soothingly. "Early in the war. After that he was in Tennessee, and now he's gone north to join General Burnside." Although he wished no discomfort for this woman or Mrs. Lincoln, he couldn't deny a certain resentment toward Mrs. Helm's presence here. It made this awful war look even more senseless than he was coming to think it. If family loyalties counted more than national ones, how important could the latter finally be? He wanted his own family together again. "My son has been a soldier for six years now," he said. The occasional drinking he was doing in these long periods away from the Pearl Street Baptist Church was rendering him emotional, and the nearby log fire was heating his spirit into a sudden despair. "He used to be a gentle, temperate soul, my Will. But now he writes of rebels and Copperheads with fierce gusto."

"Hear, hear," said General Sickles. "Mrs. Helm, since you're just from the South, perhaps you can give Senator Harris some news of his old friend General Breckinridge."

"I've not seen the general for some time," Emilie Helm replied, "so I cannot give Senator Harris any news of his health."

The thought of Mr. Buchanan's Vice President, now a rebel general, flushed the already overheated Ira Harris with a mixture of nostalgia and anger. "Well, we have whipped the rebels at Chattanooga," he said suddenly, his choice of words startling Clara, "and I hear, madame, that the scoundrels ran like rabbits."

The room fell quiet except for Sickles's laughter and the applauding thump of his wooden leg against the floor. He was delighted by his sober-sided colleague's loss of control.

Mrs. Helm rose to the challenge. "It was the example, Senator Harris, that you set them at Bull Run and Manassas." She was shaking, and Mrs. Lincoln was clearly angry with everyone. Clara watched with inert horror, even as she entertained the thought that if the President were here instead of sick upstairs, he would be amused.

"There are only three weeks until Christmas," said Mrs. Lincoln, trying to change the subject. But Senator Harris wouldn't let her, and Clara's ears could not believe what they now heard him ask the First Lady: "Why isn't Robert in the army? He is old enough and strong enough to serve his country. He should have gone to the front some time ago."

"Papa!" said Clara, who saw Mrs. Lincoln go white and General Sickles happily bare his teeth. It was common talk that the President agreed Robert should be in a soldier's tent instead of in Harvard Yard, but people generally sympathized with Mr. Lincoln's problem: if his wife were to lose a second son, she would be completely ungovernable, and wasn't he already burdened enough?

"Robert is making preparations now to enter the army, Senator Harris. He is not a shirker, as you seem to imply. He has been eager to go for a long time. If fault there be, it is mine. I have insisted that he should stay in college a little longer, as I think an educated man can serve his country with more intelligent purpose than an ignoramus."

{ 147 }

Senator Harris rose and addressed his last remarks to Mrs. Helm. "Madam, my one son is fighting for his country, but if I had twenty sons, they should all be fighting rebels."

Clara was desperate to put an end to this, to explain to everyone that her papa was speaking out of despair (and drink), not with the sort of rabid pleasure he was providing Dan Sickles. But it was too late. Little Sister was on her feet, too. "And if I had twenty sons, Senator Harris, they should all be opposing yours." Her pretty form strutted out of the room, and Sickles watched it through the bottom of his tumbler, which he emptied in a final gulp.

"Papa, we have overstayed our welcome," said Clara, going to his side as Mrs. Lincoln rose to follow her sister. They crossed each other's path as the rest of the guests murmured about getting up to go, and locked eyes for a second, in which time Clara realized that the First Lady, whose intuitions sometimes cut, like a lighthouse beam, through the great fog of her griefs and rages and enthusiasms, understood exactly what had come over Senator Harris and had already forgiven him.

Out under the portico Clara tried to rescue her father from Sickles's noisy congratulations, which ended only when the general declared he would give Mr. Lincoln a piece of his mind right now. He stumped back into the Mansion, determined to go up to the President's room.

"And I hope the President gives him smallpox in return," said Clara, nudging her father down the steps toward home. "Oh, Papa, how could you!" The senator was quiet, confused and ashamed, and as the two of them made their way back to Fifteenth and H, Clara patted his hand and calmed down, and thought of how she was every bit as sick of this war as he. She couldn't stop replaying the evening's fiasco in her head, but when she was up in her room, having delivered Papa to Pauline's avid questions, she found one shred of comfort. In shouting at Little Sister, Ira Harris had laid claim to just one son, Will: in his growing anguish, he had dropped the pretense, generously maintained for years, that Henry counted as another.

→ 24 ←

My dearest Henry,

The city has at last gotten to host its fair for the Sanitary Commission, so now I shall be able to reciprocate the excited accounts Mary is still sending of New York's. These gaudy celebrations seem a strange way to raise money to prevent plague and dysentery among all of you who have already borne more than you ever should have had to; but can one deny their effectiveness? "A beneficent blend of Baghdad and Barnum," the President whispered as we entered the Patent Building last night. In fact, the hall was bannered and bedecked and stuffed with more goods, for direct sale and competitive bidding, than any bazaar one could imagine upon the Euphrates. Beneath the clouds of bunting, a hundred booths enticed the crush of people with cakes and saddles and mufflers and bonnets and silver buckles and leather bindings — which a buyer could use to hold an autographed manuscript by Mr. Longfellow, or one by Mr. Lincoln himself, should the purchaser persist in his circuit of the booths and make a sufficiently generous offer for them as well.

There were even a few forms of gaming (the raffle tickets marked for some deserving soul in a hospital or camp), and the war has so relaxed Papa's Baptist soul that he offered no objection. What *wasn't* there to see? A puppet show, if that was one's liking; or an Iroquois war dance, if one preferred.

I came away with a lovely silk foulard for you, something

I shall keep hung in plain sight here in my room, so that I may picture you wearing it — along with myself on your arm — at the first party of *peacetime,* a word I would like to festoon with more homages than a mere underlining. I missed my chance at one novel item I considered acquiring for zealous Will: a pair of socks with the rebels' flag knitted onto the soles. By the time I'd decided to make the purchase I saw that dear old Benjamin Brown French had bought them up — with the intention, he told me, of giving them to Mr. Lincoln.

Our poor President would have been more cheered, I thought, by a kiss from one of the pretty girls selling them (fifty cents for a small buss on the cheek) at a stall toward the front of the hall. But Madame President was with him, and you can be assured that she permitted no momentary rival to get near, whatever the nobility of the cause. Little Lina, who grows pretty enough to have attracted a long line of commercial suitors, was forbidden to sell any kisses by your mother, who was not in attendance. (During the final days of the fair's preparation, she quarreled — mightily, I am told — with the bossy Mrs. Brookfield, one of the committee's principal dynamos, and so last night she withheld her presence.)

Aside from Papa and myself and Mrs. Lincoln, the President's party included General Oglesby and Commodore Montgomery and, you may believe it or not, Dan Sickles. The Christmastime contretemps has been, it seems, all patched up. Cousin Emilie is long since gone, and Mad Dan and Mrs. Lincoln were positively flirtatious with each other last night. I'm sure she would have purchased the flag-embroidered socks as a present for him — perfect for stomping out rebels — had not Mr. French gotten to them first (and if there weren't the inconvenient matter of having to fit one of them over the general's wooden leg).

My own moods and likings are — as you have reason to know — more constant than Mrs. Lincoln's, and I *cannot* permit myself to abide Dan Sickles, not since that silly, firebreathing night in the Blue Room. He made a ferocious speech last night, completely out of keeping with Mr. Lincoln's kind and courtly one. After claiming never to have studied the art of paying compliments to women, the President devoted all of his brief remarks to praising what women have done to help the war effort. I do hope all the Harris and Rathbone men of my acquaintance will take note of this — not that I have contributed overmuch to my sex's labors. For the last weeks Amanda and Louise have baked and knit themselves into an exhausted trance, whereas I have found it hard even to make my twice-weekly visits to the hospital. When I do go, I flee early, God forgive me, glad to be back home in my room with my novel, or down in the study talking politics with Papa. You have heard — perhaps you haven't — that Mr. Chase has taken himself out of contention for the presidency. His dear daughter will have to forgo her fond hopes of residing in the White House, and be content with mere visits there. Perhaps the disappointment, or at least the four years' delay, will at last make her turn her attentions to Sprague. She is the only young wife I know who still concentrates all her mind and emotions upon being a daughter.

Oh, to be no longer a daughter myself! I shall be *thirty* this September, too old to be only the apple of my papa's eye. I long to be, first and foremost and forever, *your wife*. I am not yet too old for that, am I? I may *be* the apple of Papa's eye, but to my own I am more and more a wrinkled, stewed one, stuck in a jar upon a shelf, stored for the winter and likely to be forgotten when that season finally arrives. If I had more goodness and less vanity, I could wrap myself up like one of the sour and serious nurses (just the way Miss Dix prefers them) who were everywhere at the fair, keeping one stern eye upon the rafflers and the other on the kissing booth.

I myself so lack for excitement — other than the constant rumors of battlefield catastrophe and triumph, which fill the streets each afternoon and our parlor every night — that I wished for *three* eyes at the fair, so that I might take in its every single sight, might make my eyeballs like the plates of a Daguerreotype, retaining each gay image I saw for the hours I spend alone in my room each night.

Talking of photographs: I enclose my new *carte de visite,* whose picture was taken at Gardner's the other month. I look like an old tsarina engraved on a coin. You shall want to hide this item at the bottom of your mess kit, lest your comrades think you are doting upon a picture of your mama instead of your sweetheart. (You will write back and tell me that I am really just fishing for compliments. I *am;* and I expect your next letter to overflow with passionate, reassuring ones.) As the picture was being taken, I could hear people tramping through Gardner's gallery, just beyond the wall of his studio. All of the Gettysburg pictures are yet exhibited; their horror still compels the quiet crowds who come to see them. Amanda and Louise — and Mary, on a visit — twice made tearful visits to them. I simply cannot bear them, and as I passed through the exhibit on my way to the sitter's chair, I shut my eyes and hummed a tune from Beaumarchais.

Who will end it, Henry? Who will bring you home to me? All hopes — at least here — now reside in the person of Grant, whom I have *seen,* you will be surprised to know. A week ago Tuesday, he stunned everyone in the East Room, just turned up, suddenly, at 9:30, in the middle of a reception — like, everyone said, an angel — one more avenging than merciful, they hoped. He was not to be presented with his lieutenant general's commission until the following morning, but Mr. Lincoln strode over to greet him with a step so fast and firm it might have riven the carpet in two. The crowd fell back and the two of them stood before the fire, alone, conferring like Priam and Hector.

Will it be Grant who saves us? Who ends this war and brings you back safe and whole? If he does, he will come to our wedding and have the first dance with your bride — your loving, faithful

Clara

As she sealed the letter, she could hear below her the last sounds of the servants cleaning in the kitchen. The soft singing of the youngest, Myrtle, mixed with the sound of the skillets being hung up, their iron bottoms ringing like solemn bells as they came to rest against the walls of this Washington house, far from the Rathbone foundry where they had been cast years ago. Clara wasn't sure she would ever get used to having Negro servants instead of the Irish ones who had always come and gone from the house in Albany, but tonight Myrtle's voice seemed as soothing as a lullaby.

It was late, and Clara was growing tired, too tired, she decided, to write another letter. She had meant to send one to Howard, who had been with them for the last three weeks, right until this morning, insisting that his lungs and heart were good and that the New York posting the Marines were sending him to, six months behind a desk in an office at the Battery, was truly dictated by the needs of the corps and not his health. It had been lovely to have him in the house, making his jokes at the supper table, telling the girls his traveler's tales like an American Othello, and later, in the parlor, impressing Papa's colleagues with sensible talk of the blockade's effect on the walled-in Confederates. Once or twice he had taken her out, and remained cheerfully true to his promise not to provoke her on the subject of Henry. He offered no brief against the engagement, which by now, here and in Albany, was an open family secret. She knew he was not resigned to it, but he had the good nature and self-control not to let it ruin the evening they spent attending the theater and dining at the National. That same sunniness, that same command of himself, made him wonderful company, even gave her a moment — but no more than that — when his simple normality, the reliability of his moods and expression, seemed something she might wish to have permanently. Walking on Howard's arm was like strolling through an open meadow on a clear night, whereas being out with Henry meant dodging the meteor shower of his moods. Which was why, of course, in her letter to him, she had not mentioned Howard's presence at the fair. There was no telling what might excite his jealousy.

Putting on her thin nightgown — here it was only March 19 and already like summer in Washington — she allowed herself to imagine Howard, and the charms of his equanimity. He could not have written the letters tied up in mauve ribbon and lying on her night table. If he, instead of Henry, were with the Twelfth, and writing her from all the places the regiment had fought its way through in the past fifteen months — Fredericksburg, Chancellorsville, Bristoe, and beyond — the stack would contain good-humored dismissals of all the hardships and fears he was enduring. As it was, coming from Henry's pen, they were full of exciting alternations: exhilaration by gunfire one week, a fearful reappraisal of that same exhilaration the next, followed by a heart-rending denunciation of the war itself, a plague on both the houses fighting it. Howard's letters would have been soothing and soft, so soft she would probably have slept with them under her pillow. But Henry's, there on the night table, seemed to glow, like foxfire in a forest.

The conflict within him, between disdain for the war and excitement in battle, was as thrilling to track as the war itself. Before Fredericksburg, as he waited for the pontoon bridges to arrive, the ones that would take him across the Rappahannock in full screaming charge, he wrote of the banging in his veins, from sheer anticipation — even as he cursed his susceptibility to the war's drums. "The old men who have sent us here are too cowardly and weak to pound those drums themselves, but once I hear them, I forget who hung them round the necks of the innocent boys hitting them with their sticks; my body wants only to do their bidding, like a mad Apache." But after the bridge had been crossed and the battle joined and his own killing was done (he believed he had shot two men), the bottom would fall out of his spirit; his letter would turn tender as a girl's, as he devoted two pages, their handwriting shaky with grief, to the tale of a young boy from a Connecticut tobacco farm who had died in his arms after being shot through the eye. Seven months after that, when the draft wasn't filling the army as it should, he sent her angry denunciations of whole cities, full of fury that any young man might be spared the old men's war by the old men's money. "We learn that Providence manages to send not one man into the army; thanks to the tax money she spends on commutation." That word, "commutation," had become the eighth deadly sin, a hot spice upon his tongue, something he spit out and ground into his letters every chance he got.

Howard's greatest virtue, she thought, was simply that he had been *here*, on her arm these past three weeks, a living male come into the frilly house in which she was tired of living. She was a lover of men, of their talk and their deeds and the spotlights they could shine upon one; there was no doubt that by now she preferred the Blue Room to all other places in Washington. These past few weeks, with the field clear of any male rival, might Howard have succeeded in turning her head if he had dared begin orating upon the good sense of considering his suit instead of Henry's? At last to begin living life, at thirty, without another month's dreadful waiting! Might he have persuaded her to leave this war-obsessed city, its social life and emotions forever in abeyance, and fly to New York? She might have said, yes, she was tired of waiting for Henry, and for the further uncertainties his presence always brought; she had seen the error of her ways and the logic of Howard's persuasions. Yes, she was ready to settle down right this minute and be his bride.

No, she insisted to herself, turning over on her side and cursing the clammy heat in the room. No, she would not allow herself to think of such things. Henry would return, and the time would come again when she and he and Howard found themselves in the same room, as so often in the past. And then the sensible fancies of a calm life with Howard would once more seem preposterous, like straining to admire a buttercup when the sky above it was filled with a dazzling summer storm. That is what she would make herself wait for — Henry — as she endured the company of women, with all their fine, dutiful feelings.

In the room next door, one of those women was only now taking up her pen, to write in a hand that, with the passing years, had lost its feminine swirl and grown angular.

March 19, 1864

My dearest son,

We've just this morning said good-bye to Howard, and a joy it was to have him in the house — to Clara especially, I think. He looks as healthy as I can remember him — fine and strapping and handsome as the best of the Rathbone men. What a handsome couple he and Clara made arm in arm last night at the fair (I enclose a cutting from the *Star*), even more so than when they went out to see Edwin Booth's *Hamlet* at Grover's a week or two ago. You'll be glad to know he's been such a tonic to her spirits; I haven't seen such vitality in her since we met the Russian sailors a few months ago, when they made their visit to the Mansion. I'm sure I should be leaving Clara to write all these things herself, but I couldn't resist the chance to let you have my own impressions, which are certain to reassure you, of how strong and manly your cousin now looks.

We are all so proud of you. Wherever this letter reaches you, it comes with the love of your

Mother

⇥ 25 ⇤

AT 4:30 A.M. on July 30, 1864, Ira Harris lay, trying to sleep, in a guest room of the president's house on the Union College campus. Just before bedtime the senator had written to his son about the fortieth reunion of the class of 1824. "It was a large and a good class — Time and Providence have dealt kindly with it and a large number still survive." Amazingly enough, so did Dr. Nott, ninety-one years old and sound asleep downstairs after being serenaded by the returning classes.

The letter to Will was on the senator's night table, ready to be mailed to General Burnside's headquarters first thing in the morning. It contained Harris's hope that he could soon manage a visit to the Ninth Corps, though he confessed: "I cannot comprehend your objects and plans — I really do not understand what you have been doing for the last month. There is a mystery about it that all my reading has failed to penetrate. Perhaps your *next letter* will give me some light — or must I wait until I can 'come and see'? If you knew the deep interest with which we follow you, and how often and anxiously you are upon our thoughts and tongues, you would, I think, both of you, write a little more frequently. We have feared that Henry was not quite well, but have not been able to learn from him. He is not quite *reliable* in some things. Do write some of us, if only a few lines."

It still seemed extraordinary that the two of them should now be together on Burnside's staff, Will heading up the ordnance department and Henry the commissary of musters. The senator had not liked using influence (he didn't even like the word) to put Henry where he was, but the pressure at home to pull strings (another detestable phrase) had been like nothing he'd felt before. For once, Pauline and Clara had joined forces, however different their motives. His wife resented her stepson's rise and the attentions Will was forever being paid; when the University of Rochester, the school he'd abandoned for the Point, granted him, at twenty-six, an honorary degree, she had barely been able to offer her congratulations. She insisted something be done for Henry, to the point of raising her voice one night in the presence of the girls, crying she would not have her own son's situation "occupying less of my husband's attention than some postmastership in Utica." Senator Harris had counted on Clara to come to his defense, but he waited in vain. She thought being on Burnside's staff would keep Henry well behind the lines, and she was willing to bite her tongue and watch her papa suffer for the sake of her beloved's safety.

The senator resisted for weeks. True, he took pride in his ability to play the game of patronage at a level the Dictator could now only imagine, but post offices and customs houses were one thing. Playing with lives — safeguarding his family's while draftees were being slaughtered — was quite another. But Pauline and Clara and the anxiety of three years of war succeeded in wearing him down. And hadn't the Harrises and Rathbones given their share? Even young Jared was getting ready to leave West Point for the war. So he had relented, and fixed things.

As he tossed and turned now, he hoped the temporary peace between Pauline and Clara was holding in Newport. It was strange to think that, while he idolized Will, both their attentions remained focused on Henry. But with the two boys posted together, news of one meant news of the other, and he had to admit the wisdom in having arranged the appointment. It made it easier to imagine his family as a happy, normal one.

If only this thought were enough to let him sleep! As night neared morning, his mind was still on the war and what the Ninth Corps might be up to. News of what they were calling the Richmond Campaign had been terribly grim these last weeks: he knew, however cryptic Will's letters, that his son and the other men had endured a season of marching, exposure, and incessant enemy fire. It *could* not last another year, the senator told himself, falling back on his belief in Lincoln and Grant, which somehow grew with every month the war continued. They would bring it to a close. He had faith, though he would admit that faith had been tested tonight when he watched Dr. Nott praying for the war's conclusion and noticed him quivering from his years and the enormous nature of his petition. Even he seemed powerless against this remorseless beast continuing its rampage.

On the same night, four hundred miles to the south, at Petersburg, Virginia, Will Harris looked up from the letter he was writing to his fiancée by the candlelight in Ninth Corps headquarters at Fort Morton. He grunted hello and returned to his composition: "Henry has just come in looking very dirty (for him) but delighted with his inspection of a certain part of our line."

How he wished he could tell Emma what was really going on here tonight. In a matter of hours, when they captured the rise, the war would be over. This morning he had climbed a tall tree and looked down on Petersburg, picking the best-looking house, the one he would confiscate and make into his quarters. Across the room Burnside's bags were already packed, and Generals Ferrero and Ledlie were back in their shelter with a whiskey bottle between them, playing cards and waiting for the explosion.

The war was going to end — in one great bang. Everyone said it couldn't be done, but Colonel Pleasants and his regiment of coal miners had accomplished it: a month of digging had taken them right under the Confederates' artillery salient. Six hundred feet of tunnel, with two shorter arms extending beneath the rebels' trenches. Soon four tons of gunpowder would send both arms flying upward. General Mahone's South Carolina companies would be swept away like a tableful of toy soldiers.

Will could now hear the click of Henry's silver scissors as he sat on his cot and trimmed his whiskers for the second time that day. This was distracting enough, but when his brother began to talk — "starting in," as the family called it — Will had to throw down his pen and quit.

"Tell me, Cousin," said Henry, using Pauline's solecism, which Will so disliked. "Isn't secrecy an essential component of any major military operation? That is the sort of thing they teach at West Point, isn't it?"

"Yes, Henry," said Will, blotting that portion of the letter he'd managed to complete. "Anyone who gained a position on this staff through merit, experience, and training would agree to that."

"Then I wonder," said Henry, laying his scissors down, "why I just heard so much shouting across the lines."

"And what were they shouting?"

"'When you-all nigger lovers agoin' ta blow us up?'" cried Henry in his best imitation of a South Carolina accent. "That, as you'll imagine, came from our opponents, who received an equally loud reply, shouted into the dark by our young men: ''Fore you know it, you'll be chasin' your ass back to rebeldom.'"

"Excellent mimicry, Henry. Yes, rumors of Colonel Pleasants's scheme have reached even the ordinary Johnny. But you miss the important point."

"Tell it to me."

"If their commanders truly believed that what they've heard were even remotely possible, the Johnnies wouldn't be left sitting where they will shortly be blown to kingdom come." Will looked at his pocket watch, a present from Ira Harris when he'd won the sophomore Latin Prize at Rochester. "You see, Henry, that's the beauty of this operation. It succeeds by seeming too good to be true."

"Well," said Henry, "the rebel commanders may not believe it will happen, but our own Irish and niggers certainly do. You should hear them out there, saying their Hail Marys and moaning their spirituals in the middle of the night." He paused for a second before muttering, "The poor niggers . . ."

Will spun around. "I'm telling you, it doesn't matter." The last-minute decision by General Meade, over Burnside's objections, not to use five regiments of General Ferrero's Colored Troops had certainly put a snag in the operation. It didn't matter, Meade had told Will, that the coloreds had practiced hard for a month. "If they get cut down in the first wave, all the radicals and abolitionists, like your father's friend Senator Sumner, will be screaming about 'cannon fodder.' We can't have it. I don't care how exhausted Ledlie's men are. They go in first." It seemed to Will that Meade was the exhausted one, too tired to see this operation was going to succeed no matter who led the assault. History would remember Meade only for nervousness, and Will was damned if Henry was going to make *him* nervous, too. "I'm telling you," he repeated, "it doesn't matter."

Henry rolled over on the cot and shut his eyes. "No, it doesn't."

A half hour after the explosion, when the first reports began to reach staff headquarters, Will realized he had been almost all wrong. The bomb had detonated at 4:45 A.M., and the South Carolinians were duly flung into the air, finding themselves, upon their return to earth, at the edges of a crater seventy feet wide and thirty feet deep. But when the order came for the Union forces to climb out of their trenches and capture the rebel ground behind the crater, the tired, ladderless men, gasping and choking from the fumes and soil the explosion had driven into their lungs, found it almost impossible to clamber over the top. Nearing suffocation, many of them panicked. After finally recovering breath and sight, those who managed to stagger to the edge of the crater became giddy over what their eyes disclosed: a great scoop of the earth was gone, as if a meteor or the hand of God had struck and departed.

They arrived in a scattered, desperate fashion. Units got mixed up and commands went unheeded. The crater that lay before them was almost empty (most of the South Carolina boys had landed far away), and it was natural to want to go down into it, as if it were a swimming hole they had discovered on some other summer day long ago. Once a half dozen of them had slid down, thousands of Union soldiers began whooping and jumping and piling in, until the crater filled up like a bowl of blueberries. Those who kept their minds on military objectives assumed they would just cross the clay and sand and come up the other side to find that the rebels had taken flight and left the field — maybe even the war's final victory — to them. They laughed and yelled, all distinctions of rank and outfit disappearing in the predawn carnival.

It ended in screams. The rebels had not cleared the field; they were soon rushing across it toward the western edge of the pit, firing down into it, picking off Union soldiers. Rushing for cover was impossible: the hole was so full of men there wasn't room to move. The men were bubbles in a boiling pot, ready to be popped, one by one. General Ferrero's colored soldiers, bringing up the rear they'd been ordered to occupy, succeeded in flanking the crater north and south, but they were soon driven down into it, where they were given gleeful priority by the rebels above, whose screams of vengeance never ceased, and by some of their Union brothers, who were already fighting for what air was left in the pit.

Hour after hour it continued, and by mid-morning Will Harris and Major Cutting, along with Colonels Loring, Peirce, and Richmond, were still a half mile from the crater, deep in discussion of what they would tell investigators to save themselves and General Burnside from embarrassment or court-martial. As they worked on their story, Henry sat on his cot, silent, until 8:45 A.M., when he picked up a rifle, brushed off his tunic, and headed west toward the crater. Coming toward him on the morning breeze were screams, louder with each hundred yards he covered, until he was able to distinguish those of vengeance from those pain. The smells, first of smoke and then of exploded bowels, gathered and thickened as he reached the Union rim of the crater and looked down.

There was a boy looking up plaintively, and Henry regarded him intently before realizing the boy had died, perhaps hours ago, with his eyes open. Farther toward the center, amidst patches of screaming and a hedgerow of limbs that used to belong to bodies, a pair of bayonets still parried each other, clicking like knitting needles. Toward the other side, about sixty feet from where he stood, a Negro's head exploded in a shower of pink grain. Near him lay some Union flags the coloreds had recaptured from the rebels before being driven into hell.

That, of course, was where he stood. He recognized it. It was the woodcut from *Paradise Lost,* the one inside his own father's Milton, which sat in Ira Harris's library in Albany. It was Saturday, which meant that Deirdre, an hour or two from now, would be dusting it. And when she did, he realized, his eyes scanning a thousand broken limbs and shattered skulls, he would be inside it. He now felt that everything in his life had tended toward this moment, this vision of man revealed. He stepped to the edge of the crater and looked down, whispering, "'Hail horrors, hail / Infernal world, and thou profoundest Hell / Receive thy new Possessor.'"

He stepped onto the wall of mud and sand and began his descent, and he was shot, through the top of his chest, before his feet could reach the crater's floor. He fell onto the small terrace of a ditch within the wall, where he lay for the next sixty-eight hours, passing in and out of dreams — dreams of the Eagle Tavern and his mother, of Clara, of his stepfather's apple orchards, of the girls on Quay Street. By the time the burial truce was declared, he had lost the strength to bat the flies away from his wound. He lapsed into unconsciousness, after vaguely reasoning that he should try to keep his eyes open and move some part of his body, lest the teams of soldiers coming through with shovels proceed to bury him with the rest of the dead.

➤ 26 ⬻

HE WAS BREVETED, once he'd been lifted away from the Crater. His wound had bled amazingly little, the mud having acted as a natural poultice. Exposure and exhaustion were his real complaints, and even the effects of these were abating a week after the battle. He regained strength inside Fort Morton and was urged to complete his convalescence on home leave late in August. Pauline and the girls returned from Newport in order to nurse him. The summer heat in Washington made recuperation uncomfortable, but on the third floor of the Harris house he had the best of care: Mrs. Lincoln even had the President's personal doctor following his case.

In his first week home he was so pale and mute that the family feared for his mental well-being more than his physical one. His stepson's ghostly presence made Senator Harris so nervous that he tried to provoke Henry into saying anything at all. Let it be even a denunciation of Will; that would be preferable to the inscrutable silence. The girls tried to revive him by gentler means, arranging carriage rides and pointing out such novelties as the Capitol dome, completed since he'd last seen it — all without much result. Henry could often be heard murmuring with Pauline when she went to his room and closed the door, but his mother, as if she were a lawyer or confessor, refused to share their conversations with the rest of the family.

Will, who had also been promoted, arrived at the house on September 5, staying one night only; the following afternoon he testified at the military court set up to investigate the Petersburg fiasco. He bitterly blamed the debacle on General Meade, who after the battle had suspended Burnside. It was a kangaroo court,

Will insisted at the Harris dinner table; everyone knew the judge advocate was Meade's man. Shaken by the only disaster in his charmed life, Will did his best to say as little as possible. He tried to avoid Henry's thin smile at the far end of the table, just as he avoided talk of the battle itself. Instead he swapped stories with his father and Pauline about entertaining the Grants — he at Fort Morton and they here on Fifteenth Street. Only once did he explode, while recounting some conversations he'd had on Capitol Hill: "They discouraged me more than the worst defeat on the field of battle. The heartless apathy! This criminal fault-finding with officers and soldiers is more evil than the sacrifice of human lives. We don't deserve peace."

"You're right about that," said Henry, a reply that sent his stepbrother storming out of the house and off to Cleveland, where he would spend a few days with Emma Witt's family before returning to a new post at the Allegheny Arsenal.

Over the next two weeks Henry was intermittently his old self, but that entity had always been mercurial, and it was difficult to tell when it might come and go. Appearances at the Harris home by Edwin Morgan, now New York's other senator, as well as mad Dan Sickles, roused him to a bit of mimicry and a few whispered asides, but when they were gone he tended to lapse back into silence.

On the first evening of fall, he and Clara went to dine at Gautier's. Her attempts at conversation — wasn't the pâté reminiscent of what they'd had on the rue de Rivoli five years ago? — were so cautious, and his rejoinders so unresponsive, that they might have been old marrieds, or a couple on a first, unchaperoned date — anything but secret lovers. Afraid to bring up the immediate past or discuss the future, Clara sat quietly and felt the war destroying all her connections to Henry, severing them like an enemy's rail lines. She wanted the two of them to stand for love, to be an improbable example of it, and here they were, mute strangers to each other.

"Not this way," she said after they'd left the restaurant and gotten close to Fifteenth and H. "Not home just yet. I want to walk." She took his arm and led him away from the park, east down H Street, until the twilight world of lawns and carriages changed into an unpaved one through which tired clerks and freedmen and prostitutes marched between work and home. "Up here," she said, pointing to the top of some steps at a house near Seventh Street. She had a key from Johnny Hay at the White House; the rooms, a separate apartment, belonged to a friend of his who was away on business through September. Without mentioning the court of inquiry, Hay had said he knew her brother Will was to be in the city this month; if he wanted a place to get away from the bustle of the Harris household, this friend of his would be only too happy to have him use the rooms.

They were a solid, masculine affair, book-filled and a bit dusty, but a model of neatness compared to Leander Reynolds's studio outside Munich, which was what she thought of now. The fears she'd had that afternoon were nothing next to what she felt tonight, a fear that Henry was slipping away, becoming forever unreachable, a silhouette behind stained glass. She wanted to bring him back to life, to make him crazily ardent. She wanted to feel him naked against her in the dark, pressing into her with a force that would banish the last three years of worry and sewing and feminine chatter, banish them in a thrill that belonged to no one but the two of them, here, in the dark. He had worried about the war unleashing all his pent-up anger, but now it seemed as if the war had muffled him to the point of death. As she pulled down the blankets, she imagined herself fanning the last bit of a fire that threatened to go out and leave her frozen. She got into the bed and pulled him toward her, coaxed the lightning down once more. He climbed in beside her and rested his head against her neck. She waited for his whiskers to move, for the rhythm to start; she made an urgent humming sound, and still she waited, until she realized he'd gone to sleep. She stroked the back of his head, smoothed his hair, frustrated and more worried than before, but determined that he would at least have a deep rest. She smoothed and stroked, again and again, until she herself was nearly asleep.

Her eyes opened in the darkness at the sound of a song,

something low and moaning. He sounded like a Negro, singing into the pillow, his throat vibrating against her shoulder: "*We looks like men marchin' on / We looks like men o'war!*"

><

An hour later Clara was in her father's study, pleading. "He cannot go back to his regiment."

"He must, my dear."

"Work something out — with Mr. Lincoln if necessary."

Senator Harris frowned. "I've made special arrangements for Henry before."

"Which proves they can be made again. Papa, he is about to take leave of his senses. I have heard him muttering and singing as if he were somebody else entirely, miles away."

"Your mother insists he will be well."

"Of course she does. She always insists upon her wishes. You cannot tell me she would oppose what I'm asking."

"But dear, what exactly are you asking?"

"That you contrive to get Henry completely out of harm's way. Put him at one of the camps for the Confederates."

"It's not for me to put him anywhere. He's an officer trained to muster men for battles, not to stand guard over those who have lost them. I cannot arrange for him to spend the rest of the war playing cards at Point Lookout."

"Papa, I'm not talking about a regular prison camp. I'm talking about Rock Island, out in Illinois."

"What do you know about Rock Island?" Senator Harris asked, wishing his daughter weren't exposed to all that afternoon talk in the Mansion.

"You know what they're saying. Or at least what they're arguing about. Training the captured Confederates for the Union's service."

"General Grant and Mr. Stanton are opposed to it."

"But Mr. Lincoln is *not* opposed," said Clara, leaning across the desk and making her father look straight into her eyes. "You know why, Papa. If the President keeps drafting men at the current rate, General McClellan is going to win the election.

{ 167 }

What do you think Mr. Lincoln would rather do during the next six weeks? Issue another induction call and lose Pennsylvania to the Democrats, or take some rebels into the Union army?"

Ira Harris forced himself to smile. "The war has turned even women into politicians."

"My stepmother was a good politician long before Fort Sumter." Clara took his hand. "Please, Papa."

Senator Harris pursed his lips. "You know this is not a good idea, Clara. Asking men to fight their old compatriots."

"But they won't be fighting Confederates. They'll be fighting the Sioux Indians, which means their loyalties won't be tampered with. They're wanted for service in the territories."

"I see I should spend more time in the Blue Room. The intelligence I get in the Senate cloakroom isn't half so specific and up-to-date." Harris paused. "All right, my dear. I shall speak to Mr. Lincoln."

"Thank you, Papa." She got up to get him his hat and walking stick.

"I don't mean *now*, Clara!"

"Yes, Papa, right now. If you walk over to the Mansion, you'll find him up, working with Mr. Hay and Mr. Nicolay. They're expecting late reports from Sheridan tonight."

Old Edward, the doorkeeper, led Senator Harris upstairs, where it turned out Mr. Lincoln was alone, eating raisins and an apple — "a seventy-six-inch squirrel," Dan Sickles once called him.

"Come in, Senator. I've let the boys go for the night," said the President, pointing to Nicolay's empty office. "I can use your company."

Harris took a seat across from Lincoln and in an embarrassed rush put forward Clara's proposal. The President seemed amused. "Mrs. Lincoln speaks admiringly of your daughter's sense and spirit. Here's fresh evidence of it."

"My stepson," said Harris, taking a handful of raisins from the President, "is a high-strung young man. I find it difficult to plead his particular case when so many are enduring so much, but he has seen some of the worst of this war — Antietam,

Fredericksburg, the Crater — and I couldn't help thinking as I walked over here that he might be of more use to his country right now if he weren't in the thick of battle. I fear, given the strain he's showing, that he might not be quite dependable."

Lincoln went out to Nicolay's desk and took a paper from a stack on the blotter. "This is a letter to General Grant that I had John working on. Read it and tell me if I'm having it both ways, for that's what I want."

Harris skimmed the draft and read aloud the crucial part, which acknowledged Grant's opposition but still pushed the Rock Island scheme: "'I did not know at the time that you had protested against that class of thing being done, and I now say that while this particular job must be completed, no other of the sort will be authorized without an understanding with you, if at all. The secretary of war is wholly free of any part in this blunder.'" Harris looked up, trying to find whatever words the President wished him to say.

Lincoln took the paper from him and walked it back to Nicolay's desk. "It's not the strict truth. I had a pretty fair idea of the general's point of view all along. But I intend to get this thing done. Tomorrow morning I'll go see Mr. Stanton and placate him, too. Why don't you come round to the War Department with me?"

"If you think I can be useful, sir, I shall be happy to."

Lincoln sat down at his old postmaster's desk and took out his pen. "Good," he said. "Now I'll get your stepson to help me as well." He said no more until he finished composing an order sending Captain Henry R. Rathbone to Rock Island "to make a special inspection, under instructions to be given him by the provost marshal general, of the prisoners to be enlisted." He handed the paper to Senator Harris. "That should do it."

"I'm very grateful, Mr. President."

Lincoln offered him an apple slice. "I'm sure this isn't as good as what you grow up in Loudonville, but let's finish it off. It will fortify us for our little talk with Mr. Stanton in the morning."

The two men — one tall and craggy as a totem pole, the other smooth and solid as a statue in the Rotunda — sat munching the rest of Mr. Lincoln's apple in silence, until the President, looking tired, asked, "So, is there anything else, Senator? A consulate or a clerkship for some worthy New Yorker?"

Harris blushed, but Lincoln, rising for his bedtime, brought a friendly hand down on his shoulder. "We've done good business tonight, old friend." They walked out of the office together, past the war map with its colored pins. "A year from now, less than that with luck, this war will have come to an end, and Henry and Clara will be about the business of giving you and Mrs. Harris a grandchild."

Harris looked up, surprised, but the President just patted his shoulder once more and blew out the lamp. "The Red Room is a two-way sieve. Mrs. Lincoln spills what secrets she hears in my direction."

October 14, 1864
Rock Island Prison

Darling Clara,

They lied, of course: Grant, the President and the pater. We were instructed to raise the 1st U.S. Volunteers only from persons born in the North or abroad, despite their service to the Southland. Now, to get our 1,750 men, we are being permitted to take the oath from "discouraged Southerners," too, which is a good thing, since all the captive voices I hear in this place sound just like the ones I heard calling out from the rebel lines before Burnside sprang the Petersburg mine: each as mellifluous as your old friend Miss Bashford's.

They are hungry, and the brighter ones realize they will soon be cold. It's full rations for those who come over, considerably less for those who don't. The former have been put by Col. Johnson into what we call the calf pen; on the other side of a fence lies the "bull pen," where the recalcitrant and confused remain. It's touching to see the odd bit of bread and meat being flung from the sheep to the goats — I wonder if the same generosity manifests itself at Andersonville, or if this is a species of the regional gallantry Miss B. liked to go on about.

My war has come full circle: once again I am a recruitment

officer, this time Honest Abe's personally appointed one. But what we are doing here is far worse than what we accomplished on the streets of New York. These crackers aren't being *sold* on the army; they're being *starved* into it. The denizens of the bull pen fully expect us to slaughter them once the snow falls and supplies are interrupted.

Nonetheless, I will galvanize these rebels out of their gray and into our blue — all so they can go kill the red man. If they do a thorough job of that, what say you, Clara, to our heading west once we're married? We can settle near some fort in Colorado and grow gaudily rich off the silver dug out of the new earth, and never again hear a syllable of oratory. I dreaded the war, but I thought it would at least blow away the old men and leave something new and exciting once the smoke cleared. Now I know the old men have managed to run the war as they did their businesses and law firms and all else. I hate what they've done and what I've seen. Had your Mr. Lincoln let the wayward sisters depart in peace, I'd have grown harmlessly, biliously old; as it is, a million lie dead and I, dear girl, am a wreck, deservedly so.

Kiss mother and the girls for me. I kiss you myself — right now — this moment —

Henry

She read it twice, and she decided she would not cry over it. Surely this was a *good* letter, she thought, forcing herself, as she sat in her father's study, to read it a third time. Henry had emerged from the torpor that gripped him after Petersburg. A wreck? Nonsense. He would not be looking west, and toward their marriage, if he were. This letter was a fine thing, however sad it might sound. Papa and Mr. Lincoln had saved him — *she* had saved him, right in this room, kept him alive. The war would end, and he would come home knowing that he owed her his life. And then they would make life together. A child, children, and a new life for themselves. Yes, maybe they would go west. On a shelf behind her, she looked for Papa's copy of Parkman. She carried it upstairs to read, humming as she went.

→ 27 ←

CLARA MOVED the flowers from the left side of her waist to the right. The mirror told her they looked better there, but for a moment she wondered if the shift might disrupt some symbolic meaning.

They were awash in portents. Mrs. Lincoln's latest enthusiasm was Spurzheim, the German who thought the bumps on everyone's head had significance. The day before yesterday, when the President paraded to his second inaugural, everyone decided the dark clouds meant that peace was still further off than they'd been hoping. But when the sun broke through, right over Mr. Lincoln's head as he began his speech, the crowd cried its approval. The President went on to promise moderation, not marvels, but at that moment you could have convinced anyone, even Henry, that a glorious victory was only weeks away.

Mrs. Lincoln could use peace immediately. Since the reelection she'd become stranger, even less settled than before. Last month, in a response to one of her husband's own ominous dreams, she had ordered a thousand dollars' worth of mourning. She painstakingly explained to everyone in the Blue Room that this was a way of cheating fate, not abetting it, but no one felt the act's strategic nature made it any less morbid. Clara tried to imagine her as she must be right now, across the park and inside the White House, getting into her dress for tonight's ball at the patent office. Clara knew it was white silk covered with point lace, and that she'd be wearing a lace shawl over it. She further knew, from John Hay, that the dress had cost $2,000. Still, spending two times as much on the festive as the funereal had to be a good sign.

Clara had no intention of covering her own shoulders tonight. The only thing her ensemble would have in common with Mrs. Lincoln's was the spray of violets she now pinned into her hair. Another look in the mirror proved the deep apricot silk she had on to be a marvelous choice; she was already too old for pastels and chiffons, and if she had her way tonight, she would take a giant step toward being, at last, at thirty-one, a married woman.

She could hear Pauline in the next bedroom, straining to get herself into the purple bombazine she'd bought. *Much more tasteful than bright colors during wartime, don't you think, Clara?* What Clara really thought was that, except for her beloved feathered headdress, Pauline would look like one of the Catholics' giant statues wrapped up for Lent. Her stepmother was doubly happy if she could criticize Clara and the First Lady in one fell swoop of moral fashion. Mrs. Lincoln had consistently disappointed her these past four years: any solidarity that might have arisen from mutual antipathy to Mr. Seward and Mr. Weed had long since congealed, on Mrs. Harris's part, into hostility. Indifference by the First Lady toward the whole Harris family would have been preferable to the way she dispensed social favors exclusively to Clara and Ira. Things had reached a pitch of pique on Friday, when Mrs. Lincoln insisted that Senator Harris be her escort to the swearing-in of the new, dead-drunk Vice President. Clara, now putting some jasmine in with the violets, relished recalling the sight of Pauline, looking on from a distant part of the Senate gallery and practically having a seizure over her banishment. This morning at breakfast she'd actually told her husband, "I hope that tonight you'll be cautioned by Andy Johnson's example," the first reference anyone in the family had ever made to Ira Harris's steadily greater tippling. The poor old thing had been crushed by the remark, unable to make a sound as he spooned his egg and munched the rest of his bacon. Well, Clara hoped he would take as much punch and spirits as he liked tonight. She had a small design that depended on his slight inebriation.

Bless Papa, he'd already done so much. When the Rock Island

mission was finished and she urged him once more to keep Henry away from battle, she'd never expected her father would manage to bring Henry home, six days before Christmas, with a promotion to major and a job — behind a desk! — a few blocks away in the provost marshal's office. Henry was commanding eighteen clerks and messengers now, disbursing hundreds of thousands of dollars to every regiment in the army. "In a year or two," she'd said, flinging her arms around him while he worked at a ledger in Papa's study one night, "you'll have put yourself out of business, paid the last volunteer and draftee and helped send them home. You'll shut the cash drawer and hear a nice hollow thud, and we'll know the war is over for good."

At ten o'clock the four of them could hardly squeeze into one carriage for the ride to the ball. Clara's gown billowed over Henry and Papa, and when one of Pauline's feathers found its way into Senator Harris's mouth, everyone actually succeeded in laughing together. Henry, pointing to the bunting that covered the patent office, wondered "how much commutation money this party would be eating up," but Clara decided his words were offered more in a spirit of teasing than as serious inquiry about the twenty million dollars he now knew the provost marshal had collected from men buying their way out of military service.

"Now, Henry," said Ira Harris, for once feeling confident his rejoinder wouldn't bring on a squabble, "I've got it on good authority — which is to say my daughter — that they've sold four thousand tickets at ten dollars apiece, and that all of it will go to the families of soldiers."

Just before it parked, the carriage hit a bump, bouncing the occupants and their finery. When Pauline settled back down, the same purple feather reentered her husband's mouth. The coachman, soon at the door with an apology, his arm out for the ladies, smiled at the sight of what he took to be a happy family.

"Thank you, young man," shouted Senator Harris, clapping the boy's back and pressing a half dollar into his hand. "Isn't it a fine night?" Along with the bunting, the building was also hung with huge portraits of the President and Vice President, and great torches sent up plumes of smoke that dissipated like the tops of the Ionic columns. Climbing the steps, Clara could hear an army band, and her heart beat faster. Henry had her left arm, and she gave her right one to her papa, who all week had vented optimism over the military situation. Even old Mr. Weed had sent the President a telegram conveying admiration for Saturday's inaugural address. "The nation's wounds *will* be bound up," said Harris as he marveled over the military might assembled here. Farragut, Hooker, Banks, and Halleck, all in one room. And to think that they would soon be going home to their barracks!

Clara's optimism surpassed her father's. She looked around the vast hall, nearly three hundred feet from end to end, and decided she and Henry had no need of the West and its open spaces. The two of them would be fine right here in this city. All the mountain peaks and Indian chiefs in the territories could not compete with the music, plumage, and power in this room. She squeezed Henry's hand just before the army band quit in midmarch, took a breath, and struck up "Hail to the Chief." The roar that greeted Mr. Lincoln, arriving arm in arm with Speaker Colfax, could have cleared the rebels from their last Virginia strongholds, she thought. She pulled Henry along, to the front edge of their side of the crowd, which was parting to make room for the President as if he were Moses himself. Mrs. Lincoln was on the arm of Senator Sumner, passing right by Clara, smiling into her eyes without a hint of recognition. She was on that stratum of trance-like excitement Clara had witnessed a few times before; her eyes were as bright and expressionless as the Tiffany seed pearls at her neck. "Two thousand dollars," Clara said to Pauline over the din, hoping this bit of gossip would create some feminine solidarity between them. Her goodwill extended all the way to her stepmother tonight, but Pauline reciprocated with only a small clucking sound.

The First Couple took their places on a large blue and gold sofa, the applause and huzzahs hardly subsiding as the dais filled up with members of the Cabinet. Senator Harris, his tall form on tiptoe, managed to make Mr. Seward see a wave of his hand before Pauline could retract it with a tug on his coattail. He smiled at her, misty-eyed with fellowship and craving a drink. Clara dispatched Henry to get him one.

"A poor spectacle for a republican government," Pauline shouted into his ear, pointing to the dais and its distinct air of a court around a throne, with Madame President its unchallenged queen.

"Rejoice!" Senator Harris shouted back. "Two years ago this room was a hospital full of dying soldiers. Let yourself feel our triumph. It's a good one." He was back up on tiptoe, waving to Gideon Welles with such a sweeping arc of his big hand that he accidentally bashed the headdress of Mrs. Edwin Morgan, who was squeezed up against him.

The crowding at ten o'clock was nothing compared to what happened with midnight's arrival. Supper was brought in as another wave of ticket holders and gatecrashers rushed into the hall. The scramble toward the platters of tarts and oysters and terrapin was frightening, like a reenactment of Pickett's charge at Gettysburg. The President had left an hour before, but those still on the dais risked being trampled with everyone else. The glass cases lining the walls, housing hundreds of patented inventions from the telegraph to the orange squeezer, threatened to shatter one by one, but whenever the sound of smashing glass came, it turned out to be a dish or a goblet. More people were standing on the long tables than were seated at them, and the food was grabbed with such abandon that more of it wound up on the guests' skirts and shoes than in their mouths. When it became clear that everyone was merely being mauled, and that no one was likely to suffer broken bones or suffocation, the crowd settled into a kind of pleasant mass hysteria.

"What would old Mr. Osborne say?" Clara shouted up to her father, who, like Senator Morgan, was standing on a chair to survey the proceedings.

"'It's like Andy Jackson's first day in the White House!'" father and daughter yelled together, mimicking deaf old Mr. Osborne's characterization of every family and civic commotion he'd witnessed in Albany for the last thirty-five years.

"They say fifteen thousand came through the Mansion on Saturday," shouted Ira Harris.

"And I heard how they left it, too," said Henry. "With big holes in the carpets and curtains."

A naval officer six feet away brought his sword down upon a cream cake, sending salvos of filling in all directions and exciting happy shrieks from the ladies. Mrs. Morgan scooped some cream from her husband's shirt cuff and took an approving taste while he shouted to Senator Harris atop the next chair, "The President and Sumner seemed to be getting on well tonight."

"All *manner* of thing shall soon be well," said Harris, clinking his empty glass against his colleague's half-full one.

"Henry," said Clara, "find more spirits for Papa."

This was easier said than done, but Senator Harris was already swaying from what he'd had.

"Look!" cried Clara, nudging Henry. "Robert Lincoln's over there."

"Looking well rested, too."

"Indeed," said Pauline. "Worn out from three whole months with General Grant at City Point."

"Who's he with?" asked Clara. "Mary Harlan? Oh, look, they're trying to dance." A clutch of young people stood by the Prince of Rails and his partner, laughing at their attempt to move amidst the crush.

"I wish there *were* room to dance," said Clara, slipping her arm through Henry's.

"If there were," said Mrs. Morgan, licking a finger, "you still wouldn't see Kate Chase out there."

"Why not?" asked Pauline.

"Expecting."

"To new life!" cried Senator Harris, still atop his chair and raising his long-since-drained glass.

"To your own grandchildren!" cried Clara. "Before another Congress is elected!"

"Clara Harris," said Mrs. Morgan, "what are you trying to say?"

"Ask my papa."

"Senator?" said Mrs. Morgan.

Pauline looked up with an imploring glare, hoping to forestall him, but his mood was too happy, his desire to please his Clara

{ 177 }

too strong. There was no stopping the marriage now that peace was here. Clara would redeem his four-year-old pledge the moment General Lee handed Grant his sword, so why wait for the *Star* to announce the news? Why not let it out tonight and bless it with some luck from this grand occasion?

"Yes!" boomed Ira Harris, as if he were twenty years younger and standing on a tree stump in his first campaign for the state assembly. "My son will soon be my son-in-*law.* Henry and my Clara intend to be married."

"Oh, how marvelous!" cried Mrs. Morgan, simultaneously clapping her hands and casting her own husband a look of sarcastic disbelief. "How extraordinary!"

The wonderful cat was out of its bag, at last and forever, just as Clara had hoped, thanks to her papa's good mood and empty stomach. She had seen Mrs. Morgan's glance, but she wasn't going to let it spoil her triumph.

"Isn't that Senator Hale's daughter?" asked Pauline, bitterly attempting to change the subject.

"Yes, it is," said Clara. "They say she's in love with Edwin Booth's brother. And look, Henry, there's little Fanny Seward standing next to Admiral Farragut. I must meet him." Getting to the admiral required squeezing through half a dozen couples, but Clara seemed to float over them on her own happiness. Left beside Pauline, Henry watched his fiancée make her way through, the whole vast hall now *her* Eagle Tavern, her own hour finally come round.

✦ 28 ✦

"EVENTUALLY it became apparent that some mysterious form of disease had assailed him, with which medical skill found it hard to grapple; though there were intervals in the progress of his malady, when strong hopes were indulged that it had been, or would soon be, permanently arrested." Just when, Clara wondered, had it become "apparent"? Reverend Sprague, preaching Howard Rathbone's funeral sermon in Albany's Second Presbyterian Church, made it sound as if everyone had known his condition and been anxiously discussing it for months. She had heard nothing until ten days ago, when word reached Washington that he lay dying in the New York Hospital after collapsing in the street. He had been trying to reach the railroad station, hoping to go home to Kenwood for what he surely knew was his last "shore leave."

He died on Wednesday at the age of twenty-nine. Now, Saturday, April 1, 1865, all the Rathbones and Harrises save Will stood on the tall grass of the Rural Cemetery, having come in six different carriages over the plank road from Albany to Loudonville. Clara was aware of being somewhere between the skeletons of Henry's father and her own real mother. At the top of this gentle slope, she could see Mayor Rathbone's sarcophagus, a row of sculpted rosettes beneath its stone lid, and she knew she could still find her way through the cemetery's oaks and pines toward the simpler grave into which Louisa Tubbs Harris had been placed the same week, twenty years ago.

For Howard, said John Finley Rathbone in a quavering voice, they would erect a monument worthy of his soaring, generous spirit. He had already talked to the Italian man who would carve the obelisk, and told him just what Howard wanted inscribed on the plinth, John 3:16. It was typical of Howard, wonderfully typical — offering comfort to those who approached the stone, not memorializing any virtue or accomplishment in his own short life. Hamilton Harris, shaken by the sight of Emeline Rathbone, now deprived of both husband and son, nervously tried to distract himself by asking Pauline if she knew where in the cemetery the Dictator had bought his large plot. Clara patted his hand, and he resumed listening to the minister's muttering.

She herself was thinking back a week and a half, to the night before Mrs. Lincoln accompanied the President to Grant's camp at City Point. She'd been upstairs with the First Lady and Mrs. Keckley when old Edward brought in Louise, who had run across Lafayette Square to tell her there was bad news from New York. Howard was "poorly," she said; Clara had to shake her, right in front of Mrs. Lincoln, to get the real news. It was a cancerous stomach, what it had probably been for years, and, no, he wouldn't recover.

Two days later she and Henry stood before the huge stone hospital on lower Broadway, a terrible-looking place out of a Wilkie Collins novel; she could imagine the grave robbers pulling up to it in the middle of the night with corpses for the researchers. The north building? a gatekeeper had inquired of them, assuming they were there to see a wounded soldier. No, it was the main building they needed, for that's where Howard was, amidst the charity patients and merchant seamen, for the moment too weak and hopeless to be moved. They went down the gaslit corridor, freezing from the air that poured through open windows at each end, cross ventilation trying to keep down the ship-fever germs that Irish patients carried into the country with them.

"One at a time, please," the nurse had said after telling Howard they were there. "He asked that it be that way."

Clara went in first. Howard was gaunt, in terrible pain, coughing into a filthy cloth, his big, sudden smile just camouflage for a wince. He took her hand. "I saw your announcement."

"Yes," she answered, gently rubbing his wrist with her thumb. "Mother insisted on its being in the papers everywhere, here and Albany and Washington. Determined to salvage social prestige from the 'disaster.'"

"How is Henry?" he asked.

"Fine," she whispered, fussing with the blanket. "Getting ready to demobilize the Union army from a desk in Washington. Oh, Howard," she said, prying the cloth from him and bringing his hand to her cheek. "Everything will soon be well. Can't you be, too?"

"I'm afraid I can't, Clara. I'm going home to die."

"No," she said.

He had turned his head away, exhausted. "Please bring Henry in. I want to say goodbye to him."

She had begun to cry, and while she was afraid to kiss him, had been scared even to touch his handkerchief, she took him in her arms — there was nothing but bones beneath the night-shirt — and kissed his mad-hot cheek. He was also crying, holding her with one arm, clutching the iron rail of the bed with the other, squeezing it until his knuckles turned white and he could feel something besides the pain in his stomach.

"Don't, Clara," he gasped, making her think she'd hurt him. She gently laid him back down against the pillow, but even when he was free from her grasp, he groaned, "Don't. Don't go through with it. For your sake, not for mine."

She said nothing, just put a fresh cloth into the basin of water. She mopped his forehead and hushed him and hummed a soft tune until he fell asleep. Back out in the hall she told Henry his cousin was finally resting and it was better that he not go in.

Now, as Howard's coffin was lowered into the freshly spaded earth, she thought back to the uproarious night of the inaugural ball and wondered how she might regain that hopefulness. As she started sobbing, Papa came to her side and put his arm upon her shoulders. "Don't cry, my darling. Everything will be fine. Peace will be here very soon. Howard will have everlasting life, just as his monument will say."

She dabbed at her eyes with her gloves.

"That's better," said Senator Harris. "I am going to remain here for a while helping Emeline. Henry will take you and Mother back. He will take care of you now. The next telegrams coming will be full of joy and peace, not sadness. I only hope I get back to the capital soon enough to be with Mr. Lincoln at the War Department when the great news comes in on the wire. This is the last terrible thing," he said, pointing to the grave, which some boys nearby, tugging on their caps and trying to be quiet, were waiting to fill in.

"All right, Papa, I'll be happy. Don't stay away from us long." She reached up to kiss him. Henry shook Harris's hand and took Clara's right arm. With her left hand, as they walked away, she closed her mourning shawl, a borrowed item from Mrs. Lincoln's fate-defying spree the other month. The First Lady, having no real need of it herself, had pressed Clara to take it when Louise came with the news about Howard.

"I'T'S A QUARTER PAST EIGHT," said Lina Harris. "Where are they?"

"Come away from the window," called her mother from the dining room.

"But what good is an invitation to the theatre if you miss half the play?"

Laughter came down the stairs with Clara. It floated ahead of her pink satin gown, which descended to the approving shriek of her young half-sister.

"A little lateness is to be expected," said Clara. "The war may have ended, but I suspect the President still has a few things on his mind." Lina kept her at the bottom of the stairs, circling the dress, admiring and fluffing, preparing her for the inspection of Henry, who was waiting in the parlor.

"Well?" asked Clara, striking a pose so pretentiously regal that both her fiancé and Lina understood her to be imitating that young queen of Washington society, Kate Chase Sprague.

"Stunning," said Henry, before he returned to his *Evening Star.*

"Hmmph," said Clara, pretending to be miffed. Toward Lina she made a confidential gesture with her fan. "Our brother can't be expected to appreciate these things. I'll let *you* attend me on the sofa." They went across the room, giggling, though they both stole an anxious glance at the clock, which now showed the time at 8:18.

In the dining room, Clara could see Pauline Harris arranging lilacs and jonquils and feigning indifference to the President's arrival. She had been silently furious ever since this afternoon, when Mrs. Lincoln's footman arrived with the invitation. If Senator Harris had been here instead of in Albany, she would have everyone believe, the invitation would have been for the two of *them*, not Henry and Clara. This was ridiculous, Clara knew. Actually, General and Mrs. Grant had probably been the First Lady's preferred companions, but Papa and Pauline had certainly never been in the running.

"Here's the proof," said Henry, reading an item from the paper that corresponded to what Clara was thinking and they had all discussed at dinner:

> LIEUT. GENERAL GRANT, PRESIDENT and Mrs. Lincoln have secured the State Box at Ford's Theatre TO NIGHT, to witness Miss Laura Keene's American Cousin.

Pauline came to life in the dining room. "I'm afraid the theatregoers will be disappointed," she called.

Lina pinched her older sister and the two of them stifled laughter. Pauline simply would not let Clara enjoy it, would never forgive Ira Harris for being away with his two other daughters.

Sitting across the parlor, Henry looked almost his old self to Clara, fuller in the face behind his red whiskers and mustache. He hadn't put on the foulard she'd bought him at the Sanitary Fair, but still, how wonderful it was to see him out of uniform, in shoes instead of boots.

But it was 8:20 now, and even Henry could no longer concentrate on the *Star*. He folded it up and crossed his legs, drummed his fingers on his shin and picked at the velvet sofa, the same sort of nervous movements he had made all day in the adjutant general's office as he toted up the blood money, the government's filthy take from commutation, each $300 of it a bullet that one Northerner had fired into another's back. When his disgust got the better of him, he would take a break and look at Clara's photograph from Gardner's studio, which sat on his rolltop desk, and he would try not to imagine, once more, the romantic farewell he was sure she and Howard had taken of each other in the New York Hospital.

Pauline entered the parlor and took a chair beside him. "Of course," she said, "I've already seen Miss Keene do this play, six or seven years ago at her theatre in New York. It wasn't long before we took our European trip." Clara was about to say something, but she stopped herself. Her spirits were too good tonight; she would not be drawn into any war of oblique words with Pauline. She would listen to the tick of the clock, smooth her handkerchief, and imagine herself a little while from now, standing in the golden glow of the gaslight at Ford's, between Henry and Mr. Lincoln, as the audience came to its feet.

"The story is crude but amusing," said Pauline. "A lot of fuss over an inheritance. But you'll be amused by Lord Dundreary's silly affectations. Sothern was marvelous in the part. He —"

Lina shrieked.

"Let the *girl* get it," cried Pauline, but it was too late. Her youngest child had already raced past the maid to the door, opening it for Charles Forbes, who took off his hat and inquired, "Major Rathbone and Miss Harris?"

"They're right in here," said Lina, pointing from the hallway into the parlor.

"Please tell them that the President and his lady are here."

Before Lina had a chance to follow his instructions, Henry and Clara had come into the hall. "Good evening, Mr. Forbes," she said. He smiled at this one of Mrs. Lincoln's favorites and stepped aside so she and Major Rathbone might precede him to the coach. Lina followed the three of them with her eyes, straining for a glimpse of the President inside the carriage that had just made the brief journey from the Executive Mansion. But he and Mrs. Lincoln were seated in the hooded half of the coach, and Lina couldn't see him in the dark. Henry and Clara were taking the open seats behind the driver's box. The coachman looked ready to snap his reins, and Pauline was about to close the door. But just then, in response to a smile and gesture from Clara, the tall man in his high black hat leaned forward and waved to the wife and daughter of Ira Harris, his loyal, if irritating, supporter from the state of New York.

The carriage clattered into H Street, heading toward Fourteenth. The pink satin of Clara's dress caught a ray of lamplight, and Mrs. Lincoln shrieked with a piercingness that outdid Lina's display five minutes before. "So beautiful!" she exclaimed.

"Not so pretty as yours," said Clara, smiling at the President as she returned his wife's compliment, and thought of all the times she had accompanied the First Lady in pursuit of what her husband called "flubdubs," expensive dresses whose making he endured for the brief elevation they gave to his wife's mood.

"My apologies for our lateness," said the President. "I had Speaker Colfax and then Congressman Ashmun. I wouldn't have gotten away at all if Mother hadn't threatened the three of us with bloody reprisals."

"At least you didn't have Senator Harris," said Clara, whose gentle joke on her favor-seeking father coaxed a smile from Mr. Lincoln. Not long ago the President was reported to have said, "The last thing I do before going to sleep at night is check under my bed for Senator Harris," a remark that made its way through Washington and to the house at Fifteenth and H, where Pauline had failed to find it amusing.

"Where is your good father this week?" asked Mr. Lincoln, looking first at Clara and then at Major Rathbone, unsure which one to put the question to. To his mind they were both Harris's children, and when Mrs. Lincoln burbled the secret of their engagement to him last year, he had stood for a moment without saying anything, just feeling that it was a peculiar thing for a boy and girl raised together as they had been to be marrying each other.

"Papa is in Albany on family business. Henry's cousin Howard died last month, and Papa is helping his widowed mother get things in order. Also, my sister Amanda is getting married next month, and he's been dragged into the preparations."

The President just nodded, but his wife burst into renewed speech. "Clara, we must start thinking about your own wedding. Have you set the date? You *must* set the date, right now. We don't want you two to waste a minute of peacetime."

Clara was happy to see her in such high spirits — she'd witnessed her low ones and her rages — but she feared her mood might be too good tonight, a dance upon a precipice; her high-pitched chatter made a jarring contrast to Henry's silence and the President's amiable exhaustion.

"Father!" the First Lady cried, grasping his long forearm. "I insist that Major Rathbone and Miss Harris have their nuptials in the Mansion. In fact, I want you to give Clara away. Her papa can't very well give his daughter away to a young man who's his son!" She laughed loudly, turning for appreciation first to the President and then to Henry, who smiled politely.

Clara's heart leapt at the thought of being married in the White House, but the President was not rushing to embrace his wife's excited suggestions, and Henry, who had spent most of his life insisting that he was *not* Ira Harris's son, was just looking out of the coach, westward, into Fourteenth Street.

"Mother," said the President at last, "I suspect Mrs. Harris will have some ideas of her own about her children's wedding. Wait to hear her will in the matter. Senator Harris and I are occupied with less explosive affairs, like the demobilization of the rebel army and the reconstruction of the Union."

Clara waited out the moment, crossing her fingers beneath her fan. The President's joke might provoke a storm of anger or merriment or anything in between from his tightly strung wife. Fortunately, it was Mrs. Lincoln's shrill laughter that filled the carriage as it rounded Fourteenth Street and turned onto F. Clara looked toward Pennsylvania Avenue in the distance. Some white victory torches and a triumphal arch were visible through the evening's clouds. The night was enchanted, its perfection safely beyond the reach of anyone's moods and sorrows. Even Henry had joined the conversation.

"Are you expecting the surrender in North Carolina, sir?"

"Any hour now, Major. That's what Secretary Stanton tells me. There may be a few scattered engagements before it's all over, but over is what it appears to be."

Mrs. Lincoln rapped the President's gloved knuckles with her fan. "From now on, the only talk of engagements will be about the kind Major Rathbone and Miss Harris are having."

"All right, Mother," said the President. "We shall exchange the martial for the marital." They all laughed.

"This is our second carriage ride today," Mrs. Lincoln said suddenly, putting her hand on Clara's knee. "During the first, this afternoon, the President and I made a pact that we would both be more cheerful from now on."

"A fine idea," said Clara, who could remember all the black days she'd endured alongside Mrs. Lincoln, especially after Willie died.

The carriage had turned into Tenth Street and was in sight of Ferguson's restaurant and the theatre. The street was lined with the coaches of people already inside watching the play, but the waiting drivers, mostly Negroes, turned around on their boxes for a look at the President and his party, tipping their hats and softly cheering. A small crush of people, enough to require the attentions of a policeman, waited in front of Ford's. Someone was struggling to lay a wooden crate down in the gutter so the ladies wouldn't muddy their dresses as they descended.

"Goodness," cried Mrs. Lincoln, delighted by the little crowd. She straightened her brooch and put on a grander air. "It reminds me of the night we all first met. Do you remember the mob outside the Delavan House? Do you, Clara? Do you, Henry? Father?"

The President took her hand. "Your memory is a formidable thing, Mother. That was four long years ago." The coach came to a stop. Clara was sure she could recall that night even more vividly than Mrs. Lincoln: the terrible commotion; the struggle to get through the crowd; her first sight of Mr. Lincoln's long, kindly face, so much less ravaged than it was tonight.

The spectators outside the theatre were clapping for the President, who stepped down from the carriage and tipped his hat with a trace of embarrassment. Charles Forbes extended his arm up to the First Lady. Once she had alighted, Henry helped Clara down, lifting a flounce of her gown away from the gutter. The ushers cleared a path through the lobby. The President shook hands and murmured apologies for their lateness. Clara could feel herself and Henry being stared at by people who thought they might be the Grants. Once these people realized their mistake, their eyes quickly shifted to the Lincolns, but one woman, convinced that Henry was commander of all the Union's forces, whispered to her companion, "He's so young!"

A man handed them programs while they mounted the stairs at the theatre's south end. Walking the length of a narrow aisle toward the room leading to the state box, Clara could hear the sounds of the play through the wall. It was curiously quiet when they entered the box. Mrs. Lincoln made a whispery fuss of arranging them all: the President in a rocker, herself beside him, Clara on a chair to her right, and Henry on a small sofa behind his fiancée. "Will you be able to see?" Clara asked him. Everything, she noted, was red: the floral wallpaper, the carpet, the damask of Henry's couch. The balcony seemed a toy world, like the doll's house her father had given her years ago in Albany, the Christmas just after her own mother died.

The President leaned over to show himself to the audience, which applauded and cheered just long enough to stop the action onstage. The play resumed so quickly that Clara was disappointed. She had hoped for a longer demonstration and the chance for them all to stand. The little orchestra might have played "Hail to the Chief," but it didn't. She reached over the balcony's railing to touch the red-white-and-blue bunting and finger the lace curtain that hung along the indentation separating her and Mrs. Lincoln. They were so close to the stage that they might almost be on it. As it was, their box seemed better decorated: the sets, Clara could see, were threadbare. She looked across the theatre to the opposite box. It was empty, she was sorry to discover. She was in a mood to be watched tonight, and she wondered how she would be able to sit through the rest of this silly play until the moment came when she and Henry could descend, with the Lincolns, into the envious, excited crowd.

The performance didn't seem to be going over. There had been scarcely a laugh since they took their seats, and the actors were shouting their lines in sweaty near desperation. Miss Keene looked like a fool, all the paint and powder adding years instead of subtracting them. She was affecting the gaiety of a girl, and the results were grotesque. Mrs. Lincoln might be too old for what *she* was wearing tonight (Henry had given Clara an amused nudge about the low cut of the First Lady's gown), but at least her childlike animation was something that bubbled up from her own complicated nature, not something pinned on like one of Miss Keene's curls.

Clara leaned back and glanced at the President. It would be a pleasure to see him laugh tonight, after all his trials of the past four years, from the rivers of blood he had been forced to navigate, to the inveiglings of her own dear prolix papa — not to mention the frights and tantrums of his wife. Even here he wasn't safe from bother. A few minutes after they sat down, Clara heard a man out in the hallway telling Mr. Forbes about a dispatch the President must see.

"Yes," Harry Hawk shouted from the stage, making one more joke about Lord Dundreary's dyed red whiskers. "About the ends they're as black as a nigger's in billing time, and near the roots they're all speckled and streaked." She turned back toward Henry, whose fire-colored mustache had always been the subject of family jokes and her own twirlings. He smiled at her, though she was sure he hadn't caught the line, or much of anything else. She knew where he was, could tell from his expression: back in Virginia, awash in blood and screams and flying bones at the battle of the Crater. Had he noticed that General Burnside was in the house tonight, down there in the front row, having arrived even later than the four of them?

How strange that they should all be sitting here. How extraordinary, too, that she and Mrs. Lincoln had managed to stay friends — even after the night Papa had asked why Robert wasn't in the army. But the First Lady's nature was more forgiving than it was ferocious; Clara had seen that again and again, on all the occasions when she and others had unaccountably displeased her.

Poor Mr. Lincoln was cold. He'd looked around for his coat and was awkwardly putting it on. The gesture reminded Clara of the only one of his wife's séances she'd attended. (If her Baptist papa ever found out!) The spiritualist hired to conjure up the presence of Willie kept asking them if they didn't feel the sudden rise or fall in the room's temperature — observations that had the ladies tearing off or reaching for their shawls. It was hard to tell whether Mrs. Lincoln's imagination brought her more comfort or pain on that occasion, but right now there was no disputing the blessing it was to her, supplying the evening with all the little touches of glory Clara thought it missing. The First Lady was delighted with the play, fizzing with joy, unable to sit still or keep herself from talking. The President had taken her hand a few minutes ago, and now Clara could hear her playing the coquette, asking him, "What will Miss Harris think of me?"

"Why, she will think nothing about it," he replied.

She will think nothing about it. He was only trying to quiet her, of course. Surely he wasn't thinking, *How can she think anything about it? After all, she's about to marry a man who's virtually her own brother.* No, it was foolish to worry about that. She was too sensitive on this point. But after just one month of being openly engaged to Henry, she was tired of having to explain to people who'd just met them, and were confused, that there was no blood between them.

She would not start thinking about that now. She would force herself to be interested in this play, which alas had no intermission. "People sometimes look a great way off for that which is near at hand," said the fortune-hunting Mrs. Mountchessington to Asa Trenchard. Mrs. Lincoln laughed, and Clara smiled. Perhaps there was a little life in this old chestnut; Mr. Lincoln showed signs of dozing, but the audience seemed to be warming up. Mrs. Mountchessington was certainly a perfect stage version of Pauline: "I am aware, Mr. Trenchard, you are not used to the manners of good society, and that, alone, will excuse the impertinence of which you have been guilty." The tone and the bearing were comically approximate. Did Henry see the resemblance too, and should she risk trying to share the joke with her mother-worshiping fiancé? She turned around to him, but he wasn't even looking at the stage. He was gazing intently at the door to the box, as if imagining the moment they could all get up and go.

"Don't know the manners of good society, eh?" bellowed

Harry Hawk, so loudly that Clara immediately resumed looking down at the stage. "Well, I guess I know enough to turn you inside out, old gal — you sockdologizing old man-trap."

Clara felt the muscles of her arms jump inside their puffed sleeves. A trap door must have been sprung onstage, a play on "man-trap." The loud crack was some bit of stage business, like this burst of blue smoke she could see and smell. But that had to be wrong, she realized, turning left in her seat: the smoke was behind her. The box was filled with it, and before she could turn far enough to see Henry, she realized that he was on his feet, along with another man who was now in the box, whose face she couldn't see behind the smoke. There was a gleam, which she suddenly recognized as the long silver blade of a knife. The faceless man was plunging it into Henry.

She felt herself trying to scream, but she couldn't; the only voice she heard belonged to the unknown man. He had just hissed the word "freedom." He was coming at her now, his bloody knife in one hand and a pistol in the other, but he wanted only to get past her. He was trying to climb over the edge of the box, to find a grip amidst the bunting. Henry had come after him and was reaching for his coat, just barely touching it, when she felt a hot liquid spraying her face. It was in her mouth and tasted of metal. Her dress was wet.

The man got over the railing, but she never heard him land on the stage because by now Mrs. Lincoln was screaming. Clara moved toward her, colliding with Henry, who was leaning over the balcony.

"Stop that man!" he shouted.

For a second there was no sound but Mrs. Lincoln's wail, like a train whistle in the dark. Clara saw the audience rising to their feet; here and there drawn pistols glinted like stars.

"Oh, my husband's blood! My husband's blood!" screamed Mrs. Lincoln. She was pointing at Clara, who now realized that her dress and face and mouth were covered with blood, but blood that could only be Henry's, since the President was still sitting, undisturbed, in his rocker.

"Water!" Clara heard herself screaming, as if the balcony

really were part of the stage and she had finally come to her lines. "Water!"

She was now crazed with fright and could think only of getting the blood off her face and out of her mouth. But the blood was everywhere, an ocean of it. Below her the crowd roared, and some of its members leapt onto the stage. She heard a furious pounding, a hail of fists on the door to the box, and she looked toward it, crying "No!" She was sure a gang of men were about to come in and kill them all. "No!" she screamed again as she saw Henry struggling to open the door and let them in.

A square of light revealed several blue army uniforms. One of the men — a colonel, Clara could tell — hurriedly spoke with Henry. A very young soldier, a doctor, was rushed toward Mr. Lincoln, whom he touched gently, like a large animal he was afraid to wake. His hands hovered over him, searching for something. He asked the others who were filling up the box to help him lay the President on the floor so he might cut away his clothing. Another doctor, just as young, assisted; the two of them felt for a pulse, and they blew breath into Mr. Lincoln's mouth and nostrils.

"I am bleeding to death." It was Henry's voice, near the door of the balcony, but the small space was now so packed with people, even Miss Keene, that Clara couldn't get to him. A soldier had moved her and Mrs. Lincoln onto the sofa from which Henry had watched the play. It was soaked with blood, but Mrs. Lincoln had ceased screaming; she now held out her arms mutely, grasping at nothing.

Clara began to weep. With all the men in the balcony, she thought, someone must be attending to Henry, but she couldn't see him clearly, and her attention was distracted by all the loud voices arguing over whether the President was to be kept here, or taken home, or moved somewhere else.

After a minute of this, during which Mrs. Lincoln resumed screaming, the colonel took charge, and suddenly everyone was on his feet and filing out, deliberately, as if a train had just arrived for boarding and Mr. Lincoln's limp form, preceding them, were a trunk that had to be carried on first. A tailor's house, across the street from the theatre, the colonel explained, was being prepared to receive the President.

They left the theatre the same way they had come in, through the narrow corridor and down the stairs to the lobby. As they walked, a great roar grew ever closer. It came from the street, which was so full of torches that the late hour seemed more like a brilliant twilight. Police and soldiers were everywhere, pushing back the crowd, keeping the torches away from the theatre, and cuffing those who clamored for it to be burned to the ground. People desperate to get close to Mr. Lincoln screamed the question "Is he dead?" over and over. They were answered by shouts of "He's dead!" or "He's alive!" from onlookers too far away from the limp form to tell. In the shoving and chaos, the President's gold spectacles fell into the mud of Tenth Street.

Halfway across the gutter, Clara at last reached Henry's left side, gasping when she saw the knife wound that ran almost the length of his upper arm. A strip of pink flesh hung like a ribbon through the rip in his sleeve. His face, pale and shocked, stared straight ahead as he moved like a phantom, steadied by an army major and propelled by the crowd.

Now Mrs. Lincoln was calling for Clara, pushing her way toward her. She saw Henry's tall form and immediately grasped his forearm with both her hands, pulling on it, as if imploring him, oblivious of his wound. "Oh, why did they let him do it?" she wailed. The pain of her touch sent his eyeballs up into their sockets, and even with the other major's assistance, he looked ready to faint. Clara begged, through tears, "Ma'am, please, *please* let go of him," prying the First Lady away, pushing her the last few steps to the tailor's house.

"Where is my husband?" Mrs. Lincoln shouted when they reached its threshold.

Inside, soldiers were lighting candles and clearing a path to a room at the back. The army major assisting Henry told Clara his name was Potter. He was joined by another man in uniform. They took Henry into the hallway, where he sat down on the floor and at last passed out.

"Please do something for him," cried Clara, one more urgent plea in a house that was ringing with them. Only now did she understand how gravely Henry was injured; for the first time she was seized by the idea that both he and Mr. Lincoln might die here. "Please take him home," she begged the second soldier as Major Potter tried to bandage the arm. "Please take him to my father's house," she said, aware of some strange courtesy making her say "my" father instead of "his," as if she were paying a respectful gesture to the dead. She feared that the soldier going for a carriage would never secure one in the infernal street. From outside, the screams for vengeance and the shrieks toward heaven came through the open windows of the parlor, where other soldiers were trying to get Mrs. Lincoln to sit down on one of the black horsehair chairs. Alternating between wails and silent supplication, she begged to be brought to the back room where the President had been laid on a bed — diagonally, according to a soldier who came out muttering with awe at the size of the wounded man.

"I've got one! Now!" cried Major Potter's helper, rushing back into the house and urging that Henry be hurried into the waiting carriage. As the two men hoisted his insensible form out the door, Clara kissed its white forehead, recoiling at the small blood smear her own cheek left on it. She dabbed at her face with a handkerchief, and another soldier, or a policeman, she wasn't sure, asked her to help calm Mrs. Lincoln, who had at last sat down on a sofa. Clara took a place on the cushion next to her and tried to put her arms around the First Lady, but this succeeded only in agitating her again. "It's the blood," said Clara to one of the soldiers, pointing to her dress as the source of Mrs. Lincoln's new cries. Helpless, Clara gave way to sobs for the second time since the gun had been fired.

She now knew that that was what the loud crack and blue smoke had been, just as she knew, from bits of rushed, overheard conversation among all the doctors and politicians streaming in and out of the house, that one of the President's pupils was wildly dilated, that his heart was functioning at only forty-four beats per minute, and that the catastrophe was thought to have been perpetrated by Edwin Booth's younger brother, who had apparently escaped. Senator Sumner had arrived, and Robert Lincoln came in with Secretary Stanton, who insisted the President's wife be kept from his bedside, which was now littered with mustard plasters, hot water bottles, and dried blood. The doctors were trying to keep the tiny puncture behind his ear from clotting; the pillow, Clara heard Stanton tell Sumner much too loudly, was a terrible sight.

It was the middle of the night before Clara heard the tick of the front parlor's clock above the diminishing roar in the street. The crowd had been pushed back, but until two A.M. its sound came through the window like the noise of the ocean each summer in Newport. She was exhausted and her mind kept wandering, back to Albany and the days of her childhood, before returning to this time and this room, which had come to feel like eternity. By three A.M. it seemed as if they were no longer waiting to see when Mr. Lincoln would cross the border into another world; it was as if all of them already had crossed over, and this was it, a world in which they would forever reel, growing always more sore and exhausted. At one point Mr. Stanton came out from a back parlor, where he seemed to be running the whole government, to ask Clara what she had observed in the box. She made an effort to tell him, but he became impatient with her imprecision and went back to his business like a storekeeper who had a richer customer to see. Sometimes Mrs. Lincoln seemed as unconscious as her husband, but no one considered moving Clara from her side, not even when Miss Keene took up a plaintive position, on her knees, in front of the First Lady.

Nor did Clara herself think of moving, though at any moment she might have asked one of her father's colleagues, who continued tramping through the house, to take her home. She was afraid that if she returned there, she would find Henry dead, or that she herself would be murdered en route: the statesmen shuttling between the bedroom in which the President lay and the room in which Mr. Stanton worked talked as much of Mr. Seward as Mr. Lincoln, of how he had been stabbed in his bed at home in Lafayette Square, and would probably die with the President. A strange feeling that she had been painted into history, inserted into a tableau, also kept her from moving. It was a terrible feeling, though at moments exhilarating — this sense that she would forever be as she was now, arrested, like the play across the street, which would never move beyond the second scene of act 3. If she tried to leave, the tableau would come to life and move toward an even more terrible climax, some dramatic revelation that would destroy her. And so she stayed.

More than an hour after Clara first heard the clock, Mrs. Lincoln succeeded in her demands to see her husband. Clara and Miss Keene were asked to assist her in the bedroom. The First Lady proved silent, even stoic, at the sight of the President's head, with its blackening right eye. She put her cheek against his, tenderly, without agitation or theatrics, until he let out a long, tormented breath that startled her into shrieks. Mr. Stanton became furious, and she was not allowed back in until long after dawn, after the newsboys could be heard screaming in the streets. Robert Lincoln escorted his mother into the bedroom, while out in the parlor Clara listened to the last minutes of the waiting, which ended with the First Lady's terrible cry — "O my God! I have given my husband to die!" — and the murmuring of prayers by the Lincolns' family pastor, the Reverend Phineas Densmore Gurley, who had been busily introducing himself in the parlor, announcing his ridiculous name over and over, like one of the characters in the play.

Mrs. Lincoln was brought through the hallway and led from the house. Miss Keene was suddenly nowhere in sight, and Clara realized that she herself was at last free to go, that in fact she must go. A soldier she had not seen before found a carriage for her, and she made the journey back toward Fifteenth and H alone, along the same Z-shaped route she had traveled with the others twelve hours before. Beyond the carriage's half-covering hood, the rain fell on her absurd dress, wetting the satin and bloodstains. The bells from every church in the city swung and banged, again and again, as if pulled by the fast-moving hooves of the horses.

Lina opened the door and flung her arms around Clara.

"Don't cry, Lina darling. You must let me get upstairs to see Henry." She closed her eyes and clenched her fists, bracing herself, waiting for her little sister to say that Henry was dead.

But there was no terrible news. "Papa is coming" was all that Lina said. "They reached him with the telegraph."

Clara mounted the stairs. Through the open door to Henry's room she could see Pauline sitting at his bedside. Her stepmother rose and came toward her, stopping to say only "My son nearly died" before relinquishing Henry to his fiancée. Pauline brushed past Clara as if the younger woman had tried all their patience by staying out at a ball until morning.

Henry lay still, his white forehead furrowed with pain. Clara knelt down and softly put her hand on his chest.

"Is he dead?" he asked.

"Yes," she whispered.

His eyes looked past her, toward the door at the edge of the room, just as she remembered them doing before the loud crack and the blue smoke.

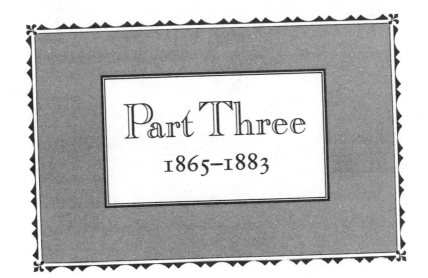

Part Three
1865–1883

⇾ 30 ⇽

My dear Mary,

I received your kind note last week, and should have answered it before, but I have really felt as though I could not settle myself quietly, even to the performance of such a slight duty as that. Henry has been suffering a great deal with his arm, but it is now doing very well, — the knife went from the elbow nearly to the shoulder, inside, — cutting an artery, nerves & veins. He bled so profusely as to make him very weak. My whole clothing as I sat in the box was saturated literally with blood, & my hands & face — You may imagine what a scene. Poor Mrs. Lincoln all through that dreadful night would look at me in horror & scream, Oh! my husband's blood, — my dear husband's blood — which it was not, though I did not know it at the time. The President's wound did not bleed externally at all — The brain was instantly suffused.

When I sat down to write I did not intend alluding to these fearful events, at all — but I really cannot fix my mind on anything else, though I try my best to think of them as little as possible. I cannot sleep, & really feel wretchedly. Only to think that fiend is still at large! There was a report here yesterday that every house in the District of Columbia was to be searched today. I hoped it was true, as the impression seems to be gaining that Booth is hidden in Washington. Is not that a terrible thought!

Mr. Johnson is at present living in Mr. Hooper's house opposite us. A guard are walking the street in front constantly —

It will probably be two or three weeks before Mrs. Lincoln will be able to make arrangements for leaving. She has not left her bed since she returned to the White House that morning.

We expect to be able to leave next week for New York, but on what day, it would be impossible yet to say. I will write you in time however. So that I shall be sure to see you, while there.

Please give my love to all the family, & believe me

Ever truly yours
Clara H.

Clara shook the blotting sand off the last sheet of the letter and reached for an envelope. Her stack of fresh ones lay atop a copy of Mr. Stanton's latest reward poster: $50,000 for the capture of John Wilkes Booth. "THE MURDERER OF OUR BELOVED PRESIDENT IS STILL AT LARGE!" it proclaimed, with as much panic as vengefulness. Papa said they had lost count of the number of people arrested, with or without a reason. No other official had been struck down since the President and Mr. Seward were attacked ten days ago, but everyone in the square remained fearful. It was two A.M. now, actually the twenty-sixth of April, Clara realized as she glanced again at her letter to Mary Hall. Everyone else in the house was asleep, and she would not allow herself to retire without checking the bolt on the front door one more time. From her window she could see the guards puffing on their cheroots next to Congressman Hooper's house. President Johnson must have long since gone to bed, and the only sound came from the boots of some pickets stationed farther up the street.

She no longer followed a normal human schedule. She slept whenever fear and memory let her, but even then she was awakened by Henry's moans from the room above — either the wakeful groaning he had from his arm or the dull cries he let out during nightmares. When she was up late, as now, she relived the days since the assassination over and over in her head.

→←

When she'd arrived home an hour after Mr. Lincoln died, and gone up to Henry's room, he seemed on the verge of telling her something. His eyes had a despairing urgency, as if he were trying to bring himself to communicate some vital matter that had been lost in the violence and chaos. But he succeeded only in upsetting himself, and his pain and loss of blood sent him in and out of consciousness. For the rest of Saturday, on Pauline's orders, only the army surgeon was allowed in his room.

The following day, Easter Sunday, Pauline sent Lina to church, and while she was there, Judge Olin of the District of Columbia's supreme court showed up to take statements. That Henry was in no condition to give one counted for nothing. The judge was insistent, and Pauline, possessed by the fright that had taken hold of the city, relented. So Henry, behind a closed door, set about answering the judge's questions as well as he could, his murmured replies interrupted at frequent intervals by louder cries of pain. Clara busied herself downstairs, putting lilies into vases and refusing to cry.

In the middle of all this, Papa finally arrived from Albany and, in a burst of decisiveness that no one in the family had seen from him in years, put a stop to the interrogation, telling Judge Olin that he himself, as a United States senator, would take statements from his daughter and stepson, and that would be the end of it. He personally handed the judge his hat.

But as the full extent of Washington's panic made itself clear to him, Senator Harris proved unable to shield his stricken family from it. An hour after leaving, Judge Olin was back — on orders from Mr. Stanton, he said: the secretary's investigators were making a survey of the box at Ford's, and Miss Harris was wanted for help in arranging the chairs as they had been when the assassin struck. The senator weakly questioned the need for this, but within minutes Clara was tying her bonnet and getting into a carriage with her father and Judge Olin.

The awfulness of what was being asked of her registered when she saw they were traveling the exact route to the theatre that she had ridden less than forty-eight hours before. All the victory torches were gone, and most of the houses, even those she recognized as belonging to secessionists, were hung with crepe and portraits of the President. In the last hundred yards before the theatre, the carriage had to make its way through a crowd of the curious, similar enough to the one that had greeted them on Friday night to make her feel she was in a dream: day had been substituted for night, her companions in the carriage changed.

Papa held on to her as they mounted the theatre's stairs, but she felt no real weakness until she was in the box itself and saw Henry's blood everywhere, dried to a dull brown. "Good God!" Senator Harris exploded, to Judge Olin's complete indifference. The investigators went about their measurements and drawings like a team of decorators hired by some unseen chatelaine. No one asked her to sit down, and she could not have done so in any case. Only Judge Olin took a chair, the President's, after she positioned it in the spot it had occupied during the play. His purpose in sitting was to determine if Booth might have fired through the hole that had been bored through the wooden door behind the chair. But most of the investigators thought it more likely the opening had been used as a peephole, before the assassin made his entrance. They noted the evidence of fresh drilling (the sharp knife marks where the shavings had been dislodged), as well as the arrangements Booth had made to brace the door shut once he was inside.

She followed the conversation and surveying with care. She was trying not to recall what had really taken place here, was glad to concentrate on these engineering details, which seemed so remote from the horror, even though it was all the drilling and bolting and bracing that had led to the screams and gore, by making the box into a trap, ready for springing. The carefulness of the assassin's preparations had made the tragedy inevitable, and for some reason this realization came as a relief. Nothing could have prevented it. The portents had been there all along: Mr. Lincoln's fatalistic dream had been the true harbinger, his wife's mourning purchases a futile defense.

A half hour after she and Papa arrived, while she was staring down at the stage set — its chairs and papier-mâché window still ready for the entrance of Miss Keene, whose next line would have been "What do you mean by doing all these dreadful things?" — Judge Olin told them they could leave, and the two of them rode home in silence. It was still midafternoon, and when they reached Fifteenth and H, she told Papa she wanted to be by herself for a while, that she had not been out of the house since yesterday morning and needed to walk. So she strolled down H Street for many blocks, past more crepe and engravings of Mr. Lincoln, past more soldiers, until she reached Sixth Street, where a crowd as large as the one outside Ford's was peering at the shuttered windows of the boarding house where the assassin and his accomplices were said to have hatched their plans. It was, she realized, just a few doors away from the rooms of Johnny Hay's friend, where she and Henry had gone last September. It was only at this moment, turning and starting for home at twice the speed she'd come here, that her tears began flowing, in great sobs beyond anything she had cried Friday night. She and Henry were being racked and squeezed like creatures in a tale by Edgar Poe. They had fallen into a nightmare, and as she ran back along H Street, disbelief competed with her anger and calculation. The only way they could escape destruction was to hurry their marriage, to be safely joined as one, stronger than madness and murder.

Henry did not leave his room for a full week, and even then, after just ten minutes sitting in the parlor, he was in such pain that he had to be helped upstairs. If he could not sleep, he would never recover, but Papa could not get the soldiers outside Mr. Hooper's house to cease their tramping over the paving stones. The crowds wanting a glimpse of the new President were even noisier, chattering all the while they stared at Congressman Hooper's windows, their backs to the Harris house, ignorant of the part its members had played in Good Friday's events. Two or three times newspaper reporters came looking for her and Henry but were firmly turned away by the parlor maid. Mr. Hooper's own servants came by, at least once a day, to borrow items from the Harris kitchen: their employer was home in Massachusetts, and even President Johnson's modest wants couldn't be satisfied from the meager stuff in the pantry.

Over the past few years, Clara had been to Mr. Hooper's parties on several occasions, always a little uncomfortably, since he was a great ally of the treasury secretary, and Mrs. Lincoln didn't want her enjoying the hospitality of someone in league with Kate Chase's father. On Tuesday afternoon she had started remembering all this, and was struck by how last week's life now seemed a decade in the past. She had been assailed by a sudden longing for Mrs. Lincoln. Throwing on a shawl, she left the house and crossed the square to the Mansion, but old Edward told her that the First Lady was still seeing no one but Robert, Tad, and Mrs. Keckley, her Negro dressmaker; she had not been downstairs since Saturday morning, and no one expected to see her in the East Room for tomorrow's funeral.

Only seven women held any of the six hundred tickets given out for the ceremony, and Clara was not one of them. She remained at home, out of sight of the funeral procession to the Capitol, which she heard making its turn onto Pennsylvania Avenue at the corner of Fifteenth Street, its drums and dirges growing louder. When the sounds receded, the silence was frightening: for the next two hours not a whisper or a moan was heard from Henry's room. When Papa arrived home from the Rotunda, he went in to check on his stepson and came down to the dinner table looking very grave. "He is beside himself" was all he would say, a figure of speech whose aptness only she really knew, having seen, after Petersburg, one Henry, a strange and ghostly one, displace the other, assume its mortal shape and banish it to a corner of the room, from which it never wholly disappeared.

Papa had planned to leave with the funeral train on Friday the twenty-first to oversee the reception of the President's body in Albany, as he had the arrival of the President-elect four years ago, but he became so distressed by the state of his own household that he decided to remain in Washington through the weekend. He would catch up with the train on Monday, in New York. So for the next few days telegraph boys ran between the Harris house and the War Department, carrying communications between Papa and the Albany organizers, who planned, he told her, to bring Mr. Lincoln's body to the assembly chamber on a catafalque drawn by eight white horses. John Finley Rathbone would command the militia guard on the brief journey from the railway station.

The train was scheduled to arrive in Albany at midnight on the twenty-fourth, and Clara realized, an hour after sealing her letter to Mary Hall, that Papa must now be putting himself to bed on Eagle Street. She imagined his exhaustion so sympathetically that some of it seemed to seep into her, allowing her at last, at four A.M., to fall asleep.

It was late afternoon before she awoke to the sound of newsboys selling an extra edition of the paper to the little crowd outside Mr. Hooper's. As she dressed, Pauline came into her room with a copy, which carried the news that John Wilkes Booth had been shot to death in a barn in Port Royal, Virginia, around the time she had been writing her letter to Mary. She read down the columns as fast as she could, avid for details — he had broken his leg fleeing the theatre — until she reached the speculation that Mr. Stanton would now persuade the President to proceed with a military trial of the remaining conspirators.

Good, she thought. It would happen quickly, summary justice, and then be over. Henry needed to know this. She finished dressing and went downstairs to tell the cook she would bring him his beef tea and chicken herself. She found him awake, staring at the wallpaper, the pile of books and letters on his end table still untouched.

"What's happened?" he asked, pointing toward the window, through which he'd heard the excitement of the crowd in the next street.

"I'll read it to you." She pulled the wicker chair close to the edge of the bed.

She got no further than the second paragraph. As soon as she read that Booth had died saying nothing more than "Useless, useless," while regarding his own murderous hands, Henry closed his eyes and sighed, as if a great slab had been lifted off his chest. She continued reading, but for the first time in eleven days, Henry had fallen deeply asleep.

⇢ 31 ⇠

WEEKS PASSED without their being able to leave for New York. On May 15, Clara was escorted past the fashionable ladies, curious soldiers, and souvenir seekers thronging the corridors of the Old Penitentiary Building. She took a seat on the left of General Holt's huge improvised courtroom, amidst several spectators she took to be military friends of the judges, and nodded to Henry, who was already at the table where witnesses gave testimony. She was part of an audience for the first time since the night at Ford's, eager for Henry to get through his part and be done with the killing forever. Though no one had scrupled about making her return to the blood-stained box on Easter Sunday, it had been determined that Henry's testimony would be sufficient for both of them today. Whenever the judges finished conferring at their round table across the room, and the reporters stopped chattering at their square one in the center, Henry would speak his piece. All the windows were closed, making the buzz of conversation louder and increasing the heat to the level of a midsummer day.

There was only one other woman here, and she too was fanning herself, behind a heavy veil. Clara started with the realization that this was the boarding-house keeper, Mrs. Surratt, at the far end of the row of conspirators, all of them seated behind a railing at the front of the room. They weren't wearing the hoods she'd read about, and Clara looked at each one, her eyes lingering over the magnificent form of Lewis Paine, who'd stabbed Fred Seward and his father; she wondered how he maintained his physique while chained up in the basement.

General Holt finally rose and walked over to Henry. As a courtesy, the chief judge would himself lead the major through his testimony, which he now invited him to give in a single long statement. In a voice much softer than the one he used to use in the dining room on Eagle Street, Henry began to drone. After a couple of sentences, Clara recognized most of what he was saying as an exact memorization of the affidavit Papa had written for him on Easter Sunday: ". . . When the second scene of the third act was being performed, and while I was intently observing the proceedings upon the stage, with my back toward the door, I heard the discharge of a pistol behind me, and, looking round, saw through the smoke a man between the door and the President. The distance from the door to where the President sat was about four feet. At the same time I heard the man shout some word, which I thought was 'Freedom!' I instantly sprang toward him and seized him. He wrested himself from my grasp, and made a violent thrust at my breast with a large knife. I parried the blow by striking it up, and received a wound several inches deep in my left arm, between the elbow and the shoulder. The orifice of the wound was about an inch and a half in length, and extended upward toward the shoulder several inches . . ."

The precision of the recollections was so at odds with the vagueness of Henry's demeanor that some of the twelve judges appeared embarrassed, as if they were watching a cripple. Clara wanted someone to put a stop to this right now. But Henry went monotonously on: "The clothes, as I believe, were torn in the attempt to hold him. As he went over upon the stage, I cried out, 'Stop that man.' I then turned to the President; his position was not changed . . ."

Why, Clara wondered, her anger rising, must any of this be gone into? Booth was dead. The question of his cohorts' guilt depended on what dealings they had had with him *before* he entered the box. What transpired once he went in was now moot. Could no one else see that?

Colonel Clendenin brought a bowie knife over for Henry's inspection. Even from where she sat, Clara could see that its long blade still held Henry's bloodstains. Surely, she thought, this would animate him; but he just continued droning: "This knife might have made a wound similar to the one I received.

The assassin held the blade in a horizontal position, I think, and the nature of the wound would indicate it; it came down with a sweeping blow from above."

Colonel Clendenin entered the knife in evidence, and Henry was permitted to step down. A buzz of conversation resumed at the reporters' table, and the judges' as well, everywhere but in the row of conspirators. As Clara closed her fan and straightened the black silk flower on her hat, she heard one newspaperman say to another, in a hiss of sarcasm, "'Stop that man.' For Christ's sake, why didn't *he* stop that man?"

Clara stared at the two of them in disbelief.

"'Intently observing the proceedings upon the stage,'" mimicked the second one. "What a fine idea a week after Appomattox! Couldn't imagine there'd be trouble!"

"The man's a fool," said the first one.

"Or worse," his companion replied.

Nine days later, his arm still in a sling, Henry stood with Clara on Pennsylvania Avenue and watched 150,000 soldiers parade by in the Union's official victory celebration. The Twelfth New York was marching, and Clara, Ira Harris, and Pauline had all urged Henry to march with it. "You are a *hero*," his mother had insisted. "From Antietam to Petersburg. You should be with your comrades. You should not be leaving the field to Will." But he did not relent. He had come to realize, in the weeks after Ford's, that many of those who read the newspapers and talked endlessly of the assassination had formed a very different view of him than the heroic one held at Fifteenth and H streets. The monstrous injustice of the whispering — the absurdity of the idea that Henry might somehow have prevented the killing of the President — was never discussed by anyone in the Harris house. Its members tried to ascribe his refusal to join the parade to anything — physical pain; modesty; perversity; just being Henry, the *old* Henry — except the shame they feared he was feeling. What he actually thought remained unclear. He spoke little to anyone, including Clara; the two of them avoided the only topic on their minds.

So there they stood, on the sidelines of a city still crazily split between celebration and grief. The hotels were full, and visitors who couldn't get into them were once more sleeping on porches and bathing in the fountains, as they had before Mr. Lincoln's first inaugural. As the troops marched by to screaming huzzahs, the Capitol remained hung with crepe, and the Treasury Building decorated with the flag torn by Wilkes Booth's spur. The parade went on and on, regiment after regiment, from dashing Zouaves to colored troops shouldering pickaxes, all of them moving between the White House, where Johnson and Grant and the Cabinet occupied a reviewing stand, and the Capitol, on whose steps a vast, disparate choir sang everything from "The Battle Hymn of the Republic" to "When Johnny Comes Marching Home Again."

Soldiers from the Twelfth passed Henry without recognizing him. Clara looked at the laces of her shoes and thought of the conspirators' trial, which was still going on in the penitentiary. She was so cheated by fate that she might as well be wearing one of the plotters' hoods, with no one to recognize or care about her. "Let's go," she said to Henry after twenty minutes at the avenue's edge. "It's time." They walked in silence back to the corner of Fifteenth and H and climbed into the carriage they had told to wait. The driver now asked if the circuitous route he had in mind for getting to the station would do, and Henry said yes, anything that would get them around the parade. The terminal was bound to be chaotic, but their seats to New York were reserved. Papa and Pauline and the girls would follow tomorrow, and they would all be back in Albany in time for Amanda's wedding.

When the carriage came as close as it would to the Mansion, Clara thought of Mrs. Lincoln, who two days ago had left it at last. She reached her hand over the rim of the coach, as if trying to touch or signal her spirit. Then she turned her head back toward Henry, and they rode in silence until he spoke in a tone he had never used with her before this moment. "I'm surprised you didn't spend the last six weeks in there with her," he said, gesturing toward the Mansion. "In fact, I'm sometimes surprised you came home at all that morning."

→ 32 ←

"YOUR PAPA SAID Mr. Vassar's hired a lady astronomer to teach the girls down at his college." Mary Hall pointed to a bright star as she and Clara sat on the front porch of the Harris home in Loudonville on the third Friday in November.

"Yes." Clara laughed. "And she's going to live with *her* papa in the observatory."

After eleven years of knowing Clara, Mary still didn't always understand her humor — the private thought waiting behind the expressed laugh — so she paused to let her friend continue. "That would be a good life for me, Mary. Alone with Papa, just study-ing the moons of Jupiter through a telescope."

They were the only two still awake in the house full of women. Amanda was living away from home with her husband, but Pauline and Louise and Lina were asleep upstairs, and all the men were gone: Will and Jared (now graduated from West Point) were away at their posts, and in the week since coming up here for "Thanksgiving" dinner — the custom revived by Mr. Lin-coln two years ago, in 1863 — Ira Harris and Henry Rathbone had been back in Washington.

"Do you think a woman can really be an astronomer?" Mary asked.

"Of course," Clara said. "You surprise me, Mary. You think the black man is the equal of the white one, but you never seem able to imagine the women of any race being equivalent to their men!"

"That's not true. I simply don't think *everything* should be meted out in like measure to men and women."

"Mary," said Clara, who had been irritable since late this morning, "don't you dare bring up Mrs. Surratt again."

"I wasn't going to."

"Yes, you were, and I'm not going to have another discussion of it. I'm glad they hanged her with the rest of them, just as I wish they'd hanged Mary Hartung six years ago after all the abuse and whispering Papa endured."

"All right, all right," said Mary. "Have you heard from Henry?"

Clara, wondering if the word "whispering" had prompted Mary to pick Henry as the change of subject, answered, "Yes, today. He's writing an enormous end-of-the-year report, all about the dismantling of the army."

"That's wonderful," said Mary.

Clara wanted to ask the question that had been on her mind all week — whether Mary had heard people in New York talk of Henry's conduct on the night of the assassination. But she couldn't. Instead it was Mary who screwed up the courage to ask, "Do you have a date for the wedding yet?"

"Soon," said Clara. "But still no date."

"A little more waiting isn't so bad," said Mary. "It will put the war further behind you."

"You make the war sound like a summer in Newport or last year's birthday, Mary. Something that will soon be completely and neatly forgotten. It's not that convenient. Do you suppose Sybil Bashford will ever put the war behind her?"

"Yes, I rather think she will."

The two women surprised themselves with sudden, uproarious laughter. "Oh, Clara," said Mary. "God forgive us."

Clara settled down, relieved. "I do love you, Mary, and I'm sorry I've been so grumpy. I promise to be better in the morning." She kissed her friend good night, and the two of them went upstairs, Mary to a room at the top of the house and Clara to her old window seat, where she lit a candle and took out two letters from the pocket of her dress. The first had come from Henry:

... your father is only beginning to realize the tone this new session of Congress is taking. "Smiler" Colfax, Thaddeus Stevens, Sumner — they've all got their scissors out, ready to cut up Andy Johnson and his Reconstruction plans faster than he ever trimmed a pair of breeches back in Tennessee. Darling, the mild, Whiggish Republicanism of Senator Ira Harris is finished: the radicals intend to scald his portion of the party with the same lye soap they'll be using on the South. Your papa thinks he can put himself in their good graces, catch up to their runaway train and jump on. But they know his heart isn't in it, and they don't settle for anything but purity. He and his moderate friends will be packing their bags a year from now. This fellow Conkling, who struts like a turkey but is much more glamorous than his name, means to have your father's seat. And he probably will. The fight that's getting under way is the same bloody game of parlor oratory all these "statesmen" played in the years before the war. Its most eager spectators are the misfits and pansies who never found the battlefields, the little clerks who now buzz about politics in the taverns and sashay into the galleries of Congress to look down on the players . . .

She shook her head and set the piece of paper aside. The second letter, from Papa, had been written the same evening, three nights after his and Henry's return to Washington, and it contained what he hadn't been able to tell her face-to-face here in Loudonville last week:

. . . Henry alternates between vociferation and anomie. I cannot keep track of his movements or moods. He is doing superb work for the Adjutant General — I know as much from my friends — but his overall reliability seems more questionable than ever. The other night some fellows from his office came by, and he was the old Henry — merry and saturnine by turns, sarcastic throughout — but when the conversation among them turned to General Grant and Mr. Lincoln, he abused the General and the President's memory in the most shocking way, and was unrecognizable for the rest of the evening. (The soldiers who fought the war, on either side, are now saintly in his mind; the politicians who prosecuted it are, to a man, devils.) I fear he is still hopelessly dislocated by what he expe-

rienced on the battlefield and at Ford's, and however much I
dread telling you this, my dear, I must: I want you to postpone
your marriage yet a little further, for another year at least, so
that we may see what stability he comes to . . .

This was the third time she had read these letters since their
arrival this morning, and she was determined never to read a
pair like them again. To think of these two men, alone in that
house except for the servants, sitting in different rooms, neither
one communicating with the other, each complaining to her —
it made her furious. She loved them both, but she would not be
the victim of Henry's anger and Papa's dithering; she would no
longer be crushed between their cross purposes. So she brought
the candle to her table and commenced writing two letters of her
own. As she flexed her hands, squeezing the last of the late
autumn cold from them, she felt herself taking control of matters once and for all.

Dear Papa,
    I will postpone the wedding for one year — not because I
share your alarm, only because I don't wish to add to it.
    You must know that I lived through the war on the strength
of your promise, and I will not allow you to break it — I shall
not become Louise, who is *six years younger* than I and already a skitterish spinster. If I allow you to delay the fulfill-
ment of this promise, then I have the right to set some conditions of my own. When Henry and I marry, we shall remain
in Washington, whether or not you are returned to the Senate.
If you must come back here, we shall buy the Washington
house from you. I know that you will fight hard to be returned, just as I know your good service makes that the only
just eventuality, but you must realize by now that the odds
against it are growing long. Mother does not speak of it, but
I know that *she* is resigned to being back in Albany a year
from now. You must have noticed how the trunks she packed
to precede us on this last trip up here contained more than the
usual assemblage of clothes that had fallen behind the fashion.

I notice bibelots laid out on tables here and on Eagle Street that I haven't seen at these latitudes in five years.

She is preparing for the next portion of her life, up here, and I do not mean to share it with her. I do not mean for Henry and myself to pass our marital existence as an exotic hybrid inside a forest of Rathbones and Harrises. I mean for us to have our own life, in Washington, the only other place I really know. There will be plenty for Henry to do there — you yourself admit his talents for administration — and if he does nothing but live off the Rathbone money, that will be fine too.

It is time for me to be insistent. You are to discuss this letter with Henry before you come back here for Christmas, and when I see you we shall plan a new announcement of the marriage, with a new date, in 1867, *during which year I shall turn thirty-three.* You must not doubt my love for you, but you must now exercise yours for

> Your devoted daughter
> Clara

Without pausing, she reached for another sheet of paper.

I have sent Papa a letter. You are to discuss what it says with him. I insist on everything that is in it. I shall wait no longer than I promise to in that letter. I shall not allow us to drift, to be latter-day victims of the war, like soldiers dying of resurgent infections. If you love me as you say, you will agree to what I propose — and you will let the better angels of your nature conquer your anger and sorrows. I mean to be happy, and to make you happy too.

She feared losing the courage to mail both letters, so she hurried downstairs and put on her coat and went out to the box at the edge of the plank road. The boy would pick them up early in the morning. Crossing the lawn back to the house, she realized that she had quoted Mr. Lincoln to Henry: "the better angels." This was probably not a good idea, but either he wouldn't catch it or any feelings it pricked would be overwhelmed by the rest of the letter's urgency.

She could hear frost crunching beneath her feet. It made the only sound in the cold blackness, until she neared the front door and heard a scream. Her eyes darted to its origin, Louise's room, where some candlelight flickered. She raced upstairs, throwing off her coat as she went. Mary Hall, candle in hand, had already arrived at Louise's door and was asking what was the matter.

"The dress," said Louise, who was sitting on her bed, shaking and trying to apologize.

"Be quiet," said Clara.

"I couldn't sleep, so I went back to work on the closets," Louise rushed on. "I opened the box, thinking it was just one more that Mother had shipped up here."

"And so it is," said Clara, picking up the pink satin dress from where Louise had dropped it. "I don't know why I meant to save it. It seemed important to, six months ago. It no longer does." She took the gown and shook it, and the crusted blood flaked off it and fell to the floor like iron filings. Mary gasped, and Louise began to cry again. "Stop it," said Clara, throwing the dress back into its carton. "I'll dispose of this in the morning. I said stop it, Louise, and I mean it. You've seen blood before, and you'll see it again. Now go back to bed, both of you. You'll wake Mother."

⇀ 33 ↽

"MAJOR Henry Rathbone and Miss Clara Harris!"

Stepping into the French minister's ballroom on the evening of February 9, 1866, Clara felt as many eyes upon her as she had sequins on her dress. Even the Marquise de Montholon, the minister's wife, jeweled fleurs-de-lis all over her, the Order of Napoleon dangling from her bosom, was looking.

Clara knew exactly how a hundred conversations were proceeding. "Isn't that the couple . . ." would be the question from one woman to another. "Yes, can you imagine the horror of it . . ." would come the response. "But you know," would add the first — and here fans would go up to mouths, and voices would drop to whispers — "isn't it peculiar that he was unable to . . ."

She kept smiling, moving down the line of hand-kissing men, and meeting the gaze of each of their wives, as Henry came stiffly behind her. When she got to the end, she decided, she would unclench her teeth and begin to enjoy herself. This was not, after all, just a White House reception hosted by Mr. Johnson's daughter, or another party at the Chase mansion on E Street; this was the greatest affair the city had seen since before the war, and she was going to delight in it as much as anyone. They owed it to her, all of them — Henry, Papa, Fate.

There were army officers, senators from both sides of the aisle and across the great divide within the Republican Party, beribboned diplomats of every complexion, Kate Chase Sprague in white moire and a diamond tiara. All of those things were predictable, she thought, working her way down the receiving line, taking kisses, extending her hand, passing the huge vases of poinsettias and the swinging censers. What seemed odd was the reappearance of so many Southerners, older men and women who had lived on in the District through the war without ever venturing forth to a party given by Mrs. Lincoln.

She reached the end of the line as the orchestra returned from a break. Henry spotted friends from the adjutant general's office and headed across the marble floor in their direction, handing Clara over to old Gideon Welles, who professed his delight. "Though I'm afraid my legs have grown too stiff to dance," said the navy secretary.

"Then we'll just stand and have a look together," Clara replied, patting his hand. "All these Southerners! What do you make of it?"

"It was the same at a party my wife gave, and at the last few receptions in the Mansion. They're showing the flag. It has less to do with the last war's being over than the one we're engaged in now, with these radicals. A terrible business. We need all our troops. Where is your father, Clara?"

"Just back from Dr. Nott's funeral in Schenectady."

"How old was the man?"

"Ninety-two."

"Good Lord," said Welles, laughing. "I'll see the twentieth century if I go on that long. You've made me feel younger than I have in months."

"Then I'm glad I came out tonight." She wished that a realization of Dr. Nott's antiquity would make Papa feel younger, too, but the funeral had had the opposite effect. He'd arrived home the other night looking, at sixty-three, like an old man. Dr. Nott had been alive longer than the Republic, and his continuing presence had kept a part of all the Union men of his time feeling like boys, needful of instruction from the little wizard in the pulpit at the front of the college chapel. Now he was gone, and the years had suddenly tumbled down on Papa like a snowfall.

"You tell your father to come see me over the weekend. We need him back in the game immediately. The President needs him."

"I shall do that first thing upon arriving home."

Mr. Welles would need luck with Papa, who'd be an exasperating ally, trying to trim a moderate course, hoping to do what Mr. Lincoln would have wished, but still trying to curry favor with Thad Stevens and the radicals. He needed someone to lay down the law to him, the way Mr. Weed used to years ago, but there wasn't anybody like that now. Clara was sure he would be back in Albany in twelve months' time, bewildered. For that matter, she suspected Mr. Welles would soon be home in Connecticut, editing his old newspaper.

But she would stay right here. She had had her way about the wedding date: July 11, 1867. It still seemed distant, but it was fixed, and she finally had an engagement ring on her hand. When the house was theirs and their lives their own, she would give her own parties, not so grand as this, but good enough to match Kate Chase Sprague's. They would be a good investment of Henry's money. If he could learn to hold his tongue, there might be a Senate seat in his own future. But that didn't matter. When she truly had him, her ambitions would be fulfilled, for the first time since she'd unconsciously realized them, twenty years ago at the Delavan, at Papa and Pauline's wedding breakfast.

She wished Mr. Welles would relinquish her. There was much she wanted to learn tonight, and she needed to get out on the floor. Where, she wondered, was Alice Hooper? She was always a good source of information; she, if anyone, could confirm the astonishing story Clara had heard the other day, that Kate Sprague was dallying with Ira Harris's young rival, Conkling.

"So, Miss Harris, where are your papa and mama?" boomed a friendly, whiskey-laden voice coming up beside her. "Two of the best hosts I ever had. Your brother, too, though in somewhat less grand circumstances."

"General Grant," said Clara, actually curtsying, her heart thumping a bit. "Mrs. Grant."

"Hello, dear," said plump Julia Dent Grant, looking uncomfortable in her gown. "Go on, Ulys, take Miss Harris for a spin. I'll inflict my company on Secretary Welles in the meantime."

So Clara's first waltz of the night turned out to be with General Grant himself. The other couples glided away from them, like ripples made by a brilliant stone that had been splashed onto the dance floor. Some even stopped to applaud.

Why such kindness from the general? she wondered. It was

probably Mrs. Grant, said to be mindful of how it had very nearly been she and her husband sharing the box at Ford's; the general's wife still insisted that Booth and three of his band had been across from her at lunch at Willard's on the day of the assassination. Clara was grateful for the solicitude, but wished that Grant would favor Henry, across the room, with at least a handshake. That would put an end to the whispering once and for all.

"My wife," said General Grant, pleasantly in his cups, "reminds me that there's to be a wedding. When will it actually occur?"

"Shortly before you begin your run for the presidency, sir."

He laughed, and twirled her a little faster, and as the night flowed on, she became his favorite. He came back to her three times, between her turns with a half-dozen other politicians — including Roscoe Conkling — and a small assortment of undersecretaries and army officers. At midnight, the general even escorted her to the supper table's orderly arrangement of fruits and foie gras, whose fastidious ingestion was as different from what went on at Mr. Lincoln's second inaugural as a carriage ride from a steeplechase. The dancing resumed after that, and Henry remained a distant presence, smoking a cigar with the men of the adjutant's office, every so often getting one of them to hold it while he gave a spin to some ambassador's daughter, dark girls mostly, wearing official-looking sashes. He would return to his colleagues as soon as the band hit the last note in its selection, as if he were trying to win a game of musical chairs. An hour went by before he even caught Clara's eye, as she and General Williams, who had married Senator Douglas's widow, cut a corner. Henry raised a champagne glass in ironic salute, as if to ask if she was happy now that she had her way.

The first cotillion wasn't called until dawn, and for the first time all night she and Henry touched as dance partners. He twirled her with a harsh, fast grace, through one round of a complicated minuet. At breakfast she sat beside the son of the Danish minister, smiling, without a common language, watching some golden crumbs of toast get lost in his identically colored beard. It was seven in the morning before the party ended, the women and men going off to do social and bureaucratic battle without bothering to change out of their finery. She had no calls to pay and didn't set off with the ladies. She would have Henry walk her home. He could change uniforms at the house; meticulous as ever, he refused to see the charm of spending Saturday morning at the office in clothes he'd worn Friday night.

The February air was very cold, and they could see their breath before them as they walked away from the marquis' residence. The sounds of departing carriages and revelers began to fade, and he put his arm around her shoulders to keep off the chill. They walked quietly along H Street, her folded fan swinging beneath her gloved hands, timing their progress like a metronome.

Finally, in a toneless voice he said, "Well, you've outshone my mother in her heyday."

"Meaning?"

"The dozen men you had clustered about you."

She wasn't sure if this was being offered out of admiration or jealousy. She hoped it was the latter.

"I've always had to function as your mother, my sweet." She swatted his free hand with the fan's ferrule. "Ever since you were a disagreeable little boy of eleven."

As if she hadn't spoken, he said, evenly, "This will be your town, you know, not mine."

"I intend to make it *our* city, Henry. I'll give my own marvelous parties, and our pack of beautiful children will look down on them from the top of the stairs in their pajamas. And the men will *still* be clustering around me."

"Take care, darling," was all he said; she didn't know whether he was cautioning her against extravagance or other admirers.

"You mean my trentogenarian self can excite your jealousy? I'm so glad, darling."

"You may not always be."

"All right, dear," she said, squeezing his bad left arm just a little. "Next summer on the lawn at Kenwood I shall dance only with you and Papa."

They continued walking east into the orange sun, a great medallion still rising in the sky.

⇒ 34 ⇐

AT 28 EAGLE STREET the unlit candles were going soft in the evening sun. Had the wedding presents on the parlor table not been sterner stuff — ivory knives, silver kerosene lamps, mahogany mirrors — they might be melting too. The heat inside the Pearl Street Baptist Church, as the Reverend C. DeW. Bridgman wed Clara Harris to Henry Rathbone, had been stifling, and afterward, the five dozen guests who jammed the Harris house couldn't down their punch and dripping ices fast enough, so eager were they for the day's real treat, a lawn party down at Kenwood, Joel Rathbone's old estate. An endless convoy of carriages — "more cavalry than I've seen since Gettysburg!" shouted Dan Sickles — was organized to take them two miles south, to the little village once called Lower Hollow, where the rolling grasses and shady trees would soothe their overheated brows. The notes of "Beautiful Dreamer," Mr. Foster's very last song, wafted in greeting from a small orchestra at the edge of the huge lawn, where a hundred wicker chairs sat like whitecaps on a green sea.

"Bonnets are smaller this year," said Lina Harris, now seventeen and mad for clothes. Her older sister Louise, wearing the same straw hat she had donned the past three Easters, took little interest in the tulle and crepe and lace that topped the heads of all the Albany and Washington women. She just nodded. Lina, still aggrieved that Pauline had not bought her one of the white mohair suits that all young girls now wanted, consoled herself by imagining what outfit Mary Hall was helping Clara into somewhere inside the house. "I'm predicting gray poplin," she said. "If you trim it with gray silk it's very fashionable. I love to think of what she'll be wearing once she and Henry get to London. They say that bodices have dropped to the point where the women there are hardly wearing anything at all above the waist. Do you think Clara is too old to be *décolletée?*" Louise, fingering the paper rose at her neck, said she didn't know, and Lina, undiscouraged, asked, "Did you hear that Tom Thumb has managed to raise a mustache?"

The slow, schooner-like strains of Stephen Foster gave way to something like a tugboat blast as the orchestra launched into "There's a Good Time Coming." A few feet away from the girls, their Uncle Hamilton Harris and his friends began to shout a bit louder amongst themselves.

"So are we really going to have some Negroes in the United States Senate?" asked John Finley Rathbone.

"To hear Sumner tell it, I'd say the answer is yes," said Hamilton Harris. The two of them shook their heads, more in amazement than anything like clear approval or distaste.

Nearby, Ira Harris was having a bourbon with Indiana's Henry Lane. They had been seatmates in the august body being discussed, until Roscoe Conkling and the radicals had sent Harris packing six months ago. "Ira!" called Hamilton Harris, always solicitous when his brother's fortunes were in a downturn. "Come over and join us. Bring Mr. Lane."

"Quite a feather in your cap, having the chief justice in your parlor," said John Finley Rathbone when the two men arrived. "What's his thinking on impeachment these days?"

"Oh, you'd have to ask someone else," said Ira Harris, who had been thrilled to get Chase up to Albany, even if he'd declined this second party here at Kenwood. "I'm just a professor at the Albany Law School now. For political intelligence, you should try my old friend Lane here."

"Nonsense," said Hamilton Harris. "You're still at the center of things. Delegate to the state constitutional convention. Busier than ever. Did you know," he asked Lane and John Finley Rathbone, "that he was in the assembly chamber last night to hear Lucy Stone? 'Votes for Women!'" cried Hamilton in imitation of her troops, the idea more strange to his manly nature than the notion of Negro senators.

"What's that for women?" asked ancient Mr. Osborne, looking up from his lawn chair before subsiding back into his nap.

"Pauline!" cried Hamilton Harris when he spotted his sister-in-law talking to Henry. "Tear yourself away from the bridegroom and join us. We want to know if you were cheering with your 'sisters' last night."

Pauline held him off with a wave. She was occupied with an important matter of social record. "Henry," she said. "Before you go, you must send a letter to the *Express* and get them to correct their error."

"What error is that, Mother?"

"Tomorrow they'll be saying in their announcement of the wedding that you've resigned your commission in the army. An old friend of Howard's who works at the paper just gave me a piece of the page proof. It must be corrected."

"Is that all?"

"It's important for people to know you are still a colonel, even if you've decided to leave the adjutant general's office."

"I can't very well stay there while I'm on a yearlong honeymoon."

"Henry," said Pauline severely. "I want you to make sure you do this. It will take you five minutes. Then you may go." She did not reiterate her disapproval of the trip's length.

"Too bad the Dictator isn't here. We could get him to correct the matter in the *Commercial Advertiser.*"

Pauline shook her head. Thurlow Weed's absence from the wedding — no matter how much power he had lost, and no matter that he'd moved away from Albany to run another paper in New York City — had annoyed her. Ira Harris could once more be snubbed with impunity. She and her husband were old now, and she didn't like it. Her nature could not content itself with the memory of his elevation in '61, or even with Justice Chase's presence here today.

Henry knew that further joking would only inflame his mother, but he had already drunk too much to do anything else. "You know, Mother," he said, "you should concentrate on the weightier items in the daily paper. Did you see what today's *Journal* has next to the news of this happy affair? Just one column to the right," he said, getting ready to intone the item he had already recited half a dozen times since the wedding: "'There seems to be no doubt of the death of Dr. Livingstone.' Axed in the head by a Mefite tribesman. Not a pretty juxtaposition, is it, Mother? Should Clara and I take it as a warning against tarrying abroad?"

Pauline pursed her lips and focused on the lawn. Noting how old his mother looked, Henry, in a burst of alcohol-induced tenderness, leaned down to kiss her lips, an action that recalled her momentarily to life. "I insist, Henry. Before you leave for the pier." Tonight he and Clara would be taking the boat from Albany to New York, then sailing for Southampton in the morning.

He was about to say all right, of course, anything for you, my darling mama, when his brother Jared, carrying a huge stein full of the Beverwyck Brewery's best lager, clapped him on the back and tried to pry him away from their mother.

"Can't you find some pigs to chase?" Henry asked him. "Isn't that your usual wedding-day trick?"

Jared burst out laughing as he recalled making the Harris girls shriek twenty years ago at the Delavan, when his mother married the judge. "Come on, Henry. Come over and join us." Thirty feet away, Jared's army friends, West Pointers mostly, were rounding into one more chorus of "We Are Coming Father Abraam, 300,000 More." Henry, who had few friends of his own here, heard the song and declined to participate, as did Will Harris, who sat on a wooden love seat with his wife, Emma, and looked impassively at the masses of Rathbones disporting themselves on the lawn. He especially avoided the glance of the bridegroom, the stepbrother who was now his brother-in-law.

A sixth round of "Father Abraam" was drowned out by sudden peals of feminine appreciation and hearty masculine clapping. Clara had emerged from the great house in her traveling clothes. Lina was delighted to find herself wrong about the gray poplin. The outfit — embroidered black silk with its trim of guipure lace — was so stunning, and the guests' cheering so sustained, that Clara wondered if she should take a bow. Instead of waiting for Henry to come and take her arm, she just smiled, beaming straight into the last of the flattering sunlight, aware that she was not a blushing bride but a woman nearly thirty-three, at the height of a beauty lit by the mature intelligence beneath it.

Reverend Bridgman, who had performed the ceremony, took her hand and Henry's in his own. "There were times, children — when Howard died, and when you both had to share Mr. Lincoln's agony — when I thought your two families would never be truly happy again. How wrong I was! How happy I am to have been so wrong!"

Clara extracted her hand in order to pat his and thank him for the sermon this morning. But he flooded on, announcing that he had one last treat in store for them. He hushed the throng with a great tamping motion of his arms, and called for ten robed members of his choir to come forth and sing an envoi for Mr. and Mrs. Henry Reed Rathbone.

The ice in the drinks had long since melted, and there wasn't so much as a tinkling glass to interrupt the song, whose harmony traveled out over the lawn, down toward the river and the setting sun, as all stood silently listening.

This woman she was taken from inside Adam's arm;
And she must be protected from injury and harm.
This woman was not taken from Adam's feet, we see;
And she must not be abused, the meaning seems to be.

Clara felt a tear coming, but she was determined not to cry through her shining hour. She looked down at her silk shoes as the choir continued, and Henry squeezed her hand.

This woman she was taken from near to Adam's heart,
By which we are directed that they should never part.
The book that's called the Bible, be sure you don't neglect,
For in every sense of duty, it will you both direct.

Henry leaned down to whisper to her, "I shall try to make you happy, Clara. I shall try with all my heart." She took his face in both her hands, brushing his whiskers with her bouquet, and she kissed him as the singers began the last verse of the white-man's spiritual they'd chosen for their serenade:

To you, most loving bridegroom; to you, most loving bride,
Be sure you live a Christian and for your house provide.
Avoiding all discontent, don't sow the seed of strife,
As is the solemn duty of every man and wife.

"Hear, hear!" shouted Hamilton Harris without looking up from his watch, which he'd been nervously consulting since before Clara's emergence. "That's sound advice, sound advice." The rest of the Baptists and Presbyterians nodded in agreement until Mr. Osborne, fully alert now, as if participating in a scene from his long-ago youth, cried, "Your flowers, child. Your flowers." The crowd roared its encouragement, and Clara feigned a fluttery indecision as she scanned the crowd and decided where she would throw her bouquet. There was no point in wasting it on Louise or Mary Hall; they were never going to marry. Better to speed up the prospects of one who was, she thought, tossing it straight at Lina, whose catch delighted the guests. "That's so *you* won't have to wait until you're twice as old as you are now!" said Clara, bringing forth laughter from everyone, including those who still harbored reservations about what had finally occurred today.

At exactly 8:20, from the direction of the river, there came a great whistle blast that startled everyone. Hamilton Harris smiled down at his watch and got on a chair to let it be known that *his* last treat for the departing couple was arranging that they not have to go back to Albany at all. Captain Christopher had agreed to stop the *St. John* right here at Kenwood. Now all Henry and Clara had to do was hop into a carriage and be driven to the riverbank; they'd be rowed out to the steamer in a dinghy strung with roses.

The crowd shouted its approval. Clara thanked Uncle Hamilton for his ingenuity and led Henry toward the rig before the captain could give another pull on the horn. She kissed her sisters in a great sequential rush, accepted a hug and dry cheek from Pauline, and assured Mary Hall that she would write her every week from Europe.

Then she saw that Ira Harris was crying. She told Henry to get inside the coach; she would follow in a moment.

"Dearest Papa," she whispered. "You mustn't. My dreams have just come true."

He leaned over to kiss her and apologized for being a foolish old man. "I have one more present for you, my darling. A letter that arrived at the house just this morning." Clara looked at the thick cream-colored envelope with Mrs. Lincoln's familiar handwriting under a Chicago postmark. "I know how happy she must be for you both," said the judge. Clara tucked the letter into the small beaded handbag hanging from her wrist and gave her father one last kiss before allowing herself to be helped into the carriage.

"The *St. John* will have you in New York by dawn," called out Hamilton Harris. "Godspeed to you both." The horses took a step and the crowd fell back, all except Jared Rathbone, who rushed through it and shouted up to his brother, "Good news, Henry. The man from the *Journal* says there's late word on Livingstone. He's alive and well after all. So you don't need to be scared of travel!"

The guests laughed and cheered, and the driver cracked his whip.

→ 35 ←

This morning Henry stopped to converse with a diamond-cutter, a
Jew, who was going about his work. The man spoke English to us
with the same care, if not exactness, that he used to chip his stones.
It was curious, I told Henry as we left, that the Jew added value to
something precious by reducing its size with his chisel. "Do you
wish I'd bought you a smaller ring?" Henry asked, taking my left
hand and making me laugh. As he caressed my fingers, our conversation moved from diamonds to gold — the news we read in the English papers about the discoveries in Wyoming. Once again Henry
inclines toward fantasy — declaring that, upon our return to America, we should seek happiness in the solitary expanses of the West,
away from the crowded parlors of Washington and Albany.

    Whenever his talk takes such a turn, I find myself frightened that
he may be serious, but then I figure out what recent event has
prompted the recurrence of The Frontier Theme (as Mary and I
took to calling it last winter). I can easily guess the cause of today's
instance: last night's supper in the hotel dining room, which, besides
ourselves, contained two tables of traveling Americans. One party
whispered throughout the meal, their stares beating a hasty retreat
toward their plates whenever we looked over. The other, during
brandy, came over to introduce themselves (three doctors and their
wives, from Philadelphia) and say that they had been unable to help
noticing our names in the hotel register when they signed it that
morning — and would we accept their best wishes, as well as their
delight in seeing how happy and healthy we looked after what we

had been through? Thanking them, as always, was left to me; Henry just regarded the lengthening ash of his cigar, and nodded.

"This is the last hotel you choose from Harper's Hand-Book for Travelers," he scolded, upon our return upstairs. Rather than face "Americans in packs," he declared that he is prepared to cancel any further reservations we have at any establishment listed in the guide. I succeeded in placating him, demanding praise for at least not having booked us into the Hôtel de l'Oncle Tom (there really is such a place) in Paris.

But I understand his distress, and only wonder when there will be no more cause for it. Two years from now? Ten? I fear that people will never tire of talking about Wilkes Booth, any more than they will of talking about the war itself. In every hotel we're in, as soon as people get wind of our presence, we feel ourselves become objects of morbid scrutiny. The worst stretch began three days before the voyage ended, when whoever wrote the "shipboard newspaper" — a detestable innovation! — decided to mention that those aboard the vessel would surely be interested to know that their fellow passengers included . . . And with that the whole story.

This being the French Line, claret was served even with lunch, and no one's tongue was ever idle for a moment; during those last three days, whenever we were in the dining room, we began to feel like zoo animals. Henry (who imagines that the whispering is more pointed and malicious than it can possibly be) twice threw down his napkin and stormed off to the gymnasium, to pound his anger into the boxing bag.

More than a month has passed since all that, but incidents like the one last night are fresh fodder for Henry's determination to be done forever with American cityfolk. So today it was Wyoming.

Though our room is everywhere domesticated by floral needlepoint, the name of the hotel means "bull's-eye." Harper's Hand-Book says so, making me think of arrows and Indians and the frontier, and my own determination that we shall resume our American life nowhere but in the much wilder precincts of Washington, D.C., which I miss even now, and of whose eventual possibilities I still believe Henry can be convinced. Yes, I'm like the Jew near the

Royal Palace: I prefer the small, finished, man-carved diamond to undiscovered veins of gold.

Hanover
November 12, 1867

We were in the Reliquarium this morning, unable to take the Cru-saders' trophies — bits of sacred tibia, pieces of holy hip-joint — with any seriousness at all. Henry the Lion brought them back from Palestine, but my Henry and I could not contain our giggling. We chased each other toward the Waterloo Platz like sweethearts half the age we are, along the way stopping at the hotel, to claim our letters.

I wish we hadn't. Because the day turned dark as we sat and opened them inside a café near the great column. One from Papa, another from Emeline, two from Will and Emma, and one from Pauline, this last full of newspaper cuttings: "Mrs. Lincoln's Second-Hand Clothing Sale," said the piece from Leslie's. Everything was sold up — or at least offered — at Brady & Co., on Broadway. An awful spectacle: cheap muslin skirts for enormous prices; silk dresses so short of hem and low of neck they raised more laughter than money. The First Lady's motives are attacked by everyone, most viciously of all by Mr. Weed, who claims the Republicans "would have made proper arrangements for the maintenance of Mrs. Lin-coln had she so deported herself as to inspire respect." He charges her with all manner of corruption and coarseness, insisting she also sold off Mr. Lincoln's shirts, all but the one he was shrouded with.

The news items brought me near to tears (and anger, as I could imagine Pauline's scissors at their gleeful work), but Henry would have none of it. He wondered if Mr. Seward "had sprung for any of the clothing" for his daughter-in-law — assuming he was in a mood to waste his personal treasury "after squandering the national one on Alaska." When this left me cheerless, he became angry, railing at what an addled woman Mrs. Lincoln has always been, "the help-meet of that bloody-minded ape." I tried to respond, but he insisted I keep silent, and that we have done with "the two of them" forever.

It is this — the two of them — that I do not understand. Abuse of Mrs. Lincoln, cruel and undeserved though it may be, was com-

mon currency before we left the States — from the President's old friend Herndon to his last radical enemy in the Congress. She is a woman, and weak, a proper lightning rod for all the anger and resentment they stored up through the war, whereas Mr. Lincoln himself is subject only to reverence — except from Henry, and Henry alone, which makes his invective all the more chilling. I know it is his way of fending off the memory of what he was made to endure that night, but surely there must be some weapon less blunt and brutal. I never argue Mr. Lincoln's merits, or for any rational perspective on that awful evening, of which Henry's memories are, I'm sure, still disarranged. Trying to get him to talk about what happened leads only to his ugly censure of everyone's behavior, mine included. I have told him I will not listen to that. And I would not this afternoon. We walked to Mt. Brilliant, the king's country house, in a silence I enforced. Once there, in the garden, beside a still-green hedgerow, the squall that had gathered an hour before blew away. The clouds lifted, and we kissed, and remembered that the war is over. We went back to being school sweethearts, and my own Henry the Lion laughed and purred and nuzzled my neck and asked for forgiveness.

*Cairo
early Christmas morning, 1867*

In my mind's eye — and I'm sure it must be so, this very instant, in Albany, a world away — sleighs are carrying partygoers all along State Street and Western Avenue, everyone anticipating the presents to be opened and rum punch to be drunk. If I allow myself to illuminate these lantern slides for more than a moment or two inside my brain, I become sick for home and Papa and Will and my sisters. So I do not show them to myself, and try instead to marvel at the strangeness of being where we now are, in three rooms of Shepherd's Hotel in the middle of the night, the donkey drivers still arguing in the street below, the merchants soon to be spreading out their brass lamps and bolts of silk as if it were any other day on the calendar — which of course it is. Here in the "Franks' Quarter" one sees an occasional little wreath, the improvised work of another

Western traveler, and the English in the hotel (who've no idea who we are) have been greeting one another with "Happy Christmas" in the breakfast room these last few days. But the Yuletide illusion is shattered by the horns calling Ali and Mohammed to their prayers. We are in another world, of mosques and massacred Marmelukes (this morning we saw some of their tombs), and when I give myself over to it — an immersion Henry seems to accomplish effortlessly — I appreciate its fascination. There are no street lamps anywhere, and the law requires us to carry a lantern when we walk about at night. The chances it offers for shadow play are endless, and Henry has frightened and charmed me with his inventions these past four nights.

He is now sleeping in the next room. How I wish the third contained a child, or two or three of them, ready to be surprised by full stockings on Christmas morning. But their arrival will have to wait. We have taken special pains not to become expectant parents while abroad, the prospects for mishap or confinement being too worrisome to contemplate. (Henry has used a method I suspect he perfected with the girls on Quay Street, so far with apparent success and no diminution of pleasure.) Back home, Amanda's baby is due any week, and I shall be Aunt Clara, a title I once thought might represent the final relation I had with children.

I could start for home tomorrow — it would be a voyage toward my own children, whose souls I feel waiting to come down from heaven and be born. But Henry is determined for us to remain abroad some months more. The further away he is from America and Americans, alas, the better he feels. His spirits have been fine these past few weeks, and so I am happy, too. Despite the longings confessed above, travel suits me well. I am lean and fit as a race-horse, my body exercised and pleasured to a degree that makes me blush. There are still mornings when we do not go out at all. Yesterday we were supposed to undertake a five-hour excursion to Heliopolis, a plan we ended up laughing over as we lay together, hour after hour, the sun rising ever higher behind the cracks in the shutter. "We are already in the city of the sun," Henry said, encircling me, and it was past noon when we rose.

By evening I was longing for a world of people and chatter —

*the world of home — but he will soon enough let me have that
again. Meanwhile, as a world unto ourselves we can be splendid.*

*I have cheered myself by writing. Indeed, I am now in a sparkling
enough mood to pen my weekly missive of unadulterated optimism
to Mary!*

Hotel Minerva
Rome
April 25, 1868

We spent most of the afternoon apart, Henry exploring the Army
Amphitheatre and I sitting on the Spanish Steps, writing letters to
Emeline and Will and looking up at the window of the little room
where Keats died. I reflected, of course, upon Howard, that other
merry, robust spirit jailed in a dying body, gone three years already.
This melancholy train of thought must have given me a poetic look:
before I finished the letter to Will, I noticed a young man, two steps
below and to my left, looking up at me with interest and concern.
He was a pretty boy of about eighteen, very thin, without whiskers,
but possessed of thick curls that crept over his collar like the paws
of a kitten. His name, he told me, after I smiled at him, was Adam
Simpson, a Bostonian who has been in Rome for eight months
trying to paint. "I have no gift for it at all," he explained, with as
much matter-of-factness as he said his name. He has been, in fact,
the model for more pictures — most of them done on the Steps —
than he's been the artist.

He is just young enough to have escaped the war, and I think he
sees his life as a demonstration of God's caprice. He is plainly
delighted to be here and alive, unsure but untroubled as to why it
turned out differently for others. We spoke of Keats, and he offered
to be my guide through the Protestant cemetery. I declined, telling
him my husband would be along at any moment. He bought me an
ice, and we recited bits of the Odes until he confessed that he
preferred anything of Shelley's to them. He knows nothing of what
is going on back home: he has a large prosperous family who write
him regularly, but he retains little of what they say. I gave up on
asking for the news, my usual hungry manner of acquainting myself

{ 235 }

with other traveling Americans. (When I mentioned Mr. Johnson's acquittal, I think Mr. Simpson took it to mean that the President had been tried in an ordinary court of law, for shoplifting or perhaps vagrancy.)

Henry soon came trotting up the Steps to retrieve me. I introduced him to my new friend, who immediately turned shy. He looked up at Henry, towering over his own slight, seated form, with a mixture of fear and awe. "We've been talking about Shelley and Keats," I explained, adding, "Adam Simpson, this is Lord Byron." Though he and Henry had yet to exchange more than hellos, little Mr. Simpson understood what I meant by the joke, and Henry, on his best behavior, laughed along with us, until I said, "We've also been speaking of Mr. Johnson," which sent an uncomfortable look across his face. I asked him about the Amphitheatre, which he proceeded to describe with tremendous precision. Mr. Simpson, whose interest in martial matters, I would venture to guess, is ordinarily slight, hung upon his every word. In wonderment, he asked Henry what he had done in the war, so Henry recited the awful names — Antietam, Fredericksburg, Petersburg — which sounded like the Stations of the Cross. Even Mr. Simpson, looking reverent and unworthy, seemed to know their import. As if ashamed, he soon made his excuses, gathering up his sketchpad, shaking Henry's hand and kissing mine, and disappearing into the Via dei Condotti, a sweet and faintly ridiculous figure.

A minute or two later Henry and I descended the Steps. "I suppose you told him everything," he said. "I never even gave my name!" I answered, something I hadn't realized until that minute, and which set me to laughing. "He didn't seem to need it," Henry countered bewilderingly. Then I understood that he was thinking Mr. Simpson had been satisfied just to swim in the deep pools of my eyes! "Oh, Henry," I said, laughing harder. "Surely he was a girl-boy. I'm quite certain he spent more time looking at your shoulders than my eyes." At this point I was upbraided for my naiveté, as well as for talking filth. Finally, sensing (perhaps) that he had been too harsh, he changed the subject slightly, to ask if Mr. Simpson had been sympathetic to the President's cause. "He doesn't even know what the President's cause is," I said. Trying to leave Mr. Simpson behind forever, I said I was glad the President had survived his impeachment, and that I was proud Papa had ceased vacillating and become one of his allies in those last months in the Senate. I speculated that Mr. Johnson was grateful for that still, a year and a half since Papa's return to Albany. This remark Henry seemed to find hugely amusing. "Mr. Johnson has far greater reason than that to be grateful to this family." I didn't know what he meant; I was only sorry that what should have been a pleasant memory of little Mr. Simpson had had all this cold water preposterously thrown upon it. We were a quarter hour into our circuit of the Pantheon — during which time Henry asked me if Mr. Simpson hadn't reminded me of Howard — before each of us regained his humor with the other.

Copenhagen

August 20, 1868

How late the summer light lingers at this latitude. Tonight we used it in the Tivoli Gardens to read our books. Sitting in our chairs, side by side, we made a comic, prematurely aged sight, especially to ourselves. "Have we grown tired of each other's company?" I asked at one moment when we both happened to look up from our pages. "Never!" said Henry, beginning a volley of melodramatic protestations we kept up for a good three minutes, our own imitation of the dreadful play we saw two nights ago at the Royal Theatre. Finally we settled back into our reading, ignoring the violinists and gymnasts and mimes quietly disporting themselves in the last hour of sunshine.

I am halfway through The Ring and the Book. Henry is making a long march through volume one of Freeman's History of the Norman Conquest. This follows a lengthy run of Macaulay and Gibbon and a dozen other historians whose books he has cogitated over with great intensity, as if gestating some complex theory of his own. The books are usually left behind in hotel rooms, along with the shoes and souvenirs we are constantly forgetting, but their sober matter seems to stay lodged inside Henry, like something he has swallowed, endlessly to ruminate.

I care no more for what he reads than he does for Browning.

When it comes to men's affairs it is Grant and Seymour, not William and Harold, about whom I want to hear. Our mail from home has been full of the election, but we will not be back for another month and a half, by which time the campaign will be nearly over. The letters from Albany clamor for us to return, and they make polite reference to the question of what it is Henry will "do" once we've recrossed the Atlantic. It is a question we have had almost no discussion of ourselves. What I shall "do" is much clearer: get us to Washington and bring forth a baby.

⇢ 36 ⇠

HAPPY BUT STILL TIRED, halfway between sleep and waking, Clara looked out the bedroom window into the moonlight and could have sworn she was seeing the silhouette of Abraham Lincoln. She squinted at what seemed attached to the glass, and in her gathering wakefulness realized it *was* the President's profile: a black paper one commemorating his birthday that some schoolboys on a charity drive had sold to one of the colored servants the other morning. It was nighttime now, Clara could see, and she wondered if it was still February 12, as it had been, amazingly enough, this morning, when her son, Henry Riggs Rathbone, entered the world. Mary Hall, who had come down from New York for the lying-in, had greeted the coincidence with awe, telling her that she and Henry *must* think of naming the boy after Mr. Lincoln. No, Clara had replied, before falling into a long sleep; she didn't think that was a good idea, at least not from Henry's point of view. Now, almost fully awake, she wondered if Henry's anxiety last night, after she had gone into labor — the wish he sent upstairs that she be a brave girl and make the effort to get through the ordeal as quickly as possible — wasn't perhaps connected to a desire that the baby be born before midnight; that is, on February 11. No, she decided, that was foolish. She doubted Henry had even remembered the date of the President's birthday until Mary reminded them this morning.

Looking once more at the schoolboys' paper silhouette, she wondered: when would her son start going to school? Just in time for the centennial, in '76, she calculated, imagining the day she would paste his own first drawings, of cherry trees and cocked hats, to the panes in his bedroom window. She was glad they had bought this house in Lafayette Square, glad they had decided not to live at Fifteenth and H. The moment she and Henry stepped into a great welcome-home party on Eagle Street sixteen months ago, she had realized the need for a complete break with their peculiarly joined parents. She had known all at once that she *couldn't* move into the Washington house that Papa and Pauline had occupied throughout the war, and when it developed that Admiral Alden's was up for sale, she persuaded Henry that buying it constituted a radical departure — even if it was just inside the square, on the other side of the park, and involved little more, as Jared pointed out, than "looking at the other end of Andy Jackson's bronze horse."

But little Riggs — as they'd be calling him to avoid confusion — had been born this morning into a whole different era of history in the square. Across the tiny park, on Madison Place, James G. Blaine, the speaker, was occupying the house where Mr. Seward once lived and nearly died. On their own side, two doors down on Jackson Place, Vice President Colfax had taken up residence in the stucco dwelling where Dan Sickles used to live and bellow. With the war five years over, men were building new houses everywhere in the city. They read stock quotations now, not casualty lists. Instead of hacking itself to bits, the country was bursting with growth. This was the good and exciting time into which her son had been born.

She was all at once desperate to see him again, and so, carefully sitting up in bed, she called through the closed door and asked Mary to bring him to her. Mary had been an angel this past week, the only person Clara had wanted to come down and be with her. Lina was too easily distracted and Louise too squeamish, but Mary's endless generosity had put up with Henry's moods and pretended not to notice the spats that flared between the two of them at least twice a day. Mary's work with the poor in New York was deepening her own natural goodness, giving her an ampleness of spirit that was lovely to observe. She was no longer just a passionately right-minded girl; she was becoming, Clara believed, a soul. Spinsterhood had already wrinkled Louise, but Mary was blooming. Still, Clara thought, hearing her steps come down the hall, how shockable she could be! The other day

Clara had confided to her that not the least reason for looking forward to the baby's arrival was the prospect of resuming relations with Henry as man and wife; the poor thing had blushed to match the crimson bell-pull. If only she knew how important this really was. The baby might be their creation, something that would finally give them a living, breathing common interest, an object of worry beyond themselves; but more important, its delivery from her body would give them back to each other, let them once more return to their nighttime world of almost violently happy lovemaking. It was daylight that always brought back trouble.

"Look who's here!" whispered Mary. Clara, extending her arms to the baby, recognized the robe he wore as one she herself had knit for Lina twenty years ago.

"My precious little Riggs," she said, taking him from Mary, who turned up the lamp. "Oh, Mary, look," she softly cried as she fingered the down on the infant's skull. "I never noticed this morning. It glints red in the gaslight, just like his papa's whiskers. Yes, sweetness, you're your papa's little man, aren't you?"

Mary moved to close the door, but Clara asked her to leave it open. "I've been shut in here all day. I'd rather hear some noise from the rest of the house." She joked about "confinement" being the right word for what she'd experienced. With relief she heard Henry turning pages in the library across the hall: the huge book of Egyptian history, she imagined, feeling calmer to know just where he was.

"Let me go back out and get the telegrams," said Mary while she smoothed the bedclothes. A moment later, after scurrying in with a pile of them and forgetting to leave the door open, she took a seat at the foot of the bed. In a voice too soft to disturb the baby, she read them one by one to Clara.

There was one from Pauline and Papa, who was PROUDER THAN EVER. Mary held it up and Clara delighted in the black capital letters made by the miracle Dr. Nott had once prophesied (that story Papa never tired of telling). Had their own "annunciation," as Henry called it, not gone out over the wire early this morning, Papa's congratulations would have had to wait a few days before arriving in a letter, and its handwritten form would have saddened Clara: the small stroke he suffered last year had rendered his penmanship unsteady.

"One from your Aunt Emeline," said Mary, "and another from Amanda and Tom."

"Does she mention that I'm still one behind?" asked Clara.

"Yes, she does!" said Mary. Amanda and her husband, Mr. Thomas Ewing Miller of Columbus, Ohio, had had their second child last month.

There was even a wire from General Schofield, on whose staff Jared now found himself, and another from Emma and Will, who was commanding the Watertown Arsenal.

"Is Will supposed to be there much longer?" asked Mary, who still felt a pang or two of curiosity about the noble young soldier she'd years ago had a crush on.

"No," said Clara. "Probably not more than a few months. When his discharge comes through, he'll be secretary and manager — I think that's the title — of the Decatur Rolling Mill Company. Henry calls it the Tolling Bell Company, but I don't see why he makes fun. It's a very Rathbone-like thing Will's decided to do: he'll soon be a mighty manufacturing man, not just another orating Harris like Papa and Uncle Hamilton."

"Has Henry been discharged himself?" asked Mary, who had been circumspect this past week in inquiring about his plans.

"He will be, at the end of the year," said Clara, before shifting the topic to the wondrous intricacy of Riggs's fingers. Henry had been unassigned from any duty since March of last year, and it was unclear to Clara what real difference his formal discharge, when it finally came around, would make. His lack of plans must seem uncomfortably evident in contrast to Will's, but she was grateful that Mary asked no further questions, just as she appreciated her not commenting on the quarrels, or on how few acquaintances called during the days and evenings Henry spent inside the house. Perhaps Mary thought everything was fundamentally all right. Well, now that Riggs had arrived, everything *would* be fine, or at least very much better.

There was a sharp rap at the door. The two women started, but the baby slept on. "You'll have to learn to start playing *pianissimo*, heart," whispered Clara, after Henry entered.

"Something from Mrs. Grant," he said, handing Mary a parcel. "A boy just delivered it." It was a bedjacket, blue quilted cotton, quite merry and not at all fancy. Clara pronounced it enchanting and wondered how the First Lady had gotten the word: "We didn't send *them* a telegram, after all." Henry supposed it was their own cook talking to the Vice President's that had started the very short grapevine needed to reach the White House from Jackson Place.

"Come look at the telegrams," said Clara.

"I've already been through them. I'm sure tomorrow will bring many more congratulations upon your feat, dear."

"Mary's done most of the hard work. I feel as light as air, but she must be ready to drop."

"Where will our son and heir be spending his first night?" asked Henry.

"I offered to put him in my room," said Mary. "I thought that would give Clara a better night's sleep. But she wants him right here." She pointed to the cradle that the maid had placed in the room an hour ago.

"That's fine," said Henry, "though I can't say what it will do for *my* night's sleep." The three of them laughed. Mary took the baby from Clara, kissed her good night, and placed Riggs in his cradle. She smiled at Henry and left for her room down the hall.

Clara wanted to see her husband pick up his son, wanted him to find irresistible the idea of waking Riggs up and hearing his little lungs. But Henry just looked down at him, in a manner that seemed disappointingly objective. She closed her eyes.

"Tired, darling?" he asked.

"Yes, a little."

"Let's go to sleep, then. And hope that he does."

He turned down the lamp and kissed her. Clara watched him shed his waistcoat and trousers and place them on the chair with his old comical neatness, more dandified than military. He put on his nightshirt and came around to her side of the bed, pausing only to peel the Lincoln silhouette from the window and toss it into the fireplace.

→ 37 ←

THREE YEARS LATER, on March 3, 1873, Henry stepped off the Pennsylvania Avenue streetcar at a point slightly beyond Lafayette Square. He was returning from an afternoon spent reading Carlyle in the Library of Congress. Entering the square on the Madison Place side, he began a slow counterclockwise circuit toward home. As always, the houses surrounding the park excited familiar reflections and long-held resentments. He walked over the spot where fourteen years ago Dan Sickles had shot his wife's lover, and he thought of Clara, advancing toward forty and, after three children, still beautiful — though too eager to be reminded, by every congressional clerk and Tuscan fop, of just how lovely and spirited she was.

No house in the square was more potent to Henry than Mr. Seward's place, as he would always think of it, even though it had belonged for some time to Speaker Blaine. Seward had died last fall, and Clara's slow recovery from the birth of their third child and first daughter, Clara Pauline, had given them an excuse not to travel up to Auburn for the funeral. Judge Harris (as everyone once more called him) had sent them an account by letter, his handwriting still more quavery after a second stroke. Even so, he'd managed all the telling details, including Mr. Weed's attempt at pallbearing amidst a flood of tears. The description was friendly, even heartfelt: the judge was content with teaching law and being chairman of the American Baptist Missionary Union, a position that provided Pauline with the small bit of social recognition she still craved, though it was nothing, of course, to the road show of lionization that Seward traveled, from Mexico City to Shanghai, after leaving office and Lafayette Square in '69.

Nobody, thought Henry, was where they had been just a couple of years before. All the army men had quit, not just himself and Will, but even Jared, who'd left Schofield's staff and gone out to California to raise horses. He'd make a success of it, too, just as the noble Will was doing with the Tolling Bell Company. But their western ventures left Henry without any desire to compete. The more he heard of them at family holidays up in Loudonville, the more inclined he was to live off his money like a gentleman, adding to it by investment, spinning paper from paper in the speculative spirit of the Age of Ulysses. His brothers could hew and haul; the precise numerical manipulations he plotted in his own library let him feel like an artist. In this town, to his satisfaction, the accumulation of money set him apart from all the men accumulating power. It was true that he hadn't yet increased his fortune — in fact, he'd so far lost more than he'd made — but he knew a good return would soon come his way. If it was so important for Clara to stay here, fine; but he would carve out a separate existence for himself, and she would have to agree to a few months in Europe each year, when he could shed Americans like his itchy winter coat.

It would all have turned out differently, he thought — passing the great house where McClellan had quartered himself during the war — if preposterous Little Mac had managed to beat Lincoln in '64. But he hadn't, and it had come out the way it had, and at just this moment Henry would not allow himself to think about it, would put one foot in front of the other as he turned the corner onto H. He would not look down toward the old house at Fifteenth. He'd look instead toward the Wormley Hotel, wondering if one of the diplomats nested there was planning a party that would interfere with Clara's tonight.

Well, good luck to her. He wouldn't be staying to the end of it anyway. After an hour he would slip out to gamble at John Chamberlain's or dine at Welcker's, where he could sit amidst walnut panels instead of the floral wallpaper that now filled his house. At Welcker's he could look at women, not wives, and converse with some honest bookmaker instead of the politicians who, except for the odd poet, would make up Clara's whole guest list. At Welcker's the crowd changed from night to night, and he could sit there without having to make friends, without getting to know anyone well enough that they'd dare ask him anything he didn't wish to be asked.

He was passing Senator Sumner's house now. And wouldn't you know, the old gentleman was out in front, his neck tilted backward, the better to warm his face in the fading afternoon sun. As he heard Henry's walking stick approach, without even opening his eyes, he asked, "How is your father progressing, Colonel Rathbone?"

"My father-in-law does very well, sir. He walked the length of Mr. Seward's funeral procession and came home to write us all the details."

"Well, that's one good piece of news to come out of such a sad occasion." The old man brought his head down and looked at Henry. "No matter how many years go by, I still miss having Ira Harris at my 'evenings.' Though your wife's presence is a beauteous substitute."

"I shall pass the compliment on to her, sir."

"Please do that. We always hope to have you join us yourself, Colonel."

"It's always good of you to ask," Henry responded with a tip of his high hat. He continued walking west, past St. John's and then old Montholon's place. Clara's own parties must seem in-expensive to her, he thought, given the way she could remember the French minister's famous ball every time she looked out her windows.

It was only four-thirty, and he didn't want to go home yet, so he went into the park and sat on a bench that afforded him, through the now bare magnolia branches, a sight of both the White House and Seward's old home. He thought, as always, of the gigantic Lewis Payne crashing up the steps of the latter just as Booth was doing his work at Ford's. Doing his work right in front of Henry himself. Carlyle maintained that all history de-pended on the will of great individual men. Nowhere did he acknowledge what resulted from one man's doing something he had neither planned nor understood. This, Henry felt sure, was the other mainspring of history, the second one, which he would someday, after many more volumes and much more reflection, figure out. At that point he would have his peace, and the rest of the world a new parcel of enlightenment.

It was quite dark before he got up and crossed Jackson Place toward number 8. Reaching the door, he could hear Gerald's wailing and Riggs's chattering. The nurse, who had Clara Pauline in her arms, let him in. He handed her his hat and went into the main parlor, where Clara was sitting on the carpet, finishing a romp with the boys and soothing a freshly raised bump on Gerald's forehead. They were both their mother's creatures. They had little affection or curiosity, and she no mothering, left over for him. She had a peculiar way — admirable, he thought at times; embarrassing, he believed at others — of entering their world completely, of making herself their equal. This was one of those moments; it was only his entrance that caused her smile to fade. She looked up while replacing a hairpin.

"It's six o'clock, Henry. Six o'clock at least. *You* should be larking about with my darlings. I have a dozen things yet to oversee." She rose from the carpet and wiped the dust off her dress. She offered him her cheek, which he kissed, before asking, "At what hour may we expect the rush of peacock feathers?"

"Eight o'clock," she answered.

"And for what fare?"

"Chicken cutlets, sweetbreads, charlottes, two wines — no, three, but only three. Oh, Henry, I can't remember it all. Ask cook, if you must."

Henry, who prided himself on his dining discipline, and whose stomach was as hard as it had been at Union College, smiled. "I trust the wines will be good ones. Their luncheon oysters will barely have traveled south from their gullets; they'll need something fine to slide them on their way."

"The wines are quite modest, actually. And I haven't stuck a diamond in my bonnet, like Mrs. Sprague."

"You know I want you to do things in style, dear."

"Yes," she said, straightening some ferns. "I do know. And I trust you'll tell me when I've begun to spend our capital."

"I shouldn't worry," he said, accepting the rolled-up *Evening*

Star from Riggs, who had manfully toddled in with it from the hall.

"The secretary of war is coming," she said, attempting a playful, wheedling tone. "I should think, with the President's second term getting under way, that thirty-five is just the right age for a new undersecretary."

"Not interested," said Henry as he allowed Gerald's tiny fingers to explore his boot buckle. "I made *them* what they are, in any case." He opened the paper and sat down on the sofa. Clara shook her head over this one more cryptic bit of self-assurance. "You exasperate me, Henry. Mind that Gerald doesn't hit his head again. Betty! There you are. Come in, please. Tell cook to set out a punch bowl in the library. And tell Edwin not to let the gawkers get too close to the front steps when the guests are arriving."

"Yes, ma'am."

"And take Riggs in for his dinner, please."

Now she could get dressed. She made one last glance toward Henry, who had quite forgotten Gerald at his feet. "I'm counting on you to be here from beginning to end," she said, and left the room, envying Kate Chase Sprague, who, with or without a diamond in her bonnet, had only a husband's drunkenness to worry about.

"To think it could have been Greeley!" shouted Congressman Roundtree, thinking ahead to tomorrow morning, March 4, 1873, and Ulysses S. Grant's second inaugural. Clara's guests, Republicans to a man (and to an unenfranchised woman), were raising their goblets of Madeira in a toast to the reelected President.

"Let's thank God he took his own advice and went west, young man!" cried Mr. Ralph Eaglesfield, a representative of the Pennsylvania Railroad in Washington, who reached clear around Mrs. Hannibal Hamlin to slap the back of Congressman Roundtree, two seats farther down Clara's big Eastlake table. A few feet away there was a second table just like it, whose diners brought the total in the room to sixteen.

Clara was discomfited to realize that a clear majority of them were laughing at Mr. Eaglesfield's remark. Would they not let the defeated Democrat rest in his grave? She looked around for some decently pursed lips or averted eyes, and could find only those belonging to Mary Hall, old Mr. Hamlin, and his wife. "Poor Mr. Greeley," said the latter, with a gentle bipartisanship that Mr. Eaglesfield and Congressman Roundtree must be finding quaintly obsolete. "To lose his wife, his newspaper, the presidency, and his own life — in the space of a few weeks! I think we should toast his memory," said Mrs. Hamlin.

Gratefully, Clara raised her glass and thought something kind about Mr. Greeley. In fact, though it was twelve years too late, she wished that the New York legislature had chosen him instead of Papa for the Senate seat. How different everything would have been.

"Well, I've still got some malice toward one," said Mr. Eaglesfield — another good one that Congressman Roundtree would appreciate, and which a back number like Mrs. Hamlin could be counted on to recognize.

The congressman was not the only one in Clara Rathbone's dining room caught up in the Crédit Mobilier scandal. His name, she knew, had appeared on the *Sun's* list of those given Union Pacific shares by Massachusetts's Oakes Ames. Nothing can stop them, thought Clara, not even a scandal as big as this one. In November, the Republicans had made huge gains in the House, including the two new men at the next table, the kind of men who, even ten years ago, her papa would have had trouble bidding a good morning to. She did not like the unstirrable mixture of her own guests: crude, green buccaneers and white-haired relics. (Dear old Vice President Hamlin, back in the Senate since '69, had shown up tonight in his black swallow-tailed coat.) The old ones were mostly true friends; the new ones would chew on any leg of mutton or hand extended in their direction. The people in between, the ones who really made things happen in Washington, were, with the exception of the secretary of war, absent. She was finding them harder to attract than she'd expected when they bought the house three years ago. Curiosity drew her first-time guests; was it Henry's peculiarities that kept many of them from coming back?

Oh, dear. Mary, bless her true-blue heart, was about to say something. Couldn't she be stopped? Apparently not. A look from Clara failed to close her friend's lips, which were trembling on the verge of utterance.

"That's not the spirit of *my* Republican Party, Congressman."

Roundtree moved his gaze to her. "And what spirit would that be, ma'am?"

Mary searched her mind for a moment and declared brightly, "Why, the spirit of men like William E. Gray and John Ray Lynch."

Oh, she *would,* thought Clara. Naming two of the Negroes who'd actually been allowed to address the convention last summer. Roundtree and Eaglesfield were now leaning across Mrs. Hamlin to roll their eyes at each other. At the other end of the table, Henry seemed amused, wondering how Mary would, as always, dig herself in deeper.

"Anyone else?" asked Mr. Eaglesfield.

"Well," said Mary, sputtering a bit, "Senator Hamlin, of course." He bowed his head gratefully. To Mary's mind, he had been a bit late in coming to the abolitionist cause (she could always tell you just what year in the 1850s any Northern politician had "turned"), but as Mr. Lincoln's Vice President he had safe conduct into her pantheon. Even so, her heart really longed for the moment when the other guests would all be gone and she could slip across the square to Senator Sumner's house, bringing that grand old radical a leftover cake and her own most humble good wishes. She made this pilgrimage every time she came to visit Clara in Washington, her awe never diminishing a jot.

"Mrs. Rathbone, how is your good father?" asked Hamlin, deliberately changing the subject.

"He does very well, sir. He's a bit stiff in his legs, but he still works hard for the American Baptist Missionary Union."

"Past seventy now," said Mary Hall, full of ecumenical admiration. Her own father, the Episcopal bishop, had passed away the previous year, leaving her alone in the house on Beekman Place.

"And your brother Jared, Mr. Rathbone? Still on General Schofield's staff?"

"No, out in California, Senator. Raising horses and pursuing some mining ventures."

Clara looked solicitously at Mr. Hamlin. She knew he must be requiring his pipe by now, and she gestured for the server to speed things up and bring in the cheeses.

"Good for him," said the senator. "Too many men have been staying on in the army longer than it needs them. Even fine West Pointers like your brother. The war's long over. We're friends again, and blessed with a protective ocean on either side of us. We can do with a smaller service. We need talented men like your brother to be settling the great open spaces."

"So long as Congress allows them to," said Mr. Eaglesfield.

"Sir?" inquired Hamlin.

"So long as Congress doesn't fence off half the West into some giant preserve. Some of you men on Capitol Hill won't be satisfied until they make this Yellowstone Park a hundred times bigger than it already is."

"Nonsense," said Hamlin, putting a wedge of Stilton onto his slice of pear. "There will always be plenty of room for the entrepren —"

"I'm afraid Eaglesfield is right, Senator," interrupted Congressman Roundtree. "The country's got to grow. We can't be fencing off great parcels of it just because —"

"Am I the only one here who's read Mrs. Southworth's new book?" asked pretty Mrs. Eaglesfield in her silvery voice. She seemed to mean well, looking first to Clara and then Mary, hoping to tame the men before they got into a real row.

"No," said Mary. "I'm afraid not. But I have just finished Mr. Charles Reade's *A Terrible Temptation.*"

Mrs. Eaglesfield blushed. "It sounds quite scandalous."

"It exposes abuses in the regulation of lunatic asylums," said Mary, an answer that brought forth a hoot of laughter from Mr. Eaglesfield. His wife just said, "I see," clearly perplexed by the thought that a spinster like Miss Hall should interest herself in such dreadful things. She looked away from the table, toward the Japanese prints on the far wall. (Clara was determined to keep up with the fashion in furnishings.) Mrs. Hamlin, by way of compromise, mentioned how much she had enjoyed Mr. Roe's *Barriers Burned Away*, all about the Chicago fire of two years before; but this new offering failed to light any conversational sparks. Mr. Eaglesfield, who by now had drunk too much wine, had picked a pomegranate from the fruit bowl and, leaning backward behind Mrs. Hamlin, was waggling his wrist to demonstrate to Congressman Roundtree the newly approved baseball throw, which allowed the pitcher to put a bit of spin on the ball, even if he was still prohibited from throwing it overhand.

Clara knew that Mr. Eaglesfield was one of nature's bullies, the kind of man who, if he were still a boy, would be out in the gutter hurling insults at whoever was attempting to master the bicycle. He had looked down the low, feather-trimmed neckline of her dress when he'd come through the door tonight, fresh from Capitol Hill, where he had no doubt been applauding the victory all his well-paid congressmen had won over salacity this afternoon, when they passed the Comstock Act. Clara was willing to put up with these hypocrites if they could make a difference to Henry's situation, but the evening would soon be over and he had made no real effort to talk to anyone, including the secretary of war. If nothing happened when the men went up to the library with their cigars, she would soon have to put on yet another dinner like this one.

"So what's your theory?" shouted Mr. Eaglesfield to Congressman Roundtree, both of them now leaning forward, the question going straight down the table and across poor Mrs. Hamlin.

"Theory of what?" asked Roundtree.

"Yes, of *what*, Mr. Eaglesfield?" Clara asked, hoping to bring the table into one last round of unified conversation before the sexes rose and went their separate, post-prandial ways.

"Theory of the *Mary Celeste*, of course," said Eaglesfield, surprised that she should even have to ask. The mystery of the American ship had, after all, been in the papers for days. She'd been discovered by the *Dei Gratia*, a British brigantine, floating between the Azores and Portugal, still carrying her 1,700 barrels of alcohol, but without a sign of her seven-man crew, or her captain, or the captain's wife and daughter, who had accompanied him on the voyage out of New York. The lifeboat was missing, too, but what had possessed anyone to get into it? There was only a little water in the hull, according to the crew of the *Dei Gratia,* who had boarded the drifting ship on December 4, and since then testified to a court of inquiry in Gibraltar.

"It was a mutiny," Congressman Roundtree said definitively.

"Couldn't have been," shot back Eaglesfield. "Mark my words, this Captain Briggs was conniving with the skipper of the *Dei Gratia.*"

"You mean with the captain who discovered her?" asked Senator Hamlin. "That seems fairly preposterous."

"Yes," said Mary Hall. "And it doesn't explain where everyone else is."

"Something went wrong between the two of them," said Eaglesfield. "Some sort of falling out. The *Dei Gratia'*s man ended up having to get rid of his confederate and all the rest of them. Don't forget the bloody sword they found on board."

By now the eight guests around the other Eastlake table were tilting their heads toward Clara's group. The *Mary Celeste,* about which everyone in the country held an opinion, had unified the conversation beyond her expectations.

"That blood you're referring to turned out to be rust," said Senator Hamlin. "That's what the board of inquiry says."

"Indeed," declared Mr. Eaglesfield. "That's what they *say.*"

"Oh, I'm sure they abandoned ship in a moment of panic," said Mrs. Eaglesfield, giving her husband a conspicuously adoring look, one that told the other guests it was her happy duty to calm the male feelings of her imposing spouse. "There's the theory of the waterspout," she reminded them. "That bit of water in the hull came in in such a great rush, they didn't realize it would end up being just a small pool. They feared they were about to be overwhelmed, and they made too much haste toward the lifeboat. Panic can make people overreact. Or sometimes it can make them fail to react at all." She looked to her right, to the head of the table, and straight into Henry Rathbone's eyes. Within seconds, all the other heads and gazes in the room traveled to the same location. No one said another word; they just waited for him, this recognized expert on panic and inaction, to say something.

The sound of ringing startled them back to their former postures, and their manners. Clara shook the white china dinner bell once more, until the butler came to pull back the ladies' chairs, and the other servants began the clearing of plates. "The gentlemen to the library," she announced as gaily as she could. "And the ladies into the parlor." Mary helped her herd the rustling silk-and-feather-clad women, while the men began climbing the stairs and talking gruffly on some other topic they could pretend they had been talking on all along. Henry went with them, smiling stiffly and saying nothing. His wife watched him, now wishing he *would* go off to Welcker's and get himself away from these rude sensation seekers.

Dear old Mr. Hamlin took her arm and gave it a small squeeze as he passed her on his way to the landing, a sign of solidarity. He had told her years ago that he wished fate had been less cruel to her and Henry; his own escape from that violent night's disruptions had always struck him as an undeserved mercy. After all, Lincoln might have run with him again in '64 instead of Andy Johnson!

Clara gave him a grateful look, then let him catch up with Henry, where he tried to restart that discussion of Yellowstone Park. She excused herself from the ladies, pleading an obligation to check on things in the kitchen, though she actually made her way into the alley, where she stood under the stars for a moment or two, losing her anger, and then gaining it all back when she realized she was looking vaguely northward, toward Tenth and F, where Ford's Theatre still stood, in perpetual mockery of Henry. It had been purchased and remodeled by the government to house, among other things, the adjutant general's office! It now held the pension files of the men who had fought Mr. Lincoln's struggle. To Clara's mind, this was grotesque; why could they not pick another vacant building? Let them tear down that detestable place.

She closed her eyes and smoothed her dress and made herself the same vow she had already made a number of times in the past year or two: to her own list of admitted faults — her stubbornness, her love of admiration, her lack of piety — she must not add self-pity.

She returned to the house and climbed its back stairway to the children's rooms on the third floor. If the boys were already asleep, it would be a small miracle, but she heard nothing from their room. It was from the nursery that she heard soft, soothing sounds. She went to the door and opened it.

"Beautiful dreamer, wake unto me . . ."

"Henry?" she whispered.

He didn't seem to hear her, didn't turn around, just kept singing softly to the infant daughter in his arms, the two of them in a rocker near the window, looking out into the square. She felt her eyes glisten at the sight of her husband stroking the hair of this baby he had named for his wife and mother. What it must be like for him, she thought — though this was more a feeling, a rush of sympathy as strong as what she had felt the morning she came home from Ford's to find him moaning in his bed. For eight years now he had lived with this. Those people downstairs, eating his food and drinking his wine, would never let it be otherwise. How could she get this agony out of him? Might it have failed to root itself if she had gone home with him, instead of staying with Mrs. Lincoln, in those first hours? Why had she been afraid to? Was he failing her now, failing their children, because she had failed him? She had to remember that for all his bad moods and his frequent unkindness, he had done nothing wrong. He was Booth's second-worst victim; he had suffered more even than Mr. Seward, who, once *his* stab wounds had healed, was again whole in his mind. She had to remember that the real Henry was the man in front of her, the man crooning to this little girl he loved, the man who would rather be with her, and his wife, than with the great men of action in the library.

She walked slowly up behind him and touched his shoulder. He wheeled around, his face going white in the moonlight.

"Darling," she whispered, "don't let that awful woman downstairs upset you. We know she's wrong, and that's all that matters."

"Yes," he said, reaching up to take Clara's hand, as the baby slept on. "She *is* wrong. I didn't panic. I was very clear about what I did."

→ 38 ←

SHE DIDN'T WANT to go in and talk to him. He had been in a terrible humor all morning, ever since a letter he wrote nearly a month ago, requesting advice from his old friend Jack Barnes about shares in the Toledo & Wabash Railroad, had been returned by the mailman, crumpled and dirty, despite its having been correctly addressed. The week he wrote it, he'd been angry at the poor performance of Toledo & Wabash; the week before New Year's he'd been angry at Jack Barnes for not bothering to respond; and today, January 16, 1875, he was angry at the United States Post Office.

Clara recognized the Christmas season as a bad time. This one had been especially so. With Aunt Emeline's death last August, Henry seemed more surrounded by Harrises than before. Out in Loudonville he was scampered over by Will's and Amanda's children as well as his own three, who were all now full-throated and fast on their feet. Even Pauline had less attention available for Henry, though she would not in any case have acknowledged his strange new tempers and withdrawals. What wounded Clara, what made her feel lonely and vulnerable during the family frenzy, was Papa's apparent unwillingness to notice these problems. Her own veiled complaints about her husband, her measured confessions of distress — each one made at high cost to her pride — he immediately deflected, as if they were more than an old man who had suffered two strokes could be expected to bear. But she believed that his alarm over what he gleaned from her hints — as well as whispered reports from his other children, and the observations of his own failing eyes — was secretly greater than her own. And what right had she to ask for his worry now? Would he not just remind her of his warnings fifteen years ago? No, he wouldn't. That was not his way, any more than it was hers to doubt that she had done the right thing.

She certainly wasn't going to start fearing her own husband, and so she crossed the hall into the library. He could fume all he liked over his bad investments (if only Toledo & Wabash were the worst of them), and he could rail as he pleased over the vagaries of the U.S. mails, but she wouldn't allow him indifference toward his own children.

"Henry, I want Dr. Carter to look at Riggs." Her sons and daughter were usually healthy, and while she was not a nervous mother, she was determined that nothing was going to happen to them, the true success of her married life.

"You'll condition him to think that it's normal for every sneeze to make a doctor appear, like a genie blown out of a lamp."

"For one thing, genies are *rubbed* out of lamps. You'd know that if you ever bothered to read your children fairy stories. And for another, he hasn't sneezed at all. His ear is hurting him, so badly that he's crying. He'd howl if he weren't afraid to. You'd do well to remember Eleanor."

This mention of Amanda's baby, who'd died two years ago from what started as an ear infection, stumped him, as if Clara had just brought up Eleanor of Aquitaine in connection with her son's ailment. But turning back toward his desk, he said, "Suit yourself. Just don't summon Carter by mail, or Riggs will be dead by the time he gets here."

"Thank you," she said sarcastically, starting for the door.

"Seen the paper?" he called after her.

"No," she said, hesitating.

"It's full of the Beecher spectacle. Your papa's old vanquished senatorial foe, Mr. Evarts, is going to help out with the defense. He'll have quite an audience to play to. 'Three Thousand Persons Seek Entry to Brooklyn Courtroom.'"

"Poor Mary," said Clara, unable to smother a laugh. Her friend's tottering idol, Henry Ward Beecher, was now accused of seducing a parishioner's wife.

"What's she written you about it?" Henry asked.

"Very little."

"Probably disappointed it wasn't herself. I always thought she was jealous of those colored girls — 'Eliza' and 'Sarah' and whatever else they were called — the ones whose freedom he got his congregation to buy." He laughed at the memory of it. "The abolitionists' slave auction!"

"Don't you dare make fun of Mary," said Clara, turning to go, her mild amusement now extinguished.

"Tweddle Hall," said Henry in a tone of quiet reminiscence. "Do you remember that night we heard him, way back in 'fifty-nine?"

"Yes," said Clara, pretending to look for her gloves on the cluttered hall table just past the threshold. She wondered where he was going with this.

"It was the night your papa proposed his grand tour, never knowing I would crash the party."

"Yes, it was," she said, walking away. He rose from his swivel chair and came up behind her shoulders and neck with his arms. "I was at least as good a seducer as Dr. Beecher, wasn't I?" She felt herself getting warm, wanting to turn around and lead him into the bedroom, the one place where their aggressions still, on occasion, transported them to peace.

"Leave me alone," she said.

She hurried down the stairs, put on her coat, and went out of the house to get Dr. Carter, whose consulting room was in Vermont Avenue. The January air struck her full in the face, and she felt tears coming. But she would not give in to them, would not let the ladies of Lafayette Square see them on her face. She didn't care how cold it was; she would compose herself inside the park. Crossing Jackson Place, she entered the nearest gate and looked for a bench. She was distracted by the sight of a girl thinly wrapped in a shawl, a housemaid she vaguely recognized, standing by a Spanish chestnut tree, just west of Andy Jackson, with her eyes closed, intently whispering as if in prayer. She *was* in prayer, Clara realized: this must be the "wishing tree" her own housemaids sometimes talked about. Her foot cracked a dry twig, and the girl, realizing she was being watched by one of the neighbors, opened her eyes and took off, as if the tree's magical bark were like the bread in all the pantries on the square, the rightful property of the house owners. Clara felt embarrassed for both of them, but when the girl was gone she touched the tree herself and looked over at the late Senator Sumner's house. "How is the colonel?" was the question he used to ask whenever she went to one of his evenings. These days any such inquiry would bring a hush to the room, as everyone waited for Mrs. Rathbone to give what they knew would be only a polite, correct answer, but which still interested them, charged as it was with the electricity of her odd, absent husband.

She hadn't given a party of her own in months, and wondered if she'd been imagining things the last time she had, when the stack of regrets seemed a little higher than the time before, elevated, she thought, by the growing reluctance of the neighborhood ladies to go to the house of this man who was evidently peculiar, spending the days inside poring over his investments and history books, and now, it was said, his "writings." Of the latter Clara could tell them no more than they had heard rumored; whatever historical tract he was laboring at, Henry never offered to show.

Was it too late for him to do something real? She had just passed forty, and he wouldn't reach that age for another two years. She touched the ordinary-looking chestnut tree, this apparently magical growth at the center of all the vast nation's power, and silently made a wish, not for a new prince but for a *job*, something that might still take her husband out of himself, if not away from her.

⇥ 39 ⇤

JUDGE HARRIS suffered his third and final stroke at home, late in November of 1875, while sitting at his desk cracking walnuts and writing a testimonial to the character of an Albany Law student. He was seized all at once, violently; a walnut slid, uncracked, across his desk and onto the carpet, and a moment later the judge fell down beside it. Pauline used the telegraph to draw his children home to Loudonville, addressing the Washington wire to Clara, treating the judge, as always, like a circumstance only incidental to Henry. Still, it was assumed that whatever turn the judge's condition took, Henry, lacking any business of his own, would stay in Loudonville with Clara and the three children through Christmas.

On Thursday evening, December 2, Ira Harris's life was nearing its close. Pauline, tired from her vigil, went to bed after dinner. Little Clara and Gerald were left to play with the kitchen maid, and Henry took charge of Riggs. On their way out of the house to walk in the orchard, father and son passed Clara, who was about to join Will at the judge's bed, which had been made up in the study where he was stricken.

"Where are you taking him?" she asked Henry. "He's not dressed warmly enough to go out."

Riggs kept his eyes on the hall carpet.

"For a short walk," said Henry. "I'm going to explain death to him."

Oh, this would be a wonderful speech for a five-year-old, she was certain. A piece of ill-informed grandiloquence designed to convince a shivering boy that what was happening to his beloved grandfather was all connected to the bloody harvests of men from Thermopylae to Fredericksburg.

"Don't keep him out there long" was all she said, moving past them, brushing Riggs with her skirts and a quick caress.

As she entered the study, Will nodded rapidly to her, to indicate that the end was approaching. The judge's breathing was loud and spasmodic. Unable to move or talk, he still had the disconcerting use of one eye, which he had half open, appearing to take a last inventory of his possessions. His vision traveled to a piece of mission art that Jared had sent from California; to the letter knife his old partner, Julius Rhoades, gave him when he was elected to the assembly; to the tin tray with the painted apples, on which he had stacked letters for the last thirty years. Now he remembered the piles of them that arrived after Louisa's death, and wondered who in the house would answer the ones arriving after his own, which he knew was at hand. He moved his eye in Clara's direction and struggled to make a sound.

She leaned over and said he mustn't strain, as she pondered the cruelty of this speechlessness that had settled upon her father after a lifetime of words, too many to be sure, but sincere as they were prolix, all of them uttered in the comforting baritone she knew she would never again hear. If only men might devise some way of preserving sound, so their voices might be kept with photographs and engravings, not just sent out from the body to die upon the air. She stroked her father's cold, immobile hands and listened, in her mind, to the flourishes of his voice as she had heard them in the Senate gallery during the debate on Senator Bright — "Oh, how it must satisfy the rebels to know that as they assault our lives and property, we may be counted upon, ourselves, to destroy the honor of the finest among us" — or as they took their stately annual wing, like returning birds, over Union College commencements. How many times had she heard him send boys "into the sunlight, to find their lives and serve their Lord." These were the words she tried to hear now, not the paternal flummery of the last few years. "Henry is a fine man," he would tell her, in panicked reassurance, on those occasions when she allowed her fright to spill over the proud fortress of denial in which she had come to live.

"Papa, don't try to speak," she said, smoothing his white hair, which lay on the pillow, still thick but now in an unfamiliar tangle.

As the evening wore on, the judge's breathing became ever more raspy. The movements of his left eye, random now, un-nerved Will into occasional bursts of declamatory conversation, which his father was beyond comprehending. "There's been a letter inquiring after your condition from President Raymond down at Vassar, Papa, and Governor Tilden sent his personal representative to convey his best wishes." During these loud speeches Clara would touch her brother's arm, signaling their futility. As the hours passed, she thought of little stories she might have told her father and offered them to Will. "A day or two before we came up here, I was out walking in the square with Riggs, and he pointed to the Mansion and asked me, 'Do all of General Grant's soldiers live there with him?'" Will said, "That's Henry's doing," and Clara replied, "Yes, he's already filling him full of the war."

A few moments after this, a spasm seized the judge's face and turned it toward the right side of his pillow.

"He's gone," said Clara to Henry an hour later, after telling Pauline the news. She got into bed.

In the dark, in his own bed on the other side of the room, Henry lay with his eyes open and struggled with himself, trying, from a sense of form and a weak flicker of tenderness, to find something to say. But nothing came to him. Clara knew he was hardly thinking of Papa at all. He was putting his memories through their nightly mill grind. Perhaps Petersburg, maybe Ford's, or the money he'd lost in the '73 panic — she didn't know what-all. But his agitation cast a charge across the room, like a spark coming off the counterpane.

Her instinct was to shield herself, and her father's spirit, from the electricity she could feel dancing over her husband's silhou-ette. As if to repel it, she spoke the first bromide that came to mind: "There was nothing that could have been done. Not since Friday morning, Dr. Crane said."

"I've taken care of Riggs," said Henry, he too using words as a repellent, this time against that detestable phrase — *nothing that could have been done* — which he'd heard spoken and whispered, as a question, to his face and behind his back, for the past ten years.

"What do you mean, 'taken care of Riggs'?" asked Clara. "You didn't know Father was dead yourself until this moment."

"I mean I've instructed Riggs in the general idea of death. He'll now find understanding this particular instance of it easy enough."

Even a year ago, she would have snapped back, said something like, "Ah yes, Union College, Mental and Moral Philosophy. It was the *second* part of the lectures you were fined for not attending, am I right?"

As it was, tired and unsure of herself in the dark, and aware of being in new waters, stripped of even the flimsy protection of her father's love, all she replied was, "I'll see to Gerald and little Clara myself."

The next morning Henry rose before everyone but the kitchen girl. When Clara came down she found him in the dining room reading the newspaper. "There's nothing in the *Argus*," he informed her, "but Dr. Crane has gotten the word round. A memorial photographer was here to ask if we wanted a picture of your father's corpse. I told him no. I've taken the liberty of opening up his letters. I know the one on top will interest you."

Springfield, Ill.

My dear friend Judge Harris,

It is with the greatest sorrow, that I learn through the papers, of your very severe illness. Dearly, did my noble husband & myself, love you & my deeply afflicted heart goes out to you in my prayers, for your speedy recovery.

Please present my warmest love to your wife & family, and accept for yourself, dear & honored friend, my sincerest love.

Most affectionately yours,
Mary Lincoln

"From Springfield," said Henry. "I was unaware that they'd unlocked the asylum in Batavia and let the widder-woman out. 'Ow, yes, Mister Ratboon,'" he continued in the Irish accent of the servant girl, "'the dair thing's been allowed 'oom since September.'"

Clara put the letter into the pocket of her dress and reached for the next one on the pile.

❧ 40 ❧

Paris
20 November 1876

I see I've even begun to write my dates like a European — that's how long and often we've been over here. The children, bundled onto train after train, week after week in country after country, look up at me perplexed when their ears realize it's a different unintelligible language they're now hearing. Henry promises to get us home by January, in time for the season, but it won't make up for all I've missed this year, especially the election (the result is even now in doubt). To read Uncle Hamilton's accounts of warring Stalwarts, Half-Breeds and Carpetbaggers, you would think he was writing from the Dakota Territory instead of his desk in the state legislature.

I am sick unto death of Europe, heartily and forever sick of holding the chain of my children's hands as we rush for the next ferry or coach or streetcar. There are mornings when I would rather drown them all like kittens than get them ready for another day of touring. I would also rather go out my own front door and look ten times a day at Washington's silly monument, still unfinished, than have one more glance at a perfect Saint-Cloud. I want to hear Riggs sliding his bare feet across the linoleum in the kitchen; here he's squeezed into little leather shoes that go clicking across the marble corridors of whatever museum is in Henry's plan for the day. We have missed the Philadelphia Exhibition, which Amanda and Tom say they went twice from Ohio to see: we read their accounts of machines that "type" and ones that sew after we've spent hours looking at glass-encased crossbows. But it isn't only novelty and sleekness I crave; it's also the familiar shabbiness of home — the Negroes and the mud, the very stench upon the District's summer air.

*Henry and I had a great discussion (I mean, of course, a fero-
cious fight) last night. I think we have a compromise, though what
he chooses to remember of it will no doubt change by Christmas. I
told him I would not come over here again without a fixed abode
and the chance for my children to spend time, much of it and
regularly, with their own countrymen; and since the best way to
achieve such an end would be a diplomatic posting, I have declared
that that is what we must seek for Henry once we get home. I am
beyond being fed up with his investing and scribbling, and am
determined that my sons shall observe their father in some posture
other than angry idleness.*

*I have, for what it's worth, his word. Perhaps he will keep it;
perhaps he finds appeal in the idea of being some chargé who gets
to tyrannize baffled American travelers and would-be emigrants.
Either way, I told him it is the only circumstance that will get me
once more across the ocean.*

*How difficult will it be to find such a position? (I have no doubt
that the finding of it will be left to me.) The Harris family's political
connections are not what they used to be, but I think I have made
enough friends of my own to do the trick, assuming the State Department proves to be President Hayes's and not President Tilden's. If the
Republicans remain, I will talk to Hal Tomkins about the possibilities. I already suspect — to my shame — that what will motivate
him on my behalf is pity.*

Rutherford B. Hayes — "His Fraudulency" to Henry Rathbone
and millions of others — was sworn in on March 5, 1877, after
the Electoral Commission declared he'd won the presidential
election with fewer popular votes than Governor Tilden had
received. "Mr. Evarts's silver tongue serves some peculiar causes,"
said Henry. "But he does seem to get his way." The man Thurlow Weed had had to ditch for Ira Harris back in '61 won the
day for the Republicans with his argument before the commission, just as two years ago his speech to a Brooklyn jury had
saved Henry Ward Beecher from conviction. There had been
jokes in '75 about how he might expect eternal salvation as his

fee, but there was nothing speculative about the reward this time: William Evarts was the new secretary of state.

The atmosphere in Washington had been made so tense by the election dispute that there was no inaugural ball, just a reception at Willard's to which Clara could not secure an invitation — a circumstance that left her feeling apprehensive about the campaign for office she was ready to begin. But her spirits lifted within a week of the swearing-in, when Hal Tomkins, her versifying friend at State, returned one afternoon to his widowed mother's house in J Street, which Clara had taken to visiting each day, and told her there was an opening that just might suit Henry: chargé d'affaires in Copenhagen.

Clara thought back ten years, to her honeymoon, to the two of them reading in the late summer light at Tivoli, and to two other visits they had made to the city during their endless European treks, before she replied, "I think Denmark will suit my lord Hamlet very well."

She began her work that night, telling Lillian, the children's nurse, that she would be unable to read them a story. She went into the sewing room, at the back of the house, taking with her a bottle of the brightest blue ink she had: the letters needed a feminine appeal, a sort of exuberant helplessness that would make their male recipients eager to assist. The tiny room had a strong lamp, and though the March wind came through the poorly sashed window, within a few minutes of starting, Clara had so warmed to her task that she scarcely noticed the temperature. Within an hour she had drafted a half-dozen witty, imploring letters to everyone from Uncle Hamilton and Bishop Doane in Albany to General Schofield at West Point and Governor Hartranft in Pennsylvania. She made a list of the names on the back of an envelope containing one of Mary Hall's letters (could Mary enlist the mayor of New York? Her father had been a friend of his) and vowed to add another dozen to it by March 20. Before she was finished, she would pull out more stops than Papa had for any postmaster or customhouse controller.

Two weeks later she spent every afternoon in Mrs. Tomkins's parlor, sympathizing with the old lady's neuralgia and joining in criticism of her married sons, none of them attentive like her darling Hal. Like many other young Washington men, the skinny, sparsely mustached Hal Tomkins showed a tendency to crush upon the beautiful Mrs. Rathbone — so clever, so teasing, so self-assured, and yet, surely, somewhere inside, so sad? — and each day, when he came home just before five, out of the sight of his mother, he showed Clara the testimonials that had begun to arrive on the Department of State's mahogany desktops.

The first round were from the Harris family, whose enthusiasm for Clara's undertaking had already been expressed in notes addressed solely to Mrs. Henry Rathbone at her home address. The letters they wrote to State were more professional in tone, but they beat the drum unflaggingly. From Columbus, Amanda's husband Tom Miller noted that he would also be appealing directly to the President, a fellow Buckeye, on behalf of this model brother-in-law, "a gentleman of high culture and stainless character, a good soldier, a staunch Republican always reliable and of prepossessing manners." He was about half right, Clara thought, grateful that Henry still put money into Republican coffers in Albany and New York, if only to help his investments. There was no need, she thought, for the Buckeye in the White House to know that the subject of these letters of tribute had not actually voted in the past two presidential elections, not when Tom Miller went on to say that "he adds to a kind heart and amiable address an excellent collegiate education and knowledge of the French." Well, maybe Henry would now be thankful to old Union, and perhaps she could count those European hours, when he strained to converse with potted old veterans at the Invalides, to have been not entirely wasted.

"He is a warm friend of mine," wrote Uncle Hamilton, who was still giving him the benefit of the doubt, twenty years after he'd extended it at his law office. "And Mrs. R. is my niece. Hence I have a personal interest in his procuring such a position. Aside from that, however, I believe his appointment would be highly reputable and strengthening." Strengthening? The word seemed to betray an awareness of Henry's unhealthy situation, or her own. So much of what was written seemed telltale, to have a text beneath it in invisible ink, a hidden charge ready to backfire as soon as the phrase was properly decoded. When letters from the generals began arriving, she wondered, for instance, if Schofield's, saying "Col. Rathbone is too well known in Washington to need any endorsement from me," might be taken as evidence of notoriety instead of approbation. No, surely what counted was the general's declaration that Henry was "precisely the character of man whom those Americans who are jealous of their country's good name would most desire to meet abroad as the representatives of the intelligence and refinement of their countrymen." And yes, General Sherman might be stretching things — bless him — in saying, "I have known him since the war intimately," but what counted was the fact — it *was* a fact, she decided — that Henry would "worthily represent the better elements of American character abroad."

Walking home on these first afternoons of spring, looking at the crocuses already up in the park, she rehearsed favorite passages from the letters swinging inside her reticule, and tried to imagine a life in Copenhagen. They would be respected, enviable, with Henry made social and useful, not to mention grateful for the part she would have played in the transformation. Hadn't Bishop Doane written that the colonel's wife "is a most charming lady, and while the interests of the Government would be more left in his hands, the best social and personal traits of a people will be represented in Mr. *& Mrs.* Rathbone"?

Each afternoon her fantasy held until the time she would mount the stairs to the second floor of the house and pass her husband, who had fallen asleep over a book and a tumbler of whiskey in his library, the vein on the left side of his head, like an extension of the scar on his arm, throbbing angrily through his unquiet nap. She would hear Lillian through closed doors, warning the children — who instantly heeded the warning — that they mustn't disturb their father; and it was then that Clara admitted to herself the real reason she'd asked Hal Tomkins for copies of the incoming testimonials. It was not to keep track of the progress of her campaign; it was for the flickering illusion that the man discussed in them was the *real* Colonel Rathbone, the true adult aspect of the boy she had fallen in love with thirty years ago. As the weeks went by, she stored the letters not in the top drawer of her writing desk, but in the wicker box at the bottom of her closet, the one that contained such ancient treasures as letters from Howard, handkerchiefs her real mother had embroidered, and a small wooden decoy that she and Will had carved for a birdhouse in Loudonville.

After two months, she finally summoned the courage to ask Hal if he didn't think there should be some hint of a response by now, and in the nervous blink of his eyes, before he could even mumble about the slow pace of things at State, she realized the truth. Secretary Evarts wasn't trying to balance the surface endorsements against the subliminal hints of trouble, wasn't attempting to square Henry's war record with the whispers of failure and unreliability that had trailed him in the years since. No, it was all too painfully obvious, as it should have been from the start. Evarts was simply ignoring them, for why should he take any trouble to think about doing a favor for Ira Harris's son-in-law — or was it his son? — sixteen years after the judge and the Dictator had cheated him out of the Senate seat that should have been his to occupy all through the war, with real purpose and distinction, not just as a lock in the canal of patronage. Hal needn't have troubled to write out copies of the letters; for all the attention they were getting, he might as well have given her the originals. She thought back to that afternoon in '61 when Mr. Weed came huffing and puffing up Eagle Street ahead of the newspapermen, and Pauline sat in her parlor like Queen Victoria, and Uncle Hamilton nearly wept at the news of his brother's elevation. She was the only one to have seen it as trouble, the sudden undertow that would sweep them all too far out, as it had. But even she could not have foreseen such petty little ripples as this, sixteen years later, spraying her like cold rain.

In June she read in Miss Snead's column that the Copenhagen post was about to be filled. In a fit of embarrassment, Hal told her it looked as if it would go to someone owed a favor for "particularly important services" rendered during the election dispute last fall. Two weeks after that, they were off to Loudon-ville for a summer so isolated they didn't travel the plank road to Albany more than half a dozen times. She and Henry went for weeks without speaking of what had happened. Pauline said something about the job's having been beneath Henry's abilities. Clara herself brushed off commiseration from Uncle Hamilton and Mary Hall with a resigned smile and knowing jokes about "politics."

But she was not resigned. The episode had left her not just angry at Evarts, but frightened. She could see the next decades before her, stretching past the turn of the century: the children would be grown and gone, and she and Henry would still be traipsing through Europe, floating from country to country like the shades of Paolo and Francesca, lighting for a few months each year back on Jackson Place, where they would gradually stop being called upon and, finally, cease being invited.

She would not accept Mr. Evarts's refusal. She would mount a second campaign, not for the Copenhagen post but for any in Europe. She would dare the secretary to insist there wasn't a consulate on the entire Continent that could use the services of the kind of man whom all the letters described. She solicited another round of them, and this time Tom Miller sent a copy of the letter he'd mailed to his old "friendly acquaintance," President Hayes. She felt no embarrassment at its urgency: "It is with great diffidence that I once more appeal to you in behalf of Col. Rathbone . . . I only beg as an especial favor, for which I must be ever loyally grateful, that you will give the matter your *personal* attention . . . If you think of it, my wife, who truly loves the Chief Lady of our land, desires to be remembered to her — Mrs. Miller seriously thought of coming to you to make personal application for her brother, but her courage was not as strong as her sisterly solicitude." Well, *brava,* Amanda, for even considering it. Clara found the contemplated gesture no more extreme than a recent one of her own: asking General Burnside to send a copy of Henry's military record to Evarts (as if he needed another one) with a personal note attached.

This, of course, she had not told Henry; knowing she'd asked the overseer of the battle of the Crater to come to his aid would be more than his temper could abide. But otherwise he had been willing, even eager, this time around, to hear of every new development and stratagem. She had come across the draft of a letter he had himself written to Jack Barnes, to accompany the gift of two expensive books of naval history. It announced: "I intend going into action the last of this week and hope that you will find yourself able to help me in the way you indicated." His rejection, she realized, had shocked some part of him, not the one accustomed to feeling himself the target of whispering conspiracies, but the old proud part that couldn't help expecting Evarts or any other man to anoint him to the post, once he'd condescended to permit his wife and friends to advertise his availability. It was this portion of him that had now been jolted into competitiveness, and Clara welcomed its assertion. She only wondered how long he would be able to sustain and modulate it before it exploded into pique or was extinguished by the stronger tendency toward righteous withdrawal. He had been shocked back to his senses, but she knew how easily he could be shocked back out of them. She'd been reading Riggs *A Pilgrim's Progress* and *Alice's Adventures in Wonderland,* and wondering if her son's effortless entrance into these bedtime allegories came from his being already so used to his father's moods, where what was good and what was bad turned into each other as fast as Riggs could make a ball come bouncing back from the wall. What she had to do was keep at bay the taste for aggrievement until her second effort had a chance to succeed.

She would do anything. One noontime in the middle of November she was on the verge of going over to see President Hayes, when she looked through her bedroom window at the front of the house and noticed one of the most handsome men she'd ever seen. He was strolling up Jackson Place, heading into the park through the gate she entered whenever she went to talk to the wishing tree. What could this young man possibly have to wish for? He was tall and slim, though broad-shouldered, with fine wavy hair and a face so cleanly beautiful she could almost smell the soap on it. She closed her eyes and folded her arms in front of her, pressing them against her waist, which Henry had not circled with his own arms for more than a month. She took a deep breath and, with her eyes still closed, imagined what it would be like actually to smell this glorious young man's cheek, to put her hand into his wavy hair and take a strand of it in her mouth.

When she opened her eyes and quietly raised the window for a better look, she noticed two old ladies passing in front of the Parker house and whispering to each other. One of them, with the gloved hand not covering her mouth, now pointed to the young man. Well, Clara thought, if these two, old enough to be his grandmother, find him an Adonis, she could scarcely, being only old enough to be his mother, feel ashamed herself. But when she saw the second lady squinting and finally nodding, she realized it was not the young man's beauty, but his celebrity, that was causing their discreet excitement. Suddenly she too knew who it was: the smooth, stunning face belonged to Webb Hayes, son of the massively bearded President. She had read and heard all about him, even though, like alcohol, she had yet to be invited into his mother's White House. He was just out of Cornell, a footballer, serving as his father's private secretary. In the months after the disputed election he had functioned as his bodyguard: even in Europe she and Henry had heard the rumor about a bullet being fired through the Hayes's Ohio dining room window.

Fully awake from her romantic daydream, she raced to open the bedroom door. "Riggs!" she called, not caring if she disturbed his father. "Get your ball right now. And meet me just inside the front door. Lillian, put his coat on him. Right away!" She combed her hair as she ran down to the first floor. At the mirror in the hall she checked her face before rummaging the clothes tree for a shawl with a bit more color than the one she had on. At the same time she rummaged for facts: he had a sister, Fanny, about ten, and a much younger brother — Sam? Scott? — not much more than five or six, who had a — pony? well, at least a mockingbird. "Riggs! Lillian! Hurry!"

The nurse rushed the boy from the kitchen into the hall,

buttoning his jacket as she pulled him along. He looked up at his mother with a confused expression, holding his biggest red ball out toward her, wondering why it was so important for them to go out and play with it right now. She licked her fingers and wiped a smudge from his face, and together they dashed through the vestibule, stepping on the letters that had just come through the mail slot. But before they went down the front steps, she knelt and whispered to him, "We're going to go into the park and play a game. When I signal to you, pretend to throw the ball to me, but I really want you to hit the back of the man I'll be standing next to. Can you do that?" Riggs, looking very grave, nodded to indicate that he thought he could.

They reached the park in no more than a minute.

"Oh, I'm sorry!" cried Clara as soon as her son had carried out her instructions.

Webb Hayes turned around and flashed his white teeth. "That's all right," he said with a laugh, scooping up the ball in a single elegant movement. He tossed it back and asked the boy, "What's your name?"

"Henry Riggs Rathbone."

"We call him Riggs," said Clara.

"Like the bank," said Riggs.

The President's son laughed again and extended his hand to the boy. "I've got one of those last-name first names, too. Mine's Webb. It was my mother's name before she married my father."

The boy seemed to have no idea this was the President's son, but instead of enlightening him, the beautiful young man turned to Clara and said, "I am Webb Hayes. I take it you are Colonel Rathbone's wife."

"Yes," said Clara, nervous about what part of Henry's reputation had preceded her into the park. "Do you walk here often? I've not seen you before."

"Only once in a while. My father usually keeps me at work during lunchtime. He dictates letters between bites of his chop. There was a change of plans today. He's over at the British legation having a proper meal, and since I wasn't invited, I decided to stretch my legs. I didn't know I'd have a ball game into the bargain. Come on, Riggs, throw!" He faded back and extended a long arm into the air. Riggs's throw came nowhere near it, but Hayes still managed to catch it with one hand.

"You should be entertaining your own little brother instead of being so kind to my boy."

"Oh, fat little Scottie is probably riding around on his velocipede. I just bore him."

"Does he ride it in the Mansion?" Clara asked, remembering the way Tad Lincoln used to drive his goat through the hallways.

"No," said Webb Hayes, jumping to net one of Riggs's throws. "His mother can be quite strict."

"I remember that Mrs. Lincoln —" she began, but there was a sudden loud shout from across Jackson Place. It seemed to Clara that the ball froze in midair.

"Riggs!" cried Henry's distant voice. "Come back here right now. And bring your mother."

Riggs rushed after the ball, and as soon as he had it began tugging at his mother's skirt. She tried to stall him, to get just a few more words in, dreading all the while that Henry would shout something else or, even worse, come over to the park.

"You saw some terrible things with her," said Webb Hayes, calmly getting back to the subject of Mrs. Lincoln.

"Yes," said Clara. "But they were in the service of our country." She hated the pomposity, the idiocy, of what she'd just said, but she was determined to press on with it. "Since then, my husband and I have spent much of our time abroad. As a matter of fact, he is now seeking a diplomatic position." She looked pleadingly into Webb Hayes's eyes, blue as two huge cornflowers, before saying, "Excuse me. I should be going. My husband needs me."

"Riggs," called Webb Hayes to the boy, who was already running back to the house. "Come to my house with your mother some morning around ten. It's over there." He pointed to the White House. Clara saw her son's eyes pop as he realized this man lived where General Grant and all his soldiers used to. She laughed for joy. "Thank you, Mr. Hayes."

"We'll see what we can do."

"Come on, Riggs," said Clara, gaily catching up with her son, hurrying him out of the park as she waved goodbye to Webb Hayes. "I'll race you to the house!" She and Riggs darted across Jackson Place, bumping into the old Negro vegetable man. Running up the steps, Riggs shouted, "I won!" and banged the knocker to signify his victory. But the door was already open. Henry was standing just inside, holding the letters he'd picked up from the tiles.

"I have something to tell you," said Clara.

"Go upstairs," he said sharply to Riggs. The boy did as he was told.

"Henry, listen to me," said Clara as she took off her shawl. She hung it on the clothes tree, over the brown one she'd rejected five minutes before, and then turned around to deliver her good news. Her face was met by the full force of Henry's open hand. She fell backward into the little space between the stairway and the parlor wall, scraping her head against the portrait of the two of them that William Merritt Chase had done, and which even now she was aware of hating for the way the artist had put them in different chairs, as if they were watching the play, as if he wanted to fix them in their famous moment for all time.

"Don't you ever," Henry said, coming closer. "Don't you *ever*," he said again, looking down at her, his eyes devoid of all the normal ambition she'd seen in them this morning. "Don't you *ever* conduct one of your disgusting flirtations in front of my son."

Before she could rise from the floor, he had thrown down the clothes tree and left the house.

⇢ 41 ⇠

"HE'S HUGE," said young Henry Riggs Rathbone.

"*I* could ride him," said his even younger brother, Gerald, who squeezed between Riggs and their Uncle Jared to look at the tintype of Electioneer, the prize sire on Mr. Leland Stanford's Palo Alto stock farm.

"You could not!" cried Riggs, cuffing the younger child away from the breakfast table, on which their uncle had laid various emblems of his life in California.

"Boys," said their mother gently as she braided their little sister's hair. Jared looked at the girl and her mother and smiled. "I remember watching you do that twenty years ago, for Lina."

"Yes," said Clara, smiling as she tied the last of the ribbons. "I would have expected to be done with this by now. But here I am, a forty-three-year-old woman with a five-year-old daughter."

"Well," said her brother-in-law. "The war kept you from getting an early start."

"Yes," said Clara. "The war." She said no more about it, just gave a final smoothing to her daughter's honey-colored hair and picked up the novel Jared had brought her as a present.

"Thank you again for this."

"I thought you could appreciate it better than most."

"You're right," she said, flipping through the pages of *The American,* by Henry James. "Though I could do with a bit less Europe."

"Then maybe it's good this Copenhagen post never came through?"

"No, it was a terrible defeat. For him, and for all of us. Really,

Jared, I shouldn't mind our being abroad under those circumstances. As it is, I'm sure Henry will have us back in vagabondage before another year goes by."

"Why not come west? Visit Maria and me in California. Bring all the children. She'd love to fill the house with them. It appears we can't have any of our own, but she dotes on all the ones that come near her."

"Does she still paint?" asked Clara, not responding to the question of a visit, moving away from the subject as if it were a self-evident impossibility. The maid began to clear the table, and Clara told the boys they could take the turquoise buckles with them if they went into the parlor and agreed to play quietly.

"Yes, she paints flowers mostly," said Jared Rathbone. "Great blazing western ones you wouldn't believe. They're everywhere on the ranch, unlike anything you've seen. If they popped up in the Harris yard in Loudonville, you'd scream in horror."

She laughed. "Tell me more about what you do for Stanford. The children were all over you as soon as you came in last night. I hardly heard a word."

"We're raising trotters now," he began, happy for the chance to expound on the work he loved. "What we've got at Palo Alto, Clara, isn't just a stud farm. It's a sort of college for horses. Well, at least that's what Maria calls it." He laughed at his own grandiosity. "We train them according to the latest scientific methods. Look," he said, hunting for a photograph amidst the pile the boys had disarranged. "Here, this one."

Clara stared at it, perplexed. "It looks like a cake that the mice have gotten to."

"No, look closer. It's a rubber floor covered with flour. The depressions are the ponies' hoofprints. We study the pictures to see exactly how they move."

She pushed the photograph back to him and smiled. "I don't think even Dr. Nott could have imagined this."

Jared laughed. "Eliphalet Nott! I haven't heard that name in years."

"Nor I," said Clara, thinking of her father.

"Well," said Jared, "Dr. Nott was all for the future, and so am I. Clara, you should think about coming west. All of you."

"Do we live too much in the past?" she asked.

"I fear that you do."

She looked at her brother-in-law, a smaller, softer version of Henry, still in possession of all his red hair.

"I'm afraid there's no escaping it, Jared."

"Isn't there?"

She shrugged, managing a wan smile as she straightened the photographs and little presents he had carried all the way from San Francisco. She didn't want to tell him her troubles, but she was glad he was here. After all these years, she was feeling guilty about the scant attention she and the rest of the household had paid him when the Harrises and Rathbones were united. Will and Henry were the stars by which the girls had steered their way toward womanhood, while Ira and Pauline had both been too fixed on their firstborns to be much occupied by Jared.

She tried to change the subject. "It's wonderful of Maria to let you make the journey. I only wish she'd felt up to coming with you. It still seems a —"

The doorbell rang.

"Boys!" she shouted, hearing them run for it. "Don't answer it!" She got up to make sure they didn't. "Excuse me, Jared. I'll be back in a minute. They don't understand. It's Thursday the thirteenth. Betty! Where are you?" She hurried into the hall, nearly colliding with the parlor maid.

"It's only the mailman, Mama," Riggs told the two of them. "He says there's postage due."

"Oh, is that all?" asked Clara. "Betty, can you pay him what's owed?"

She came back to her guest in the kitchen. "I never have a cent on me," she explained to Jared with an embarrassed laugh. "Thank you, Betty," she told the maid, who put the letters on the kitchen table. "I'll pay you later. Or you can get the boys to give you the penny from their banks." She turned back to Jared. "With all the children and commotion, I can't keep anything straight."

"Not even the date," said Jared, smiling. "It's Saturday, not Thursday."

"Oh, 'Thursday the thirteenth' is just an expression of mine.

{ 279 }

The day before April fourteenth is always, to my mind, a Thursday, and usually unlucky, since it brings the newspaper reporters around. They do anniversary stories. I was afraid it was one of them at the door. They come and ask questions, stupid ones that upset Henry. It won't be so bad this year, but three years ago, on the tenth anniversary, it was constant. And goodness knows what 1885 will bring. When that year gets here, I intend to shut myself up in a box for the entire month of April."

"Exactly what questions do they ask?"

"Oh, from me they only want some little story of Mr. Lincoln's kindliness, or some lie about what last wise words he spoke in the darkness of the theatre. I just close the door as politely as I can."

"That doesn't sound so bad."

"It isn't. It's what they ask Henry, if they catch him instead. They've even lain in wait for him on the sidewalk. 'Good afternoon, Major Rathbone. Could you tell us what you're thinking today? What do you think President Lincoln might be doing if he were still alive? Do you ever think about how different the country might be if you had been able to stop Booth?' He will always be 'Major' Rathbone."

"What does he say to them?"

"He gives them odd answers about history, ones that confuse them and which they end up not printing. But every year, if we're not in Europe when the date comes around, they're back for more."

Jared said nothing, and Clara began to examine the letters. "There's one here from Louise, which will make the children laugh. She writes the same thing from Loudonville every other day, all about how the custard's just gone into the oven now that the chicken has come out, and how she wishes Pauline had more of an appetite. I don't think it's yet occurred to her that your mother is going to outlive us all. Here's one from Will."

"I'd be ashamed to tell you how long it's been since I've been in touch with either him or Louise," said Jared.

"There's nothing to feel guilty about. You've made a fine life in a truly new world, and I know they are only pleased for you."

She paused for a moment. "The Harris and Rathbone blood never really mixed, except in little Lina."

"And in your own children, of course," said Jared.

"That's true," said Clara, shaking the crumbs from Riggs's and Gerald's napkins.

"How is Will?"

"He's very well," said Clara. "Still making steam shovels and raising his boys. His and Emma's letter is bound to have a bit more news than Louise's. They're usually adding a room or buying another horse."

"Then it sounds as if he could afford the right amount of postage!" Jared joked.

"No," said Clara, "the penny was due on this one." She handed him a letter postmarked Virginia City, Nevada. "I don't know who Eller Browning is."

"I do," said Jared with some surprise. "He was in the Twelfth. I knew him slightly, Henry somewhat better. I think he stayed on after both of us had left the army." He turned the letter over in his hand. "I'll take this upstairs to Henry. I didn't find much to break the ice with, when I got in last night. Maybe this will help."

"He'll be up in the library."

Jared climbed the stairs to the second floor, passing the brass sconces, which were missing a candle here and there and in need of some polish. He'd been surprised yesterday evening when he'd arrived on the dot at the station and found no family carriage to meet him, just a ragged old driver whose hack had been hired off the street and sent to fetch him at the last minute. He had no clear idea of how Henry spent his money, or how much of it he had left. In what state of dishevelment, Jared wondered, did he spend his mornings? How did his brother occupy himself?

In fact, Henry was sitting straight-backed at his desk. His grooming was as rigid as his posture, his whiskers precisely shaped above a starched white collar and a tightly knotted cravat. His newspaper lay folded at the edge of his desk, and he sat before a half-filled sheet of paper, his pen poised a few inches above it, awaiting his next thought.

He calmly greeted his younger brother.

"Jared, come in," he said, getting up to take his hand. "I'm sorry we didn't have much chance to talk last night. I was so tired, though I'm sure not as tired as you were after the last leg of the trip. I hope it wasn't rude of me."

"Not at all, brother," said Jared, sitting down on a chesterfield sofa across from the desk. "I was hoping to see you at breakfast this morning."

"I'm afraid I never eat with the children. The noise makes me nervous."

"I can understand that," said Jared. "It took a bit of time for me to get used to the sound myself. But I envy your having them. I'm afraid I may have to content myself with being an uncle." He looked to Henry, expecting some words of inquiry or sympathy, but his brother regarded him with a thin, bland smile. Jared couldn't be sure what he'd said had really registered. "I brought you up a letter," he went on. "Eller Browning. Does that name ring a bell?"

"Oh, yes," said Henry, reaching across the desk to take the envelope. "He writes me once or twice a year. He's still with the Twelfth. A good man, rough old bachelor. Got badly hurt at Fredericksburg." He slit open the letter. Jared was relieved that there would be something to talk about now.

Henry read silently for a moment, lifting an eyebrow and frowning, more alive to Eller Browning's presence than that of Jared directly across from him. At last, *in medias res,* he began reading aloud:

The railroad ruined us as a civilization, I always thought, and you can be damned sure it was the horse ruined these Nez Percés — turned them from fishers into hunters, and then into warriors — this tribe so accommodating to us white brutes that they once *asked* us to send some Christian missionaries out their way! I never heard of any group so friendly to our coming in. Someone should have told them to beware, for sure enough our lust for gold has done them in. That's what started this war — *our* pushing *them* around — and don't you let the papers or any friends you still have in Adjutant's office tell you any different. Last June we were ordered up to San Francisco from Fort Yuma. Spur of the moment, underfinanced as usual, barely enough money to hire the red scouts we needed to lead us from S.F. into Montana. But we got there, and we were told to wait in the valley of the Big Hole until they needed us. And, sure enough, the time came when Gibbon did: after he'd roared into their camp one night and cracked their sleeping skulls and killed half their babies. He didn't figure on the counterattack their braves were able to mount, and that's when we had to go help him. When we rode into the Indians' camp, I was more sickened by the sight than by anything I've laid eyes on in forty years of life, including those long-ago four when we were sometimes together. You would be ashamed of your old regiment. General Howard even let his savages, those expensive Bannock scouts, dig up the Nez dead and mutilate the corpses, after which we pursued the living ones into Yellowstone. One night they raided us, and when I found myself wishing they'd gotten away with the cavalry as well as the pack horses, I knew it was time for me, after twenty years in, to get out. Otis Howard went into Virginia City for supplies, and I went in with him and resigned from the United States Army. I've been at this hotel all these months since, thinking over my next move . . .

It was a terrible story, and Jared didn't want Henry to go on with it. His brother looked to be morbidly involved by the narrative. His brown eyes were moist, and his hand holding the paper had begun to shake.

"I suspect he did the right thing," said Jared. "I can't say I know much about this tribe or what the Twelfth is like these days."

Henry put Eller Browning's letter back into its envelope and set it aside. He looked at Jared with a sudden brightness. "So how is the driver of the golden spike?" he asked.

"Stanford's all right," said Jared. "A good boss. Maybe even a great man. I don't see how any of us could ever have suspected he'd finish a transcontinental railroad, certainly not because his father built that little spur between Albany and Schenectady."

"Yes," said Henry, "but that was a pretty grand feat in its day. I remember our own father used to talk about it as an amazing thing. He used to go on and on about the changes it had made in his business. Do you remember that, Jared?"

"Yes, I do," said his brother, noting how warm and normal Henry's smile now seemed, how connected it was to the ordinary words he was speaking, words of pleasant memory, of simple fraternal conversation — ones that seemed to bring him at last into the room, as if from some far country. Jared grinned back at him, hoping he could capture Henry like a wild horse, hold him in this domestic light and keep him from racing back to that unintelligible realm. "Do you remember Jane Lathrop?" he asked. "She's the girl Leland married."

"No, I don't," said Henry, getting up and walking over to his bookshelves, which ran from the ceiling to the floor.

"Sure you do," said Jared. "A pretty girl, about Clara's age. I remember Clara saying, around the time Mama married the judge, that she was jealous of how Jane got to go to the Albany Female Academy."

Henry said nothing. The normal, connecting smile was gone. He was lost in thought, and Jared decided to try something bolder.

"Why not come out west?" he asked. "You and Clara and the whole lot of you."

Still Henry didn't reply.

"Think about it, brother. Leland has his finger in a dozen different pies, not just horses and railroads. He'd know a hundred men who could use you to do law for them. Or anything else you'd enjoy doing. It's a place where people *make* things, Henry. It's the place to fulfill the Rathbone in you. It's a shame things didn't work out with that consular post, but put it behind you. You've been in Washington too long. Come out to San Francisco and make a fresh start. It's a beautiful city —"

"I couldn't," said Henry, as if stating something as factually evident as the temperature. "There's no fresh start for me." He continued looking at the shelves, all of them filled with histories, huge tomes about civilization from the Incas to the industrial age. Half a minute passed in silence.

"Henry?"

He turned around to face Jared. He again wore the distressed expression he'd had when reading Eller Browning's letter. "Those Indian mothers and their children," he murmured. "They're probably better off dead, better off than if they'd awakened to what was left of that camp."

"Henry —"

"And the worst of it is, Jared, that if I'd been there with the Twelfth, I'd have made the loudest noise and come away with the bloodiest hatchet." He sat back down at the desk, tired out, it seemed, from his own imagining.

"Nonsense," said Jared, who went quickly back downstairs, where he found Clara still in the kitchen.

"Something in that letter upset him. I left him looking as if he were somewhere else entirely."

"He *is* somewhere else, Jared. Whether it's the Crater, or Chancellorsville, or Ford's, I don't know. He goes deeper into his memories every month."

"Does he have delusions?" asked Jared, not sure that was the right word for what he had in mind.

"No," said Clara as she put some coasters into a stack. "I don't think so. I think he just suffers from his real memories. Although," she said, her reluctance to speak breaking up, "lately he hasn't seemed quite . . ."

"Clara," said Jared, "sit down with me." He took her hand and tried to lure her to the table. She would not budge, so he stood next to her as he spoke. "I know I've been too occupied by my own ambitions these past ten years to pay enough attention to even the Rathbones in my family, let alone the Harrises. But I want to try to amend that. That's one of the reasons I've made this trip. Maria is right in what she's told me: without children of our own, what else have we but the families we've come from? I know my own letters have been poor things, with intervals too long between them, but I've read your own attentively, and I've read Henry's, too, and I know from them that Henry is not right. I know that he is in the grip of some affliction that is making you suffer, too."

She turned away. She was not ready to discuss this. "Jared, some things cannot be avoided. Whatever our fates, whatever our crosses —"

"But fates can be undone, Clara. Crosses can be lifted." He went over to her at the sideboard. "Clara," he said, turning her around to face him. "I was in London only recently, selling Stanford's horses. There are streets there being lit with electricity. They've managed to move Cleopatra's Needle there from Egypt, and a block away from it people are eating beef that was shipped frozen all the way from the Argentine."

She smiled. "You sound like Dr. Nott again."

"But these things are true, Clara. Not just visions. Do you know there are doctors looking at strains of bacteria, magnifying them to look like insects in a garden? Doctors who are trying new means to cure afflictions, even ones inside the brain? There are doctors who might be able to help Henry."

She pushed him away. "We have a doctor just blocks away, Jared."

"I'm not talking about some purveyor of bromides and laxatives, Clara."

"Jared, Henry is not one of your racehorses. He's not going to yield up his sorrows and secrets to somebody who comes at him with a measuring tape and a camera, if that's the kind of thing you're thinking of."

"No, Clara, not —"

"There is only one thing that can help him, and that is love. No matter how useless it may seem. I am the only one who can give it to him. That is my duty, Jared. You know," she said — her voice breaking, her face collapsing like a flower in the rain — "I still love your brother. With all my broken heart." She reached for a tea cloth and wiped her face.

"Henry," she cried, heading out of the kitchen to stand at the foot of the stairs. "Won't you play teatime with little Clara Pauline? She wants you to, I know she does."

"Yes, darling," he called back. "I'll try to come down."

⇢ 42 ⇠

IT WASN'T A CITY, it was a city-sized sanitarium. And at that, she thought, looking out the waiting room window at the plumes of steam curling through the pine trees, the whole place looked more infernal than healthy. They had come to Carlsbad four days ago, on the train from Prague, to find this medicinal resort that seemed more like Lourdes, which she'd seen, than her idea of Hot Springs, which, despite its being in her native land, she hadn't. Down below her, the town was a jumble of stage sets, the granite pillars of the new Mühlbrunnen Colonnade appearing to have been set up for the production of a Roman tragedy, while the gabled gingerbread houses looked ready for someone's dramatization of a fairy tale.

This almost *was* the seacoast of Bohemia. The town's two parts, on each bank of the river moving through it, supported all kinds of strangeness and contradiction: the old and sometimes twisted bodies of the guests, wrapped in bathing costumes, climbed paths from one spring to another, as all the bubbling hot water they craved lay in sight of snow-covered peaks. These restorative pools for soaking and drinking actually contained, she was told, traces of arsenic, the magical secret perhaps, working with the topsy-turvy logic of inoculation. At this moment she knew Henry was inside the new iron-and-glass Sprudel Colonnade, being blasted with a jet from the 164-degree geyser beneath — as if whatever fluids running inside him needed heating up instead of freezing.

It had been Henry's idea to come. The waters, he had decided, would be good for the maintenance of his forty-two-year-old physique, of which he was still justifiably vain. The mineral springs might also help the dyspepsia he claimed to suffer from.

The discomfort was nothing remarkable, he insisted, but why not see if, incidentally, the waters might relieve it? For once the children would be home in Washington with Lillian, so he and Clara could "pamper themselves": that is what he'd said upon unfolding the itinerary he'd devised for this, their third trip abroad since the chargé d'affaires fiasco two years ago.

Accustomed to defeat, she had agreed to the journey. He had not struck her since that day in '77, but he had not apologized either. It was as if they'd made an agreement never to speak of the incident, to pretend it had never taken place — a fiction that, as the first months went by, she knew was the best she could hope for. It was only later, after more than a year had passed, that she realized, with some fright, that Henry truly believed it had never happened; he had no memory of it, and none of the incident that had "provoked" it. She had never again seen Webb Hayes, except once or twice from the bedroom window. She had not gone out to speak with him and never taken Riggs to the White House. Henry now joked about the whole office-seeking episode, recalling it the way one might a New Year's resolution that had been made and quickly broken.

This afternoon she had lied to him, told him she was joining a group of English and American ladies for a carriage ride to Dallwitz and a tour of the porcelain factory there. She would be back by dinnertime. Fine, fine, he'd said, in a peculiar good humor as he got ready for his geyser. She'd hurried here instead, to the office of Dr. Heinrich Beierheimer, taking care not to be seen by any of the acquaintances they'd made in their four days here. She had arranged the consultation by mail three months ago, before they'd left the States, with the help of Jared. As soon as Carlsbad was on the itinerary, she'd swallowed her pride and asked him if one of these innovative doctors he'd talked to her about last year might be found amidst the spa's bubbling springs. Henry's brother, after calling on some of Leland Stanford's cosmopolitan connections, replied confidentially that while there she ought to make Henry see this man Beierheimer, a disciple of Wilhelm Griesinger. This name meant nothing to her until she accompanied Henry to the Library of Congress one afternoon and, on the other side of the reading room, engaged in some research of her own — "looking up a few things about Words-worth," she'd claimed.

"Frau Rathbone," the physician now said, hitting the *t* quite hard.

"Herr Doktor."

"Welcome to Carlsbad. I hope you have been enjoying a pleasant stay. Won't you come inside to the consulting room?"

Jared's letter had mentioned the doctor's five years in London. His English was as correct and formal as his manners, and his office furniture, most of it maroon-colored leather, betrayed an Anglophilic fondness for men's clubs. He sat her down on a sofa in front of his desk, and in the still-bright afternoon light she appraised his large head. Its thinning blond hair rested atop a protuberant brow whose skin was so fine as to seem translucent, the minimum coverage required for all the mental matter under the skull.

"Tell me about your husband," he said. "Just, for the mo-ment, verifiable data of his life, a sort of *curriculum vitae.*"

"He is about your age," she began, relieved that he was making her start out in the precincts of established fact. "He was born in Albany, New York, the state capital, in 1837. His father was that city's mayor for a time. He has one brother, a few years younger than himself. Mayor Rathbone died in 1845, and three years later the boys' mother married my father, a widower. From the time I was thirteen and Colonel Rathbone was eleven, we were raised as brother and sister, though our families liked to call us cousins."

Dr. Beierheimer said nothing, but made his first note.

"Colonel Rathbone was educated in a nearby city called Sche-nectady, at Union College, the alma mater of many public men, including my father, a United States senator, and Mr. Seward, the late secretary of state."

"Yes," said Dr. Beierheimer with a smile. "Seward's Follies."

Clara didn't stop to correct this one solecism. "Henry briefly studied law in my Uncle Hamilton's office, but when the war came he joined a regiment of infantry and saw two years of very brutal fighting."

"Gettysburg?" asked the doctor.

{ 289 }

"Nearly everything but," replied Clara. "Antietam, Fredericksburg, the battle of the Crater."

Beierheimer nodded sympathetically and made another note.

"As I told you in my letter, we accompanied Mr. and Mrs. Lincoln to the theatre on the night the President was killed. My husband was —"

"He was your husband then?"

"No, not yet. My fiancé. He was badly wounded by the escaping assassin, had the length of his upper arm slashed with a dagger. But he recovered, and we married two years later. That is, twelve years ago."

"Children?"

"Three. Two boys and a girl. They're not with us on this trip, though they usually accompany us on our travels through Europe. It has been our habit to spend some of the year in Washington and the rest of it over here."

"Does your husband still practice the law? When you are at home?"

"No. He looks after his investments. He inherited a great deal of money before the war — the Rathbone family are very wealthy. He also writes."

"What does he write?"

"I'm afraid he never shows it to me. But I believe he is composing a theory of world events. He spends hours each day reading the great historians, especially military ones."

The doctor made a third note, and Clara realized she had reached the conclusion of her chronicle. As she regarded the carpet and played with one of the buttoned puckers in the upholstery, she felt ridiculous, like someone escaping a building whose interior was aflame, only to remark, to the first person she met outside, upon the structure's handsome cornices and columns.

"Now," said Dr. Beierheimer. "Tell me what you think is wrong with your husband."

"He suffers from periods of melancholy," she said, hurriedly speaking the language she had rehearsed this morning. "He is sometimes enraged, occasionally against me. From an early age his mood was cynical — Byronic, if you will — but as the years go by it becomes —"

"Disconnected?" the doctor suggested. "From the realities of the world?"

"Yes," said Clara with the first trace of enthusiasm she had felt.

"Frau Rathbone, you mention Byron to me. And 'melancholy.' Have you read Goethe as well?"

"Yes," she said.

"Romantic nonsense," said the doctor, putting down his pencil. "The mind's moods do not simply descend upon it, like a witch's curse or the morning dew. They are all manifestations of the physical. Every one of them."

"There is nothing physically wrong with my husband," Clara answered, more in disappointment than irritation. "Other than his war wound and the injury he suffered at the theatre —"

"You do not *know* what may be physically wrong with him. So much of the physical is hidden — the brain and the nerves . . ."

"How does one determine their condition?"

"You must bring your husband in and let me examine him."

"He will never come," said Clara.

"If he will not come," asked Dr. Beierheimer, "then why is he here in Carlsbad?"

"He's come to take the waters for his general good health, as well as occasional stomach trouble."

The doctor seemed moderately intrigued by the last piece of information, and he made another note. As he did, Clara asked him if the hot springs really did anyone any good.

"Perhaps," said Dr. Beierheimer with a shrug. "Some somatic distractions may be minimally useful. The baths are certainly more beneficial to people with mental complaints than bleedings and purgatives have been. Tell me, Frau Rathbone, have you consulted a physician at home?"

"No," said Clara, who had just noticed, on the table behind the doctor, beneath a framed diagram of a dog's skull, a black box with a dial.

"The brain runs by electricity," he said, spotting the focus of her interest and swiveling his chair around to it. "Shocks to its specific sectors can make the body move in particular, predictable ways. It stands to reason that the exact locations of all the mind's feelings and moods will one day prove detectable."

"What bearing does all this have on my husband's character?"

"Differences in personality may really come from different wirings of the brain. Think of the old 'doctrine of the humors,' but with electrical impulses, not fluids, accounting for our discrepant natures."

"And injury to the 'wires' leads to mental defect?"

"Yes," said the doctor. "Precisely."

Clara looked out the window, at a bird flying through a plume of steam, and thought about how little this could possibly have to do with Henry, as if he were the key on the end of Benjamin Franklin's kite. She was too tense to sigh, but her attention was beginning to wander.

"Does your husband have any phobias, Frau Rathbone?"

"Phobias?"

"Unnatural fears."

She thought for a moment. "He imagines people whispering about him, just out of the range of his hearing. For a time, after the killing of the President, this may have been true, but it's long since ceased. Even so, he —"

"Obsessions?" asked the doctor.

"He is more and more preoccupied with his food. He lives, sometimes for days, on small portions of vegetables, professing a horror of animal blood and tissue. He associates different dishes, single ingredients, with different states of mind." She paused again to think. "I suppose his preoccupation with history is an obsession. And he may be obsessed with Mr. Lincoln himself. On those occasions when he permits himself or others to speak about him, he abuses the President's memory in mystifying ways." She was once more absorbed in this conversation with the doctor, excited by its possibilities. But then Dr. Beierheimer inquired, "Does he have any abnormal sexual practices or enthusiasms?" He pronounced the last word with a kind of juiciness, a function, she was sure, of his accent, but even so, he made the word sound concupiscent, and she felt herself blushing, as if she were Mary Hall.

"No. We had a happy life together. It is gone now, but it was happy." She wouldn't, she couldn't, tell him of the vigor of their nights together — the shouts and scratchings, the games and sometimes terrible language. She was sure these things were "abnormal," had always been sure of that, but they had always been normal to her and Henry, and that was the only standard she had held them against, all through the days when they banished the world and made her — made the two of them together — happy.

"Has your husband ever suffered from syphilis?"

The word, which she had never heard uttered by any man in any room she'd sat in, struck her like a hand. Her eyes widened, but she made no response.

"*Any* venereal disease?" the doctor asked. Clara felt naked to his gaze and thoughts, and she was astonished to hear her own disclosures. "None that I know of," she said, fixing her eyes on the drawing of the dog's head. "But in the years before the war he was sometimes in the company of prostitutes. And I have my suspicions that he may again be with them now, from time to time, when he travels by himself to New York."

The doctor made a notation.

"Do these diseases play a part in disordering the mind?" Clara asked.

Dr. Beierheimer, who seemed to have lost interest in his own question, closed his eyes and shook his head and touched the dial on the black box behind him. "We don't really know," he said. "I would certainly have to see your husband to begin to make a determination."

"I'm afraid that's impossible," said Clara.

"Then why," responded the doctor, a hint of irritation curling up from his smooth manner, "did you come here?"

"Because of my brother-in-law," said Clara, preparing to leave. "His intentions, and mine, were honest, but perhaps naive. I had hoped that you would be able to suggest something, even without seeing Colonel Rathbone."

"Sit, please, Frau Rathbone," said the doctor, urging her to unclasp her shawl and go back to the leather couch. "There," he said when she once more appeared at ease. He put down his pen and pushed his notes aside, and for the first time since bringing her into the consulting room, he smiled. "Tell me," he said, and Clara leaned forward, hoping that this new question would be easier than the last ones. "Tell me what President Lincoln was really like. I've heard so much about his moods."

→←

There were towels everywhere, strewn about the hotel suite. Steam danced out through the open doorway of the bathroom, where Henry, in an exuberant mood, was shaving.

He stopped his humming when he saw her.

"No plates?" he asked, noticing she was empty-handed. "Not one china cup, or even a thimble, after touring a porcelain factory?"

"No," Clara answered, untying her bonnet. "They didn't give anything away, and I didn't think to make purchases."

"You need to indulge yourself more, my dear wife." He banged his razor against the enameled sink, shaking loose the blood-flecked lather. She watched him dry off and comb his hair, which had retreated an inch in the dozen years they had been married and now had strands of gray amidst the red. The vein at his left temple, like a crack in the sidewalk, asserted itself more strongly than it used to.

"Are we going out tonight?" she asked. "Or only to the dining room here?"

"Out," said Henry, emerging from the bathroom and surprising her with a quick kiss on his way to the armoire. "We're going to that little restaurant near the colonnade, and we have guests: Monsieur and Madame Gilles, from Bordeaux. He's a fine fellow. Makes farm equipment. I think I see a good investment."

Clara reacted cautiously. "Where did you meet him?"

"At the Sprudel geyser."

"What did you say?"

"Oh, he knows all about us. He was a great sympathizer with the Confederates, told me he'd loved doing business with the old

Southern planters in the years before the war. He's a friendly type, not at all like a Frenchman. He also happens to be hideously ugly. I can trust you with him."

"Stop it," said Clara, who realized she was staring at her husband's forehead, contemplating it as he put on his shirt, wondering about the "wiring" beneath it and whether that prominent vein wasn't a diversionary channel, rerouting the whole system toward a place it oughtn't go. "If he wants your money, all right," she said over Henry's whistling, "but I hope you didn't entertain him with our life story." After years of his almost frantic silence about Ford's Theatre, her husband sometimes now volunteered a string of reminiscences to near strangers. She could never tell if he was seeking their approval, trying to shock them, or testing some limit in himself. The subject would be closed as quickly as it came up, with Henry apparently on the verge of recounting some crucial detail — and then thinking better of it.

"So what if he's interested in what happened to us?" asked Henry. "As the years go by, I'm more and more convinced I did fine that night."

"That's what I've told you for years," said Clara, warily hopeful, "every April fourteenth when the newspapers hound us and you feel such distress. No one could have done any more."

"You're right," said Henry, sticking the pin into his cravat. "No one could have done better." Clara helped him find his studs in a jumble of pins and jewelry, shaking her head in confusion. Had Dr. Beierheimer cured Henry through a kind of magical sympathy? Perhaps some electrical currents had floated across the air from his consulting room to the hotel.

"You should listen to this fellow tonight," said Henry, taking a pair of horseshoe-shaped cufflinks from Clara. "On the subject of the South, especially. They were a good people. We should have let them go. No, my darling," he said, pushing one of the links through its hole in the cuff, "I did fine that night."

Her small hope faded to nothing. Here comes the rambling, she thought — one of the peculiar chains of associations she could not follow. She said nothing, just helped him with his cuff.

"You're the one whose behavior I'll never understand." He said it quietly, as if in a spirit of sincere inquiry. "Why did you leave me that night?"

"I won't go into this again, Henry. Yes, I did 'leave' you. I let you go home to Papa's in the company of a surgeon, whose work I should only have interfered with by being in the carriage. I stayed with Mrs. Lincoln because that's where people thought I was needed."

Henry's tone changed to something more sarcastic. "Even after Miss Keene arrived to provide her with some feminine support? Even after the Prince of Rails managed to bring himself from the White House to his mama's side?"

"That's the end of this discussion," she said, letting go of his left arm and quitting the room. She took a seat on a sofa in the suite's tiny parlor.

No, she would not talk about this again; she wouldn't even let herself think about it. It was useless, a trivial matter from the past that he brought up whenever he wanted to accuse her of faithlessness. But still the question bothered her. She had never really understood why she didn't rush back to Fifteenth and H that night, why even when the morning came, after the long fatal vigil at the tailor's house was over, she somehow resisted returning home, amidst the drizzle and bell ringing, to her future husband, who needed her. She knew all the explanations: she had been frightened; the tailor's house was safer than the streets and the unguarded Harris home; Mrs. Lincoln had genuinely needed her; she would only have been in the way while Henry was properly bandaged and surveyed; she wasn't thinking clearly. Over the last fourteen years, she had told herself all these things any time he forced the absurd subject, but she knew that if she was honest with herself, she would admit how her own behavior *had* been odd, would acknowledge that she had not returned home for some more unsettling reason. Could it really have been an instinctual love of the limelight? The possibility was grotesque, and the fact that Henry had more than once thrown it into the buckets of abuse he poured over her had let her dismiss it as irrational. The real truth, she thought, although she didn't understand it exactly, was something worse, something having to do with a fear of Henry — not the mild fear she had always had, or the near-constant one she would suffer in the years after that night, but some vague fear particular to that moment, a fear that if she went back home, he would tell her something awful, a hideous detail, something that would make the horror reenact itself more clearly and terribly inside her mind — something that would forever keep her from getting over it.

Now he stood in the doorway to the little parlor with yet another look on his face, so plaintive and innocently frightened that for a second she thought she was seeing not Henry himself but some bewhiskered version of their son Riggs.

"You're not going to leave me *again,* are you? You wouldn't, would you?"

"No," she answered, in the same tone she used to soothe her children out of their repetitive worries and questions. "Of course not."

"Good," he said, smiling, happy and relieved, his mood altered as suddenly and completely as Riggs's or Gerald's or little Clara's would have been. He was ready to go back to the armoire and his dressing, but not before again saying, "Good," and then, after a pause, adding, "Of course, I wouldn't let you in any case." His boy's expression vanished, like a sheet of paper being torn from a tablet. The next look, sly and confident, was more familiar. "Come, darling," he now said. "Pick up the pace. Change into your purple dress, and let's not be late."

⇀ 43 ↽

SHE WAS without him tonight, alone in the parlor on Jackson Place, the children and Lillian playing upstairs. He had gone to New York to talk to Jack Barnes about his investments, and right now, at nine in the evening on January 15, 1880, she expected he was patronizing some red-lit brownstone off Union Square, along with a lot of other sporting males, the sort he would, a dozen years ago, have scorned for being beneath him in education, breeding, and money in the bank. When he arrived home tomorrow, he might admit having gone to a concert saloon, and leave her to infer the rest, from telltale observations and the rumors that came from friends insisting on their good intentions. She didn't care. His dalliances were the least of her worries, inspiring more relief than competitiveness. She had no more illusions about her own charms, no need to look in the mahogany mirror to know that, at forty-five, she was growing heavier, had gray hairs, and signs of untidiness in her dress. She was overly fond of gaudy jewelry and looked too old, too eccentric, to be the mother of the small children playing upstairs.

But she was devoted to them, determined they should survive all the frights and uncertainty surrounding them. Little Clara had, at seven, just learned to mimic her papa, to hold up the newspaper and say "Traitors and scum." When her mother first heard the imitation, she begged that she never do it again, only, of course, to hear her perform it two days later in front of Henry himself. Clara had stood in the next room with her heart in her mouth, ready to fly to the aid of her girl — but Henry decided to roar with laughter and crush his daughter in a delighted embrace. He might just as likely have decided (if his faultily wired brain were truly capable of "deciding" anything) to give the girl a dose of verbal terror and some grotesquely inventive punishment.

Yes, she loved her children, but they gave her as much fear as delight, and for all her attentiveness toward them, she found herself drifting, more and more, as the years of her marriage passed, into memories and long blank reveries. She had no more desire to feed her mind than to care for this house, so infrequently was it occupied between forced marches through Europe. The wallpaper had faded and the family furniture grown shabby, any new items having no more style than what they found in all the hotel suites that were more truly their home. She knew it was only a matter of time before they left here altogether, after selling the house to a new Cabinet officer or tiny country, to serve as its embassy. They would stash themselves up in Loudonville during the shorter and shorter periods Henry permitted them to come home. And when they had left Washington, she knew she would not care; she would find whatever peace she could in the shade of her father's apple and cherry trees. The "lust for limelight" — what Henry sometimes still called it in mid-tirade — had long since been driven out of her. They had no more friends, and few acquaintances, absence and the dread of "scenes" having driven everyone away.

In fact, right now, when the front doorbell rang, she almost didn't recognize its sound. She couldn't remember the last time she'd heard any but the one on the back door, when the grocer or iceman tried to summon the maid to deliveries. Her heart pounded with surprise and exasperation: it could only be Henry, and he wasn't supposed to be here. She was entitled to one more night by herself. He'd either forgotten that, along with his key, or had deliberately decided to deny her this evening of peace. For all she knew, he had developed another jealous fantasy this afternoon, and raced back to put a stop to one more imagined tryst between his wife and all the handsome gentlemen he claimed she summoned into his home and bed.

But it *was* a handsome gentleman — two of them, she discovered to her astonishment when Maggie (the latest housemaid in the dozen they'd had) opened the door and showed them in.

"Nope, not a day older," said the first of them, the one with the close-set brown eyes and long mustache. "You were quite right, Cameron. She's not a day older."

Clara rose from her chair and squinted, until she realized who the speaker was and went over to hug him. "Johnny Hay, you wonderful liar. You good old friend!" It was *he* who looked no older than in Mr. Lincoln's time. He was finally past forty, but his tiny features still seemed more a boy's than a man's, his long brown hair falling from a part near the middle of his head, and the long mustache, that would-be walrus, just two long pampered wisps.

"Dear Don," she said, releasing Hay and taking both the hands of James Donald Cameron, who had not long ago replaced his father, the Harris family's long-time friend from Pennsylvania, in the Senate. It had been a year since she'd seen him.

"Is Henry around?" he asked.

"No, he's away in New York until tomorrow. On business," she said, making the phrase sound proudly normal, even while she was embarrassed to see Cameron and Hay's relief at the news.

"Well, we'll have to see him another time," said Hay. "But tonight we can still see you, dear Clara. I was having supper at Wormley's with Cameron here, and he suggested we take a chance and drop by."

"I hope we're not intruding," said Cameron, who now realized that they couldn't have picked a better time.

"Not at all," said Clara. "You're making me so happy. Maggie, please bring us some coffee and some cake — do we have any? Good. Sit down, Johnny. You too, Senator Don. We're going to have a lovely visit, and then I'll have my three darlings come downstairs to shatter your ears."

Hay had returned to Washington two months before as assistant secretary of state, before which he'd been living in Cleveland. The first thing he told Clara, as they settled themselves in the parlor, was that he'd gotten used to running into Will Harris at his club.

"I know," she replied. "He's told me in his letters. He also tells me you've got a Clara of your own."

"Indeed I do," said Hay, as charmingly eager to talk about himself as he'd been during the war. "For the past five years. My company has probably aged her ten, but she's getting a good respite from me right now. She's not going to join me here until I can find us someplace suitable to live. Meanwhile, I mail her all the calling cards I pick up on my social round — all those powerful names foreign and domestic — and she dazzles our Ohio friends with them."

"What houses have you looked at?" asked Clara.

"Dozens, alas." Hay sighed as he took a chipped coffee cup from the maid. "But nothing seems right. If I were sure I was staying longer than a year, I'd have a mind to build one of my own, right here in the square. Everything I've seen scares me off for one reason or another. My friend de Hegerman offered to rent me his, but he warned me of one small drawback: rats. Or, as he trilled it, '*Wrrats!* I meet dem on de stairrs and efry vere.' He tried to solve the problem by dressing one of them up in a red flannel cape, a sight he was told could be counted on to scare the others to death."

"With no success," chimed in Cameron, who had already heard this three or four times.

"The other rats are probably just clamoring for little red coats of their own," Clara speculated. "Doesn't the Washington winter seem colder than the ones you remember?"

"Yes," said Hay, "but on the other hand, the whole place seems so plush and paved now. I'm constantly aware of all the changes since the war. I can't help being so, because half of me is still living in those old days."

"You mean for your book?"

"Yes," said Hay. He and John Nicolay had been at their Lincoln biography since 1875. "We've got years and volumes to go. I'd contemplated running for Congress, but then I thought better of it. Even this little stint under Mr. Evarts is more distraction than I ought to be allowing myself."

Clara nodded uncomfortably. "And what is that like?"

"Well," said Hay, "times may be less tumultuous, but I think I appreciate these men of power more than I did back in Mr.

Lincoln's time. I was too young and blinkered then to feel half the awe I feel now. I tell you, Evarts is a phenomenon. He has every detail in his grip, but never loses sight of the big things sweeping through the sky, never fails to notice what's behind and ahead of the present moment."

"Give me an instance," said Clara, who still had the skills of a belle in flattering the male talker.

"Take the current men of the South," said Hay. "Evarts only wishes they knew how much better off they'd be had Mr. Lincoln been left alive. He'd have eased them back onto their local thrones much more quickly; as it is, they were left to wait and fear the future, and while they did, the shadow of Negro suffrage just paralyzed them with fright. Maybe permanently. 'The fear of the suffrage is the weak point of all public men in an educated and intelligent democracy.' That's what Evarts told me one night before Christmas. He says a man's better off fearing a lion, for at least he can measure one. He's *very* bright, Clara, a pleasure to work for, not just another credential collector. Most of the people in this city care nothing for history, even as they're making it. I suppose that was also true in the days we shared. But he's got a steady, long view of the whole thing."

Don Cameron watched Clara's careworn face politely nodding up and down. He was pretty sure Hay knew nothing about Evarts's refusal to give her husband a job (both Cameron and his father had joined the letter-writing campaign), and certain he had no idea of the great "history" Rathbone was always rumored to be writing — a subject of sadness or snickers among those in the District who knew him. Still, the conversation was making poor Clara uncomfortable, and he wished Hay would ramble toward some other topic.

Within half a minute he had: "You know, the biggest change I've noticed between 'sixty-five and now is all these female clerks everywhere. State and War and Treasury — everywhere I go, I find the offices crawling with them. Poor, single, ink-stained, practically living on apples. What a lot! How did they all wash up here?"

Clara shook her head in sympathy and disbelief. Any woman with three children and a husband and a large house could not courteously express herself otherwise. But what she was really thinking as Hay chattered on — what even Don Cameron couldn't read on her face — was how lucky those girls were. She saw them all the time walking along Pennsylvania Avenue, knew and surmised enough about their lives to envy their impoverishment and freedom and to imagine herself as one of them, toiling away all day at an inkwell and coming home to a boarding house on Fifth Street, with nothing but some candles and the moonlight to intrude upon the perfect peace and darkness of her room.

"You haven't said a word about the election, either one of you," said Clara, looking from gentleman to gentleman.

Cameron, at last getting a word in, declared his desire for Grant's return. "He'd attract a lot of Democratic votes. I think even Mr. Hayes would welcome it, if it stopped Conkling from taking over the party."

Clara asked Hay if he agreed, but before he could make it through the second hundred words of his considered opinion, all three of them looked up toward the sound of the front door. Henry Rathbone's boots were coming toward them, crossing the threshold of the parlor. Clara thought quickly: what did he once say about Johnny? "The President's pipsqueak; he'd be better off as a drummer boy." But Don's being here will make things all right. Two men are safer than one, and he actually liked Don's father. I shall keep calm and things will be fine, there will be no scene, if —

"Henry, you're home!" She jumped up to kiss his whiskers and squeeze his good arm, as if some long-ago part of her might be able to signal some long-ago part of him to do something sweet for her, simply, please, to *behave*.

"My business took less time than expected," he said, returning her kiss and dropping his muffler on a table. Maggie took his coat, and Clara thought that things might be all right. If he was agitated, he would have made the word "business" a double entendre, flicked it toward her with a cruel little snap.

"Well, I've been having a delightful evening. Look who've surprised me, Henry. John Hay and Senator Cameron. Tell these old friends they don't need to get up."

Henry did as he was asked, shaking their hands and gesturing for them to resume their seats. But he appeared confused, as if trying to figure out how Hay could be so old and Cameron so young.

"Colonel," said Hay. "It's been too many years. I don't believe I've seen you since just after the terrible events in 'sixty-five."

Yes, thought Clara, it might be all right. He might not say anything about Johnny Hay's being at the White House that night, studying Spanish with Bob Lincoln while she and Henry were all but being killed at the theatre. Still, she wished he'd say *something,* not just continue with that confused stare. To fill the silence, she spoke herself: "I'm going to go upstairs and see if the children are still up. They always want to see him when he's gotten home," she told Hay and Cameron, who both smiled nervously. "Henry, I hope you've remembered to bring them something." Her gaiety was paper thin, and she knew her guests could see it.

"There's no need for you to go, darling," said Henry. "I'll check on the children myself. Will you excuse me?" he asked Cameron and Hay. "I'll join you shortly."

"Good," said Clara, smiling too broadly, fluttering her hands until she thought to call out to Maggie to prepare more coffee and a drink for Colonel Rathbone.

She noticed Hay and Cameron conferring with a glance, and told them, "No, you mustn't go yet." They couldn't leave the house until they could take with them some happy domestic illusion, like leftover cake on a covered dish. "Johnny, you haven't told me nearly enough about your triumphal return. I want more tales of adventure. Who's been lucky enough to have your company? Anyone from the old days?"

"One or two," said Hay, lowering his eyes and voice, sufficiently encouraged to launch into another party piece, this time a somber one. "Old General Holt, whom you'll surely remember." Clara nodded silently, wishing he had mentioned almost anyone but the judge to whose military court Henry once swore his version of the events at Ford's, as the reporters on the chairs next to her snickered and speculated. "He's retired now, all alone in the world, rattling around in his big house up on Capitol Hill, like a ghost."

"Speaking of ghosts," said Cameron, by way of a cue, as if the quicker he could get Hay to complete his repertoire, the quicker they could make their way out of here.

"Oh, yes," said Hay. "Mrs. Sprague. She's alone in a *little* house, on Connecticut Avenue."

"Is her divorce soon to go through?" asked Clara, who still read Miss Snead's column in the *Evening Star,* even if she no longer went to the dinner parties that supplied its items.

"Yes," said Hay. "She's very proud, but I suspect she fears pauperdom. She's fallen so far so fast, she can't see any reason she shouldn't crash to the very bottom. But a minute after fretting over it all, she can be bold as brass. She paints her cheeks now — it's a sad sight — and she invited me to join her for dinner at the Conklings'. Imagine, dining *à quatre* with her and her paramour and his wife!"

There were a dozen questions and comments, both charitable and feline, that Clara could have spoken, but she could focus only on the thought of divorce — that unspeakable possibility she had herself entertained, never for more than a moment at a time, in the middle of the night, lying awake beside Henry. She thought of it now, but with her heart already going from the evening's unexpected events, she forced herself to change the subject.

"Too depressing, Johnny. Tell me about your *new* friends."

"Friends?" asked Hay in mock astonishment. "I have no friends, only hosts and hostesses. None so fine as you, but a few exotic ones here and there. Zamacona, the Mexican minister, gives some good feeds, and Mrs. Bancroft sets a beautiful table, prettier than the one laid in the White House, I can tell you. Lord, the place is shabby, Clara. I was over there at Christmas; all the decorations couldn't hide the torn curtains and loose floorboards. The whole house needs a thorough overhaul."

There was a time when she would have faked a knowing expression, tried to mislead him into thinking she regularly had lemonade with Lucy and waltzed in the East Room with Webb

Hayes, but there was no point in trying to create such misapprehension, not when her own house was looking more neglected than the Mansion could possibly be. Still, Johnny's talk — all the names, all his silly exuberance — seemed to give her energy, a dose of hope, enough to make her think she might still somehow recover her vitality, even a piece of her old Washington dream.

The boots were coming back down the stairs.

"Senator Cameron, Mr. Hay," said Henry, ignoring the tumbler of whiskey that Maggie had brought in. His wife's guests both stood up to a height much lower than his own. "I'm afraid," he said, "that my children are braying for a story. I'm going to read them a very brief one and then retire. I've had something of a headache since I got on the train in Jersey City. So if you'll forgive me, I'm going to let my youngsters exacerbate it into something truly skull-cracking and then head off to sleep. My charming wife will, I know, continue to entertain you."

It was *he* who was charming; wonderfully so, she thought, silently praising the Lord for letting this particular mood be the one her husband rode into the house tonight.

Hay shook Henry's hand, and Cameron did the same. "Good night," said Henry to each of them, before adding, to Cameron, "I'll tell Senator Harris you came by. I know my stepfather will be pleased to hear you called."

Now, as he kissed her good night, Clara knew what his earlier puzzled expression had meant. He thought that Don Cameron was his father, Simon; thought, she realized horribly, that Johnny-now was Johnny-then, that the war still raged and Papa was alive, and that somehow, children and all, they were still in the house at Fifteenth and H. Her heart was racing, and she knew that she had reached a lower and stonier depth than Kate Chase Sprague was ever likely to strike.

She would pretend not to have heard, pretend that Hay and Cameron hadn't either. She would get them out the door, and Henry to sleep, and then she would sit here alone, facing the moment that had arrived: the time when, instead of restarting her Washington dream, they must sell this house; leave the city forever; go home to Loudonville and hide.

⇥ 44 ⇤

UNCLE HAMILTON came to see Clara and the children once a week, and she was always grateful, since otherwise there was almost no one to talk to. The house in Loudonville, which had had rooms and dormers added over the years, was now so large that the children could war amongst themselves in some distant corner of it without her even hearing them. There were hours during these hot September days when her solitude was more lonely than peaceful, and the arrival of her papa's quick-moving younger brother — his sentences still as neat and clipped as his mustache — inevitably cheered her. She was even more appreciative for knowing that these Saturday visits afforded him so little pleasure of his own. He would make some quick inquiries about how they were all getting on while he glanced nervously around the premises, as if he'd just heard a strange noise. In the Harris family manner, he outwardly assumed the best and never probed her polite assurances that everything was fine.

Sometimes he went into the library to greet Henry and give him some cigars, but mostly he stayed with Clara out on the porch, catching the children as they flew past and telling their mother a few bits of gossip about those men in the legislature she might still remember, or amusing new ones, like Theodore Roosevelt, "who intends to be minority leader before he's twenty-five!" Though he had left the state senate himself, punctilious Uncle Hamilton was more influential than he'd ever been. He headed the board of commissioners charged with rebuilding the state capitol, and generally exercised such power behind the Republican throne that politicians now joked about Ira Harris's having died and come back as Thurlow Weed — in the mortal envelope of his brother.

With Clara he seemed embarrassed about his influence, about having learned to play the game better than her father had, so he tended to talk to her more about the past than the present. Today, along with the stack of books he always brought, he had included a pamphlet sent to him by John K. Porter, a friendly adversary back in the 'fifties, when he'd been district attorney. Porter had just achieved a measure of fame for prosecuting Charles Guiteau, the hapless fanatic who had killed President Garfield last summer. His courtroom questioning of the assassin had been deemed so effective that now, months after Guiteau's hanging, a transcript of it was available in a little book. It made a peculiar present, but Uncle Hamilton was famous for the well-intentioned gaucherie of his gift-giving: a waffle iron for the boys, gloves four sizes too big for their sister.

When her uncle was gone, Clara opened the book:

MR. PORTER: Do you feel under great obligations to the American people?

GUITEAU: I think the American people may sometime consider themselves under great obligations to me, sir.

MR. PORTER: Did the Republican Party ever give you an office?

GUITEAU: I never held any kind of political office in my life, and never drew one cent from the Government.

MR. PORTER: And never desired an office, did you?

GUITEAU: I had some thoughts about the Paris consulship. That is the only office that I ever had any serious thought about.

MR. PORTER: That was the one which resulted in the inspiration, wasn't it?

GUITEAU: No, sir, most decidedly not. My getting it or not getting it had no relation to my duty to God and the American people.

The pamphlet was thin enough to tear in two, and that's what Clara did, before tearing it again, into quarters, and walking to the bin at the edge of the orchard. Tomorrow the illiterate boy from Rensselaer could burn it with the rest of the rubbish when he came to do his chores. She wouldn't have it in the house. This printed interrogation, coming up from the page with such quiet madness, unsettled her more than it should have, but the affinities between Guiteau's voice and Henry's were inescapable. People said that Secretary Blaine remembered brushing aside the office-seeking assassin whenever he was accosted by him in the months before the killing. Who knew, she wondered, what crazy fantasies Henry might have entertained, even five years before, against Mr. Evarts and President Hayes? Guiteau had claimed credit for Garfield's victory in 1880, on the basis of some mad speech he'd written and never delivered — a boast oddly like Henry's own occasional assertions that he was the cause of various events from which he stood far removed. As she picked a skirtful of apples, she felt sick recalling how, when Mr. Garfield finally expired last September, Henry had said he was thinking of offering his services to the new President, since, after all, Chester Arthur was a Union College man and might be in need of him.

The eighty summer days during which Garfield lingered and suffered, rallied and relapsed, had been dreadful for anyone reading the newspapers: the ghastly paragraphs about drainage and pus; the unhealing wound that the physicians' fingers probed again and again; the attempts to cool the sickroom by blowing air over a huge box of ice. Every Sunday the sermons were full of it, as the congregation at Albany's Cathedral of All Saints fanned themselves and nodded with equal fervor over mercy and retribution. She had been prepared for the congregants to stare at herself and Henry, since memories of Mr. Lincoln's killing were newly revived, but there turned out to be fewer eyes on them than she'd expected. It was as if this second shooting of a President in sixteen years had at last made the first one old news. The glances, when they did come, were mostly the sort that villagers might direct toward any couple who, after long absence, had come back to live among them.

This summer was nearly as hot as last, and as she rinsed the apples in the kitchen, she felt grateful for the coolness of her father's house. So much of what was here had been his. In these last few years she and Henry had acquired almost nothing of their own, had come back from Europe so empty-handed that customs agents eyed their trunks with suspicion. Even now she was aware of slicing the apples onto a painted tray that her mother had given Papa forty years ago. She should put it away for her daughter, she thought, not keep adding knife marks to it; and she should do the same with other items, for Amanda's children. She had asked Amanda please to come this summer and bring them all with her, but her sister hadn't been able to. There were times when Clara almost wished for Pauline's cold, aging presence in the big house, but she had gone to Newport and taken Lina with her. Mary Hall, merrily working herself to death at some charity house on Canal Street, had declined her invitations, too. Louise and Lillian were here, but Louise scurried away from Henry with the same speed she used to avoid a field mouse, and the businesslike briskness that allowed Lillian to cope not only with the children but with the oddities of their father made her, alas, not very relaxing or intimate company.

The house ran on a needlessly rigid schedule, and since it was now past three in the afternoon, the day's history lesson had begun in the dining room. She could hear it going on, more a recitation than a lesson, a two-hour drone from father to sons, no interruptions permitted. She stilled her paring knife to listen to Henry's strong, invisible baritone: *"Upon discovering the position that Lieutenant Benedict was in with his company, I ordered him to fall back with his company to a ditch near the cemetery, and from thence to the cemetery itself, if possible. Previous to Lieutenant Benedict making the move, he had lost seven men wounded, and while making it, he himself was wounded severely and one sergeant mortally. I then determined to occupy the tannery (which was a good brick building), and after making loopholes in the end, and posting a few good men at them as well as at the windows, succeeded in keeping the enemy's fire under until midnight, when we were relieved by a portion of Couch's division of volunteers."*

She smiled in spite of herself. It wasn't violent, just deadly. It was some officer's dispatch from Fredericksburg, printed word for word in *The War of the Rebellion,* the official history of the Union and Confederate armies, which the government had begun issuing two years ago and would go on issuing for years to come, in dozens more volumes than Nicolay and Johnny Hay would need to cover Mr. Lincoln. Colonel Henry R. Rathbone was a charter subscriber to this clerkly bookkeeping of the apocalypse he once prophesied; the document-filled installments now arrived in Loudonville with only a little less regularity than *Harper's* and *Leslie's.*

Little Clara was exempt from the recitals, but the boys were too scared to ask for even temporary leave. They just waited hopefully for their father's next trip to New York, which would come unannounced and leave them to climb the trees and play ball and once in a while take a carriage into town to play with their Rathbone relatives. Clara no longer asked Henry where he went, and upon returning home from the city, he offered no evidence to make her think he'd been with Jack Barnes. Since he could hardly go satisfy himself along the quays here in Albany, she hoped for his own mad sake that he was staying out of Manhattan's rougher dens; she didn't want to have to tell her children their father had been murdered in the streets. While he was gone she liked to think he was in one of the fancier houses of assignation, some quiet and nearly respectable place not far from the house Chester Arthur still owned on Lexington Avenue.

Sitting down at the kitchen table with a peeled apple and a glass of cold water, she thought of this dapper President-by-accident, who had, she'd read, hired a French chef, Monsieur Fortun, for his midnight suppers. If Johnny Hay was still in Washington, he must be pleased at how the new tenant had started fixing up the Mansion from top to bottom, trying to make it as perfect and polished as his green carriage with the morocco trim. His first state dinner, for the Grants, had included eight different wines, and poor Mr. Hayes had been appalled. "Nothing like it ever before in the Executive Mansion — liquor, snobbery, and worse," he'd said. The worse must be that Arthur, on top of everything, was Conkling's man.

But she liked him, liked the idea of him, this tuxedoed beau she'd seen years before at a college affair Papa had organized. He was running the sort of White House she had once dreamed about, and she was missing it all, left to feel as Pauline must have fifteen years ago when Conkling's ascent forced her and Papa home. But even the indomitable Pauline, past seventy and as selectively perceptive as ever, was closer to the center of things. The President was spending his summer in Newport, and when Pauline arrived home in September, she could be counted upon to report her hand having been kissed by his lips, as Clara, who would be filling a trunk with woolens for yet another ocean crossing, politely nodded and asked for details.

She came out of her daydreaming when Gerald, who would turn eleven next week, crept into the kitchen and whispered, "Papa says I can have a glass of water." She reached over to smooth her son's hair, and in a loud voice, the kind she wished her children weren't afraid of using in front of their father, said, "You'll have a lovely glass of cold, sweet cider. And your brother will have one, too." She got up to get the pitcher from the icebox. "Your papa can have the water — for his speaking voice — if he can pause long enough in his oration to take a breath." She poured two glasses of cider and placed them on the tray, after clearing it of apple slices. "Did you know this tray was your grandpa's? And that it was given to him by your grandmother?"

"Grandmother Louisa?" asked Gerald, still whispering. "The one I never met?"

"That's right," said Clara, lowering her own voice, not interested in having Henry hear this part of her conversation with her son. This was the sort of history, bits and pieces of family lore and better times, that she wished the boy were learning.

"Do you still miss her?" Gerald asked.

Clara thought for a moment, trying to give him the kind of truthful answer she believed was good for children. "No, sweetheart," she said. "It's too long ago since she left. I was only your age. That's more than thirty-five whole years ago."

"I'd still miss *you*," Gerald said quietly as he experimented with managing the tray.

Clara took it from him and set it back down on the table. "Would you?" she asked, in a whisper so low the boy had to strain to hear it.

"Yes," he said, looking up.

She took him into her arms and pressed his head against her cotton dress. "I'm not going anywhere, Gerry. I'll be right here," she said, stroking his red hair.

"But you'll be coming to Germany, won't you?" he asked, pulling away, looking anxiously up at her and forgetting to whisper.

"Germany?"

"Papa says he wants us to live there. He says that Germany, thanks to Bismarck and the emperor, is 'where you can really see history at work.'"

⇀ 45 ↼

SIGHTING THE FIVE-STORY, cast-iron immensity of A. T. Stewart's, Clara pulled the check string on the coach and waited for the driver to stop his horses. She passed her fare up through the hole in the carriage roof and prepared to alight at the corner of Broadway and Tenth Street. She was surprised at how the sunlight had established itself since she'd left Reverend Hall's house on Beekman Place an hour ago. She had walked all the way west to Fifth Avenue before hailing the carriage, too excited by the long-forgotten sensation of walking about, just herself, to mind the drizzle. She had arrived in the city yesterday, giving Mary no more than a single post's notice of her intention to come down. In fact, she'd not had much more notice herself. On Sunday afternoon Pauline, just back in Loudonville from her winter in St. Augustine, had urged her to go, to see her friend and the city before, yet again, she had to board a ship for Europe. They would be sailing Saturday. "A little time for yourself will be refreshing, Clara. You can rendezvous with Henry and the children right at the dock if you like."

Clara's need for refreshment was, to Pauline's way of thinking, attributable to her contrariness and ever-waning energies, defects Pauline had long since decided were of her own making. Clara was willing to assent to this fraud, no matter how insulting, if it sanctioned a journey away from the house. Besides, Pauline was surprisingly good with the children. Clara would never have gone off and left them with Louise, who was harrowed by Henry's moods. Pauline's presence would induce her son's adoration and calm. So, as Clara wrote Mary to tell her she was coming, her only regret came from realizing it was her own absence that would give her children their three most peaceful days this year. Otherwise, as she'd left the house for the Albany train station, she'd had a feeling of joy, a sense of being sprung from a box far more confining than the small carriage she was now getting out of.

It was years since she'd been in Stewart's, and the midday bustle filled her with excitement. She couldn't recall where any item was to be found, but she remembered the bank of elevators, and headed for it straightaway, pausing only once to look up at the great rotunda, arching her neck and allowing her head to swim for a delicious moment. She got out on the second-floor arcade, still unsure of her exact destination but eager to look over the railing onto the great main selling floor — high enough to enjoy the strangeness of the perspective, near enough to make out the faces of the shoppers. They moved below her like figures in an old genre painting, skaters, heading toward cases and counters with wonderful free-willed speed. Dozens of ushers stood like sticks frozen into the ice, around which the shoppers spun. The classes mixed freely, shopgirls and ladies and servants all in casual pursuit of what their money could buy.

"Madam?" inquired a callboy.

"I need summer suits for my two sons. I have their measurements written on a piece of paper," she said, reaching into her dress pocket. "They're nearly as big as you, and I hope they haven't grown since I wrote these numbers down on Sunday."

"Let me take you to the salesman, if you please, ma'am."

"Thank you," she said, falling in step beside him.

"It's ready-made suits you're wanting, am I right? This is the floor for them."

Clara paused, losing her gaiety in a rush of indecision. Whatever she decided now would leave her vulnerable to Henry's sarcasm or rage. If she had the suits custom-made, she would be attacked as a spendthrift; buy them ready-to-wear and she would be charged with dressing her children like newsboys. Suddenly she felt depleted, heavy, and wanted to let herself down from the giddy height of the arcade. "Are the custom goods on the first floor?"

"Yes, ma'am."

"I had better go there, I think. Thank you."

Within another ten minutes she had ordered two fancy linen suits in which she could picture poor Riggs and Gerald — ridiculous to themselves and pitiful to her — having to sit for long, silent hours on hotel patios in Nice and Wiesbaden and Geneva as their father showed them off to titled frauds and vacationing financiers. "Please have them sent to Number Four Beekman Place. You really can have them there by Friday afternoon?"

"Rest assured, ma'am," the clerk said.

Clara headed out of the store, onto Broadway. She walked north toward Eleventh Street, past veterans selling pennywhistles and popguns, women hawking candy and cigars. A half hour ago she would have found the loud street life appealing, but the boys' suits had forced her mind toward Friday and the passage to France. Her immediate destination, McCreery's, exposed her to the same conundrum she had rehearsed on the second-floor arcade. If she went in to have a new ball gown made up, she would be scalded with charges of extravagance; fail to go in and, come summer, Henry would rail at her for shabbiness. When should she take delivery of his abuse? She would schedule it for the summer, she decided; the hot weather would leave Henry with less energy to dispatch the insult. It might spoil the quicker and be discarded with the custards and creams rotting on the hotel patio.

So she would not go into McCreery's. Besides, she had long since lost her appetite for clothes. Years ago she would stand inside the White House like a Maypole, Mrs. Lincoln with her dressmaker whirling round her, festooning her simple frock with silk flowers and paste jewelry. She had once or twice come back to Fifteenth and H so done up that her sisters couldn't decide between admiring exclamations and fits of laughter. In fact, she was rather shabby now. The dress pocket from which she'd pulled the list of the boys' measurements was torn at the corner, and on her collar there was a small sauce stain that just this morning she'd noticed but not bothered to remove. Looking as she did, she knew it was no wonder the callboy back at Stewart's had assumed she wanted the ready-made suits.

She was tired, torn between starting back for Mary's and continuing to savor her free movement through the city. She decided to walk east, through a gay gantlet of balloon men and shoelace sellers, toward the Astor Library on Lafayette Place, where she could sit down by herself. Once inside its reading room, she took a volume of Wordsworth from behind the grille and smiled at the memory of her father, who years ago had gently suggested that Bryant might be better nourishment for an American girl in the Hudson Valley. But until her twenty-first birthday it was Wordsworth she had loved; then she fancied herself outgrowing him for the wickedness of Byron and Thackeray, writers who seemed proper companions for the clever-tongued woman everyone said she had become.

> *As if but yesterday departed,*
> *Thou too art gone before; but why,*
> *O'er ripe fruit, seasonably gathered,*
> *Should frail survivors heave a sigh?*

Why, for the sake of self-pity, naturally. She sighed, even now, over the departure of her long-lived father, and could feel some remnant of her former witty self rebuking the naiveté of the even earlier girl. And yet, the next verse reminded her that the poem left plenty of room for grief over the death of that person closest of all to her:

> *Mourn rather for that holy spirit,*
> *Sweet as the spring, as ocean deep;*
> *For her who, ere her summer faded,*
> *Has sunk into a breathless sleep.*

It was she herself who was dying. She was expiring beneath the force of Henry's misery, just as he was being crushed by all the hateful history he worshiped, and in which he'd been caught. Just look at it, shelf after shelf of it, all around the upper reaches of the reading room, oppressing the poetry shelves beneath: Tacitus and Livy and Gibbon and Carlyle, all of it laden with doom, some of it — right at this hour in Loudonville — being poured into the uncomprehending ears of her sons.

Mr. Astor's library closed each weekday at four. Clara stayed, turning the pages of Wordsworth and *McClure's,* until the chime rang at 3:50, after which she started not for her temporary home at Mary's, but farther southward into the city, down Broadway, block after block, with no purpose, as far as Broome Street, the corner on which Mrs. Prevost's Theatre used to be, where Pauline and Emeline saw John Wilkes Booth play Henry V one night in 1862. Newsboys were hawking the afternoon editions. She got through several competing packs of them before deciding that with a paper under her arm she might walk in peace. So when the next group came up — "News of the day, ma'am?" "*Telegram? Telegram?*" "Only two pennies, only two pennies" — she took one from the smallest boy she could spot, thereby earning him a few good pokes in the ribs from the rest of the gaggle, before they dashed off to another possible patron. "There you go, ma'am," said the boy, making change from Clara's nickel. "That's a nice cartoon of Ol' Mutton Chops we've got today, ain't it?" He pointed to a caricature of the widowed President Arthur shying nervously away from the seductions of Britannia.

"And what if I were to tell Old Mutton Chops that that's what you call him? He was a friend of my father's, you know."

"Yer foolin'."

"No, I'm not," said Clara, laughing. "And what's so astonishing about that, anyway? Don't you think you yourself might be President of the United States someday? Or at least senator from New York?"

The Irish boy was laughing with her now. "Nah," he said. "Senator from the Dakota, maybe. That's where they'll be sendin' me, soon as they can find someone ter make use of me out there."

"Where do you live now?" asked Clara.

"Down at the Newsboys' Lodgin' House. Right down at Park Place," he said, rather proudly, pointing down Broadway toward Printing House Square. "Lots of us winds up out west. A good deal all around, doncha know."

Clara smiled down at this marvelous boy, so full of nerve and ginger that Henry himself wouldn't be able to dash the life from him. She'd half a mind to take him back to Loudonville and make him change places with Gerald, just like the boys in *The Prince and the Pauper*, Mark Twain's new book, which she'd given them at Christmas, and which Henry promptly condemned for making penny candy out of history.

"You take the rest of this nickel," Clara told the boy, giving him back her change. "You'll need it for seed money, for making your fortune out west." Before she could change her mind, the boy tipped his cap and ran off into the late afternoon.

Clara did not arrive at Mary Hall's until seven. She walked every step of the way back to Beekman Place, lost in her thoughts, unwilling to relinquish the unaccustomed solitude. A cloudburst soaked her with rain as she trudged north through Murray Hill.

"Come upstairs and let me undress you," said Mary when she saw her in the entrance hall. "Never mind the maid."

"It's my own fault, Mary. I couldn't persuade myself to take a carriage." Clara shivered and allowed her friend to lead her up the stairs. The saturated dress with the torn pocket came off, as well as the undergarments. As Mary dried Clara's back, she seemed to search her naked form for clues.

"No, Mary, you won't find any bruises. It's not like that."

"Then what is it like?" asked Mary, surprised by her own boldness. "I mean lately."

Clara closed her chenille robe and sat down at the foot of Mary's bed. "Lately," she said, "if one can call the last two years that, it has been very . . . lonely," she said, choosing the word carefully, deciding that she would not cry. "Pauline no sooner returns from Newport than she's off to St. Augustine. From Cleveland, Will inquires into nothing. Louise is supposed to join us in Europe later in the year; meanwhile she scurries away in terror at Henry's very approach. Tutors come to teach the boys, but Henry sends them home before lunchtime, sure that he can more effectively impart wisdom to his sons than they can. No tutors for little Clara. I'm keeping her ignorant, just like me. Riggs uses every ounce of strength he has to deny the strangeness of his situation. Gerald, I think, hates him.

"You won't be surprised to know that I'm not looking forward to Germany and all the Old World wanderings that will precede it. I shall soon have quite enough of closed carriages." She stopped to laugh, theatrically — a sign, thought her friend, that she desired interruption, some question or challenge. At a loss for the right one, Mary remained silent, and Clara resumed: "We shall sit amidst speculators and heiresses, the former pretending to solicit Henry's advice. He will relish the chance to appear shrewd, a man of consequence, but they will be too rich already to have much interest in swindling him. They will just keep him talking and talking, hopeful that he'll somehow wander into that precinct of conversation known as What Happened At Ford's, so that they can have their own brush with the history their newfound companion so reveres. Chances are the hoped-for conversation will never take place, since even speculators have acquired too many manners to push him towards it, though as more and more whiskey is consumed, the electricity of risk will once or twice enter the air — and Henry may just be in the mood. The heiresses will look to me as a source of maternal advice, while their mamas will regard me as a potential purveyor of worldly wisdom, though the years since I was 'Mrs. Rathbone, Lafayette Square's notable hostess' have begun to recede."

"Must you go, Clara? Must any of you go? Is there any point to one more trip abroad?"

"Yes Mary, there is, albeit a hopeless one. There's a stop in Geneva that's been scheduled. A medical matter. That's right," she continued, avoiding Mary's eyes, which had widened in surprise. Telling her what no one outside the family knew, she said, "It's for Henry. For his mental condition. It's not the first time this has been tried, either. Four years ago we sought out a man in Carlsbad, but it did no good. Once more the doctor comes on Jared's recommendation, some bit of intelligence he picked up on his European travels for Mr. Stanford."

"But surely this *is* a hopeful sign, Clara."

"No, Mary." She now looked into her friend's eyes. "I'm afraid it isn't. Henry sees nothing whatever wrong with himself. He will sit and listen to the doctor and compliment him on his erudition. Then he will leave the consulting room and pour the doctor's advice, along with his potions, down the hotel bathroom's drain."

"Then why does he go to these doctors at all?"

"He *agrees* to go. He fears that Jared will try to cheat him of the rest of Pauline's money after she's dead. He's decided that going to these physicians and talking sweet reason in their presence — you know, he's become a much better actor than Wilkes Booth was — will be, in the eyes of some probate court one day, a clearer demonstration of goodwill and sanity than adamant refusal to act upon family advice regarding his lapses into 'melancholy.' How I love that elastic word!"

"But perhaps this doctor really can be of some help, in spite of Henry's resistance. Oh, Clara, I'm just certain things will have improved by Christmas!"

"Oh, Mary," said Clara, coming across the room to embrace her friend, to hold Mary's head against her own damp hair. "You sound just like my papa."

↬ 46 ↫

Nice
10 August 1883

We arrived here in the usual unpatterned way. (Riggs charts our "progress" — no word ever meant more its opposite — on a map, and the lines he draws create a mad cat's-cradle, resembling what I still think of as Henry's "wiring.") Our previous location, for all of four days, was Amsterdam, where we saw one more world's fair. Had we been abroad last year, I am sure we would have attended Moscow's. I have seen half a dozen of them over the last fifteen years — but never one in my own country.

I don't know when our German residence is supposed to begin, or where exactly we're supposed to spend it. The pace of our travels has so quickened that I wonder if Henry will ever be able to brake us; perhaps we shall go on forever. I think he believes that moving like dervishes will keep us all together, by some sort of centripetal force. He has once more been asking the question he put to me in Carlsbad four years ago: "Are you going to leave me?" He has asked it a half-dozen times since we've been over, in every possible manner — panicked, imploring, angry, and just casually curious, the way the children used to inquire whether streetcars could fly.

This afternoon in the hotel garden we paced mechanically — twelve times around it, in one of those mathematical repetitions Henry sometimes insists upon. On most of the circuits we were accompanied by a fat gentleman from Manchester, who looked like the Prince of Wales and told us about his investment in this train the papers are full of. Less than two months from now, the Orient Express will depart from Paris toward Constantinople, carrying forty people through Munich and Vienna and Budapest, stuffing

them with caviare as they go. The furnishings sound beyond anything I can recall from the Vanderbilt: Turkish carpets, silk sheets
and wall coverings, a different bathroom for every two couples. A
gipsy band will come aboard somewhere in Hungary, and when the
whole Barnum-like production rolls through Bulgaria, King Boris
III, who has a passion for trains, will put on a pair of overalls and
take the controls.

By the time the Manchester man was through with his description, Henry was prepared to write a check for shares in the company. Of course, we shan't see any of this train ourselves. Henry is
in the trough of his mental economic cycle, preaching frugality and
sacrifice to me and the children. When his mood arrives back in the
extravagant part of its arc, I hope we are through with the German
experiment and home for good.

We are a train, a runaway one, with mad King Boris at the
controls. Henry goes on playing at life, according to whatever impulses run through his wires, and the rest of us follow behind, like
motorized mannequins. A month has passed since the "consultation" in Geneva, which took just the course I anticipated. Henry
was exceptionally plausible, and charming, getting this "specialist"
to believe it really was just dyspepsia he suffered from, and that he'd
only made the appointment to placate his beloved but alarmist wife.
We left with two prescriptions, one for his stomach and another for
my nerves. Back at the hotel, I noticed how he carefully put the
doctor's receipt with his most important papers: as "proof," I am
sure, of good intentions and mere physical malady, to any court that
might one day be interested in the matter.

All I ever saw him do with the bottle of medicine was stare at it.
He read the label a dozen times over, until he had entranced himself
and was on one of those frightening trips back to the war. He
seemed to think he was looking at a bottle of liniment in a hospital
tent, the one he'd actually been in after the Crater. For a quarter of
an hour he was calmly, genially, out of his mind — during which
time Riggs and Gerald came into the room and for the first time
witnessed their father being quite unaware of who they were. I
summoned Louise, who hurried the boys into the next room, telling
them the stomach medicine had had some adverse effect upon their

papa and that he would soon be well. But I am sure they knew otherwise: Gerald had gone white, and Riggs, in his manly little way, urged Louise not to go back and sit by Henry's side "until his stomach settles." I wish, instead of the two of them, that little Clara had been the one to see Henry this way: she has a sharper instinct (and tongue) and is more resilient than her brothers. I think she is entirely aware that her father is not "right," and I believe she's been so for the last few years, since she was six or seven. No matter, I eventually got everyone to bed, and I ended the evening by looking at my own bottle of medicine, the tonic prescribed for my "nerves." The skull-and-bones on its label shrieked that not more than a teaspoonful could be taken every twelve hours, and had I not known just how ineffective it was (I had tried it that morning), I might have contemplated swallowing the entire contents — "That I might drink, and leave the world unseen."

Hanover

10 October 1883

Last week at this hour we were passing through the Hartz Mountains, staring up from the coach at the Brocken, all of us marveling, even Henry, at the white mists surrounding it. We felt ourselves to be flying rather than pulled along terra firma by a team of bays. But only hours later we returned to the mundane earth — in the form of this city — with a great bump. I do not like Hanover; I never have since that day sixteen years ago when we had a terrific fight in the Waterloo Platz (over what, I cannot now remember). Henry has managed to settle us into a damp-filled boarding house, with the children crowded into a single room. (We are still near the nadir of his economic cycle, and such places as the Hotel de Russie are out of the question.) He told the landlady that he was determined to keep us here for the "extended experience" of Germany he is bent on having. (Solemn remarks about Bismarck and the emperor and the nation-state, to which Riggs and Gerald are expected to attend, emanate from him every several minutes.)

Up until yesterday I was grimly adjusting. I had discovered a small community of Americans and English among whom the chil-

dren might find some friends (I no longer bother to seek any for myself), and I was determined I would find the courage to order that Henry's German experience be fully "extended" and complete before Christmas. But then yesterday morning he announced his intention to remove us all to Berlin, so that he might read history in the national library. This undertaking required a special pass, he thought, and so he piled us all onto a train for nearby Brunswick, where he could talk to the American consul about getting one.

While Henry called at the man's office, I was left to explore the town with the children. Henry would not give us the $2 fee to visit the palace, so we went off to the cathedral instead — one more cathedral, one more set of Henry the Lion relics. After perusing them, the four of us returned to the open air, walking along what once were ramparts, and deciding that Brunswick is a much nicer place than Hanover. Everywhere below us were lovely houses upon green hillsides. We chased and ambushed one another along the walkways, playing tag and singing in rounds. There I was with my three beautiful American children, ridiculously — but for a moment so happily — bellowing "Oh! Susannah" into the German air. For the first time in months I felt happy to be alive, rebellious, or — my old favorite word — encouraged. I believed I might yet overcome the disaster of my life, this disaster of my own making, created from my stubborn, blind love.

And then the day was over. We arrived back here in the dark, all of us silent in the face of Henry's bad humor, which was brought on by the consul, who had denied him whatever application he sought. He would not eat his dinner, and would not allow the children, despite my angry protests, to touch anything but the vegetables on their plates. Today he has spent all day in the next room. ("Menschenscheu," I heard the landlady whisper to her husband when he wouldn't come to lunch — "Shy of human beings.") He did not permit the children to go out (they are now playing — happily enough, according to my ears — in a shuttered room), and he has forbidden me to sit by the window.

I am calm. I am clear. I shall now hide this book (an absolute necessity always) and write Will, who must, I have decided, come over here and get us. He must take us all home, and after that he *must take us away from Henry. It is the only thing left to do. I do not know how we will end up once we are back in America; right now I must concentrate on getting us home, on rescuing my children by destroying my family. What lies ahead will be ugly and dangerous. My mind is already racing with plans and contingencies. It occurs to me that yesterday's visit to the consul was a blessing. This man, whose name I now know, Mr. Fox, will perhaps remember the strange gentleman who called on him, and be disposed to help the man's wife. I must tell Will his name in the letter, which I will ask Louise to mail for me. I need her now, and she must not fail me with her fearfulness. She must not fail the nephews and niece that, in her stifled way, she loves.*

I must not fail myself.

O my love, my life — for nearly forty years! I am finally ready to surrender you, to save for my children what little is left of myself, to go away from you — if need be, never to see you again — to let others keep you under lock and key. I sit here in this small room, afraid to approach the window, surveying the little wreckage of my life, but I thank the Lord for one last great gift: the strength, at last, to admit my heart is broken.

Hanover

30 November 1883

We are still here, destined to remain so for another six or seven weeks at least. Today a response from Will finally arrived, but this letter that Louise and I have been watching for every single day, and are now contriving to keep out of Henry's sight, has only made my heart sink further. Will says he is alarmed by what I've said, but along with his concern I detect an equal measure of embarrassment. This pillar of Cleveland never expected such family disgrace to shadow his own dignity. I am so far removed from my normal wits that I mistrust my ability to read between the lines, but in addition to everything else he says, I can't help but notice a small sense of triumph over the stepbrother who always despised him: Will sees Henry's mental incapacity as a vindication of his own character. My good brother would be ashamed to admit, even to himself, this delicious feeling, but I'm sure I see it lurking on the watermarked pages of his letter.

He says that if I cannot convince Henry to take us home before the New Year, then he will sail for Europe on January 5 and do what he can to fetch us back to America. He may bring Amanda's Tom with him, for he fears terrible scenes and complications. Jared is too far away in California to be of help, and Will doesn't want to drag Uncle Hamilton away from Albany, since he will be the one required to make the delicate arrangements for Henry once we have gotten him back home. Pauline, who has gone with Lina to St. Augustine for the winter, will be told nothing until all is accomplished.

I should be cheered by these plans, but I despair to look at all the weeks I shall have to endure until they are executed. Will does not know how things have worsened since I wrote. Henry is physically unwell, chiefly due to his frequent refusal to eat. (He has, thank goodness, been so preoccupied with his own food-aversion that he has let the children do as they please with their stomachs.) He is pallid and gaunt, and will not leave the house. Last week the landlady helped me summon a doctor from the next street, but he could only tell us the obvious, that Henry should eat more. Henry is for the most part silent, staring off at the wallpaper without a sound. At intervals he becomes messianic, though calmly so, wondering aloud whether Mr. Blaine, if nominated for President next year, will ask him to explain how he managed to make that happen. Once or twice he has sworn that voices are emerging from the picture in the hallway (a print of the Angelus), and he is often under the impression that Eagle Street lies outside our window. He mentions no enemies, but insists upon going to bed with a revolver under his pillow.

I now sleep in Louise's room, a dereliction that has so far met with no resistance. It is, after all, only mothering he wants now — endless soothing, and reassurance that the children and I are not planning to leave. He once more allows them to play outside, but will not let me leave the house with them. I am able to go off with Louise, but only after lengthy explanations of the nature of our errand.

My chief fear is that he will harm himself — this worry much

*heightened by my discovery that he has written a will. It is incoher-
ent — I cannot make any clear sense of what is being left to whom,
but its first sentences seem to indicate that he thinks his demise will
come soon.*

*For the last two hours, since the arrival of Will's letter, I have
wrestled with the desire to make Louise send him a cable in Ohio,
one that says we cannot wait until the 5th of January for him to
leave. I am held back by a fear that sending it would convince me
the situation is even worse than it is. That would lead me to panic,
whereupon I will be no good at all to the children. So far I have
managed well enough (though I, too, have grown thin, from the
strain); I tell myself I can manage several weeks more, through
Christmas, which will distract the children and perhaps coax Henry's
mind from the terrible jail it is in.*

*The truth is that I have never loved him more than I have this
last month. I have wanted to wail with pity over him, as if he were
a corpse, and I a widow. He mutters more than ever of our hours
in the box at Ford's, forcing me to think of them too. I realize I shall
be the last alive of the five persons who were in there once Wilkes
Booth entered. When Will gets here, I shall be sending Henry into
the same dark afterlife that Robert Lincoln banished his mother to
before she actually died. For all my own suffering, and for all my
certainty that no other course lies open to me — not if I am to save
my children — I am stricken with guilt. The action, however rea-
sonable, feels like treachery. And even now, no, I cannot bear the
thought of losing him — my love! — forever.*

⇥ 47 ⇤

A FRESH MAT of snow covered George Street, and the little opera house was festooned with gold torches and silver bells. Approaching the entrance with Henry, Clara squeezed her hands inside her red velvet muff, not just to keep them warm, but to give herself a pinch, to make herself believe she wasn't dreaming. No, here she was in Hanover, two nights before Christmas, actually out with her husband like an ordinary wife, waiting for him to hand their tickets to the usher so they could go inside with the other American and British couples, to hear a local chorus attempt the *Messiah,* in English.

After this morning, it seemed a miracle. Henry had slept late, troubled by dreams an hour past his usual time to get up. She had come into the bedroom to find him thrashing, shouting at some pursuers to shoot him — to come and get him and get it over with, for God's sake! When she grabbed hold of him and shook, she noticed that his nightshirt was soaked through. Once he came round, he was exhausted and docile, eager for her to stay as he ate every item on the breakfast plate that had been warming on the little porcelain stove in the room.

Afterward, he even let her go shopping without Louise, which is how she came to linger long enough in the bookshop in Frederick Street to encounter Mrs. Carswell, who shuffled in, huge and cheerful. A retired British major's wife whom Clara had met her first week in Hanover, Mrs. Carswell was so naturally bossy and well intentioned that today Clara found herself pouring out her own story, right down to Henry's morning nightmare. It was Mrs. Carswell's matter-of-fact nodding, her complete lack of surprise or censoriousness, that made Clara wonder if here, too, as in Mr. Fox, the consul, she might have an ally when the time came to impose her will on Henry. Faced with Mrs. Carswell's monumental patience and person, she felt a desire to rest her head like a schoolgirl against the woman's great bosom, to fall asleep on it, in peace.

"He's in a terrible slump, isn't he?" said Mrs. Carswell, with no more alarm than she might have expressed in diagnosing a child's head cold. "The poor dear. He needs strong medicine, and I don't mean pills and potions. I mean *sunshine*, and people. You've got to force company upon him, my dear. You've got to let a lot of new faces crowd out this mood of his; you've got to let them *trample* it down to nothing. You won't get him out of it if you stay in that boarding house with your little ones. Get him *out,* Mrs. Rathbone, and don't wait 'til Christmas morning. You get him out and about right now. Today. Or at least to-night," she said, reaching into her great beaded bag and extracting two tickets to the evening's recital. "You do yourselves a favor, and Herr Wenzel, too. The choirmaster — a darling man, have you met him? You show up with your husband tonight and let him hear the Lord's good news sung to a crowd of happy people. English words and English music! I don't care what Herr Wenzel says, to me George Frederick Handel is an Englishman. Don't you agree? In any case, you take these tickets and you use them. Show some *courage*. You'll find me there tonight with Major Carswell. Look for the red and green plumes of my hat — it *is* Christmas, and I intend to wear it, even if it blocks the view of whoever's behind me. Keep an eye out for me, and I'll toss you all the encouraging glances you need."

Clara didn't know if this woman was incalculably sensible or just as silly. She only knew she wanted to do what she was being told, wanted to let Mrs. Carswell shake her up, just as forty years ago the Harrises' Irish housemaid would scrub young Clara's tear-stained face with a rough, soapy washcloth. So she went home with the tickets and told her sister she had a treat for her. Louise could spend the evening here alone with the children; she and Henry were going out. Mrs. Carswell had filled her up with such confidence that she didn't even consider the possibility of failure. Henry's pliant morning mood would continue, it had to, long enough to make him agree.

And it was soon settled. He would let her take him to the theatre. That is what he made it seem, a willingness to be led, to put himself in his wife's motherly hands. He spent what was left of the morning following her around, giving her occasion to use terms of endearment she hadn't spoken in years. Once or twice she almost lapsed into baby talk, a form of expression that had never been part of even their best days, when their intimate words had always been about their bodies, brutal, thrillingly so. Today he seemed as sweetly obedient as Gerald. Her heart was light. If this kept up for even a few days, they would have a last Christmas together that approximated happiness. His docility would also buy her time, let her conserve her strength for the showdown that would arrive next month with Will.

All afternoon she decorated the front room, and Henry kept out of sight to finish carving a wooden doll, a present for little Clara. He was clumsy at it, using a new long knife with an ornamental handle, one too delicate for the task. When he purchased it a week ago and began work, he had cursed himself each time the blade slipped, but today, when she checked on him, he seemed amused at being all thumbs. *The normal human character is marked by a sense of humor, a notion of its own occasional ridiculousness* . . . There were so many sentences she could quote from the books of mental hygiene she'd consulted year after year in the Library of Congress, and the Albany Public, and the English-language bookstore in whatever city she was passing through, statements of bland good sense whose inapplicability to Henry always caused her to quit reading. This suddenly apt one, *a notion of its own occasional ridiculousness,* came back to her now, like some sweet echo of her mother's voice, and cheered her further. She returned to the damp little parlor ready to whistle, and she fastened sprigs of holly to the windowsills and hung the cards from Amanda's children on the fireplace. The landlady, Frau Kiesinger, came up with a pot of wine for them to mull on the bedroom stove, a gift that Henry accepted peacefully and set to stirring between bouts with the wooden doll.

There was only one bad moment, which came from letting down her guard. Gerald, seeing the cards on the mantel, remembered last Christmas and declared that he missed his cousin

Louis. He was afraid the boy would forget him if they stayed here much longer. "It's all right, sweetheart," Clara reassured him as she put some walnuts into a bowl at the edge of the room, forgetting that her words would carry down the hall to the bedroom, through whose open door the spicy smell of the wine was drifting. "You'll be seeing Louis very soon." "Really?" Gerald said, running toward her at the same time Henry, with a worried expression, came out of the bedroom and started down the hall.

Her heart sped up, the way it did a dozen times most days, like a fire catching a bellows. But she caught herself and laughed, and kissed both her men, saying to Gerald as she stroked his hair, "Whenever your papa is done with his studies, dear. That's when we'll go. You must have patience. Louis won't forget you. The day after tomorrow you can write him another letter telling him all about the presents you got for Christmas. All right?" She smiled at Henry, trying to effect a look of parental conspiracy; but she was aware of her effort, aware that this was the sort of smile she usually gave to little Clara when her papa had said or done something particularly odd.

But the crisis passed. Henry appeared calm, and she urged him to join them in the parlor as they strung paper balls for the tiny fir tree on the table. Why didn't he sit here and read the London *Times,* which she'd picked up in the bookshop this morning? It was from two weeks ago, but already full of Christmas tidings. "Look," she said, opening it to the third page as she moved him toward the sofa, "Matthew Arnold is going to be at the White House on Christmas Day. He and Mr. Arthur may even go to church together." Henry took the paper and smiled, as if she'd brought up some pleasant family memory from long ago. While she and Riggs held opposite ends of the wire, Gerald and his sister strung the bits of paper around it. Clara glanced nervously at her husband. This gentleness, this respite, she thought, was a new form of torment: if he were no worse than this, shouldn't she remain a good wife and take care of him, be glad to have him at her side for the rest of their days?

⇥⇤

The purple robes and golden stoles of the entering choir brought a murmur from the audience. Along with everyone in the mezzanine's first row, Henry and Clara leaned forward for a closer look. As she gripped the wooden railing, Clara caught sight of Mrs. Carswell, who down below was giving her an emphatic wave: well done, it seemed to say. The gas lamps were lowered, and Herr Wenzel raised his baton. Henry inserted his left hand into Clara's mink-trimmed muff, which lay between them. With her right hand still inside it, she took hold of him and smiled like a young lover. He was so thin, she thought, feeling the fingers. Except for the receding hair, he could, in these dim lights, pass for a college boy, or a young man the age his cousin Howard was when he gave her this muff one Christmas long ago, before the war.

Every valley shall be exalted, and every mountain and hill made low, the crooked straight and the rough places plain. As the nervous young tenor sang these words in his German-accented English, she could remember Reverend Bridgman reciting them in the pulpit on Pearl Street as she sat next to her papa, his Roman head nodding in silent appreciation. Right now it would be midafternoon in Albany. She tried to imagine the sleighs on Broadway and State Street, and she wondered what pantomime might be on tonight at the Leland or the Levantine. Was Washington perhaps getting one of its rare snows? Were Lafayette Square and Andy Jackson's cocked hat right now dusted with just a bit of white? It was amusing to think of President Arthur, all powdered and primped, climbing the steps of St. John's on Christmas morning, arm in arm with that dour scholar-gypsy Matthew Arnold. Whatever would they talk about? Below her the choir soldiered on through Handel, afraid to take their eyes off their big square song sheets, which reminded her of the children's books she used to stack in the sewing room. She wished her sons and daughter hadn't passed the age when they wanted to be read to. Would Louise have gotten them to sleep by the time she and Henry made it home?

Thus saith the Lord of Hosts, boomed the bass. *Yet once a little while and I will shake the heavens and the earth, the sea and the dry land; and I will shake all nations; and the desire of all nations shall come.* Henry's eyes, she could now see, were too attentive, too intense. Once or twice he had turned around to see over his shoulder, and she'd patted his hand inside the muff to get him to return his gaze to the choir. But now his eyes seemed riveted, as if convinced the choir were singing man's true history, not his mere hopes. She patted his hand once more and wished that Herr Wenzel would reach the point where the alto sang soothingly of the Virgin.

Before long Henry seemed calmer, leaving her to be the one struggling for control of her emotions. Like a horoscope, every verse in the recital seemed meaningful, and when the bass began to sing of how *The people that walked in darkness have seen a great light; and they that dwell in the land of the shadow of death, upon them hath the light shined,* she felt her own tears coming, for they were singing her own guilty hope for deliverance, which one moment felt still too dangerously far off, and the next just selfish, something she ought to be too faithful to need. Still, perhaps all manner of thing *would* be well. Henry would leave them, but just for a time. Her children would grow up strong, and then he would return to them, old, but well and whole. He would come *home* someday, an old campaigner through madness, scarred but full of lucid tales of what he'd soldiered through. And she, his Desdemona, would listen to him, marveling and grateful, as they spent their winter years together, a long miracle, by the fireside. They would be rewarded for their suffering, for what they were passing through now.

Henry, too, had a glint of moisture in his eyes — she could see it in the dimmed gaslight — as the chorus sang of all the torments heaped upon the Savior, the sort that for years had been heaped upon Henry himself, all because that night he had failed at being superhuman, the savior people wished had been present. *Surely He hath borne our griefs, and carried our sorrows! He was wounded for our transgressions; He was bruised for our iniquities; the chastisement of our peace was upon Him.* She patted his hand as she looked down on the crowd, too warm in their coats, with all their gloves and scarves and Homburgs piled upon their laps. It was a vision of self-satisfaction, while up here in the balcony she and Henry were doomed to keep twitching and suffering. But suffering *together*, she thought, grateful for this reunion with him, however painful, that she was feeling.

She was so tired. She turned her eyes back to the choir's regal coverings, to the holly and poinsettias all over the stage, and let herself be lost in the music instead of the words, until the end was near, and the bass voice came like a gong: *Behold, I tell you a mystery: We shall not all sleep; but we shall all be changed in a moment, in the twinkling of an eye, at the last trumpet.* She nudged Henry and motioned that they should go. She did not want to be caught in the departing crowd, sprayed with its holiday chatter, did not want to exchange bromidic winks with good Mrs. Carswell. She wanted to get home to her own hearth, damp and alien as it was. She would put her poor husband to bed, and with a small blessing from God — just a little favor, not the apocalyptic Good News promised by the choir — tomorrow would contain moments of contentment like the ones today had brought. Henry looked up at her, gentle and confused, but content to be led. They muttered their apologies and exited the mezzanine's front row, before finding a staircase that led out of the theatre.

Back on George Street, Clara put her arm through her husband's.

"Are you warm enough, dear?" he asked.

"Yes," she said. She now had both her own hands inside her muff, and the two walked for a full minute with no sound but Henry's boots crunching the snow. "I'm fine," she assured him. "I'm only tired, that's all. I'm glad we came out to hear the music."

"Yes," said Henry. "I'm glad you brought me. The singers were rather good, didn't you think?"

"Yes, though a little comical, too. Those German accents made me think of Johnny Nicolay, when he used to talk about 'army bensions' and the slowness of the 'bost office.'" Henry said nothing then, and she realized she had ventured into risky territory by making even this casual reference to Lincoln's Bavarian-born secretary.

While it provoked Henry to neither sarcasm nor anger, the

calm reply he made was nearly as dismaying: "I'm trying to recall if before tonight we'd ever sat in a balcony — since Ford's."

"I'm sure we have, darling. More than once, I'm certain, at theatres in New York, in the first years we were married." She walked faster, pulling him gently by his right arm, as if a quicker pace might succeed in changing the subject. "Let's not think about that," she added. "Let's look forward to Christmas. Do you think you'll have Clara's doll finished in time?"

"I should," said Henry.

"Good. I'll put it into her stocking tomorrow night."

"It's such a plain thing," he said. "I wish it were something fancy, like that frilly Marie Antoinette we bought for Lina years ago in Paris. Do you remember?"

"Of course I do," said Clara. "But what you're making is lovely. Much nicer than this gaudy thing. Look," she said with a disapproving face, directing his attention to a shop at the corner of their street, through whose darkened window one could still see the crudely painted figures of a Santa's workshop. They quietly walked the last fifty yards to the steps of the boarding house.

"The children are asleep," he said, looking up at the second-floor windows. "Louise is, too."

"Even Frau Kiesinger and her husband." Clara pointed to the shutters a story below.

They shook the snow from their shoes and climbed the stairs to the apartment. In the faintly lit hallway, Clara moved to kiss Henry good night and go off to join Louise in her room. But he gently restrained her. "Clara, stay with me tonight."

"All right," she whispered, pleasant surprise outweighing any wariness.

Once inside the bedroom, she sat down on the upholstered wing chair, instead of the straight-backed one at her vanity. She undid her hair and began brushing it. Henry went into the bathroom to perform his still-meticulous nightly wash-up. The softness of the chair and the rhythm of the brushing soothed the tension from her; she felt like a cat whose fur was finally settling down, and before she knew it she had dozed off, the brush falling onto the cushion with the hairpins. A minute or two passed before she opened her eyes and found that her husband was still not in bed. "Henry?" she called softly, wondering what could be keeping him this long at the sink; but when she looked through the door of the bathroom, she saw it was empty.

"Henry?" she whispered, venturing out into the hallway.

She saw that the door to the children's bedroom was open, and she walked toward it, relieved to find him standing just inside the room. It was a sweet sight. He had his back to her, his arms crossed in front of him, regarding his three sleeping off-spring in the moonlight coming through the window. She came up silently behind him and slipped her arm through his, as she had ten minutes ago on the street. But this time her hand struck something sharp. As Henry turned his head, calmly, to look at her, she glanced down toward her own bare arm. It had been nicked by the ivory-handled knife he was holding in his left hand. For an instant she closed her eyes and offered what she swore would be the last prayer she ever prayed if only it were granted: *please let his other hand be holding the wooden doll.* But when she opened her eyes, she saw that it contained the revolver he had kept for the last few weeks under his pillow.

She knew what it was like to feel her heart hammering, but at this moment she thought her blood had frozen, that her heart had stopped entirely, and that she would faint at his feet. But she squeezed her fists and gathered her last wits and whispered, "Henry, come away from here."

"No," he said quietly, exercising the same care she was in not waking the children. "This is something I must do for us."

"What do you mean?" she asked, affecting reasonableness, trying to keep him calm.

"I must keep us all together. I can't let us come apart."

"We're not coming apart."

"Yes," he said in a spirit of gentle contradiction. "We are. I'm sure you're going to leave me. You've been planning it for years, and you're going to take the children with you. So I'm going to arrange things differently. I'm going to keep us all together, in paradise."

"Henry, stop." Her voice was louder now, but only a little. She realized the impossibility of rousing Louise, who was behind a closed door at the far end of the hall, without waking the children.

"No," said Henry, raising his right arm and pointing the revolver at little Clara. "I must."

"Stop it!" she cried, not reaching for the gun but swerving around behind him, to his other side, where she took hold of his damaged left arm and squeezed it with all her strength, until he groaned with pain and both arms fell to his sides. He growled, but quietly, as if he, too, still wanted to avoid disturbing his sons and daughter, who had all begun to stir. Clara again pulled hard on his left arm, this time dragging him backward, across the threshold and out into the hall. She pulled the door closed and began beating on his chest, punching and pushing him toward their own bedroom. As he moved backward under the rain of blows, he looked at her without any anger, just perplexity over her failure to see the wisdom of his plan.

"Henry, get inside!" She succeeded in forcing him into their room, but her hopes of rushing back out to the hallway to wake Louise and Herr Kiesinger were now thwarted. Henry had gotten behind her and locked the bedroom door.

He put down the knife on the porcelain stove, but he kept the revolver at his side.

"Why did you stop me?" he asked quietly, though his calm was finally shattering and he had started to cry. "I never stopped *him*."

For a second she didn't know what he meant, but then she realized, of course, that he was talking about Wilkes Booth, and she decided she would not scream for Louise, that she would gain control of the situation by having the same conversation they had had so many times over the last eighteen years. As he stood before her with a revolver, a moment after trying to kill their daughter, she told him that he mustn't be so hard on himself.

"Henry, let it be. You did everything anyone could have."

"No," he said through his tears. "No, I didn't. You don't understand."

"I *do* understand, Henry. People have been foolish to think —"

"No!" he shouted, gesturing with the pistol as if it were merely a part of his hand. "No! You *don't* understand! And neither do they! I did *not* do everything I could, and I was not negligent, either. *I saw him open the door,* Clara. I saw him stand there for a good five seconds. I never got up from my chair. I *let* him do what he did!"

"No, Henry. You're imagining this."

"Our eyes locked, Clara. His and mine. I let it happen. I *wanted* it to happen."

"No!" she cried, as if what had just taken place down the hall lay eighteen years in the past, and her present frantic business was to thwart the murder of Mr. Lincoln.

"Yes, Clara, I *wanted* it to happen. I wanted to avenge all the soldiers he'd sent to die. I wanted to hurt all the old men who'd made the war."

"Stop, Henry! I shall go mad!"

"I regretted it the moment the gun went off, and then I leapt to stop Booth. I tried to tell you. Tried to tell you crossing Tenth Street, but I couldn't, because the widder-woman kept pulling on my arm, bleeding me to death!" His tears were no longer coming. The baffled, childlike gentleness was gone, replaced by bellowing rage. "I tried to tell you the next morning, when you finally came home. But I could hardly stand to look at you, because I knew you'd spent the night with *her.* You left me! The way you've always left me ever since, for any man who stepped into our house!"

She couldn't attend to the rest of the tirade, though it had the peculiar comfort of familiarity. She could see only what she had seen eighteen years ago, yet remembered and understood only now: his eyes, as they had been in the dark of the box, looking toward its door. From the moment it had happened, she had sensed there was a secret sewn into the violence of that night. She had been afraid to go home for fear of what he would tell her, and so she'd stayed across the street past dawn, locking her suspicion in the cellar of her mind, until this minute, when he'd at last dragged it up and let it out.

"You won't leave me now!" he cried, raising the gun.

"No!" she cried. "I won't. Oh, Henry, let me live!"

She had fought for her children's lives, but beyond this plea, she would not fight for her own. She closed her eyes and heard him fire the gun at her, once, twice, three times, the sound, it seemed, not the bullets themselves, knocking her onto the bed. There was a great roaring in her ears as the blood rushed up from her chest and into her mouth, spilling onto her face with the same warmth she remembered from that night. She knew that she was dying. Louise's shouts and her knocking at the door seemed irrelevant. Clara wearily opened her eyes, as if the noise were an unnecessary imposition. She wanted to tell Louise to go back to bed; she wondered why Henry wasn't telling her to do that, why instead he was standing over her with the knife he had picked up from the stove.

"Don't," she whispered as he plunged it into her already gaping chest. She knew, quite calmly, that she was thinking her last thoughts. Everything was clear. Henry had turned into Booth, and she into Henry. He was using the knife on her as Booth had once used it on him; he was killing her for saving the children, killing her for doing what he hadn't done eighteen years ago. All that remained was for him to kill himself, to thrust the knife into his own body. She saw him withdraw the dagger from her heart, saw her own blood clinging to its blade, which he now drove through his white shirt.

A look of peace came over him, as if he were satisfied that their blood was now finally mingled, that they were at last brother and sister, as they had been husband and wife. The last of her attention and strength ebbed away, and she wanted to say, again, "Don't." She saw him take the knife from his own breast, to begin hacking at his arms and trunk and thighs. He was drenched in blood as he dropped the dagger and walked to the door, opening it at last for Louise, whose screams at what she saw competed with the sound of Herr Kiesinger's boots bounding up the stairs. Henry ignored both of them as he went back to the bed and took Clara into his arms, kissing her saturated hair and whispering the last words she would ever hear. "Who could have done this?" he asked. "Who could have done this, my darling?"

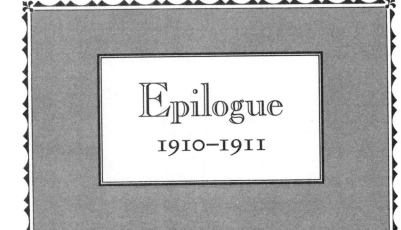

Epilogue
1910–1911

"TELEPHONE, Curtis."

"Yeah, Sally. In a second. First come have a look at this." Young Bill Curtis couldn't stop laughing over the sight below his fourth-floor window. Outside the creamy, iced-wedding-cake offices of the *Evening Star*, the paper's cantankerous treasurer was trying, without success, to crank his new Packard to life. As soon as she arrived at the window, Bill slipped his arm around Sally Kenyon's waist and directed her attention to old man Hubbard, sweating and swearing in the noontime sun as his car sat there like a mule. Sally laughed and removed Bill's arm. "You'd better get your Princeton mitts around the phone, Curtis. It's Hammersmith, and he sounds in a hurry."

"Yes, *ma'am*," said Bill, stealing a kiss and sprinting back to his desk at the far end of the newsroom. Before the receiver was up to his ear, he could hear the features editor barking.

"Yes, Mr. Hammersmith. Right away. Lafayette Square."

Bill walked to the supply cabinet to get a new reporter's pad, losing any interest in the assignment as he went. He sat down beside Sally, trying to shift the girl's attention from her typewriter to him.

"What's old Yammersmith want?" she asked without letting up on her keyboard.

"Some old houses being pulled down on Jackson Place. Jeez, the things that guy thinks are *stories*."

"It's summertime, sweetness. Stories are scarce, if you haven't noticed."

"Why can't we leave town with Fatty Taft?" Bill whined. "How about it, just you and me?" He reached over to tickle her wrist.

"We stay because we're wage slaves, Princeton. At least those of us without trust funds." She returned the carriage so fast it nipped his hand. "So quit bothering me and go about your business. You can take me out for a soda when you get back." She handed him his straw hat, which had been on her desk all morning, since he'd made the first of half a dozen trips over to it.

It was blazing hot on Pennsylvania Avenue. Making things even less comfortable, drowning out the clip-clop of the horses, were all the proud belching cars, thousands more of them than when Bill first came to the capital three years ago. He was drenched in sweat by the time he passed the White House and turned into the square. What in hell did Hammersmith expect him to come back with? he wondered, lifting his suspenders to peel the shirt away from his chest. It was just some guys with a steam shovel, taking a bite out of a house and cursing the temperature as they worked — plus a little crowd of onlookers, heat-whipped clerks from Treasury who'd come to Lafayette Square in search of some lunchtime peace and found this instead. They didn't know any more about what was going on than he did. What did Hammersmith want him to do? Find some old-timer who could wax nostalgic about Benjamin Harrison and bemoan the march of progress that had taken the country to 1910? The only old man he could spot was a colored fellow in a waiter's jacket, and Bill knew that Hammersmith, who hailed from Birmingham, wouldn't want him serving up some darky's dialectal reminiscences. Still, it was a start.

He tapped the waiter on the shoulder. "You know what they're doing?"

"Tearing it down," the old fellow replied, looking a little sad under his grizzly white hair. "Making room for an extension of the Cosmos Club."

"Ah," said Bill. It was even more boring than he'd thought. "That where you work?"

"Yes, sir," said the colored man. "Over forty-two years."

"You don't say. Do you know who was living here before now?"

"Oh, I've known most of 'em, going almost all the way back to the war."

Bill smiled. The old man seemed sharp, and better company than half the fellows in the newsroom would be this afternoon.

"This used to be the colonel's house," the waiter said.

"Who's the colonel?" asked Bill. "And who are you?" he added, extending his hand. "Name's Bill Curtis, with the *Star.*"

"My name's Johnny," said the man, not sure he preferred the handshaking ways of these young white fellas to the older gentlemen he was used to waiting on. "The colonel was Colonel Rathbone. He and his wife and his children lived here, thirty, forty years ago. Used to see her in the morning when I'd cross the park to go to work. Found her lots of times out by the wishing tree. That's gone, too," he said, looking through the wrought-iron fence toward Jackson's statue.

"The wishing tree?" asked Bill.

"Yeah, the wishing tree," interjected a sharp New York voice. "Like in, where you'd go to make a wish you were somehow gonna come back from this place with a story."

Bill laughed. "Hey, Eddie." It was McClanahan, his opposite number at the *Post*. "Meet my friend Johnny."

"A pleasure," said McClanahan, not offering a handshake.

"Johnny's telling me about the neighborhood, about some old colonel."

"I know who he's talkin' about. The guy who was with Lincoln on closing night. Booth cut him up on his way out of the theatre. Years later he killed his wife. Over in Germany. Emptied a whole barrel into her chest."

Bill cast an inquiring glance at Johnny, who confirmed McClanahan's account with a quiet nod. Well, *that* would be a story, if it hadn't happened about thirty years ago, and if McClanahan, who liked to point out that his education stopped at P.S. 5, not Princeton, didn't already, as usual, have all the details.

"So what happened to the colonel after that?" asked Bill.

If Johnny knew, he decided it wasn't his place to say; he let McClanahan rattle on with the story: "Nothin' good. They threw him in some German jail. He couldn't've lasted long. He'd cut himself to ribbons after he shot the wife. 'A sordid story,' as we like to call 'em on page eight."

The steam shovel was now buzzing at a higher pitch, making

all three men wince. Over the din Johnny mimed that it was time for him to go back to work, and McClanahan shouted that this demolition was for the birds. He was going to head on over to the morgue instead. "Girl there dead from an 'illegal operation,' as we also always say on page eight. See you around, Curtis. Don't let the ivy grow over your eyes." He swatted him with his pad and took off, leaving Bill to stare at the bedroom wall left exposed, by a bite of the steam shovel, on the house's second story. You could still see the squares of unfaded wallpaper over which the last owner's pictures had hung.

He was too hot and too lazy to stay here and get the lowdown on the Cosmos Club's architectural plans. As it was, nothing he did today would satisfy Hammersmith. He might as well just hunt up a sketch of the dead colonel. They could run it beside a picture of the crumbling house, and he could do a "historical notes" caption. With any luck that would pass for a day's work, and by four he'd be sitting over a phosphate with Sally Kenyon, pushing his luck as far as he dared. As he walked west to the Pension Building, thinking they might have a clipping or a sketch inside the colonel's file, he entertained his fantasy of Sally, and worked up his lines. He'd get one straw from the counterman instead of two, and when she asked him where his was, he'd just say, "Yours'll be sweeter," and see where that got him. Hurrying down F Street, he looked toward what had once been Ford's Theatre, still boarded up after it collapsed and killed all those clerks, poor sons of bitches. Happened years and years ago, when it was still offices. Lucky the colonel wasn't there *that* day.

He'd never much liked the Pension Building, those times he had to go to it. The outside was grand enough, all the soldiers and sailors going round and round it, frozen on the frieze, but the inside was crazy, halfway between a hive and a stadium, thousands of clerks toiling around that huge fountain. Anyway, here he was, striding through its Corinthian columns and checking his pocket watch, 1:35 P.M., and figuring he'd be back at the *Star* in another hour.

He filled out the form and showed the silver-haired clerk his press card, which didn't speed things up. Even so, the file appeared in ten minutes, and Bill put out his hand to receive it.

"Can't do that," said the old man in a Mainer's accent.

"How so?" asked Bill.

"Living pensioner. Private file."

"*Living?*"

"Living. Which is to say none of your business."

"Where is the man?" asked Bill, his tone more respectful, even a bit hushed.

"Can't tell you."

"Oh, come on. He was a famous man in his day. I'm here on newspaper business. Historical interest."

"You kin of his?"

"No," admitted Bill.

"Then I can't help you."

"Well, who can, then?"

The old man squinted through his glasses at the handwritten notes on the file's jacket. "Pensioner's nearest kin is his son, Henry Riggs Rathbone. Least he's the one getting the checks, at Sixty-seven West Washington Street, Chicago, Illinois. The Land of Lincoln," the old man added in a little flourish, before frowning at the sight of another notation.

"What are you looking at?" asked Bill.

"Unfortunate," said the clerk.

"What's unfortunate?"

"Oh, suit yourself," said the old man, either tired of Curtis's manner or unable not to be the bearer of bad news. He pointed with his immaculate index fingernail to the designation "LUNA-TIC," before retracting the file once more. "The man is confined to an asylum in Hildesheim" — he pronounced it, slowly, as *Hildy-shame* — "Germany. He's certified, according to the act of June 27, 1890, as possessing 'a permanent physical disability not due to vicious habits.' His son administers the pension and has since the death of the man's brother-in-law, one William Hamilton Harris, in 1895. And that's all I'm going to tell you, son. It's far more than I'm supposed to." With that, he took the jacket of papers away with him, back into the vaults where the Union dead took their official, statistical rest.

➔✦

Six months later, Bill Curtis turned up the collar of his alpaca coat and walked up the hill to the gates of the old Benedictine monastery in Hildesheim. He showed his letter of introduction, stamped by the American consul, to the gatekeeper, whose scrutiny of it was interrupted by the shouted greeting of Dr. Israel, the provincial asylum's director, a genial bald man bounding down the path from the main building and instructing the guard to let the young American in. "Yes, yes," said Dr. Israel, shaking Bill's gloved hand, "I know all about you. You're here to write about our colonel. We got your editor's letter," he said in his fluent English. "We're all ready for you. And so pleased you've traveled all this way to see him."

"Actually," said Curtis, trying to keep up with Dr. Israel's fast pace, "I'm over here to write about the German army, but since last summer I haven't quite been able to get the colonel out of my mind. My editor thought it might be worth taking a side trip to come see him."

"Excellent," said Dr. Israel. "Your editor writes that you have just received a promotion."

"Undeserved," said Bill with a smile. Getting shifted to the foreign desk, away from Hammersmith, had been a gift horse whose mouth he hadn't looked into.

"I'm sure it's otherwise," said Dr. Israel, leading Curtis into the building and instructing a woman in white — a secretary or nurse, Bill wasn't sure — to bring them some tea and cake. "Come, sit down," he said, laying Bill's coat over a heavy wooden table. "Despite its current function, we owe this great building to Ludwig the Pious, son of Charlemagne, not the *mad* King Ludwig of later days."

"Has he really been here the whole time?" asked Curtis, eager to get on with what had occasioned this long detour. "Colonel Rathbone, I mean. I've had no cooperation from his son, and I don't know much more than I found out from my visit to the army's pension office."

"Oh, yes," said Dr. Israel. "The local authorities agreed with your State Department to discontinue criminal proceedings if the colonel were confined to St. Michael's. The sister sailed home with the children. The brother from Ohio, a model of a man by all accounts, brought them up. The colonel, had he been in his right mind, could not have asked for more. All this was taken care of early in 1884. It happened very quickly, given modern communications. Did you know, by the way, that your President Arthur got the news as he came out of church on Christmas day — right on the steps, I was told — less than two days after the incident?" Dr. Israel, who seemed proud of being not merely the colonel's physician but a historian of his case, explained that he had heard all the details years ago, when he first came to St. Michael's, from old Dr. Rosenbach, the royal Prussian district physician.

"Where is the colonel?" asked Bill.

"He is out," said Dr. Israel, reaching for his meerschaum pipe.

"Out?"

"Yes, on a drive. He keeps a carriage."

Bill laughed incredulously. "He keeps a carriage? A lunatic on a soldier's pension?"

Dr. Israel held a lit match to the pipe's bowl and sucked it to life. "Even though the colonel remains rather wealthy in his own right, the family have always taken the pension. That's how the rich stay rich. The colonel is a gentleman, so we let him live like one. The 'servants' in his dining hall are really guards, but what harm, after all —"

"His *own* dining hall?"

"Oh, yes, Mr. Curtis. Come, I'll show you his apartment. I see you're too impatient for my chatter. All you young American men have the energy of your Mr. Roosevelt. Well, more power to you!" Dr. Israel smiled and led his guest out of the office, through two long halls, to another wing of the building, where they entered a small library with British and American magazines on a table. From there, with the help of the doctor's key, they entered a small bedroom, sparsely furnished and militarily neat.

"Is that a picture of Mrs. Rathbone?" Bill asked nervously, pointing to the dresser. An oval frame contained the photograph of a gray-haired woman.

"Yes," said Dr. Israel. "But of the preceding Mrs. Rathbone. The colonel's mother. Later Mrs. Ira Harris."

"I see," said Curtis, noticing the absence of other photographs. "Are there no pictures of his children?"

"The colonel has no curiosity about them. His brother, Jared, who became the American consul in Paris twenty years ago, would visit him from time to time, but most everyone has lost interest by now. Miss Harris, the sister, an old lady, still sometimes writes with news of his grown children, as does an elderly lady in New York, a Miss Hall, but he ignores the communications. It is cold in here. Let us go back to the office and have our tea."

Over plates of chocolate cake, Dr. Israel explained the colonel's initial symptoms, in 1884, to his visitor, who took notes. "When he came here, he was entirely under the influence of hallucinations and the mania of being persecuted. He believed himself to be surrounded by enemies who made him drink liquids through the wall. He thought poison was being given him in his medicine and victuals, and refused to take any food which had not been tasted before his eyes."

"Does he hear voices now?" asked Curtis.

"Oh, yes," said Dr. Israel. "And sees specters. But ones that have grown familiar to him. His early fears were much worse. The hallucinations were manifold. At times he believed himself to be persecuted by other patients in the asylum; he thought the ceiling would come down on him; he feared people would go to his rooms during his walks in the garden and injure his clothes; he feared he would get a yellow complexion from drinking the water. And he believed that he was kept in the asylum to be experimented on."

"How is he physically?"

"For a seventy-three-year-old man, his condition is satisfactory, though it is always hard to keep him eating adequately. He complains of pain, but that is in his mind. The pupil of his right eye is slightly dilated, always. But that is irrelevant. The cause of his difficulties is not physiological. In most respects the Romantic writers were correct. You see —"

The woman in white had come in. She spoke softly to Dr. Israel and exited with a sociable smile in Curtis's direction.

"The colonel has returned," said the doctor. "Shall I take you to him?"

"Yes, please," said Bill.

"Ignore any strange requests," the doctor suggested as they went back down the hall to Henry's apartment. "Treat them matter-of-factly."

Trying to imagine what these requests could be, Bill remained silent. They strode past the monastery's old stone walls.

"Colonel," Dr. Israel called into the library. "You have a visitor from Washington."

Henry stood up very straight, extending his hand as he lowered his head. Bill noticed that the American colonel's manners were more formal than those of his European physician. He was thin to the point of gauntness, and his hair, what was left of it, had gone white. The enlarged pupil of the right eye was noticeable, and disconcerting, as was the slightly throbbing vein at the left temple.

"I'll leave you," said Dr. Israel, startling Bill. The doctor discreetly nodded to indicate that things would be all right, and he exited.

"Sit down, Mr. Curtis."

"Thank you, Colonel."

"'Mister' is fine. I retired from the army more than forty years ago."

"Of course."

"Would you examine one of these?" Henry passed him a plate of biscuits. "They are trying to kill me with them, I'm sure."

"After twenty-seven years here, sir? It seems unlikely." Bill politely declined to take anything from the dish. "I just had cake in the doctor's office."

"May I ask you something?" said Henry.

"Certainly."

"Would you kill me with that knife?"

"No, Mr. Rathbone," Bill replied. "That wouldn't be wise."

Henry, as if long accustomed to having such favors withheld, changed the subject without any fuss. "I don't think Taft will be nominated again, do you? I think Roosevelt is coming back." This statement startled Bill even more than the request to kill his host, and Henry seemed to perceive that. "I get most of the magazines and newspapers I want," he said, "including the *Star*. It comes very late, several weeks, but Mr. Thompson, the consul, sees that it gets through."

"I'm not sure about President Taft," said Bill, who realized not only the preposterousness of the conversation, but also that he was probably less informed about American politics than his host. "I doubt he was encouraged by the off-year elections." There was a short pause, and he decided to change the subject. "How are you feeling, sir?"

"I am well, for the most part, though the walls contain an apparatus that blows gas and dust into my room at night. This is what causes my headaches."

Bill, taking a risk, said, "I believe Mrs. Lincoln had a similar complaint when she was confined."

"I do not know the lady," declared Henry, calmly.

"Do you eat well?" asked Bill.

"I neither like nor trust the food. I have suffered from dyspepsia for many years, and I have always disliked fleshiness, so I eat sparingly. Several months from now I plan to stop eating altogether."

Bill noticed that the man was almost skeletal. He was afraid Rathbone would see he was staring, and take offense, but then he realized that his host was looking off into the middle distance and smiling. He decided that he had to bring himself to ask about Clara.

"Your wife —"

"Did you hear that? That gliding? That rustling out in the corridor?"

"No," said Bill, "there's no —"

"I had no wife," said Henry.

"Clara?"

"Clara Harris was my sister."

"Sister?"

"A woman of great beauty and virtue. I miss her very much."

Bill Curtis avoided the man's eyes, but made a quick note on his pad. He wanted to leave. Madness, he decided, was finally uninteresting; its arbitrariness put it beyond profitable inquiry. But he had to ask about 1865. That was why he had come.

"You've seen so much history," he began cautiously.

"I write about history," said Henry.

This was something Bill had not heard from even Dr. Israel. "Really?" he asked. "May I see what you write?"

"I'm not quite ready to reveal it," said Henry. "It is a theory of the Accidental Man. The right man in the wrong place at the wrong time. He turns the wrong place and time into the right ones. It is complicated." He directed Curtis's attention to a top shelf with dozens of black notebooks, presumably filled with his own words.

Bill noticed, on the same shelf, a rack of pipes and a small wooden doll. He made a note on his pad. "I'm afraid I'm baffled," he confessed.

"You won't be when you see it," Henry said.

"About the history *you* saw — Mr. Lincoln —"

"I never discuss him," Henry said quite firmly, but without losing any of his politeness.

"Not even in your writings?"

"Not one word. My own experiences have given me insight into *analogous* situations. But I do not need to discuss myself, any more than an architect needs to leave a scaffolding in front of a building he has built."

Feeling at a dead end, Bill looked around the room.

"I think you need to go outside," said Henry. "I'll take you to her."

"Her?"

"Miss Harris."

Bill stared.

"Her grave," said Henry.

The younger man assumed this was a delusion, and he wondered how he could conclude the visit. But Rathbone was reaching for his coat and hat, as if to go out. Was there an attendant Bill could summon before the man wandered off?

"Gunther!" cried Henry, before explaining, softly, to Curtis: "My manservant."

Gunther, a large curly-haired youth, came in from the hall. Henry introduced him to Curtis, adroitly alternating English and German. Gunther gave Bill a knowing smile, and Henry, in German, issued Gunther an order. "'To Miss Harris's grave,'" Henry translated for Curtis. Gunther nodded to the patient and indicated that it was quite all right for the visitor to follow along. The three of them walked down one more stone corridor leading away from Dr. Israel's office, and came out the back of the monastery. It was not possible, thought Bill. Surely they brought her home with the children, to be buried in Albany or Ohio.

"You'll want your coat," said Henry.

"I'm fine," said Bill.

"The coach contains blankets."

Bill put one of them over his knees as they rode in silence over the snowy winter landscape, its brown outcroppings straining for the weak warmth of the sun. They were soon at the edge of the village graveyard, "something right out of Thomas Gray," Bill wrote in boilerplate on his reporter's pad. Gunther stopped the carriage in an automatic way that suggested the place was a frequent destination. He alighted from the coachman's seat and came around to let Henry out. The old man's frailty was evident as he stepped down. Gunther motioned to Bill for one of the blankets, which he draped over his charge's shoulders. The three men walked no more than ten yards, past a few bordered graves, before they reached a simple headstone.

CLARA H. RATHBONE
1834–1883
A mind at peace with all below,
A heart whose love is innocent!

Bill's heart pounded. He had been a poor enough student at Princeton, but even he could recognize the last two lines of "She Walks in Beauty."

"This is where I shall lie," said Henry, pointing to an empty plot of snow-covered earth, already bordered, next to his wife's. "As soon as I finish my work and cease eating."

Bill said nothing.

"Byron was her favorite," said Henry, "though our father disapproved of him. She had this in her pocket the day she died. Here, look," he said, offering Curtis a folded, disintegrating paper from his own pocket. Bill opened it carefully, afraid it would rip at the creases and scatter on the winter wind. The ink remained surprisingly vivid; the hand was distinctly feminine:

> *There was in him a vital scorn of all.*
> *As if the worst had fall'n which could befall,*
> *He stood a stranger in this breathing world,*
> *An erring spirit from another hurl'd;*
> *A thing of dark imaginings, that shaped*
> *By choice the perils he by chance escaped;*
> *But 'scaped in vain, for in their memory yet*
> *His mind would half exult and half regret . . .*
>
> *You could not penetrate his soul, but found,*
> *Despite your wonder, to your own he wound;*
> *His presence haunted still; and from the breast*
> *He forced an all unwilling interest:*
> *Vain was the struggle in that mental net,*
> *His spirit seem'd to dare you to forget!*
>
> — Byron, "Lara"

Henry motioned to take the paper back from Curtis, who refolded it gently.

"She copied it out two days before she died," Henry explained. "At a desk by a small porcelain stove in her room. It's the last time I can remember seeing her."

AUTHOR'S NOTES

AND ACKNOWLEDGMENTS

Henry and Clara is based on a wide variety of research material: published histories of the Civil War era; diaries and correspondence of the Rathbone and Harris families; contemporary newspaper accounts; military records; pension files; census reports; alumni records; State Department documents in the National Archives. Insofar as the historical record exists, I have tried to find it and, in most cases, adhere to it. The essential facts of Ira Harris's political life and Henry Rathbone's army career, as well as the chronology of births, marriages, and deaths among the Harrises and Rathbones, are true to life as presented here. Nearly all the book's principal characters, and most of its minor ones, were living persons. Nearly all the extracts from letters and journals that appear in the text are made up, but in places quotations from actual material are included. The letter from Clara Harris to "Mary," for example, which opens Part Three of the novel, is a real letter in the possession of the New-York Historical Society. The identity of "Mary" is not certain, but my discovery of this letter led to the invention of the character of Mary Hall, who in the novel is made its recipient.

The available documentation of Henry and Clara Rathbone's story — substantial in places, almost entirely lacking in others — amounts in the end to no more than a scaffold, and the reader should know that I have taken liberal advantage of the elbow room between that scaffold's girders and joists. The narrative that follows is a work of inference, speculation, and outright invention. Nouns always trump adjectives, and in the phrase "historical fiction" it is important to remember which of the two words is which.

Still, the facts have been the seeds of the fiction, and I am grateful to the many people who helped me gather and make sense of them.

Chief among these are Melinda Yates of the New York State Library and Norman S. Rice, director emeritus of the Albany Institute of History and Art. During the past few years, whether guiding me through microfilmed ledgers or cemetery rows, they have been unfailingly patient and helpful, and I am deeply in their debt. Thanks also to all the librarians who helped me find elusive bits of the Rathbone story: Jean Ashton (New-York Historical Society); Lisa Browar (New York Public Library); Barbara Durniak (Vassar College); Ellen H. Fladger and Elaine Shull (Union College); Karl Kabelac (University of Rochester); Sally Marks and Dane Hartgrove (National Archives); Linda J. Long (Stanford University); Sam Streit and Jennifer Lee (Brown University). Mrs. Sumner Crosby, Jr., and Mrs. Edward Hart Green, present-day relations of the principal characters, supplied me with information, and the distinguished Civil War historian Stephen W. Sears gave me useful advice. Professor Edith Toegel of Hamilton College translated correspondence with officials in Germany, where the Rathbones' story came to a close.

As the facts grew the fiction, I depended on good advice from Cindy Spiegel, Janet Silver, and Laurence Cooper of Ticknor & Fields / Houghton Mifflin; my agent, Mary Evans; Frances Kiernan; Lucy Kaylin; and the incomparable Sallie Motsch. Thanks to all of them.

And thanks, as always, to Bill Bodenschatz.

New York City
January 14, 1994